A Stolen Rose

CORAL SMITH SAXE

Sheri Very Good!

Bestselling Author Of *Enchantment*

SWEET NOTHINGS

"You're ridiculous," Morgana said.

"And you're a dreamer," Phillip said.

"Better a dreamer than a wastrel!"

"Better a wastrel than a lovely maid."

Morgana started to retort, then stopped, openmouthed. "You're a lunatic," she muttered. "You make no sense."

"And you're the sweetest morsel I've ever kissed," Phillip said, matter-of-factly.

She glared at him, eyes narrowed. "You're a trickster."

"And you're an enchanting rose."

"Idiot."

"Angel."

"Stop baiting me, mongrel!"

"I promise I will, my dove."

"Damn you! Stop that! You—"

"Prince of your heart? Devoted suitor? Love of your dreams?" Phillip's smile was wickedly engaging, his voice cheerful.

"Stop it! Why can't you just—why don't you—you—" She couldn't help herself. She began to giggle.

Other *Leisure* and *Love Spell* Books by
Coral Smith Saxe:
ENCHANTMENT

A Stolen Rose

CORAL SMITH SAXE

LEISURE BOOKS **NEW YORK CITY**

A LEISURE BOOK®

October 1995

Published by

Dorchester Publishing Co., Inc.
276 Fifth Avenue
New York, NY 10001

The name "Leisure Books" and the stylized "L" with design are trademarks of Dorchester Publishing Co., Inc.

Printed in the United States of America.

For my sons, two of the finest knights who ever raised a sword.

Prologue

The young man tumbled down the hill like a cartwheel sprung from its axle. He was up and running again in an instant, laughter and urgent purpose mingling on his fresh young face. He skidded to a stop at the gate in the high wall. It was closed. If it was closed, then it was locked. The monks of St. Jerome's were either at prayers or in a period of silence and were not to be disturbed.

"Ah, well, no matter."

With a bound, the lad sprang up to grasp one of the thick vines trailing over the wall from the garden on the other side. Hand over hand he went until he had scaled the obstacle, then dropped, neatly as a cat, to the soft ground on the opposite side. He brushed his hands off on his leggings, settled his cap, and sprinted off down the path to the small building just beyond a hedge of deep green holly.

"Friar Theodore!"

The old man turned at the cry, not startled, but amused. He put a finger to his lips and pointed to the hourglass sitting on the rickety potting table. The sands were almost out.

"But I have to tell you—"

The man glared and held up a commanding hand. The young man bit his lips but obeyed. He bounced into the room like a joyful young hound and danced about the tables and shelves, sniffing this plant and twitching that. The old monk followed him, frowning, yet with a tolerant twinkle in his dark eyes. He rescued the teetering saplings standing in wait for their transplanting, smacked at hands that threatened the delicate shoots lining the table, and gave the boy a gentle kick in the rump when a clay pot nearly met its end on the hard earthen floor.

The lad let out a pent-up sigh of relief as the last grain dropped to the bottom of the hourglass. "You'll never guess what's happened, Father!"

"Oh, pish. I can always guess what's up with you, intemperance. You're in love."

"How did you know? Well, never mind that. I've found her at last. She's the fairest maid you've ever seen, there can be no equal to her—"

"Yes, yes." The monk snorted. "Of a beauty unparalleled and a nature so mild t'would shame the lilies. I've heard this before, boy. You were in love with Lady Gwynn only last week, so sick with love you couldn't continue life without her. And she is not the lady you speak of now, is she?"

"Well, no, but—"

"Well! No! But! When will you learn, lad? You love like a flea! Hopping here, hopping there, and with no more production for all your hopping than a few sick verses and a handkerchief about your arm." The monk noted the lad's crestfallen face and softened. "Never mind. Who is this paragon, this pearl of great price?"

"I don't know."

Friar Theodore groaned. "Saints and devils, the boy is witless indeed. He's in love with phantoms." He turned back to his gardening with another snort of derision.

"No, no. I mean, I know her. I just don't know her name." The young man looked about as if to ensure their privacy. Satisfied that there was no one about, he continued, his voice dropping to a loud whisper. "She's an outlaw."

The friar stopped his loosening of the sacking about the base of a rose plant. He turned and narrowly eyed the lad. "How would you come to meet an outlaw? A female one, at that?"

The lad puffed up at this. "I do have my dark side," he declared. "I know that a religious man such as yourself knows nothing of these things, but I sometimes frequent the inns where more cunning and desperate folk take their pleasure."

"Oh, wise pastime for the son of the richest man in the county. What a sheep to be sheared you are!"

He colored. "I'm not a fool. I don't go in finery and I don't go spreading my name about. I'm known as Black Jonny, what do you think of that?"

"I think you're a puppy at play among wolves and soon to have his ears bitten off. So this thieves' den is where you met your new lady-love?"

"Yes, at the Green Bow. Oh, friar, you can't believe the way she talked, the way she looked! She's the most daring, beautiful—I cannot sum up half of what she is. You can't imagine."

Friar Theodore looked off into the distance, as if seeing some scene playing before his eyes alone. "Yes, I can. I can imagine it."

The boy gazed at him in wonder. "You can? How could you know—"

"I wasn't born a monk."

"Well, no, of course not. But how can you know what a woman such as she can be like?"

"How can I—? Here, take these roses." The monk thrust several bundled plants into the lad's arms. "Come and help me put these in the ground. God willing, some good hard work perhaps will take the spur from your side, wild colt."

The old man and the young left the little hut in the first rays of light and walked through a maze of gardens. When they had reached the innermost circle of the maze, the old friar dropped his spade and basket of tools upon the ground. He was out of breath, even though the walk had not been far and their pace not overly fast.

"Sit." This time it was the younger man who gave the command. He motioned the friar to a nearby bench.

The friar went meekly enough. When he was seated and had gained his breath, he pointed a brown, gnarled finger at the earth that had been freshly turned in the center circle. "Dig there. Enough for twenty plants, three hands deep."

The young man grinned and lifted the spade. As he sank it deep into the moist earth, he said over his shoulder, "So. You once consorted with outlaws."

"Lad, I was an outlaw."

Wide eyes turned his way. "You jest."

He shook his head. "Never more in earnest. And once I knew a lady of that same condition. A thief, by trade."

"Was she beautiful?"

"Impertinence! Is that all that concerns you? Flesh and beauty and that which leads you around by your codpiece?"

The young man grinned. "Well, was she?"

"Great lack. Yes. In her way, she was the most beauteous lady I ever knew."

"You loved her?" The spade sank deep, turned over a new, fresh-smelling mound of earth.

"I loved her."

The lad leaned on his spade. "And you made her yours?"

Friar Theodore picked up one of the rose bushes that sat near his feet. He toyed with a bud, then winced and sucked at his thumb. At last, he looked at his young companion. "You work, young mischief. This is a story you should hear, lover of outlaws."

The young man sank his spade into the earth once more, and the old friar settled in to tell his tale. His hands worked idly at his braided belt, and as he spoke, he looked off over the walls, as if seeing beyond them into a time of old.

"She was small and slight, no more than a wisp when I met her. That's to satisfy your lusty curiosity. You will no doubt be dismayed to learn that she went about sooty and dressed as a lad, most of the time. Her small hands could strip a man of his purse in the time it takes to draw breath, and leave him unaware of the transaction until long after she had made her retreat. She carried with her a knife, silver-handled it was, and with it she could have pared a man from his immortal soul with the skill of a carver at the king's board."

"She was a murderess?"

"Listen. Dig. I'll do the telling."

The sun rose and cast its light on the two men. The young man listened, spellbound, to the old friar's tale.

"We were known in those days as the Kestrel's flock. The most skilled, most daring, most feared of all the robbers and thieves that rode the highways and walked the streets of London. There was Kestrel, and Wren, Hugh the Sparrow and Robin, Tom Throstle, and Magpie. And then, along came the one they called Blackbird . . ."

Chapter One

England, 1409

It had to be a bad omen.

Morgana Bracewell had scarcely been in the room a few moments when she saw him. She knew him immediately. He was laughing at some jest, but his dark blue gaze was scanning the crowded room. With frightening precision, those hunting eyes behind the golden mask came to rest upon Morgana. She stood, transfixed, her hand still on the latch of the pantry door that had admitted her, uninvited as she was, into this glittering throng. She almost turned and bolted back into the pantry. Still, she held her composure, adjusted the black feathered mask on her face, and looked away in feigned nonchalance. This night was too important for her to be frightened off by a familiar face.

But, hell's fires, she thought to herself as she accepted a cup of wine from a passing servant. She willed her heart

14

to stop thumping against her ribs as she sipped. *The devil take me if my luck doesn't change this night.*

She chanced another glance at the man in the golden mask. She exhaled in relief. He had turned his attention elsewhere.

She'd seen him only once before, yet Morgana knew this man, if not his name. She couldn't mistake those blue-gray eyes or that sweep of dark hair. He was the last person she and her partner, the Wren, had lured off the highway and robbed. She couldn't forget him because there had been something about the way the man had touched her, taken her arm, when, disguised as a damsel in distress, she had begged him to help her find her "missing" horse. He'd fallen easily under Wren's light cosh, and his purse had yielded them enough to live on for weeks.

But that act had also seemed to set off a chain of ill luck for both her and the Wren. And this had best not be another link in that chain, for the adventure she was about to undertake tonight would be dangerous enough without adding the presence of one of her outraged victims.

She wanted to leave, to run all the way back to the inn where the Wren waited for her. But she couldn't do that. She had to stay and relieve her hosts of their jewelry, money, and any other precious baubles that she could stuff into the burlap sack tucked beneath her skirts. If she failed, it could mean her death and the deaths of her compatriots.

She was a sworn member of the robber band known as the Kestrel's flock, and tonight several of them worked as a team. She would simply have to stay out of the sight and reach of the tall lord who wore the mask of a golden lion.

She moved into the crowd, taking in the sights and smells and sounds about her. The room was starred with the light of dozens of candles and it seemed to pulsate with music, laughter, and conversation. In her slightly worn, green satin gown, she rubbed elbows with men and women dressed in brilliant, rainbow attire. Comfortable, wealthy, aristocratic, they teased and chattered and shouted to one another, their faces flushed with high spirits and an abundance of free-flowing wines. Gold and silver dishes glittered on every table, and the merrymakers lifted thin goblets to one another in numerous toasts. Each guest wore some sort of mask, from the simplest handkerchief to the most elaborate concoction of gold, jewels, and feathers.

Morgana knew that she, with her shabby skirts only barely concealed with new trim and her thin, hard-muscled body, was not one of these well-fed, pampered folk. Indeed, if they knew the truth of who she was, she'd not see the sunrise tomorrow. But she knew how to blend in, how to use her wits, and Kestrel had trained her well. All she had to do now was wait; enjoy a bit of the food and the music, and wait for his signal.

She tried not to look at the man she had robbed, but her curiosity was too great. Touching her mask to make sure it was securely in place, she looked over and saw him make a low bow before a lady, touching his heart as he did so. The woman he greeted was seated on a special dais reserved for honored guests, and she rose with a smile that was as serenely poised as it was lovely. She was dressed in an exquisite pale lavender kirtle and a golden mask in the fashion of a sleek lioness. The hand she offered to her partner was slender and milk-white.

As the elegant pair moved out to dance in the center of the room, the other dancers drew back, forming a pathway for them. The music began. Morgana watched with pleasure as the dancers wove colorful patterns in, out, and around the dance floor.

"Young Greyfriars seems to have returned to his place in society with ease." A tall woman standing next to Morgana leaned toward her, her voice conveying all the breathless interest of a spectator at a royal joust.

Morgana started. "I beg your pardon. Who?" She had to raise her voice to be heard above the music and merriment.

"Lord Phillip Greyfriars." The woman waved her wine goblet in the direction of the tall man in the golden mask. "The son of the Marquess of Wildhurst, you know. He's been gone from London for some time and only returned last month. I must say, the Viscountess Winston has certainly recovered from her bereavement in a hurry with that young stag to comfort her!"

Something in the woman's gossipy tones rankled, but Morgana concealed her feelings in the interest of discretion. "Lord Greyfriars seems to take his ladies as he finds them. And wherever he finds them." She hoped her observations would be vague enough to pass as knowledge.

The tall woman laughed easily and helped herself to a stuffed fig on the nearest table. "Lord Greyfriars hardly has to find his partners. They find him. Have a fig, dear, they're delicious, as always. Still," she continued, hardly missing a beat between bites, "Lord Phillip's been devoted to Lady Winston since his return." She nudged Morgana with her elbow. "See how he makes a dance into more than a dance and how she leans upon his arm when she may. There's more there than civil grace." She gave a gusty sigh and finished off her fig.

Morgana peered at the handsome couple. Lady Winston, whoever she was, moved like a wraith, with easy, liquid movements, and the young lord who was her partner followed her every motion, his long legs and lean, powerful body well suited to the intricacies of the dance.

"Lady Elizabeth will be Marchioness by Christmas, I prophesy."

Morgana looked to see that another woman had joined them, this one short and plump and dressed in a gown decorated with squarish white rosettes that trembled like a storm-tossed sea whenever she moved.

"Or rather, wife to the heir," the new woman added, nibbling from a plate of candied violets.

"To be sure," said the first woman. "Unless the Grey-friars blood doesn't carry Lord Phillip into the same troubles as his sire and brother."

"Oh, fie, Jeanne," said the other. "Lord Phillip's a hot-blooded one, that's so, but I've never heard a word of scandal about him. No more than any other young buck."

"Then you mustn't have heard about what happened while Lady Winston and Lord Phillip were up in the north, Margery," said Jeanne.

Margery's eyes grew round as Lady Jeanne whispered at length in her ear. Morgana wished she could hear the words, but she reminded herself that what Phillip Grey-friars did was no concern of hers. She trained her gaze away from the ladies and into the crowd, looking for the Kestrel.

Her eye was drawn once more to the couple in the matching golden masks. They smiled and turned and dipped, but something was amiss, to Morgana's eyes. There was a hollowness in their behavior, a falsity. She couldn't identify it, but it was as if the pair were putting on a great show for this audience of dinner guests.

Damnation! He was looking her way again. Why couldn't the man keep his eyes on his own lady? Quickly, she turned and bumped into Lady Margery, spilling her wine.

"Oh, I do beg your pardon," she said, stooping to swipe at the woman's skirts with her handkerchief. "That was most clumsy of me." The image of those bright, blue-gray eyes meeting hers from under the golden mask made her hands shake.

"Oh, never you mind, my girl," the woman chuckled. "I'd do the same if I were you and Lord Phillip were

18

giving me the welcome look.'' She pulled Morgana up by the arm. ''Here, leave off, lady. I've servants to do that.'' She waved her glove at the retreating figure in scarlet and black. ''He's noticed you, that's sure. You could be a very lucky lass tonight!''

Morgana was startled. ''But what about Lady Winston?''

''Oh, to be sure, she has his heart. But they say she's holding him from her bed out of deference to her late husband. I'm more inclined to think she's keeping him at arm's reach until she's assured of the marriage. A smart lady, is she.''

Lady Jeanne leaned over with a smile and a nod. ''And no one begrudges Lord Phillip his little adventures. He's more than generous with all his lovers, I hear.''

''But what about—has he children?'' Morgana asked.

Lady Margery frowned. ''Come to tell of it, I've never heard of any. Have you?'' she asked of her friend.

''No. And that's a wonder, I'll confess. A man of his prodigious—appetite, shall we say?—should have a string of pretty bastards by now.''

The two older women went off into gales of laughter again. Morgana stared at them in wonder, then turned to look at Phillip Greyfriars as he escorted Lady Winston to her seat.

Her lip curled in disgust. A philanderer, she thought. A common chaser of women's skirts whose rapacious exploits were fair game for every wagging tongue. Just another idle, rich lord, living by his appetites. As far as she was concerned, he had well deserved to be robbed.

Something caught her attention at the corner of her eye. She looked and saw the Kestrel. He was dressed in his customary brown garb and wore a hawk mask of brown, white, and black mottled feathers, in imitation of his namesake. She smiled to herself. She'd never known him by any name other than Kestrel but she admired his skill and trusted his leadership. He dared much, and she'd never known him to fail.

She felt reassured just by the sight of him. The Robin must be somewhere about, too, though she couldn't see him. It was just as well. There was no love lost between them, and bullying Robin often made it clear that he resented Morgana's favored position in Kestrel's flock.

The Kestrel touched his mask in salute, and she nodded ever so slightly. That was her signal to begin a search of the upper rooms. She'd have to be doubly on her guard from now on.

She moved to cross the room, winding her way through the tables to avoid the dancers. The music halted, and the crowd scattered, clapping and laughing. Morgana made use of the confusion to cover her progress toward the stairs on the opposite end of the room.

She did not get far. A hand seized her arm and stopped her. She turned and almost cried out in horror.

"My lady." Phillip Greyfriars bowed. "I've been watching you and I cannot understand why some swain is not hovering about you. May I take his place?"

Morgana could scarcely speak. "I am not—that is, I cannot—"

"Come now." His deep voice was edged with mocking amusement. "Grant me just one dance, my lady. After that, if you still find me unacceptable, you may toss me aside without another thought for my aching heart."

He was already guiding her toward the center of the dance floor, her chilly hand tightly clasped in his large, warm one. Clearly, Morgana thought, Phillip Greyfriars had never accepted the word "no" as an answer. Fearful of drawing attention by making a scene, Morgana followed him numbly as the music began again. When she saw the complicated dance that was beginning, she pulled her hand back.

"No, I cannot. I—" She cast about for an excuse to get away. She seized upon the truth. "I don't know this dance."

"It's delightful. Let me show it to you." He put his hand on her waist and started out toward the center once more.

"No, please!" To her added irritation, her ordinarily soft, throaty voice now squeaked with tension. She fought to stay calm. "I would only embarrass and vex you with my clumsiness. Please allow me to go. You've time yet to choose another partner."

He halted and stepped closer. "I don't want another partner," he said softly. His smile was wicked. And beguiling. "I want the bright green bird with the ruffled black feathers." He reached out and touched one of the short, black curls that had escaped from her light veil.

She stared up at him for an instant, mesmerized by his nearness and the intimacy of his touch, as well as by the shock of fear she felt. There was something in his eyes that disturbed her, that told her he wasn't all that he seemed. . . . She shook herself away from his grasp.

"Please, my lord, if you are a gentleman, you will allow me to go without question." She drew herself up to the limits of her petite stature, mustering all the cool haughtiness she could command.

Surprise and amusement mingled in Phillip's face. He looked at her questioningly, then bowed, matching her formality. Taking her hand, he escorted her back to the edge of the dance floor. "My lady." He touched his forehead in salute.

"Thank you, my lord."

He moved away, and she felt relief flood her being. She turned toward the stairs. Before she could take a step, two strong arms came around her, spinning her about so that she was held tightly against a smooth expanse of velvet. Phillip Greyfriars kissed her so swiftly, but so thoroughly,

21

that she had neither the time nor the power to protest.

He let her go at once, smiling with such satisfaction and appealing delight that she wanted to hit him. As it was, she could only gape at him, her hand to her lips, the sensation of his kiss lingering and spreading its warmth. The people around them were applauding and calling out their approval.

"Forgive me, little one," Phillip murmured, his lips close to her ear. "I should have told you that I'm not much of a gentleman, and when it comes to temptations such as you, I almost always give in." He saluted her again and strode off into the crowd.

Weak-kneed, she turned and found her way to the stairs. She sought the passage beside them and made her way to the back of the house, where another set of stairs led to the upper floor. She made haste up the deserted back stairs and gained the top floor, breathless.

Everything here was quiet and dim. She took a moment to gather her wits. She could not recall ever being this nervous, even when she and Wren were working the highways and couldn't be certain if their quarry would try to fight them or would somehow summon help. She didn't like how alone she felt. Even Robin, with his crude comments and his boasting, would have been welcome company in this, her first attempt at burglary.

She drew a deep breath, then proceeded down the hall, counting doors as she went. At the third door, she halted, and whispered, "Grant me courage." Then she turned the latch and slipped inside.

Morgana stood still, amazed at the sheer opulence of the room before her. She'd seen riches before, but it had been many a year since she'd witnessed such luxury. In the light from the scented white candles that stood on the mantel, she could see that every wall was tapestried or draped, making the room warm as well as quiet. Every chair was filled with pale silken pillows. Every corner or ledge was adorned with some delicate trinket of gold, silver, or crystal that caught the light and sparkled like bits of fallen stars. The bed was covered in satin and furs, and fur-trimmed slippers and a heavy silken robe awaited the owner's return. The whole room looked as if it had been polished, burnished, and gilded into existence.

Music drifted up from the floor below. Morgana recalled Kestrel's warning to be quick as well as thorough, and she began her search. Trinkets were nice and would do in a pinch, but the flock was after coin, or at the very least, gems. She reached beneath her kirtle and pulled out the burlap sack that was hidden there.

A search of all the chests in the room revealed only a store of fine linens and gowns. She checked behind the drapes and tapestries but found no hidden caches there. There was a roar of laughter and applause from below, and Morgana knew that Robin had gone into his juggling act to distract the revelers for a while. But she could not afford to linger.

She tried another door and found the garderobe. The only other door led to a dark, adjoining chamber.

"I know this is where Kestrel said to search," she muttered to herself. "Where is it? Where do these people keep their money?"

She looked at the luxurious bed and thought of the Wren. He'd be waiting for her back at their dank innroom by the river, waiting on a miserable pallet of lice-ridden straw. There was more at stake here than merely the honor and safety of the flock. This one game could land her and Wren the prize they had planned for, the price of their freedom from the flock, and all that membership in it entailed. Again, she pictured Wren waiting impatiently, tossing on his bed—

She clapped her hands softly. That was it! The bed.

She rushed to the tall bed and dropped to her knees. She felt under the satin draperies for a latch and was rewarded with a clear, crisp click of metal on metal. A drawer slid open an inch or so, and Morgana yanked it the rest of the way.

"Oh, thank you so very, very much, my Lord and Lady FitzRabbit or whoever you are," she whispered. The wealth of King Midas seemed to be contained in this one drawer. Awed by the glittering riches before her, she lifted out a ring of silver, set with a ruby the size and color of a perfect dark cherry and edged with tiny pearls. Yet the ring was but a teardrop in the lake of other gems and precious metals that winked at her from the drawer. For the first time in all her days as a thief, she found she couldn't resist their lure.

She lifted a heavy chain of gold weighted with an enormous medallion. The initial "W" was engraved in its shining surface. Gleefully, she drew the chain about her neck, feeling the gratifying thump of cool gold as the medallion settled on her breastbone.

"What are you doing?"

Chapter Two

Morgana whirled about, the chain still in her hands. The steward of the house, official staff in hand, stood staring at her in shock.

Before either of them could move or speak, Phillip Greyfriars breezed through the door from the connecting chamber. His mask was gone, and Morgana stared dumbfounded at the radiant smile he gave her.

"There you are, Alyssa," he announced cheerfully. "I told you to wait for me in the second bedchamber, not the third, you silly wench. I can't allow Lady Winston to catch me dallying with you in her very chamber, now can I? Having you kiss me in that way in front of the entire party was trouble enough!"

He was across the room in an instant, taking the chain from Morgana's clenched hands. He slipped it around his own neck as the servant watched, mute and astonished.

"I think this looks fine, don't you, Edgar?" He struck a languid pose. "The Lady Elizabeth offered it to me the other night when I was here, but I said then that I thought it was too like Lord Sefton's. But now that I've seen his, I think this a much nicer piece. What do you say, sir?''

He lifted a silver mirror from the table and admired the chain against the red velvet of his surcoat. Morgana remained where she was, too stunned and frightened to move. Phillip turned to her for her opinion. She found herself nodding mutely as his smile flashed her way.

''My lord Greyfriars, forgive me, I thought the lady was stealing the chain. I had no idea that she . . . that you . . . that is—''

''Oh, quite, Edgar, I understand entirely. And with the Lady Alyssa disguised as she is, how could you have known her? She is a thief, I concede, but a thief of hearts, Edgar, a thief of hearts.''

Morgana felt herself blushing at this blather. What was he up to and what would it cost her? She didn't like to think.

Greyfriars lowered his voice to a conspiratorial whisper. ''I know you for a man of discretion, Edgar. Not a word of this to your mistress, eh? You know what I mean.'' His black brows arched wickedly.

''You have my word of honor, my lord Phillip.'' Edgar bowed deeply.

''And I shall take you at your word, Edgar. Now—'' The man in red and black broke off as a thunderous roar erupted from below. Above it all, high and bright, came the piercing call of a hunting hawk.

The steward turned and fled toward the source of the noise. Morgana started to run as well, but Phillip caught her arm and held her fast. She struggled against his grip, but he dragged her to the bed and tossed her lightly onto the coverlet. She caught his dark expression and marveled at the change in this man, who seemed to be such an elegant peacock one moment and now showed quite a different side.

"Hold there," he ordered. His voice had changed from a luxurious drawl to terse, sharp tones. "Your friends have been found out."

She stared at him. "I don't know what the devil you're talking about," she said, making for the edge of the bed.

"Your friends took the money from the coffers in the withdrawing room just below us. They were caught before they could move. It was sheer chance that I spotted you creeping up the back stairs and guessed your game. The juggler sent to distract us all failed in his mission. He's just been apprehended, if I'm any judge." He stood listening at the door to the hall, his body straight and taut with attention.

"Believe me, you're no damned judge at all," she retorted. "Now I'm getting out of here." She went over the side of the bed and ran for the door to the next chamber. He stopped her before she'd gone half the distance, catching her about the waist and carrying her back to the bed. This time he dumped her on it unceremoniously and went back to his post at the hall door.

She could feel her panic rising now. What was he planning to do to her? Why didn't he just turn her over to the constables? No doubt they were searching the house at this very moment.

Suddenly, the trailing gown and thin under-kirtle she wore seemed nothing at all. She had her dagger, but could she use it here, now? Was he planning to hold her in this bedroom? Old, painful memories welled up within her, making her feel weak and scared. She fought to stay in control.

"There, it's quieter, people are chattering amongst themselves. Lady Elizabeth won't be pleased that her party's been disturbed, however. She may come to her chambers to escape questions. We'd best be gone."

Phillip crossed to the bed, lifting off the chain as he went. He dropped it into the compartment as if it were

27

burning hot and gave the drawer a savage kick into place. Then he looked to where Morgana was crouching on the elegant bed.

"Come then, little cutpurse," he said with a sudden smile. "Yes, I do know who you are. I knew the instant I saw that delicious mouth below your mask, and heard that extraordinary voice. You didn't believe you could come to London and never see one of your victims again, did you?" He held out his hand. "Formal introductions can wait. Let's be off."

Morgana looked around her. There was no escaping this place now that the whole household had been roused. She'd been seen with the chain around her neck. If she tried to run, who knew what would happen to her? She had no choice but to go along with the charade this Lord Greyfriars had begun. No choice but to trust him. She'd break away as soon as she could. She began to climb off the bed.

He reached for her hand to help her down. She twisted away from him and jumped down by herself.

Phillip dropped his hand and stood away from the bed. "Take your sack," he said, pointing to the crumpled burlap by the bedside. "Follow as closely as possible. And agree with everything I say. Can you do that?"

"I can, if it won't make a braying ass of me," she growled, hiding the sack away beneath her skirts.

Phillip seemed amused by her words. "Trust me, sweeting, that's the last thing I'd wish to make of you." He went to the door. "We'll use the main stairs, I think. Better to hide in plain sight if you want to escape unnoticed in this crowd." He opened the door a crack and peered out. "Right, then. Let's get started."

She followed him down the long corridor, tucking the burlap sack under her dress as she went. She cast a backward glance toward the lavish room they'd just left. *So this was Lady Elizabeth Winston's house.* She should have known, after all she had seen and heard downstairs at the party. And it was plain that Greyfriars knew his way about the house quite well.

Phillip halted at the top of the stairs and turned to her. She started to back away, but he caught her and held her still by the shoulder. Very gently, he took the feathered black mask that hung on her forehead and lifted it down to her face. With deft fingers, he fastened the ribbons at the sides and adjusted the eye holes properly.

Morgana watched him, transfixed, her insides going tense. She still didn't understand what sort of payment he would demand of her for this kindness. She knew he'd want something. His kind always did.

He gave the feathers a quick brush with his fingertips and then stepped away from her. She felt herself relax a little as he released her.

"That's better," he said, nodding thoughtfully. "Everyone knows me here. They won't ask questions. It would be no surprise to them if I wished to keep the identity of my companion a secret, especially in this house."

"So I've heard," Morgana muttered.

"Have you indeed?" His voice was full of irony. "Well, there's no time to discuss my sins if we're to get you safely away from this place." He moved toward the stairs.

Morgana hung back. "What do you want of me? Why are you doing this?"

He turned and looked at her. He seemed to be weighing his thoughts. At last, he said, "Let's just say that I have a score to settle and I don't want the constables interfering."

Morgana did not like the sound of that. But there was no time to ponder his words. Already, men were ascending the stairs, their angry voices making it clear that they were intent on finding all the thieves and bringing them to swift, terrible justice.

Phillip shepherded her ahead of him, and together they descended to the main hall. The men passed them with hardly a glance. Evidently, Phillip Greyfriars was above suspicion in this house, at least as far as theft was concerned.

When they reached the bottom of the stairs, it seemed to Morgana that every eye in the room was trained on them. She turned to run, but Phillip blocked her way. She turned back, swallowing hard, and observed that the glances were accompanied by knowing smiles and chuckles. She felt a sharp flush of embarrassment rise to her cheeks as she realized what they must be thinking about her and the libidinous Viscount Greyfriars.

The guests soon returned to their gossiping and merry-making. The subject of the burglars was still on many tongues, Morgana noted, but she saw no sign of the Kestrel or any others of the flock.

"Take my arm," Phillip whispered, smiling and nodding at a young woman with a peacock mask.

"I will not!"

"Shall I leave you right here? Here comes the Lord Mayor even now. I feel certain he and his sheriffs would wish to meet you."

"Damn you to hell's hottest fires, Phillip Greyfriars!" she hissed as she placed her fingertips on his arm.

"You have the sweetest tongue, little cutpurse. Now, just pretend to be another smitten maid, if you can. You don't even have to speak. They can see it all in your loving glance."

Morgana dug her nails into his sleeve and smiled as she felt Phillip wince in pain. The Lord Mayor was upon them in a second, his ruddy face glowing from the effects of strong wines and strenuous dancing. He mopped his forehead with a linen kerchief that matched the bright aqua of his robe.

"Lord Greyfriars, bless me, I did not see you earlier! I thought perhaps you'd taken ill. That's the only reason we could find that would cause you to miss one of Lady E's glorious celebrations. That, or—?" He glanced at Morgana meaningfully and winked broadly.

Phillip made a gracious bow and managed to pull Morgana down into some semblance of a curtsy. "Thank you for your concern, Lord Mayor. But, as you can see, I am quite well and in full attendance to her ladyship." Phillip's speech had regained its deep, drawling tones.

"Well, I'd say not quite so fully, eh, my lord?" The mayor winked at Morgana again. She cringed inside herself but managed to give the man a pale smile.

"Indeed, my lord, you see my position exactly. If you'd pardon us—?" Phillip caressed Morgana's hand on his arm. She clamped down harder and saw Phillip's smile become a trifle strained.

"Oh, by all means, Lord Greyfriars. I know all about a young lad and his lass." The mayor stood aside and let them pass, giving Phillip a resounding slap on the shoulder as they went. "A merry evening to you, sir!"

"And to you as well, Lord Mayor," Phillip responded smoothly.

Morgana dropped his arm as soon as they were away. The man was truly a rake and profligate of great repute, she thought, swallowing hard against her rising fear. Even more reason to escape as soon as possible. She proceeded through the crowd ahead of Phillip, hurrying for the main entrance.

"She's more than eager, Greyfriars," a man called out behind her. "You'd best be ready right quick with that one!"

Morgana's cheeks flamed at these words, and she slowed so suddenly that Phillip bumped into her from behind. This evoked even more amusement among the crowd.

"You'll have to find a better way than that, Phillip, my lad!" another shouted.

Morgana wanted to swing on them all. Seeing her fists clench, Phillip took her arm quickly and guided her ahead.

"Pay them no mind," he murmured. "But stay with me or we'll hear more of such foolishness before we are safely away."

They found the passage to the front rooms of the house and Phillip led her to the entryway. They were alone. Morgana took her cloak from the chest by the front door. "I can make my way from here," she said as she fastened it about her throat.

"No, you cannot. The streets are too dangerous at night." Phillip donned his own short cloak and cap.

She laughed. "I've been in more dangerous places than the Strand. I can find my way and need no hindering companions." She removed her mask, tucked it into the belt at her hips, and tied the ribbons to secure it.

"I've just seen you safely out of that mess upstairs," Phillip said as he fastened on his cloak. "Indulge me once again as fair payment."

Morgana glared at him, exasperated. "A lazy lout of a noble at my side would only endanger me more. I must go alone or my friends will believe I've betrayed them. You'd be in danger, too." She started for the door.

Phillip caught the edge of her cloak and hauled her back until she was held close against him. "Don't be a fool. The streets around here will be overrun with constables and good citizens just waiting to cry 'Thief!' Where will you go? Will you lead them all directly to your friends, as you call them? What then?"

"Why the hell should you care?"

Phillip stared at her for a moment. He dropped his hold on her. "You're right. Why should I concern myself with a little urchin who knocked me out, robbed me, and now curses me at every turn when I offer her my aid?" He shrugged. "Go, then. I'll not hinder you."

Morgana looked at him in surprise. She was puzzled, but she also knew how to make use of an opportunity. She was out the door in seconds, her cloak swirling about her.

Phillip lounged against the wall and counted to twenty before following her into the streets. He spent only a second or two pondering why he was going to such lengths for the sake of this impudent little thief. But by the saints, what else was he to do? he asked himself. Stay and dance attendance for endless hours on Lady Elizabeth? God's wounds, he'd already been bored witless. Elizabeth would have enough to keep her occupied, now that the girl's companions had been caught. And the girl herself was proving an intriguing diversion for him.

He guessed that she was headed toward the river. That area was rife with pickpockets, highwaymen, and cut-purses, not to mention every other sort of criminal and predator that fed on London's riches. The girl might be a thief and wise in the ways of the streets, but she was a female and unarmed, as far as he knew. He felt himself coming awake and wary, suddenly feeling very alive after the indolent pleasures of wine and dalliance in the luxury of Elizabeth's big house.

He strode over the rough paving, guided by the dim light from the houses along the street and the half-moonlight overhead. He spotted the girl just as she was rounding the corner to head toward the Fleet River bridge. He also spotted the contingent of men who were moving on her from the right, a prisoner in tow. One of them carried a torch, and Phillip saw the badge of constable to the Sheriff of London stitched on the man's sleeve. He ducked into a side street and broke into a run.

*   *   *

Morgana was lost in thought. How was she to face the Wren? Or the Kestrel? She'd escaped safely, but she had nothing to show for all her efforts. If Robin and Kestrel had been taken prisoner, what would happen to them?

She shuddered. She knew what would happen.

If any one of the flock was caught, his or her sole concern would be whether death would come quick or slow. Theft of anything worth more than a shilling could be deemed a crime against the Crown. And a crime against the Crown carried the automatic penalty of death.

If the Kestrel was taken, what would happen to the flock? Without Kestrel's guidance and protection, she might be caught, and then the Wren would be alone and sick. They were down to their last farthing, and Wren would need more medicine before week's end. She wasn't even sure she dared go back to the inn where the Wren awaited her. Phillip had said she was in danger everywhere.

"Damn Greyfriars," she muttered. He'd offered her protection, but she knew that he would have exacted a price if she'd given him the chance. Indeed, given what she'd heard of him tonight, his price would be more costly than most. If only she could—

A shout brought her instantly to the present. A glance behind told her the shout was meant for her, and she broke into a run, quickly gathering speed as fear rose within her and lent power to her legs and feet. Her worst nightmare was coming true.

She cut around a corner, shot out into the shadows, and nearly stumbled against a peddler's cart. Righting herself, she raced on through the dark. The shouts were louder now as her pursuers gathered speed behind her.

There was a church ahead, she knew. St. Dunstan's. If she could get inside in time, she might claim sanctuary there.

Footsteps and shouts thundered behind her as she saw her goal just ahead. She made for the darkened chapel, gained the steep steps, raced up, then stumbled midway over the hem of her long gown. She fell to her hands and knees, tearing at the satin that hobbled her.

"Stop! Thief! Stop in the name of the crown!" The sound was terribly near.

She was almost sobbing with fright as she pulled free of the skirt at last. Clawing her way up the last few steps, she regained her footing and lunged toward the top. The door handle was just within her grasp. She pulled hard.

The doors were locked.

Chapter Three

Morgana turned to flee as the contingent of sheriff's men faced her at the bottom of the steps. She stood trapped like a deer in the royal woods. She halted, her hand on the iron ring of the door, her heart pounding in her ears. *Caught, I'm caught*, was all she could think.

"Well a day," a voice sneered at her from below. "Just as I told you. That's the one they call the Blackbird. She was in the house with us when we done the job."

In the flickering torchlight, Morgana saw the bulky figure of the man known as the Robin. She knew that he'd always seen her as a rival in the flock and made it plain that he resented any favors that Kestrel seemed to show her. Now, he was held fast between two constables, his hands tied behind his back, and in spite of his own predicament, it seemed clear that the Robin was about to have his revenge on the Blackbird.

"Robin, you vile, dirty, son of a wh—" Morgana began.

"What is going on here, good gentlemen?"

A robed, hooded figure strode around the corner of the churchyard. The friar came up the steps to where Morgana stood and laid his hand over hers as she clutched the iron ring of the door. Morgana stared at him in shocked silence.

"We caught this one here stealin' at a lady's house in the Strand, Brother," one of the constables volunteered. "He says the girl's one o' his band."

"I—" Morgana got no further.

"Well done to you, sirs," the friar interjected, "for catching the sinner and bringing him to justice. I can only pray for you now, my son." He waved a blessing in the Robin's direction.

"Don't pray for me, you old sod," Robin growled. His eyes glittered in the light of the constable's torch. "I'm goin' but I'm takin' her with me. I say she done the stealin', same as any of us. And there's more—"

The friar interrupted him, shaking his head sadly. "I regret that I cannot be of aid to you gentlemen in your efforts to rid our city of those who sin against their neighbors, but this one cannot go with you, even if she has committed some crime."

"Why not?" demanded another constable. "We've got proof enough. Look at the mask she's carryin'. It's just like the masks the others was wearin' when we caught 'em in that house—all of 'em birds of Kestrel's flock. She's guilty all right. One thief will tell tales upon another." The man started up the steps.

The friar shook his head and held up a hand to halt the man. "Come no further!" he thundered. "You stand upon holy ground. This girl has asked for sanctuary by coming here, and I must grant it by virtue of my sacred vows."

The man hesitated. "Naayy," he growled, suddenly uneasy. "She's not inside the church. You can't have sanctuary out here."

"Are you a brother of my order?" the friar asked softly.

"Well, nay, but—"

"Then you cannot know of our statutes. This door is a part of the Lord's own Church. No one could enter His house were it not for this door. This girl has clasped the means to enter God's Kingdom in her hand by grasping this door-latch. She shall be granted sanctuary by the authority of Holy Church."

Morgana stared open-mouthed at the brother, his face shadowed by his hood. She looked at the party of men below and saw them conferring among themselves. Still fearful, she gripped the iron ring more tightly and felt the friar's hand squeeze hers in assurance.

"Good enough, then, Brother." The sheriff's men began to back away. "The girl stays with you. She has forty days' sanctuary, the law says. But if she shows herself on London's streets any time hence, she'll be taken and she'll pay for her crimes. Understand?"

"I understand, good sir." The friar bowed, his hand to his chest. "Go with God, gentlemen."

"No! That ain't right! Why should she go free?" The Robin struggled against his bonds, his broad face twisting in rage. He lunged forward, almost breaking free of his captors.

Morgana shrank back against the church door. Robin hated her, she knew. He would do his best to have any revenge upon her that he could. The friar's warm hand held her icy one fast as the Robin was yanked back into the midst of the group below.

"Shut your mouth and come on, then, you." The constable prodded the Robin into the street. "We've got you and the others. That's enough of a haul for one night."

The men headed back the way they came, Robin bellowing protests and curses. When they had turned the corner and were lost from view, Morgana sank to her knees before the friar and kissed his hand.

"Thank you, Father, thank you!" she breathed, almost sobbing with relief. "I will do all that you say. I will—"

"Get up, please."

Morgana heard the note of uneasiness in his voice and looked up, puzzled. He reached down and drew her up to face him.

"Now," he said firmly, "I'm going home with you."

The friar tossed back his cowl to reveal his face. A brilliant smile flashed at her in the moonlight.

Morgana sagged against the church door, wordless with anger and shock. Phillip Greyfriars! She recovered her voice, but her anger was running like a forest fire, yellow-hot and out of control. "What the devil do you think you're playing at?" she demanded. "If that masquerade of yours had failed, you would have cost me my life!"

"Ah, but it didn't fail, did it?"

"That's no excuse!" she raged. "Why are you always interfering?"

"Interfering?" Phillip's eyes were challenging. "Sweet, I just saved your lovely neck. For the second time this evening, I might add."

"I don't need rescuing! I can take care of myself!"

"So I've seen."

"I can!"

"What would you have done if I hadn't put on my 'masquerade,' as you call it?"

"I'd have found a way inside."

"I see. Can you walk through wood, then? Can you unlock iron bolts with just your sweet smile?" Phillip lifted the heavy iron ring and pulled, for emphasis. The door stayed closed.

Morgana scowled. "Don't be daft. Of course I can't. But I might have run into the gardens and found another entrance. Or another, real friar might have taken me in. Or I might have given them the slip by running into the orchard behind the church walls—''

"Or a dragon might have flown to your rescue, sweeping you up in his talons and carrying you away," Phillip said, his hands making great, looping gestures over her head.

"You're ridiculous."

"And you're a dreamer."

"Better a dreamer than a wastrel!"

"Better a wastrel than a lovely maid."

Morgana started to retort, then stopped, open-mouthed. "You're a lunatic," she muttered. "You make no sense."

"And you're the sweetest morsel I've ever kissed," Phillip said matter-of-factly.

She glared at him, eyes narrowed. "You're a trickster."

"And you're an enchanting rose."

"Idiot."

"Angel."

"Stop baiting me, mongrel!"

"I promise I will, my dove."

"Damn you! Stop that! You—you—"

"Prince of your heart? Devoted suitor? Love of your dreams?" Phillip's smile was wickedly engaging, his voice cheerful.

"Stop it! Why can't you just—why don't you—you—" She couldn't help herself. She began to giggle.

Her giggling grew into laughter. She went off into helpless peals of merriment, shaking with the combined effects of fear and relief, all turned to naught with a few silly words from this—this ridiculous person.

"Phillip Greyfriars," she gasped out, "you will surely go to hell for all your lies this night. And that," she said, pointing to the dark robe which barely covered his long legs, "that act will doubtless be the sin that earns you a place of honor at Satan's table!"

Phillip seemed relieved that she was in better humor, but he feigned indignation. "Do you laugh so at a holy brother who has just saved your pretty neck?''

"You're no monk," Morgana said, still helpless with mirth. "That much have I learned about you this night."

"Oh no? What is my name?"

"Phillip Greyfriars," she said, her laughter subsiding a bit.

"Exactly. And I am a brother to my sister, Judith. Thus, I am Brother Phillip of the House of the Grey-Friars. So you see, little cutpurse, I am fully ordained and well within my bounds to grant sanctuary to whomever I choose, whenever I choose." Phillip spread his arms wide, a satisfied grin illuminating his face.

Morgana collapsed on the steps in another fit of laughter. Phillip joined her, watching her with bright eyes.

When she was calmer, she hugged her aching sides and looked at her rescuer. "Are you always such—such a madman?"

Phillip pulled the monk's robe off over his head, tousling his glossy dark hair. He shrugged. "I have my own ways."

She shook her head. "I've never seen anyone act as you do," she told him. "You've rescued me from danger twice and yet you do not even carry a sword. Most men settle all their quarrels by force and bloodshed."

Phillip was silent for a moment. The light of humor in his eyes was extinguished in a heartbeat. "I've done my share of bloodletting," he answered at last. "And I've seen others do their share and more. I prefer to use my wits. It seems a better contest."

Morgana stole a glance at him as he sat back against the step, crossing his legs before him and gazing out into the dark street below. She shook her head briefly. No wonder women raced after him, she thought. The profile he presented to her was all dark elegance, from the high, smooth forehead to the angular planes of his jaw. His height was impressive, yet there was no hint of gawkishness about him and he was of perfect proportions. He seemed at home in his body, Morgana thought, as if it delighted him and served him well. It was a characteristic that doubtless gave others cause for jealousy. His garments spoke of this comfortable pride, as well as refinement, dash, and wealth.

She looked down at her own thin, cheap satin gown, and when she caught a glimpse of the shabby shoes poking out from under the hem, she quickly pulled them in and tucked the gown down over the toes.

Morgana knew quality when she saw it. As the daughter of the late Lord Morton Langland, she'd been born into it and raised among people of quality. But all that was over. She was no longer Morgana Langland of Rushdoune House. She was Morgana Bracewell now, alias the Blackbird of London and Cadgwyth Forest, the robbers' camp to the north. She knew she was of no particular note, in terms of beauty, wealth, or worldly status. She was only a thief and a vagabond.

These recollections of her station roused Morgana from her seat on the steps. "I must go," she announced. "Thank you, Lord Greyfriars. I don't understand why you've helped me, but know that I'm grateful."

Phillip took her hand and held it fast. His eyes were bright. "You owe me a debt, little one," he drawled softly.

Morgana felt her stomach tense and then turn over. Warning bells sounded in her head. She struggled to hide her fear with a short laugh. "What do you mean, my lord? The money I took from you is long spent. I trust your head has healed—you weren't hard hit. What would I have that a great lord like yourself could possibly need or want? You know what I am."

"I do know what you are." Phillip tilted his head, regarding her speculatively. "But I don't know who you are, little one. I would know your name as my payment.

42

"That is easy. It is Jane."

"Jane?"

"Aye." She met his gaze, her brown eyes wide.

"And have you a second name, Jane?"

"Aye, m'lord, it is Protherowe."

Phillip smiled at her and released her hand. He lounged back on the steps.

Morgana smiled back at him and pulled her cloak about her. "I bid you good e'en, my lord Greyfriars. Thank you again. You've given me my freedom and I'll not forget it." She started down the church steps.

"I have not given you your freedom, little one." In one smooth movement, Phillip roped her about the waist with the long friar's robe and pulled her back down onto the steps. "I said that I'd let you go when you had told me your name."

"But I did—"

"Nay."

"I did!" Morgana struggled against the bonds that held her. "The devil take you and roast you to a turn, Greyfriars! I told you my bloody name, now let me go!"

Phillip held tight to the robe. "You lied to a liar. That's always a mistake, little Blackbird. That was what your partner called you, wasn't it? Blackbird? It suits you nicely, with all your shiny black curls. But it's no more your true name than Jane Protherowe. Or Lady Alyssa. Was it?"

Morgana was silent.

"What do you say? Will you tell me your name, or remain my prisoner, forever in my debt?" He leaned toward her, his voice deepening.

Morgana clamped her jaws shut. She strained against the robe again, to no avail. She'd have to find some other means of escaping this man. But she could never, never, tell him her true name. She might have made some mistakes of late, but she wasn't fool enough to let herself in

43

for deliberate pain and mockery—especially not from the likes of Phillip Greyfriars.

Her stepfather's name, Bracewell, was a name she despised herself. And her own father's name, Langland, was a name despised among the powerful folk in King Henry's favor. Besides, giving a name to someone who knew she was a thief was tantamount to suicide—and Morgana had no plans to leave this life just yet. She'd worked too hard at surviving thus far to throw it all away. She halted her struggle and sat still.

Phillip saw her shoulders droop in surrender and was puzzled. He'd been sporting with the girl, teasing her. But she evidently believed that he would indeed take her prisoner if she didn't give him the truth.

While he held her there, he looked at her. Even with her back to him, he enjoyed the sight of the soft curling waves of her short hair, so different from the long hair and elaborate braids of the ladies he saw every day. The set of her small head was proud for a commoner, he observed, and she carried herself with none of the stoop-shouldered weariness of the poor. Her elbows and shoulders spoke of poverty, though, for the girl was quite thin.

Yet, with all these contradictions in her, she was a most desirable bit of womanhood, with her dark hair, dark brown eyes and soft, husky voice that brought to mind the smoke from some sweet-burning wood fire. Desire had been his original motivation in pursuing her up the stairs in Elizabeth's house—a dalliance, as was his habit. He'd known what she was, and that had added all the more spice to the intrigue.

He debated with himself for a moment over what to do with this waif, then loosened the robe that held her fast. "Keep your secret, Blackbird," he said lightly. "I'll not press you."

She turned to him in surprise. Her eyes narrowed with suspicion.

"But I will ask for another sort of payment." His hand tightened the robe again.

"I knew it," she grumbled, facing forward again. "Worthless snake of an idle . . ." The name she uttered was salty enough to make a statue blush.

Phillip ignored her curses. "You will bring a single rose to my home tomorrow," he said.

"What?" She groaned.

"I want a single rose from you," Phillip continued. "You may steal it, if you must. But I want you to deliver it to my home before midnight tomorrow."

"And if I do not?"

"You will."

"Now who's the dreamer?"

"If you do not, I'll send my men throughout London looking for you."

"You'd never find me. How do you know that I even live in London?"

Phillip seemed amused by this. "An excellent point. Well, I shall just go to that fellow—Robin, you called him?—at his cell in Fleet Prison and ask him. I feel certain that he'll tell me all I wish to know."

"You—you pig! You viper—"

"There'll be time enough for pet names when you visit me tomorrow, little one," Phillip said, chuckling. "But remember, I want a single rose. Delivered to me in person, in my home. No one else may carry it to me. Agreed?"

"What choice have I?"

"None. As for directions, ask anyone hereabouts where I live—I'm known to most everyone in the Strand." Phillip stood and tossed the monk's robe over his shoulder. "I'd best return this garment now. It's just occurred to me that there's a naked friar lurking somewhere hereabouts. An awesome prospect." He gave her another of his flashing, wicked grins. ''Fare thee well until tomorrow, little one.''

He strode away whistling, until he reached the orchard walls. Then he stood beneath some hanging willow branches and watched her go. Would she come tomorrow, he wondered? She was a liar, a thief, and a foul-mouthed urchin, he reminded himself. And she seemed utterly immune to his charms.

He smiled. He found his interest in the chase growing the more objections he could find against it. She'd not be an easy conquest, that was certain. Perhaps he'd never win her.

Ridiculous. He'd won every woman he'd so much as smiled at since he was twelve. Earlier than that, if his old nurse and his mother could be counted.

Whatever the outcome, he wanted to know more about this wild little waif. He'd know her name and more before tomorrow was out. He shook his head in wonder. Something about her made him ready to ransom his soul for a smile.

That gave him pause. Was he getting sentimental over a bit of skirt?

He thought of Elizabeth Winston. Perhaps he should be more cautious with this new attraction. He still had a task to accomplish, and it wouldn't do to anger the volatile Lady Winston. He needed her confidence in him or his whole plan would fall apart.

Should he be more cautious?

Never. He'd conclude his ''business'' with Lady Elizabeth *and* have a wonderful taste of the little thief with the luscious rose lips. Even if he had to steal to get it.

He threw the friar's robe over the wall where he'd found it and hurried off to make plans for the next day.

And when he arrived home to discover that, once again, his purse was missing, he only laughed.

*　　*　　*

"Wren, I'm going out. I've an errand to do."

"No."

Morgana fastened her knife and sheath at her hip and straightened up to face her friend. "I have to go, Wren. It's something that I cannot put off."

The Wren was sitting on a bench near the narrow slit of a window that supplied as much dirt and odor as it did light to the close, dank inn-room. He frowned at Morgana as she prepared to leave. His brown eyes were bright with irritation at his young friend's bravado, and his ordinarily calm face looked disturbed.

"I'll be fine. I was a woman last night, remember? Today, I'm young Master Tom Black again." She did a quick turn before him, showing him the dark woolen tunic, plain black leggings, and sturdy boots she wore. "There'll be no danger to me."

She came over to the bench and touched Wren's shoulder. "I'll return before midday, I swear it. And if I'm delayed for any reason, you have food and money. I've told old Fletcher to look in on you today, and he's given his word."

Wren gave her another irritated glare.

"Yes, I know you are better and can look after yourself. Yes, I know that Fletcher has the touch and manners of a plow-horse," Morgana said, smiling. "But I would not have you ill and without aid if I'm . . . detained." Her voice became firm with stubborn pride. "You found me and helped me when I was just a stupid fourteen-year-old girl wandering about London. You wouldn't have been attacked by that wild boar in the woods if you hadn't been protecting me. And the Kestrel isn't around to protect us. He may be in prison at this very moment. It's my turn to help you as I see fit. Trust me! I'll be back."

Wren looked at her with narrowed eyes. She sighed. "You know I won't take foolish risks. We have a plan, you and I, remember? A plan to get us out of this place, out of this kind of life. I'm not going to do anything that could put that in jeopardy.''

After a few more words of reassurance—reassurance that she didn't truly feel—she started out for the market-place in the early morning drizzle. Despite the weather, the merchants were out in force, their stalls set up along the row to display their goods to the hundreds who were already thronging into the area. She strolled past the flower carts, and chose one that was busy with customers. While the owner was making up a fresh bouquet of gilly-flowers, Morgana selected a single white rosebud and skillfully palmed it up into the loose sleeve of her tunic. She casually inspected several other blooms and then melted into the crowd with practiced ease.

Following the directions a tavern keeper had given her to Phillip's house, she saw that it was one of the most magnificent houses in the Strand: high, wide, and metic-ulously kept. She went around to a side entrance, hoping to avoid drawing attention to herself.

The light rain had let up for the moment. In the side dooryard of the building, a cart and horse waited, the cart loaded with a large chest and bundles of linens. The path to the entrance was strewn with barrels and crates. Mor-gana picked her way among the boxes and went to the open door.

She rapped at the entryway and received no answer. She heard a clatter from within and ventured into the back hall. "Is anyone here?" she called as she followed the passage to the kitchens.

She got no answer but she heard footsteps in the pan-tries. She crossed to the doorway and called into the dim room, "Who's there?"

A stout woman with a pleasant, round face came back-ing out from behind a stack of flour sacks. She carried two enormous bundles in her arms. Red-faced, she tot-tered toward the door, and Morgana ran to help her.

"Oh, thank you, lad. That's too kind of you," the woman puffed as Morgana shouldered one of the bundles. "I have to get this out of here in a trice. Thank the blessed saints, that's the last of it."

The woman led the way to the kitchens and dumped her bundle on a table near the door. Morgana did the same.

"Now," the woman said briskly. "What can I do for you, m'boy?"

"You can tell me if this is the house of Lord Greyfriars." Though her voice was naturally a bit husky, Morgana lowered her voice a bit to add authenticity to her disguise.

"Nay, 'tisn't his," the woman said.

"But I was told it was. Whose house is this?"

"It's Lord Elyot's now, young sir. Bought and paid for this very morning at cock-crow. Lord Greyfriar's gone, I'm afraid. Left London, oh, five hour ago."

"Gone? But he told me just last night that I was to deliver something to his home before the end of this day. He told me nothing about his leaving."

The woman's eyes brightened. "Oh, aye, so you're the one he spoke of! Well, come along then, young sir. Lord Phillip will be anxious if we aren't there soon."

She grabbed up a cloak and headed for the back door, going at a great rate. Morgana, recovering from her shock, followed her. "Wait, please, there's been a mistake—" she began.

"Oh, I know, but it couldn't be helped." The woman waved a dimpled hand in agitation. "When his lordship come to me last night late and said he was bound to leave, well, I couldn't get done any faster. And then, when I come face to face with the butcher's man and he said that I—" She halted and whirled about as they reached the cart outside. "Oh, my saints and garters, there's the tapestry in the north bedchamber, still! It's his lordship's

49

favorite. Ralph! Hoo-hoo, Ralph!'' she shouted, waving her arms at the upstairs windows.

Morgana waited impatiently as the woman ordered a boy to fetch the tapestry out to the cart. She interrupted before the woman could start up again.

''Good woman, when I said there'd been a mistake, I meant on my part. I thought your master had told me to come to his home today. But since he's gone, he must mean that I should forget my errand. Good day to you.'' She touched the edge of her hood and started away.

''Did you not bring the rose for his lordship?''

Morgana turned back. ''Aye. I have the rose here.'' She lifted it from her belt and offered it to the woman.

''Well, then, boy,'' the woman said briskly. ''You've only done half your errand, and I'm not going to complete it for you. Not that you look a bad sort, mind. Lord Phillip wouldn't have you in his house if you weren't a fine lad. But just you get up onto that cart now and we'll be off at once.''

Morgana stood where she was.

''What are you waitin' for? You gave your word, Lord Phillip said. I'm the one who's to take you to Cygnet House this day. Now move, lad. My sainted grandmother, but you're almost as slow as my Ralph! Get along, boy!''

She herded Morgana to the cart as young Ralph came out with the tapestry rolled over his shoulder. He handed the bundle up to Morgana in the back of the cart and she lifted it into place. The woman kissed her son good-bye and climbed up into the driver's seat with much puffing and many references to her numerous blessed saints.

She turned to look at Morgana, her eyes narrowing for a moment, as if she were trying to recall something that was just beyond the grasp of her memory. ''Did his lordship say it was to be a lad, or a lass?'' she murmured to herself. ''Must've been lad, 'cause sure enough here you are, rose and all. Well! Time's wastin', Sarah me girl, and by the blessed Saint Michael if it ain't startin' to rain again.''

Sarah pulled her shawl up around her graying head, clucked to the horse, and the cart rattled toward the street as the soft rains began to fall. Morgana sat down heavily on a bundle of linens and gazed at the flower in her hand.

''Damn you, Greyfriars,'' she muttered as she was jostled along the road north out of London. ''Just you wait. You'll be sorry you ever crossed my path.''

Chapter Four

Morgana was sleeping beneath an old tablecloth when she felt the cart turn into a lane. Tossing back the heavy damask, she sat up and looked about. They'd been driving most of the day and now were climbing a little hill as the last rays of the sun broke through the clouds on the western horizon. She looked ahead to their destination.

A tall house stood on the crest of the hill. It was not a castle but it was well defended by a tall, sturdy wall and by crenellations at the roof line. The building was made of some light stone, so that it seemed to be silvery in the weak gray light. Thunderheads were building away to the west, casting odd lights and shadows on the grounds below. All around were vast green meadows dotted here and there with dense copses where oak trees, their leaves faintly tinged with early autumn color, clustered dark and thick. A stag raced across the road in front of the cart, its hind legs kicking high as it cleared a shrub and bounded toward the woods beyond.

"What is this place?" Morgana asked her driver.

"Cygnet House, like I told you," the woman said over her shoulder. "It's not the family house, but it's where Lord Phillip stays most times."

As they passed through the gate, Morgana saw exquisite gardens and small, neat outbuildings. Everything was in perfect order, from the deep red roses climbing the southern walls to the crisp scarlet and black banners that hung from the archway of the main entrance. It seemed a place of serenity and unusual style, unlike any other home Morgana had ever seen. A henchman in black approached Morgana as she jumped down from the cart just inside the archway.

"Follow me, sir. Lord Greyfriars waits in his withdrawing room."

Morgana looked at the old woman who was driving the cart.

"Go on, lad. Do as he says. Y' must complete your errand before you can leave."

Morgana shrugged with irritation as the woman drove away. Lord Greyfriars might hold power over her, but she wasn't about to surrender to him without a good fight. How dare he play such games with her! She might be a mere thief, a nobody, but he had no right to send her on wild chases across the countryside just to fulfill one of his whims!

She followed the man in black through a small entry in the huge main door and crossed a great hall that was bare and quiet. She had a vague impression that her surroundings were costly and tasteful, but her mind was so focused on her anger at the master of this house that these sights made little impression on her. The servant led her to a door in the far wall, opened it, and stood aside. Morgana didn't break stride, but marched into the room and straight toward her enemy.

"What kind of trick is this?" she burst out when she saw Phillip. "I agree to your blasted errand and then I'm dragged away to this, this nobleman's barn in the bloody middle of nowhere! What do you mean by dragging me over half the kingdom just to bring you a cursed posy?"

Phillip looked startled for a moment as he took in her costume, but he recovered quickly and leaned against the hearth with a smile. His dark eyes traveled up and then down her body with a studied attention that made Morgana want to fidget. "Welcome to Cygnet House, Blackbird. Or is there some other name that you're using today?"

Ignoring his teasing, she ripped the rose from her belt and threw it at his feet. "There's your token and payment." She spat the words. "We are even, now."

Phillip bent and picked up the rose. It was wilted and battered from being carried in her belt. He laid it in his palm, looked at it, and nodded to himself. "Somehow I knew you'd bring a white rose," he told her lightly. He put the flower in a tiny crystal bowl on the mantel.

"By rights, I was free this morn at cock-crow, according to your serving woman," Morgana said. "You told me I should bring this rose to your home. When I got there, you'd left. That house isn't even yours!"

"True." Phillip lounged back against the hearth, bright humor in his eyes. "I sold it to Lord Elyot last night after you and I parted. He's coveted it for so long, I almost made him a gift of it. But it seemed wiser to let him pay, especially as I found myself without a purse when I returned home. Do you suppose I could have lost it somewhere near St. Dunstan's, Blackbird?"

"You deserved to lose your purse," Morgana said. "And I deserve to be hanged for coming all this way like a fool!"

"No, not like a fool. Like the honest . . . lass you truly are." He arched an elegant black brow at her attire, then continued. "You wouldn't go back on your word. I counted on that. And I didn't go back on mine. Cygnet House is my home. My only home, since I've given up my house in London. By coming here, you've completed your errand and are free to go." Phillip left the hearth and came toward her. "Though I wouldn't advise it."

"What now?" Morgana's eyes narrowed. She shrank inside a little at his approach.

"It is nightfall. You have no horse. There are no inns nearby and no houses to steal from. You have no food, no drink. You're unprotected." He shrugged. "I know that you're capable, but these lands are not safe for anyone after dark, alone and defenseless."

She glanced up at the light fading from the high windows. How could she have been so stupid? It was all a trick! She'd allowed herself to be driven here and now she was trapped with this lunatic—this—this man!

"I'll go anywhere I choose. I've managed in towns and forests all over England. I have my knife and my wits. That's all I need." She turned to go.

"So, you would go hunting?" He stepped in front of her.

She sighed in exasperation. "Yes. I can eat what I kill."

"How far away from this place could you get, on foot, before your hunger bids you kill for your food?"

"You and your questions! Say what you mean."

He spread his hands. "Could you go ten miles? Or twenty?"

"Aye. Maybe not twenty, but I could go ten."

"I see. And are you ready to come back here when you're caught poaching on the lands of the Viscount Greyfriars?" He nodded at her widened eyes. "I own all the land for more than twenty miles round about this house. To take one of my animals without my permission would be a crime that I could not endure."

She took a step back. "You are the lowest, the vilest—"

"I am. It's true. Ask anyone who knows me." He took another step toward her and watched her back away again. "But you may ask them one other question, Blackbird. And they'll tell you the truth. I have never harmed a maid in my life." His voice was soft but clear. "You need not fear to take shelter in my home."

"I do not fear you," she sneered. "But neither do I trust you. I'm going."

He shrugged. "Then I'll go with you. I'll not have you alone on the roads in this storm."

"You will not come with me! Leave me alone! I can manage well enough on my own."

"Can you? As well as you managed at Lady Winston's house? As well as you managed at the Church of St. Dunstan?"

"Damn you for a skulking dog, Greyfriars! Keep away from me! That is all I will say to you!"

She strode to the door. Flinging it wide, she encountered the startled face of the man who had escorted her into the house. She brushed past him and hurried across the tile floor of the great hall, kicking up the rushes as she went. When she reached the main door on the other side, she flung that open, too, and marched out into the rain.

The wind was rising. She pulled her hood down over her forehead and set a course for the front gate. A sentinel was on duty, dressed in the black livery of the house. He saluted her quickly and let her out without a word. Morgana passed through the gate, her anger setting her pace, and proceeded down the lane as the first roll of thunder sounded in the west.

"Damn the man!" she muttered. The rutted road began to fill with water. "I was faithful to my word and he tricked me. I was doing well on my own without his interference. I could have managed to get out of all those places. I don't need him. I don't need anyone!''

She was soaked through in no time as the wind gusts drove the rain against her. Still, her anger pushed her forward.

She'd get back to the Wren and they'd send out some inquiries and learn the truth about Kestrel and the others, she planned. Then she'd have her revenge on Phillip Greyfriars. The prospect was tantalizing.

''Perhaps we'll lure him out with some lady—oww, damn and blast!'' She stepped into a puddle and sank farther than she had anticipated. Losing her balance, she went down into the mud. Cold, dirty water splashed into her face.

She got up as another clap of thunder sounded, this time nearer. Lightning flickered in the distance. Brushing herself off was no use, she saw. She decided to let the rain wash the mud from her clothes, face, and hands. She threw back her hood in defiance and resumed her march down the hill. ''Kestrel will know what to do.''

But her anger was fading, and uneasiness was taking its place. What if Kestrel had been taken? His was one of the most infamous names in the land. If he was caught, even now his head could be the ornament of a pike on London Bridge. She shuddered. And the Robin. What of him? He could tell the sheriff about her and the Wren. They could search at the White Stag and find Wren, alone, still weak from his injuries.

She had to get back.

A flash of lightning lit the sky over the western woods. Thunder sounded so near that she felt the noise inside her. She glanced about anxiously. There was no one in sight, just as Phillip had said. No houses, no lights, no smoke from a chimney. Even the animals had gone to ground to get out of the weather. Everything and everyone had taken shelter. Only she was on the road in the growing storm.

Coral Smith Saxe

A painful memory intruded on her thoughts, unbidden and unwelcome. In the next flash of lightning, she was a fourteen-year-old girl again. She saw the dark, heavy shape bearing down on her in the London house—as it had too many times already—saw the hands reaching at her, clawing at her kirtle, and she sensed that this time it would be worse than all the times before. She could almost smell the stench of ale on his breath. It had been stormy that night, too . . .

She began to run, feeling somehow that she could outrun the storm and the fears that were threatening to overcome her. Mud splashed up around her, and she found the going slippery. She moved off the road and followed along on the grass. Lightning flashed so close that she could smell the heat of it, and a tingling spread along her spine. Thunder followed within seconds of the flash, and Morgana felt her heart surge with fright.

She realized at last that she was in danger. She had to find shelter. But where? Everywhere she looked, there was only open meadow. The woods were too far to run to, especially across open land. She wanted to stop and turn back, but that way was closed to her, too.

Biting her lips, she raced on. The wind flung more rain into her face and she was blinded. She stumbled again, cutting her knee on a rock. Scrambling up, she spied a crumbling wall a few yards ahead.

"Thank God," she gasped, racing toward it. It would provide some small shelter from the elements.

She thought the sky had split apart when the next flash came. There was no gap between the light and the thunder this time. They were simultaneous, combining forces in such a way that the whole world seemed to shake with their power. Morgana screamed as a lone tree nearby exploded into flames. She swerved away from it and fell again, landing on her injured knee. She cried out with pain, but staggered to her feet once again. She was growing tired.

Fear took the place of her anger. She was running for her life.

Another flash and then a burst of thunder. Another tree exploded to her left. On her right, the western forest was dotted with smoking fires. Terrified by the fury around her, she didn't hear the sound of hooves until the horse was almost upon her.

"Give me your hand," Phillip commanded.

"No!" Morgana cried. All her fears had concentrated within her. She was like an animal in the wild, desperate for help but too terrified to accept it. She began to run, crazily, toward the flaming tree.

Phillip didn't hesitate. He spurred his mount and bore down on her. As he passed her, he bent far out of the saddle and scooped her up to him. He dragged her into place before him and circled the horse around to face back up the road. The big animal needed no urging. It broke for home at top speed, laying its long neck out flat as the rain pelted them all.

Phillip heard her scream as another thunderclap drove the horse to even greater efforts. He bent his body over hers, sheltering her from the rain and keeping them in balance on the horse's back.

They tore up the muddy hill amid the flashes and thunder, toward the big house with its pearl-colored walls. With the horse pulling hard, they streaked through the gate as though pursued by hellhounds. The stallion took a full turn about the courtyard before Phillip could get him under control. He leaped from the saddle as a groom ran up to hold the horse's head. Shouting for the man to get the horse inside, he pulled Morgana down into his arms.

She wrapped her arms around his neck as he carried her to the house. Thunder sounded again, its rumbling seeming to shake the ground beneath them. To his utter surprise, she buried her face in his neck and burst into tears.

He carried her to the fire in the great hall and sat down with her on a bench before the bright flames. The sound of the thunder barely penetrated the thick stone walls of the house, and the lightning was only a faint flicker in the high windows.

Servants hurried toward them, but Phillip motioned for them to keep back. Wrapping his cloak about her slender legs, he held Morgana close in his arms and stroked her damp curls. Silent and still, he let her cry, her small body wracked with sobs, until she could cry no more. His eyes were dark with feeling as he stared at the fire over her head.

When she was quiet at last, Morgana still clung to him, her face hidden in the folds of his cloak. Signaling to a servant to bring a cup of wine, Phillip took the goblet and offered it to Morgana.

"Here," he said softly. "Drink this. 'Twill warm you."

She lifted her face at last and took the cup in both hands. She managed a couple of swallows and then handed the cup back to him. Shyly, she lifted her eyes to meet his. "Thank you," she whispered.

His face was grave. "No. Do not thank me. I was a fool to bring you here by such a trick and an idiot to let you go out into the storm. I beg your forgiveness."

She wiped her eyes and peered at him. He could see the suspicion in her eyes, but it was tempered with something else, something he wasn't sure he could name. At last she nodded.

"Thank you," he murmured.

She seemed to be suddenly aware of where she was. She started to move off his lap but he held her fast.

"I would have you here, safe," he whispered.

"I—I am too dirty, my lord," she said. "I will spoil your fine clothes."

He chuckled. "I have a laundress. I want to hold you until you stop shaking, little one."

"I'm not shaking! I'm just so cursed cold in these damned wet clothes." She began to push away from him.

He released her. He clapped his hands, and three servants hurried over.

"Please find dry clothes for this lady, Margaret," he told the first woman. "And you, Sarah, see that a bath is drawn in the east chamber. Roger, build a fire there and bring food and drink for my guest. See that she is provided with everything she wants. And, Margaret, if you will, give the lady the key to the east chamber door."

The servants bowed and scurried off to do their jobs. Phillip stood and reached out his hand to Morgana.

"I'm in your debt, now," he said. "Please be my guest for this night. I will see that you get safely back to London tomorrow."

She got up from the bench and looked down at her clothes and boots. He saw that she was muddy from head to foot. Glancing back up at him, she gave a nod.

"Thank you again, little one."

"Morgana," she said, her voice soft and shy.

He smiled with pleasure and wonder at this surprising new softness in the girl. "Thank you, Morgana," was all he said.

A bath, good food and warming drink, soothing herbs placed on her cut knee, a comfortable bed in a pleasant chamber—all of these contributed to Morgana's drowsiness. She lay back on the pillows, dressed in the silk gown that Sarah had brought to her. It was several times her size and she had had to roll up the sleeves, but the fabric was so smooth and soft that Morgana felt she was dressed for a coronation.

She snuggled down into the feather bed and readied herself for sleep. She was glad that the thunder and lightning had moved on, leaving only the comforting patter of the rain on the walls and roof. She was ashamed of the way she'd shown her fear to Phillip, but she couldn't help it. Violent storms terrified her. That was a secret she'd carried inside her for five long years, ever since that harrowing night when she'd fled her stepfather's house, knowing that she could never return. She'd wandered the streets in that storm, running from strangers who'd clutched and shouted at her as she ran on in her torn kirtle and bare feet.

Wren had found her under a bridge on the riverbank several nightmarish days later, delirious with the fever she'd caught in the rain. The quiet older man had nursed her and sheltered her, and when she was well enough, he'd brought her to the Kestrel as his new partner. She'd watched with admiration as the two men showed her how they managed their lives outside the law, how they were no one's helpless victims. She'd been with them ever since. And though she'd learned to be both cunning and daring under their tutelage, she'd never ceased to fear thunder and lightning, and she never slept without a knife at hand.

Turning onto her side, she felt underneath her pillow for the comforting blade. There was nothing there! Instantly wakeful, she sat up in bed and looked about the dim room. Where was her knife?

She recalled that Sarah, the plump cart driver, had taken her clothes to be cleaned and dried. Hopping out of the high bed, she padded across the cool floor to the mantel. No knife. She searched the room. It was nowhere to be found. She felt her breath tighten in her chest. It was essential that she find it. Especially in this strange house, with its perplexing—and vexing—master.

She opened the door and glided out into the silent hall. She knew where the stairs were and she proceeded down to the lower floor. Servants' rooms were most likely on the far side of the kitchens, that much she knew from the old days at Rushdoune, her old family home. The kitchens would be connected to the great hall. The laundresses most likely had her clothing in that area, where hot water would be close at hand and fires to dry them.

She descended the stairs and turned left at the bottom. She followed a short passage and gained entrance to the great hall. Going gingerly over the rushes strewn about the floor, she passed the door to the withdrawing room where she'd met with Phillip earlier. The room was lit by a blazing fire, and she could see him seated before the hearth.

He sat in a low chair, holding a cup in his hands. He was bent forward, and his head was bowed as if he were in pain or some deep meditation. Morgana's curiosity was roused. What could possibly put Phillip Greyfriars in such a mood? He had everything in the world—riches, youth, strength, power, handsome looks, and a title. When he'd met her in London, he'd seemed a merry, witty blade, if anything. But now he seemed weighted with sadness or regret. She found herself drawing nearer to see his face.

Phillip looked up as she hesitated just inside the door. He gazed at her in wonder as he set aside his cup. In a gown so outsized, anyone else would have looked childish. But Morgana stood revealed as a woman to him now, not just a waif in boy's clothing or a pretty girl in green satin. The gown fell gently over small, soft breasts and framed a slender waist. Her hair was combed and shining in waves around her cheeks and forehead, and her wide, dark eyes seemed to catch the firelight and hold it. He felt his breathing quicken. The urchin was a beauty.

"Are you well, my lord?" she asked softly.

"Call me Phillip, please, Morgana."

"I saw you sitting so, I thought perhaps you'd taken ill in the storm."

"No. I'm quite well." Phillip felt a jolting rush of desire as she moved nearer, her legs and hips shaping the gown as she walked. In the next moment, he remembered the way she'd always reacted to even his slightest touch. She either hated him—which he doubted by her presence in his house tonight—or else she was afraid of him. He steeled himself against his natural impulses and stayed where he was. If he was to win her, he understood that he must allay her fears. "Is anything amiss, Morgana? Does your room not please you?"

"The room is beau—" She paused and her expression hardened a bit, as if she hadn't meant to reveal any weakness for fine things. "The room's plenty good. I want to know where my clothes are."

"Do you wish to leave now?" he asked, startled. "The storm is still raging."

"No, I'll stay the night." Morgana clasped her hands in front of her, her eyes downcast. "I just feel . . . that I'd like to have my things near me. Your serving woman took them from me while I was bathing."

Phillip considered a moment. "I'll fetch them for you. The servants are all abed by this time and I can find your things just as well. You should go back to bed, too, Morgana, or you'll catch a chill in your bare feet." He paused. "Use your key," he said softly. "I'll knock and leave your clothing outside the door."

She stiffened. "You may come in, my lord. It is your home, after all," she said with a cool edge to her voice.

"Very well. I'll bring your clothes to you in a moment."

"Thank you, my lord."

Morgana left the room and returned to the east chamber. She saw the key on the little wash-table near the door and almost went to pick it up. She recalled her terror and tears of earlier that evening. She felt shamed color come to her cheeks as she thought of how vulnerable she had shown herself to be in front of Phillip and his servants. She hated giving anyone such an advantage over her. She would have to be on her guard at all times now, or he would most certainly use it against her.

"No," she whispered. "I won't let Phillip Greyfriars think that I fear him or any other man!"

She crawled up onto the high bed and got under the covers. She was so tired that her eyes felt leaden, but she sat up in bed, waiting for Phillip's knock.

"Come in," she called when she heard a soft rap at the door.

Phillip brought in the bundle of damp clothing, moving quietly across the darkened room. Placing it on the chest next to the bed, he smiled down at her and bowed. "Good night, Morgana."

She nodded brusquely, glancing at the bundle from the corner of her eye. She waited for him to leave and then pawed quickly through the wet garments. No knife! She sat back, stunned.

Another rap came at the door.

"Come in."

Phillip reentered, his black velvet tunic a part of the darkness in the room. "Forgive me, Morgana, but I almost forgot this." He held up her knife, its long blade glittering in the last of the firelight.

She could only stare at him. She wanted to leap up and grab the weapon from his hand but she held still, her hands clenching the coverlet. She willed herself to stay calm, to maintain her self-control in the presence of this dangerously knowing man.

Phillip brought the knife to her and offered it over his forearm, hilt first. His eyes were unreadable in the dim light.

"Thank you," she whispered. She took the knife and held it flat across her knees.

He bowed again and departed, his tall figure swinging to the door and slipping out as silently as the shadows around him. He pulled the door shut, and she listened for his footsteps fading away toward the stairs. She wondered if he truly knew how much she needed her knife. He must, she thought, or why should he have made such a display of handing it to her?

Her hand shook as she lifted the knife before her. Slowly, she slipped it under her pillow and lay back down.

A flicker of lightning, still far off, brightened the room for an instant. Morgana felt the safety of the walls around her and remembered Phillip's vow that she'd be unharmed in his house. In the comforting warmth of the downy bed, safety almost seemed possible for her.

But when the thunder rolled again, closer this time, her hand closed convulsively on the knife hilt. She knew better than to give trust before trustworthiness had been proven. And Phillip Greyfriars, despite his blithe manners and his elegant ways, would be no exception to that rule.

If he proved false, she wouldn't hesitate to use her knife, if need demanded. God forgive her, she had certainly done so before.

Chapter Five

Phillip prowled about his solar until the storm was past and the sky outside began to lighten with the new day. He was disturbed and amazed at the turbulent feelings he was discovering within himself since he'd met Morgana the thief in London the night before. She irritated him with her constant arguments and defenses, and yet seeing her so vulnerable in the storm had touched him deeply. Furthermore, his curiosity had been roused by her need to have a weapon close at hand, even while sleeping. He could understand that she lived a life of uncertainty and danger, but there had been something else in her face when he had returned her knife, some flicker of pain that spoke more of fear than of simple prudence. What terrors could there be in this world for one so bold and clever as she?

His desire, too, had been undeniably roused by the sight of her, framed in that delicate nightdress. God help him, but he had wanted to enfold her in his arms right then, to lift that flowing gown to see her, touch her everywhere. With any other lady, he might have done just that, and experience had taught him that virtually any lady he approached would welcome and even match his advances.

But Morgana? No. He sensed the trembling in her whenever he came near, had caught the brief hint of panic in her eyes when he touched her—panic that she valiantly tried to conceal. She was afraid of his touch, afraid of him.

He flung himself down into his chair before the hearth and gave a bitter laugh. She had good reason to be fearful, he thought. Not just because he was a man, and one used to erotic pleasures, either. Nor was it because she was a thief and he a lord.

He was a haunted man. A man with blood on his hands.

And he had a heavy debt to repay.

He looked at his hand. The fire caught the lights in the ruby ring on the last finger of his right hand. It wasn't large and it wasn't precious to him, but he never took it off. He had bought it in Italy, and it had become a symbol of a vow he had made. Not a vow of love, not by any stretch of the imagination. It was a vow of darkness and hatred and revenge.

It was a vow to destroy his former lover, Elizabeth Winston, once and for all.

Until he accomplished that, until he had cleansed himself of the shame of his past, he would care for nothing and for no one. Oh, he'd still extend his hospitality to Morgana, perhaps even enjoy a day or two of her refreshing, prickly-sweet company. After all, he had tricked her into coming here and it was not safe for her in London just now. And, truth be told, he could use some time away from London and Elizabeth and the constant round of social events he was obliged to attend. But he would shake off any fancies he had about the lovely little thief who had come into his house. He would go back to London and continue to lay the trap that he had been so carefully building over the last few months. And when that trap was sprung . . .

He shrugged. He had never thought beyond that day when he would see Elizabeth's ruination. He couldn't imagine that he'd have much of a soul left, let alone a heart to give. Certainly not enough to give to a frightened, fierce little blackbird.

His thoughts startled him. He'd only known Morgana for a matter of hours and already he was willing to forsake his freedom to have her? He grinned. It was preposterous. He must be overtired and addled from wine. He'd vowed to have a taste of those sweet lips once more—he hadn't made a vow of marriage and endless, interminable fidelity!

A few days of pleasure. A diversion. That would be all.

He pushed up from his chair, took a candle, and went wearily to his bedchamber, satisfied that he had put the matter to rest in his mind.

"You see, m'lady? Them clothes ain't fit for wearin'."

Sarah made a clucking sound with her tongue as Morgana pulled the muddy tunic over her head and shivered. The rough wool was smelly and damp and felt clammy against her skin. Her hose and hood were in the same state. She wrinkled her nose and took a step forward. A squishing sound emanated from her boots.

"You can't go to London in them clothes," Sarah said firmly. "Lord Phillip said I should see they're washed and dried, and I haven't and I don't like goin' against his wishes, even for a guest."

Morgana sighed. The clothes felt miserable, she had to admit. "How long would it be?"

"I could have 'em washed and hangin' in front of the fire within the hour. Ralph could tend to your boots, too.

Meantime, I'll fetch you one of Lady Judith's old gowns. Lord Phillip's sister. There's some here from when she was a lass and they might fit.'' Sarah's keen eyes saw the words of protest forming on Morgana's lips. "Just while your clothes are dryin', perhaps?" she wheedled.

Morgana smiled. "Very well. If you would be so kind.''

"Oh, there's a good lass." Sarah helped her out of the tunic, chuckling as she worked. "Oh my saints, when Lord Phillip brought you in out o' that storm last eve, I took one look at you and I says to myself, Sarah, you old fool, that's no boy. That's as pretty a little lass as ever's been in this house since my Lady Judith went away to marry Lord Gregory. But you sure as the world fooled me into thinkin' you was a lad!''

Morgana felt her cheeks color at the older woman's words. She sat down on a chair and began to pull off her boots, hiding her face as she did so. "Your words are flattering, Sarah. But I'm sure Lord Phillip has had many ladies here who were truly beautiful.''

"Here? Oh, nay, my lady. Lord Phillip always says Cygnet House is his home—did you know he dreamed up this house all by himself? There's not another like it in all the world. Anyroad, he says that this is his home and no ladies should ever come here, save those of his family. Strict he is about it, too." Sarah bustled to the door with the soggy boots and set them outside. "His London house was the place for feastin' and such, miss. Lady Winston is always at his side there, at least since she put off her widow's weeds. And she does give the stars cause for jealousy, I will confess it. Still—well, never mind my prattle. I've work to be done!''

"Wait!''

"Yes, mistress?''

"What is Lady Judith like?''

Sarah's face lit even further. "Oh, she's a one, is Lady Redmayne. She and Master Phillip could almost be twins in looks, 'cept of course, she's as ladylike as any and he's a man and all. But they kept the household in an uproar right up until the day Lady Judith went away to her new home."

She crossed her arms, recalling. "I'll never forget the night Lord Gregory's father was to come and look at the girl for the first time, to see what he was gettin' for his son in a wife. Well, she and Phillip weren't more'n ten or twelve year apiece and they'd been up the night before, celebratin' Twelfth Night. Lord Richard, their father, had brought in traveling players to entertain. There was a dancer with 'em, a dusky kind of lady with curls every which way. Well, Judith took it into her head that that was how she was going to have her hair, and she made Phillip set up hot rods for curling." She shook her head. "I don't have to tell you the upshot of it. When Lord Redmayne asked to see what was under the girl's veil, there she was, shorn as a spring lamb. Lord Phillip had burnt the child bald-headed!"

Morgana grinned. "So he's not as perfect as everyone thinks, eh?"

"Oh, now, I didn't say that, miss. Happen it was Phillip himself who explained it all so droll-like that Lord Redmayne was not only reassured of Judith's beauty, but he accepted her dowry price without a murmur."

She clapped her hands together. "Now, that's enough of my prattle. I'm off." Sarah bundled the rest of the clothing together and scurried off.

While she was gone, Morgana sat wrapped in a coverlet, pondering the serving woman's words. Phillip was obviously blessed with a loving family. She wondered what it would be like to have a brother or sister. She'd hardly known her half-brother, Gareth. He'd been so young when she left.

71

She put the thought away. There was no point in bringing up the past. She was done with those days.

She thought about what Sarah had said about no ladies ever visiting here, save those of his family. If he was so adamant about outsiders visiting his private citadel, why had Phillip brought her here? She grimaced and shrugged. Doubtless he felt that she was no one of consequence and therefore did not count as a lady. And there was no way in which she could dispute such reasoning.

"No matter," she said, tossing her head. "In a few hours, I'll be gone from here and no one will know that a common thief sullied his house for a time." And, she added silently, the sooner she was gone, the sooner she could forget his eyes, staring at her with such knowing intensity as he handed her the knife in the darkness of midnight.

Sarah returned with a sideless gown of heavy, forest green silk trimmed with gold. She helped Morgana first to slip into a thin shift of delicate linen and then a snowy-white wool kirtle. Morgana stood as patiently as she could while Sarah fastened the dozens of tiny gold buttons that ran from elbow to wrist on the kirtle's sleeves. At last, she lifted the deep green gown over Morgana's head and smoothed the skirt down to the floor. She stood back and admired her handiwork.

"As I was sayin', mistress, there's not been a prettier lass in this house for nigh on to three year now. That was Lady Judith's gown before she grew so tall."

Morgana stood stiffly, afraid that the slightest movement would ruin the elegant costume. It had been so long. So long since silk had touched her skin. So long since anyone had helped her dress. So long since comfort and service and warmth and safety had been within her grasp. The feeling was at once pleasantly familiar and utterly sad in its reminder of all the things she had lost, first to King Henry and then to Cedric Bracewell.

Yet it wouldn't do to get too comfortable. Such comfort could only be purchased at a terrible price—that much she had learned in this life. She had to make her own way in the world, and if it was hard, fair enough—she would still be mistress of her own fate. She turned briskly to face Sarah. "Does Lord Greyfriars still wish to see me?"

"Aye, he's been pacin' the tiles off the floor of the great hall since he had his breakfast, miss." She lowered her tone confidentially. "If he don't see you soon, I'm afraid he'll burst or somesuch!"

"Sarah!"

"Oh, I'm sorry, mistress." Sarah hurried to the door. "I'd best mind my tongue, hadn't I? Lord Phillip hasn't said a word to me about you. All I know is what I see."

Morgana couldn't resist a grin. "And you see aplenty, do you, Sarah?"

Sarah's only answer was a cackle of laughter and a finger to her lips. She left Morgana at the entrance to the great hall and hurried away to tend to her laundry duties. Morgana straightened her shoulders and stepped into the big room, going carefully over the rushes in the fine doe-skin shoes Sarah had brought her and holding the skirt out stiffly at her sides.

Phillip turned when he heard her skirts rustling on the floor. The smile that lit his face made Morgana want to turn and run all the way back to her chamber. He was too faultlessly graceful in his flattery, she thought. She was almost convinced of his sincere pleasure at the sight of her.

He strode rapidly across the room to where she stood, half-turned, by the hearth. "Good morrow, Morgana. I'm glad you are well. You are well, are you not?"

She nodded, not trusting her voice to convey the nonchalant greeting that she knew she should make.

"I thought you might like to see the house and the grounds this morning. I haven't been home for several

73

weeks and would like to see that all is well. I have it in mind to improve my stables, as well. Will you accompany me?''

''I must wait for my clothes to be cleaned and dried before I can leave for London.'' She shrugged, mastering the confusion of emotions that had welled up in her at the sight of Phillip's brilliant eyes and dazzling smile. ''I might as well join you as sit idle in the chamber.''

''Good.'' He took her arm and guided her along the hall. ''This house is not so grand as Wildhurst, my father's home, but it pleases me and serves my needs.''

''Yes, I know that you like your pleasures,'' Morgana drawled.

''I do. Don't you, Blackbird?''

''I have little time for pleasures. My time is given over to surviving from sunrise to sunrise.''

''Mm. Yes, I can imagine it is.'' He slowed and stopped before a large tapestry. ''Perhaps you can take some pleasure here. Do you like this?''

Morgana shrugged. ''It is fair.'' She studied the vast scene of hunters and gatherers and harvest revelers. It was more than passing fair, she acknowledged to herself, full of vivid color, action, and texture. Her mother was a consummate needlewoman, and as a child, Morgana had loved to sit near and watch the strands of her threads come together into pictures of surpassing beauty.

She shifted her eyes to the table below the tapestry. She didn't like being reminded of those old days, of all she'd lost. Her gaze fell upon a small golden ball set on an ebony stand. As Phillip moved away from the tapestry, she palmed the bauble and slipped it into a pocket inside the gown.

They continued their tour in the great hall, where Phillip showed her his shield and arms, the many windows, the grand fireplace that could heat the whole of the vast space, even in winter. Morgana found herself alternately impressed and angry. His home was fine and well-built, full of simple, strong taste, with bits of Phillip's characteristic whimsy here and there. But each room triggered comparisons with her old home, now lost to her, and with her life as an outcast and a thief. She had set her memories aside when she left Cedric's house, and she had never allowed herself to deeply contemplate her lot with Kestrel's flock. It was pointless to pine over what she couldn't have.

She hid her pain from Phillip as they walked about the kitchens and pantries. She wasn't about to give him the power of knowing her feelings. Instead, she turned her face up to listen with seemingly rapt attention, and in each room she managed to pilfer some trifle and stow it inside the flowing gown. They would help keep her in victuals until she was back with the flock once more.

"I want to show you the yards and the stables," Phillip said as they finished their tour of the downstairs in his library. "But first—"

He wheeled her around and walked her back to the low shelf they had just passed. He stopped and looked at her, his eyes seeming to penetrate straight into her mind and being.

"What?" she asked.

He inclined his head toward the shelf and raised his eyebrows. Morgana made a sour face, reached into her pocket, and replaced the horn pen she'd taken from the shelf. She was sure he couldn't have seen her take it, she told herself. She had purposely asked questions about things on the other side of the room, to distract his eyes. The man was uncanny.

"Thank you," Phillip said. He took her arm firmly and led her out of the room and back to the kitchens. He came to a stop at the very spot where she had slid a tiny packet of salt off the edge of the oven.

"What now?" she asked.

He shook his head and reached for her sleeve. She slapped his hand away and took out the packet. She tossed it back into place and began to walk to the screens that led into the great hall.

He reached out and caught her arm. She glared at him, uneasy at the stares of the servants as they bustled past, preparing the main meal of the day.

"Will you play this game all morning?" he asked.

"What game?"

"Don't play feeble-wit with me," he said. "You know what I mean."

"It's not a game. It's my livelihood."

"Not here. Not in my home. You are my guest, and all I have is yours for the asking."

"Is it even so? Then why should you mind if I take a bauble or two? You can afford it."

"I do not care about the objects. I care about how you treat me. And yourself. You are my guest, not my prisoner. As I said, you have but to ask me."

"I'm a thief, Greyfriars. You knew that when you brought me here. Why are you surprised that a thief should rob you?"

Phillip moved her closer to the screens. "Most of what you have stolen is of such little value, Blackbird. And while you're clever with those hands, your moves were detectable to me almost every time you pilfered. If you truly wanted to rob me, you would have waited until I showed you my money chest and you wouldn't have tried to steal it out from under my very chin."

"As usual, you make no sense."

"Ah, but I think you see what I mean, angel." He held up his hand. He had somehow managed to retrieve the golden ball and a chess piece from her hiding place in her sleeve. "You were not stealing for profit. You have no need of a chess piece. Or a pen. You were stealing like a drunkard drinks, a drunkard who's long since lost awareness of the taste or quality of what he pours in his cup.''

"Thank you for your wisdom, *Father* Phillip," Morgana retorted. "I'm so pleased to have my faults explained to me."

"I'm not interested in the correction of your soul," Phillip said, leaning close to her ear.

Morgana caught her breath as she felt panic rising inside her. "I don't care about any of your ambitions," she managed to say. She reached into her gown and pulled out a handful of her gleanings. "Here," she said, thrusting them into his hands. "You're right. I have no need of anything from you!"

She twisted out of his grasp and ran to the great hall. She skidded to a halt as men carrying long tabletops blocked her way. Shifting and dodging around the obstacles, she raced for the door that led to the entry hall. Phillip caught up to her as she struggled with the front-door latch.

"Here, Blackbird, let me help you." He lifted the latch and pulled the door wide. "Run."

She hesitated, glaring at him.

"Don't you want to go? You may, of course. I don't hold my guests against their will."

"I can't go without my clothes."

"You could. My sister no longer needs that gown. Or those shoes. I'll even give you a horse."

"Oh, aye. And what price would I have to pay?"

"You owe me nothing." He leaned against the door frame. "But I had hoped to show you my stables. And my gardens. I'm rather proud of this place, you see."

"And if I choose to steal?"

He gazed at her for a long moment. "It was wrong of me to scold you for your habits. Please accept my apologies."

She studied him. He seemed sincere. She had been so wary of people for so long it disconcerted her that she couldn't seem to read him the way she could read others. Most people couldn't disguise what was in their hearts or their minds. One way or another, she could see it in the set of their mouths, the angle of their bodies, the expression at the back of their eyes. But Phillip—she just wasn't sure of anything with him.

"All right," she said slowly. "Let's see these grounds you boast of so highly."

He led the way down the front steps and through the vaulted porch that led out to the yards. The sun was beginning to show its face on the rain-soaked grounds, setting up a glittering display on the blades of grass and the leaves of the trees. Morgana drew a deep breath of the fresh morning air. It had been a long time since she had last slept in a soft bed and wakened with no need to make a plan for the day's takings. She told herself once more that it was only for one day, this one morning. Why not make the best of it?

They inspected a mews that was under construction in a sheltered corner, strolled past the kitchen gardens, and visited some of the outbuildings at the back of the great house. As they visited each area of Phillip's thoughtfully designed, well-ordered home, Morgana was again seized with remembrance and longing. She struggled against recollections of happier days at Rushdoune House, her childhood home, and forced herself to remember that this was but a moment in passing—by evening she would be on the road once more, back to life as a vagabond thief.

"Why do you call it Cygnet House?" she asked, trying to steer her mind away from her memories.

"Ah. That is my favorite part. Come see."

They rounded the corner of the house and came out onto a path lined with a shoulder-high hedge. Morgana heard the sound of lapping waters before they came through the hedgerow and saw the pond.

Clear and blue-green, it stretched to the far wall, where it narrowed into a stream that dove under the wall to the meadows beyond. All around it were young trees of many varieties, and wild lilies springing up at the water's edge. On the pond, two large swans sailed gracefully over the smooth waters. One was black as soot, the other snowy white. Proud necks raised, they trumpeted to the sky, as if in pure celebration of their own beauty and the beauty of their surroundings.

"Oh," Morgana breathed. "I have never seen such wonderful birds. I have never seen such a beautiful place." Unthinking, she moved to the edge of the water and gathered up her skirts. She tucked the skirt between her knees to keep it out of the dirt and squatted down to be closer to the approaching swans.

Phillip watched her, smiling for a moment, then pulled a little packet of crumbs from a pouch at his belt and came to squat down beside her. He took her hand and poured a few of the crumbs into her palm. "If you throw these gently, they will come nearer," he said softly.

Morgana did not even glance his way, so intent was she on watching the pair as they swam. She tossed the crumbs out onto the waters with a smooth motion. The black swan spotted the food first and sailed forward to investigate.

"The white swan is Raina. And that black brute is named Mars. They were here when I chose the site for my house. They are the first of my swannery."

"But I see no cygnets, no young swans," Morgana whispered. She held out her hand for more crumbs, her eyes never leaving the gliding birds.

"True." Phillip laughed, filling her palm again. "I had hoped they would have mated by now, but perhaps Mars is not so mighty as his name."

Morgana giggled as the big black swan preened and floated proudly on the clean waters. "He seems like enough to his owner. Mayhap you can show him what to do to win a lady's favor."

"And will you be that lady?"

Morgana felt her chest tighten for an instant. This was dangerous talk. Gathering her composure, she gave a brief laugh. "You have no need of a rough thief like me to prove your talents, my lord. Lady Winston is more the example you should seek for a dainty like Raina."

Phillip was silent. Morgana stole a glance at him from the corner of her vision and saw that his face was tight with anger. It startled her. Rage was an emotion she had not seen in Phillip, who always seemed blithe and carefree. Then she recalled the previous night, when she had seen him bowed before the fire in his withdrawing room. Perhaps he was not the vain fool she'd taken him for at first meeting. Here was a fresh wrinkle in his character, more to puzzle over.

She looked away at the swans, who had finished the bread crumbs and were sailing off in search of other tidbits. She stood up and shook out her skirts. So the man was more than he seemed, she told herself. It was of no consequence to her.

"Will you show me these stables that you think are inadequate to house the magnificent Greyfriars steeds?" she asked, her tone light.

"Just as I was thinking." He appeared to have shaken off his flash of temper, and his cool, amused countenance was back in place.

"Let me see the mount you rode last night," Morgana said as they entered the large, dim stable. "I owe him."

Phillip led the way to the stall where the big stallion stood. "Here is Saracen," he told Morgana. "He's a fine beast, descended of a breed my grandsires brought from the Holy Land."

Morgana approached the big horse quietly and reached up a hand to touch his smooth head. She had ridden a pony almost before she could walk, and her father had taught her much about the handling and choosing of good steeds. This was as fine a horse as any she had ever seen—strong, sleek, proud. The stallion snorted a greeting and paced a bit, but Phillip's voice soothed him.

"Be a good lad, Saracen. This is Morgana. She's come to thank you for risking your neck in that storm last night. What say you?" He looked to Morgana. "He says he loves risking his neck. It's his favorite pastime."

She gave a brief chuckle as she stroked the black's soft nose. "You are a lunatic, Greyfriars. All your animals have names and you talk to them as if they were people who sit at table with you every day. This beast cannot talk to me."

"No? Did you hear that, my warrior friend? The lady does not believe that you and I talk together. Is that not foolish of her?" Phillip patted the horse's neck. Saracen nodded his great head several times as if in agreement.

Morgana laughed. "The two of you deserve each other."

"True enough. Would you like to ride him?"

"Could I? Would—would he bear me?"

"See how he has taken to you already." The stallion nuzzled at Morgana's neck. "I had to ride him in an enclosure for over a fortnight before he would even obey me. For you, he would come like a lamb, I believe. I'll go fetch his harness."

Morgana spied a half-barrel with carrots and winter apples in it. While Phillip went to get a saddle and bridle, she fed Saracen an apple, delighting in the delicate way the horse accepted the fruit from off the palm of her hand. When he had crunched the apple entirely, he nudged at her arm for more.

"Oh, you are a sweet beggar," she murmured, stroking the glossy neck. "And a handsome dark devil, too, just like your master."

"You do me honor," Phillip said behind her.

Morgana whirled about, blushing quickly. "Nay, my lord," she told him tartly. "I just compared you to a horse."

Phillip pretended an arrow had pierced his breast. "Coldhearted wench!" he cried in mock agony. "What will it take to melt thee?"

"Give me the bridle."

"That is all?" Phillip was all wonderment as he handed her the harness. "And all this time I thought you impervious to any endearments. A bridle was all that was required!"

"Lunatic!"

"Sweetest lass!"

"Idiot!"

"Angel!"

"Bah!"

They saddled the horses, using a sidesaddle for Morgana in her borrowed gown, and led the animals outside. She tried to mount by herself, but the unfamiliar saddle and clothing hindered her. Saracen stood patiently while Phillip lifted her easily into the saddle. He held her still for a moment, his hands on her waist.

"Why do you look at me so?" she demanded. She wanted to pull away but was afraid that she would startle Saracen into bolting.

Softly, he asked, "Why do you fear me so?"

"Why do you always answer questions with questions? I do not fear you," she said, her voice suddenly more strident. "I just don't like being pawed."

"I see. But I like touching you very much, Morgana."

His eyes were warming her and he smiled so kindly, she thought. What indeed was there to fear from him?

Everything! The same thing that had driven her away from her stepfather's home. He would touch her, yes, she thought. And use her, and hurt her! She shrank away from him, her face tightening with fear.

Phillip dropped his hands. "I'll not touch you, Morgana, if you do not wish it. But I tell you now that I aim to win your trust. When you're ready, I will be here."

"I don't know what the devil you mean," she said with a sniff. "Now, Lord Greyfriars, can you ride as well as you talk?"

She lifted the reins and touched Saracen's flank with her heel. The big horse started away at once, and she had urged him to a trot before Phillip could mount his dapple-gray palfrey. He swung up on the horse and was after her in an instant. Conversation was forgotten as Morgana set her heels into the stallion and tore out across the western meadows with Phillip close behind.

The ride on Saracen was glorious. Morgana loved his speed, and the horse gave her all she asked for and more. He seemed to sense that his rider was a kindred spirit, wild and wary, and he obeyed her slightest command. With Phillip alongside them, laughing and calling out silly nonsense and urging them to faster speeds, Morgana and Saracen streaked toward the forest as though they were one, stopping only when the forest edge forced them to turn back.

She peered into the trees as Saracen galloped along the forest's edge, but she saw no sign of the fires from the previous night. Still, a smoky, acrid smell hung in the air beneath the trees, making her uneasy.

She guided the stallion around and slowed him to a trot. Phillip came alongside on his palfrey, his eyes alight with admiration. "You ride him as though he were created for you."

She looked away, shy under his regard. She brushed back a lock of her hair. "It isn't me. He is a marvelous animal," she said. "He seems almost to read my mind."

"I told you he was a smart lad. Now do you believe that he can talk?"

"No, you lunatic!"

"Yes, you lovely maid!"

She tried to glare at him, but he gave her such an openly wicked grin that she couldn't keep a straight face. She cantered ahead, smiling, and Phillip joined her.

They rode for an hour, or two, or more perhaps; she lost all track of the time. They talked of nothing in particular as they rode, and she began to relax and enjoy herself. She felt as if her cares had vanished for the first time in years and she was living in an enchanted land, where animals talked, and swans swam to eat from her hand, and the air was as sweet as nectar. It was nothing like the grimy room at the White Stag or the smelly streets of London or the constant watchfulness when she and Wren rode the highways. Here she was free, if only for a time.

She glanced at Phillip, who sat easily in his saddle, his strong, fine hands holding the reins with careless skill. "You're not a bad rider yourself," she said offhandedly. "For a man of silk."

"A man of silk, eh?" He slanted an amused glance her way. "Well, then, if I'm a man of silk, then you are a lovely rose."

"More thorn than flower, sir."

"Ah. But what if I reach past those thorns to pluck the rose?"

"That would be folly. You'd have only scratches to show for your troubles."

"Do you think so?" He edged his horse closer and leaned toward her. "Remember, sweet, you've already given me a rose by your own hand."

Morgana felt a shiver course through her at his low, intimate tone, at his very nearness. It was not an unpleasant sensation, but still it unnerved her. "That rose you did extort from me, Lord Greyfriars," she said tartly. "You won't catch me at such a disadvantage again."

84

"Nor would I wish to," he replied, his voice still low and caressing. "I will win my prize fairly and I will enjoy it as my just reward."

She felt her cheeks flooding with warmth. She was unaccountably pleased by his words and equally alarmed. "I think not, my lord," she said, edging her words with frost. "You would have to steal such a prize. And I am the thief, not you."

She spurred Saracen lightly and pulled away from Phillip, needing once again to distance herself from this man who asked for nothing and yet somehow made clear, silent demands on her mind, her body, her being. The sooner she was away, the better.

When they returned to Cygnet House, she would have liked to linger with Saracen in his stall, but she knew that she no longer had any excuse to stay. With a last caress of the stallion's handsome black head, she left the stables, Phillip at her side.

"I'll be off for London as soon as I've changed into my clothes," she told him as they made their way to the front doors. "I trust that you won't be arresting me for trespassing on your properties, Lord Greyfriars?"

"You don't mean that—"

"I do mean it." She pulled open the door and went inside, gathering her skirts about her.

"But I think you should consider—"

Morgana came to a standstill in the center of the hall. She stared at the man who sat before the great hearth, then spun to grab hold of the collar of Phillip's surcoat.

"You vile, snake-hearted, pox-ridden trickster!" she hissed. "Just what have you done now?"

Chapter Six

"Hold, Morgana!"

She looked at the Wren, who was pushing himself up from his chair. She whirled on Phillip again. "A thousand poxes on you, Greyfriars! What is he doing here? What the devil have you done?"

"Morgana!" The Wren's voice was louder now.

She raced across the room and took his arm. "Sit, sit! You must be exhausted, coming all this way." She glared at Phillip. "How dare you move him when he is so sick? What right have you to interfere in our lives?"

"Listen." The Wren sank back down in the chair, holding fast to Morgana's hand. " 'Twas kindness."

"Kindness? Kindness to take you out of safe hiding, sick as you are, and drag you over the countryside to this place?" Morgana was ready to fly at Phillip once more.

"Even so."

She looked down at the Wren. He was dressed in a woolen robe and a warm cap; a glass of wine stood on a table near the fire. His feet rested on a footstool covered with sheep's wool. He looked tired and pale but unharmed. She looked at Phillip. "Explain yourself."

"Gladly. I had you followed. You were not in safe hiding, as you say, for my man found you out in a matter of hours. He went to the White Stag after you left there and fetched the Wren to safety for the night. And a good thing he did, too, for when he passed the Stag again, it was crawling with constables looking for the rest of the Kestrel's band. Yes, I know all about the Kestrel," he said, in answer to Morgana's shocked glance. "And so does all of London by now. Your Robin sang many a pretty tune to save himself from the gibbet."

"Lord Phillip fetched me." Wren smiled and raised his glass in salute to his host.

Morgana sat down heavily on a bench. "Then they are all lost?" she whispered.

"Not Kestrel."

"He escaped?"

Wren nodded and made a graceful flying motion with his hand.

"And a good thing, too," Morgana said. "Now all we have to do is re-form the band. We've done it before. We can do it again." She counted on her fingers. "There are three and ten birds left at Ca—"

Wren reached out and clasped her fingers.

"What?"

He looked in Phillip's direction.

Morgana glanced up at Phillip, who was watching her with calm interest. She nodded to the Wren. "Of course. You must mend. We can talk of this later."

"Sir," Phillip said, coming to stand near them. "If there is anything you need, if there is any way in which I can be of service, please ask. I am glad to have you in my home."

"A thief?" Wren's voice was soft but amused.

"I know you are dear to Morgana. That is enough for me."

Morgana gazed at Phillip, speechless at such a statement. What on earth could he mean by it? She was no one to him but a common girl he had picked up off the streets! The man was either a prodigious liar or a lunatic—both, she suspected. But then, she'd thought that often enough in the past two days.

Wren seemed satisfied with Phillip's words. He nodded his assent and drank more of his wine. Soon his head drooped and he fell asleep where he sat.

Phillip motioned to Morgana to move away. She walked with him into the withdrawing room, with a backward glance at the sleeping Wren.

"I've had Sarah tend to his wounds. They are old and healing, but they were grievous and he's weak. He's been well cared for, she reported. That was your doing?"

"Aye. I've had some training in leech-craft."

"You've had the care of him for several weeks, I gather. You are very brave, and very kind, Blackbird."

Morgana fidgeted under his praise. " 'Twas only what one friend would do for another," she mumbled. "He's done as much for me and then some."

"Was he the reason you were in such a hurry to return to London?" Phillip toyed with an ivory carving from the mantel.

"Him and other reasons."

He put down the carving and began to pace off the edge of the room. Morgana watched him, wary.

"Master Wren cannot be moved again," he began. "Not until he is fully recovered of his hurts. Do you agree?"

"I suppose that's true."

"I would be glad to have him as my guest, but I have no one to nurse him properly. Sarah is not overly skilled with medicines, and my physician is at Wildhurst, with my family. What's more, I cannot vouch for my doctor's secrecy or discretion.''

"So?"

"So you cannot go back to London yet. It is too dangerous. The fellow who brought your friend told me that there is a large price on your head, as on all of the birds in the flock. Your Kestrel has flown and no one knows where. I would have you stay here at Cygnet House to care for the Wren and be safe for a while.''

"No!"

"Why not?'' He came to stand before her.

"Because it is impossible. I must get out of here and find the Kestrel. I cannot stay in this house.''

"And what will become of your friend, Wren? Will you leave him here while you go off to hunt in the wilds for your leader, who may have flown to Scotland or France or Ireland by now?'' Phillip rested a foot upon a stool, leaning toward her.

Morgana held her ground. "As soon as I find the Kestrel, I will come back for the Wren.''

"Even if Wren is not well enough to travel? Even if you cannot assure him that it will be safe for either of you to be on the open roads?'' Phillip's eyes held hers steadily.

"I can take care of us both. But not here! I—'' She hesitated, angry that he was forcing her hand. "We steal, Phillip,'' she said bluntly. "It is what we do. We know no other way. And we have to be where we can ply our craft.''

"I don't believe you.''

"I don't give a damn if you do! It's the truth!'' Morgana's temper was growing short. Who was this man to test her so?

"You have not always been a thief, Blackbird. That much I've guessed. You talk like a guttersnipe one moment and a countess the next. You walk as if you own castles in every county in England. You like your baths too much to be a girl of the streets and highways.'' Phillip leaned even closer, his eyes bright. ''But you may keep your secrets, Morgana. All I ask is that you stay and assure me of your safety for a time.'' His voice dropped to a whisper. ''Do this for the Wren, if not for me. I know that he would keep you safe, as well.''

Morgana looked away from his piercing eyes. How could she stay and accept this man's charity? She'd been the object of her stepfather's charity. He had reminded her of it every day. And every night, too, until she had been forced to leave her mother and young half-brother and find her way in the streets. She had vowed then that she would never again be so beholden to any man.

But the Wren couldn't move. London was closed to them. Even Cadgwyth, Kestrel's forest hiding place to the north, could be overrun with eager sheriffs, hungry for bounty. She would have to bide her time somewhere until the Wren was well enough to act as her partner once again. She would have to gamble her fate on this man Greyfriars.

''Very well,'' she said. ''We will stay. But only until Wren is well enough to ride with me to—another safe place I know. We can seek shelter there without . . .''

''Without fear?''

''No! I fear nothing. I only meant that we could take shelter there without burdening a stranger.'' She met his eyes defiantly.

''I see. Then it's settled. You will be my guests for a few days—''

''As few as possible.'' She drew herself up stiffly.

''As few as may be,'' Phillip agreed. ''I place all my house and my lands and my servants at your disposal, Morgana. Whatever you need to see that the Wren is comfortable, it will be yours. All you need do is ask and it will be done.''

She looked down at the floor, coloring a bit in shame. "Why are you so kind to me?" she muttered.

Phillip chuckled and lifted her chin so that she met his eyes. "Don't you know?"

She shook her head. His blue-gray eyes were tender and amused, both. She dropped her lashes, unable to meet his gaze.

"Then let's just say that it gives me pleasure." He leaned closer, and she could feel his breath against her cheek. "It gives me great pleasure," he whispered.

Morgana held still. Half of her was terrified at his nearness, half of her delighted in the warmth she felt from his body and the faint, already-familiar scent of sandalwood that emanated from his skin. She looked up and met the sparkling depths of his eyes.

Lightly, very lightly, Phillip touched her cheek. She winced but did not withdraw. Slowly, Phillip pulled back, smiling at her. She searched his face for some sign of mockery, of the disgust mingled with triumph that she had seen when she had had to submit to Cedric Bracewell's touch. There was none of that in Phillip's face. All she saw was tender interest and a wondering delight.

"Come now," Phillip said lightly. "Let us prepare a room for my new guest."

He straightened and held out his arm to her. Shyly, she took his arm, and they went off to tend to her friend.

The Wren slept through the rest of the day in his new room. Morgana returned to her own chamber that evening to find that Sarah had laid out her old clothes on the bed. She had also laid a fresh gown of gay lemon silk next to the dull gray of Morgana's tunic and hose. Morgana chuckled as she saw the blatant message the good woman had left for her.

"Dame Sarah has her mind made up, I see," she said to herself as she lifted the pretty gown with its flowing sleeves. She held it up in front of her and smiled. What could it hurt to wear it this once? she thought. In a few days, she would be gone and there would be no such luxuries coming her way for a long time, if ever. "Why not take advantage of what's offered?" she whispered.

The gown fit perfectly, though the hem still dragged a bit. Morgana took an experimental twirl about the chamber, allowing the graceful, dagged sleeves to flutter from her outstretched arms. She came to an abrupt halt as a knock sounded at her door.

It was Sarah. "He's pacin' the tiles again, mistress," she said in a loud, conspiratorial whisper.

"Thank you, Sarah," Morgana said, suppressing a grin.

Phillip was waiting for her at the foot of the stairs. When she rounded the landing and stepped toward him, his eyes lit up like candles. To her own surprise, Morgana did not want to run away this time. She descended to take his arm, basking in the warmth of his gaze.

For his part, Phillip looked even more handsome than ever. His high-collared cotehardie was of a brilliant, purplish blue velvet, with gold trim about the neck and sleeve hems. The color deepened his eyes to a smoky shade, and his glossy black hair shone with blue lights. Morgana smiled radiantly at him as he led her into the great hall.

Her smile faded, however, when she saw the dozens of servants and household members seated at tables in the hall. Phillip was leading her toward the dais at the near end of the room. She hung back, her eyes wide.

"My lord, I cannot sit with you!"

"Why not? You are my honored guest." Phillip pulled her ahead a few steps.

"No, it is not right. I cannot be seated above the salt! I am not—"

Phillip stared at her in amazement. "You are the greatest puzzle," he said wonderingly. "You think nothing of entering a house and stealing a lady's jewels, you fight for every scrap of your freedom, you swear like a stableboy, and yet you balk at the prospect of sitting at table with me?''

"Yes," Morgana hissed. "I cannot sit on the dais."

"Then I will sit with you." Phillip started toward the trestle tables that stood on the far side of the hall.

"No! That would be worse! What would your servants think?"

Phillip grinned. "They'd think, 'Ah, well, another antic of our lunatic master!' "

Morgana still hung back. "Please, my lord. Do not ask this of me."

Phillip looked at her for a moment. "You mean this?"

"I do."

"Very well." He clapped his hands and Gilbert, the steward, appeared at once. "I have changed my mind, Gilbert. I will dine in my solar this eve. This lady will join me there. And summon my other guest, if he is well enough to attend."

"Very good, my lord." Gilbert bowed and hurried away.

"Thank you," she said, touching Phillip's arm.

"You're welcome." His hand closed over hers and held it fast. "Let us go, then. I am famished!"

Phillip's solar was like Phillip himself: elegant, luxurious, and filled with whimsy. Morgana wandered about the room as the servants set the table by the fire, examining the many strange and funny objects that Phillip had on display.

"What is this?" she asked in wonder, pointing at a big box-frame that housed many iron wheels and cogs.

"That," he said proudly, "is a clock."

"A clock?" Morgana touched the heavy wheels with a fingertip. "I've seen them in the cities, but always so huge! How did you find one so small?"

"I built it," he said lightly. "With the help of my farrier, of course. I'm not skilled at ironmongery. But see, here is how it works."

He reached over her shoulder and touched a lever. He showed her how to set the heavy weights, and she watched in delight as the wheels shifted into motion and the gears twisted along in a pattern of measured clicks and whirs.

"And these numbers mark the hours of the day?" she asked, pointing to the circle of figures on the front of the box.

"That's right. It is much more accurate than a candle burning from hour to hour, and I need neither the sun nor the moon as a guide."

"It is truly a wonderful creation!" Morgana looked at him with delight.

"If you like my clock, then come see what I have here." Phillip took her hand and led her to a chest near the fireplace. He lifted the lid and drew out a box of bright cherry wood. He gave the box to Morgana and motioned for her to open it.

He watched, eyes bright, as she lifted off the top of the box and peeked in. She set it down on a table and drew out the object that rested inside.

"It's a horse!" she exclaimed. "A little Saracen!"

"Saracen stood as the model." Phillip handed her a tiny key. "I learned to make these toys when I was in Florence. Here. Place this in the hole near his neck."

Morgana inserted the key and twisted it. The little animal's legs began to move! She almost dropped the toy in astonishment.

"Here, allow me." Phillip took the horse, twisted the key again, and set him down on the table. The little animal began to toddle unsteadily toward Morgana, its hooves skating along the tabletop.

"Oh, it's wonderful!" she cried, clapping her hands. She bent her cheek to the table and watched the horse walk to her, giggling when it stopped short and fell on its side. "Not much like Saracen," she laughed. "But so cunning! You made this as well?"

Phillip nodded.

"Oh, that I could work such wonders!" She grabbed up the horse and twisted the key again. This time she put him on the floor and sat down to watch him creep to Phillip's shoes.

Phillip dropped to the floor as well, and sent the horse back to Morgana. She scooped it up and sent it straight back to him, giggling as he made the sounds of hoofbeats on the floor with his fingertips. He wound it tight and set it on a course to her as a pair of boots came to stand near them.

Gilbert gave a polite cough. Phillip looked up at him, smiling. Morgana looked at the toy that was crawling toward her outspread skirts, and she wanted to pass through the floor.

"My lord, your other guest is still sleeping. I did not disturb him. Shall I take away the third plate?"

"Yes, thank you, Gilbert. I will serve us. That will be all, if everything has been prepared."

Gilbert bowed and departed with the other servants. As the door closed, Morgana tilted over and hid her face in her lap.

"Morgana? Is something amiss?"

"No," she mumbled into the yellow silk.

Phillip moved to sit by her. "Then why are you hiding?"

"I'm on the floor, playing like—like a babe!"

"Aye, and a sweeter sight I've never seen," Phillip said with a chuckle.

"But your manservant saw me!" she wailed.

95

Phillip's laugh rang out in the quiet room. He put his arm about her shoulders and lifted her up to look at him. "I've never seen the like of you. I had hardly thought you'd be so concerned with appearances."

"I do not wish to be thought a fool," Morgana grumbled.

Phillip hugged her closer. "No one would ever take you for a fool. But sometimes I wonder if they might take you for a fussy old duchess." He smoothed a wayward lock of her hair. "What can be wrong with a bit of play now and again? Life is short and ofttimes hard. A bit of sport now and then can only add a taste of honey to it."

Morgana did not answer him. He touched her cheek.

"You can be anything you like with me, Morgana. You can be a woman, you can be a child, you can be a fiery little cutpurse—anything."

Morgana couldn't trust herself to speak. She looked down at the little horse that lay on the bright silk skirt. She gave a brief laugh. "And if I want to be a boy?" she challenged.

Phillip was startled for a moment, then he laughed, too. "I'd be a little hard-pressed, there, I confess. I've already grown to admire the womanly shape revealed by these gowns," he said, lifting a silken sleeve. "But I shall accept—what did you call him? Black—even Master Black, if he returns."

Morgana felt her throat constrict with emotion. She suddenly knew that Phillip meant what he said. No one had ever said such a thing to her. She knew that the Wren accepted her. Perhaps the Kestrel did, too. But never had anyone like Phillip given her his praise and his trust. It felt very good and a bit frightening. What if he discovered who she was and all that had happened to her? That her family had been outlawed and that she had been her stepfather's plaything? How would he feel then?

"Come," said Phillip, helping her up. "We shall be dignified and go to the table properly." He marched her across to the table before the fire and seated her with many scrapes and bows and ludicrous courtesies.

The meal with Phillip was anything but dignified. Each time a new dish was uncovered, he exclaimed over its nutritional and medicinal properties, rushing over to feed Morgana from his own hand or tossing it aside if the delicacy did not meet with his approval. He kept Morgana laughing from first course to last. And for her part, she ate as much as she could hold for the first time in many weeks.

When she had finished, she pushed back her chair and rose. "Thank you for a delicious meal," she said. "I'll look in on Wren as I go to my chamber."

"You're welcome, Blackbird. But I wish you'd stay a bit longer."

Morgana gave an elaborate, almost convincing yawn. "I fear I'm too tired, my lord. I wouldn't be fit company."

"Every time you address me as 'my lord,' you mean to put me in my place. Very well. I have set aside this evening as a time for play, for eating and drinking and making merry with my guest. If I am indeed your lord, then I command you to stay and keep me entertained."

"What do you mean?" Her eyes narrowed with suspicion.

He leaned forward, lowering his voice. "Only that your company gives me pleasure, Morgana." He leaned still closer. "I like the sight of you. I like the way you laugh and the way the color comes to your cheeks when you are merry." He reached out and ran a fingertip over the curve of her cheek and down along her jaw. "Stay a little longer, Morgana."

She nodded slowly, keeping her eyes downcast. "If you wish," she whispered. Then, mischievously, "My lord."

"Imp."

"Lunatic!"

"Charming wench!"

They laughed together and Phillip raised his goblet in salute. Then he rose and crossed to the hearth. Tossing several thick animal pelts on the floor, he motioned for her to take a seat in front of the fire. She spread the yellow silk out around her as she sat and accepted a cushion from Phillip. She took another sip of wine and sighed as she gazed at the fire.

"Now," Phillip said. "You must tell me a story." He sat down behind her and placed his legs on either side of her hips. His chest was inches from her back, sheltering her from the draft off the floor.

Morgana shifted uneasily, not knowing what to do. His nearness frightened her, but at the same time, he wasn't touching her. She held rigidly still as she replied, "A story? But I don't know any stories, my lord."

"My name is Phillip, not Mylord. And any sort of story will do. I like your voice."

"Oh, you are daft."

"Yes, that much we've established," Phillip chuckled. "Perhaps you could tell me of your adventures as a thief."

"I could do that," Morgana said slowly, taking a sip of her wine. She was relaxing a little in the fire's warmth. "One time, we were on the road north to Shrewsbury when a group of fat friars from York approached . . ."

Morgana related story after story as they sat there. Phillip was a flattering listener, full of questions, quick to laugh, ready to see the point of some jest, or moral. To Morgana's surprise, he made no judgments about her activity as a thief. Not once did he point out that she was a criminal, a wolf among the good sheep, as one priest had described it to her as a child. Phillip seemed not to care beyond the enjoyment of the story and the pleasure of the moment.

Morgana warmed to her task of entertaining him, sipping her wine and basking in the glow of the fire. She launched into the tale of Harold the Mountain, a quick-tempered giant of a man in Kestrel's band, and his quarrel with an ant in his bed. She was rocking with laughter before she could gasp out the final lines.

". . . And when Harold found the ant, inside his shirt, he looked about for something to kill it with. The only thing he could lay hands on in his rage was a club. He was fair ready to beat himself to death before the Kestrel could get the club away from him!'' She collapsed in laughter.

Phillip laughed too, his arms slipping about her, bringing her closer.

She went silent and still and swallowed hard as she felt the firmness of Phillip's chest come against her back. The warmth of him was pleasant, the gentleness of his embrace surprising. Still, the old fear was there, despite the wine, the relaxing fire, and the soothing velvet of Phillip's deep voice. She was torn. Part of her wanted to run from him, as far as she could get. And yet a part of her liked the protective strength of his arms, the solid feel of his chest and shoulders, looming above her. She waited, keeping very still, to see what he chose to do next.

To her utter shock, he began to sing. Softly, he murmured an old love song that she remembered from childhood.

"All night by the rose I lay, I lay;
All night by the rose I lay . . .''

His voice was clear and true and his chest reverberated with the sound of his singing. Slowly, bit by bit, she relaxed against him. The exhaustion of the day, the wine, and the effects of a good meal made her suddenly very tired. As he crooned to her before the fire, she drowsed and slept in his arms.

Phillip looked down at her in wonder as her dark lashes drifted toward her cheeks. He continued to sing softly until he was sure that she was soundly asleep. Then he stood, still supporting her, and lifted her easily into his arms. She stirred, making soft, questioning sounds as he carried her to her chamber, but she did not wake.

He laid her down on her bed and covered her with a blanket from a bench. Then he sat down to watch her sleep.

Phillip kept his vigil for an hour or more, watching Morgana in the dim candlelight. When at last he grew weary, he rose from his seat. Bending down, he stroked a hand over her forehead, smoothing one of the dark curls that lay there.

An instant later, Morgana had wound her hand in his hair and yanked him sideways onto the coverlet. She pressed her knife blade against his neck.

"Lay a hand to me again and I'll slit your throat."

Chapter Seven

Morgana sat in the corner formed by the bed and the wall, her body hunched up beneath the blanket she clutched to her neck. She watched as Phillip strode about the room, lighting candles.

It had taken only one swift movement on Phillip's part to disarm her of the knife. She had scrambled back into the corner as he had risen, still holding the knife, and gone to relight the fire. He paused for a moment now, his back to her, and she agonized over what to do next. Would he hit her? Was he planning to take her by force? Could she fight him off if he assaulted her? She winced as he turned about to face her, his eyes dark, his face working with rage.

"Who did this to you?" he demanded. His voice was low, but she could hear the straining fury beneath it.

"What?" she whispered.

"Who was it that hurt you so? Who has made you so afraid that you would move to kill a man just for touching you?"

"I—I don't know what you mean."

"I could kill him, whoever he is! And if I be damned to hell for killing him, I would meet him there and do the same again!" Phillip flung her knife into a corner with all his might.

"There is no one to kill, my lord," Morgana ventured after a moment, wincing at his rage. "I—I was startled, that is all."

Phillip looked at her in surprise. He seemed to gather some control over himself as he looked at her cowering on the bed. He came to sit by her again. "Morgana. I know that someone has hurt you, frightened you. I don't blame you for wanting to protect yourself. But you cannot live your whole life in terror. There is too much joy in you, too much love. I have seen it."

Morgana was silent. What could this man know of terror? she thought. All of his life was spent in luxury and ease and protection. She knew what there was to fear. And she knew the consequences of letting down her guard.

The rage was going out of Phillip's face. "Will you not at least tell me why you sleep with a knife beneath your pillow?"

"I need it for protection." She shrugged. "I sleep among thieves, as you know, and am often in the wild. I have but learned to defend myself quickly, else I will lose my life." She watched to see his reaction. He must not know the truth. The humiliation of his disgust and pity would be too much to bear.

Phillip rose and went to stand by the fire, his dark brows drawn. Morgana met his gaze for a long moment, waiting tensed for his contempt or his anger.

"If there is no other reason than that for your reaction just now, then you may sleep assured that there is no one in this house who would wish to harm you, Morgana. You can leave your dagger in the chest with your clothes."

"Perhaps I shall."

"And if your only concern is for your safety, then you certainly do not need to fear me. I only wish to touch you. To kiss you. To pleasure you," he said, stepping nearer. His voice was soft and brimming with warmth.

Morgana shifted the blanket up higher as he approached the bed. She bit her lip as he sat down on the coverlet.

"Does the thought of my touching you seem so unpleasant?"

"N—no."

"And will it frighten you if I take you in my arms?"

"No, I—no."

She held her breath as he reached out to touch her knee. Instinctively, against her will, her hand flashed out and slapped him away. She gasped and covered her mouth as she realized what she had done, what she had revealed.

"Oh no," she moaned as she met Phillip's eyes. She leaped up and was across the room in an instant. The yellow silk dress caught on a chest as she brushed by. She looked down at the dress, and in her confused panic, she started to cross the room to fetch her own clothes. She stopped, realizing there was no time, turned back to the door, took a few more steps, and finally came to a halt, her back to Phillip. The silence in the room was horrible.

"Blackbird." His voice was tender. "Morgana."

"What?" Her throat was tight with fear and rising tears.

"Come back, please."

She turned and saw his face, not filled with pity or anger or disgust, as she had feared. Instead, his look was pleading, as if he wanted a great favor from her. Against all reason, against all her past, against all her fear, she flew to his arms and clung to him for her very life.

He held her so tightly she could scarcely breathe, but she did not care. He pressed his lips to her hair as she sobbed against his shoulder, and he lifted her face to kiss the tears that made stars in her dark eyes. And still she didn't care. When she lifted her mouth, soft with grief and wanting, his kiss was infinitely tender. And to her surprise, she cared very much. She wanted more.

"Hold, sweet," he whispered. "Not too fast." He moved up so that he was sitting against the draperies that hung over the wall at the head of the bed, taking Morgana with him. He held her against him and smoothed away a tear from her cheek with the back of his hand. "Talk to me."

Morgana gave a shuddering sigh and leaned against the comfort of his chest. "I'm afraid," she whispered, her voice fierce with the years of frustrated anger and hurt.

"Think of this," he murmured. "They are only words. Like the stories you told me tonight before the fire. Words are all I ask of you."

Haltingly, tearfully, Morgana related the story of her stepfather's advances, how he had threatened her and lain in wait for her some nights. She had managed to fight him off each time, but each time it became more difficult. That was when she started sleeping with the knife beneath her pillow. The last time, he had come very close to raping her and he beat her cruelly for her resistance. Trying to save herself from his savagery, she had cut him badly, and in his pain, he had let go of her. She was gone from the house in seconds, into the London streets, where she had lived like an animal for several days.

"I lived under bridges and scavenged for my food," Morgana said as her shaking began to subside. "I became sick and lay down by the river, too afraid to ask anyone for help. That was when the Wren found me, and nursed me. I owe him my life."

Phillip cuddled her close. "I begin to understand," he said. "But why did you not say to your mother that her husband was hurting you?"

"I—I couldn't. He threatened to kill me and my half-brother if I told anyone. And I believed he would. He had

104

told me often that if I did not give in to him, he would hurt both Gareth and my mother. I had to let him, to permit . . .'' Morgana looked away for a moment while she fought with her panic and anger.

"Besides, my mother was grateful for his charity in marrying her,'' she said, disgusted. ''And he would ever play upon that theme to us—how he took her in, a woman of more than five and twenty, with a brat not of his own making, and a sniveling girl at that. Who else would have her? I couldn't tell her what he was doing. It would have been too much for her to bear, after all the . . .''

"After all what?'' Phillip murmured.

"After my father's death and all,'' Morgana finished hastily. ''My mother has a gentle nature. She suffered enough. In leaving, I believe I did what was best. That way, she could be at peace.''

Phillip was quiet, his hand stroking her arm. ''Your mother's daughter has a gentle nature, as well.''

"I?'' Morgana scoffed. ''Nay, I'm rough as thorns, as I said. I've had to be. It's what I like.''

Phillip shook his head. ''You have sweetness untold. I have seen it many times in the past few days.''

"You're daft.'' Morgana yawned.

"So you say.''

A comfortable silence overtook them both. She was exhausted after all the turmoil of the day, and the comfort and warmth of Phillip's arms were making her drowsy again. The relief of telling her secret after so long left her feeling calmer than she had felt in many years.

Phillip lifted her chin and kissed her gently. Her response was sleepy and shy. He pulled the blanket over them and slid down so that she was lying across his chest. Reaching out, he drew the drape across to block the candlelight from her eyes.

Morgana was asleep in moments. Phillip smiled down at her and shifted to a more comfortable position, never letting her slip from his arms. His desire for her rose up with considerable force as she snuggled close to him, making contented little noises in her sleep.

"Soon, Blackbird," he murmured. "As soon as you are safe."

When Morgana awoke, she was still held close in Phillip's arms. She turned to face him and smiled as she looked into his sleeping countenance. She recalled all that she had told him and felt a fresh quiver of relief within her.

She had never told anyone of what Cedric Bracewell had done to her. She had often tried to imagine what it would be like to tell someone, even Ariane, her cousin and only female friend. But she had always seen only pity or disgust in their eyes when she conjured up the scene. They would despise her for putting up with a man like Cedric for so long, or pity her weakness, or shun her as unclean. They'd say she urged Cedric on, and while she felt sure she hadn't, she didn't know a great deal about the matters between men and women. Perhaps she had been guilty of unwittingly lewd conduct. She was still a maiden. Yet who would believe her? Phillip was a man. It wouldn't surprise her if he responded to her tale with revulsion and ridicule.

Phillip had not reacted in any of those ways. She chuckled softly. Leave it to Phillip Greyfriars to do the unexpected.

She reached out a wondering finger and touched a lock of glossy black hair that fell over his brow. She was amazed at herself. She was lying in bed with this man and she was perfectly relaxed! Indeed, all she wanted to do right now was touch Phillip, to explore that handsome, peaceful face before her.

She sighed and let her hand fall away from his face. He was absolutely perfect, she thought. From the rich tones of his hair to the exact proportions of his ears, Phillip was perfect. What must the rest of him be like? she wondered idly, studying his eyebrows.

She blushed as she looked into his blue-gray eyes. She backed away a bit as he smiled and stretched.

"Good day to you, Morgana."

"Good day to you, sir."

"And what shall we do today?" he asked, casually smoothing back a curl by her ear.

"Mm, I don't know," she said, stretching luxuriously. "Perhaps we could go for a ride on Saracen?" she asked eagerly.

"We?" He laughed. "You mean you, don't you?"

"Well, if you are willing to share him . . ." She was suddenly shy, realizing that she had no right to ask for anything from him.

He sat up, shaking his head. "After all your spoiling of him yesterday, I'll count myself fortunate if the beast will let me inside the stables, let alone ride him. He is yours to command."

Her smile was radiant. He hopped over her and stood, stretching in the gray morning light. "We'll leave as soon as we've broken the fast."

Saracen welcomed Morgana with enthusiasm and seemed as eager as she to be out and racing over the wet meadowlands. After they had had a glorious run, Phillip led the way north through another rolling vale until they came to a steep, grassy rise. They rode to the top and stood to survey the land around them.

"All this is yours?" Morgana could hardly take it in.

"Mm. Much of it, yes. Yonder, to the south and east, is a chase that belongs to the king. No one may hunt there but the royal party. And some of the lands belong to my father."

"Where is your father?"

"He lives east of here, at Wildhurst. He and my mother are like so many who lost kin in the plagues. When April comes, they leave London, without fail, lest they be caught in the city's contagion." He shrugged. "I see no such danger to me."

"Plague is the least of my worries, also. If death sees fit to take me that way, then so be it. But more likely I will meet my fate on some highway, when I grow too old to cry 'Stand and deliver.'"

"We shall see," Phillip muttered.

"What?"

"Nothing. Let us go see what is beyond the next vale." He cantered ahead, guiding his horse down the other side of the rise with a sure hand.

A little while later, they halted the horses by a quiet stream that cut through the rich lands. Phillip dismounted and helped Morgana down from Saracen's back. She was wearing the green sideless gown again, so the sidesaddle was mandatory. After allowing the horses a long drink from the stream, Phillip tied them to a stump and pulled their saddles off.

"Look in my saddlebag and see if you can find anything to eat," he said to Morgana.

She did as told and found a delightful lunch for two, including cheeses and bread and fresh fruits. She laughed as she spread the food out on his cloak, which he had laid on the ground as a tablecloth. "You always have a plan, don't you?"

"Mm, no, I like spontaneity as well. But sometimes careful planning may lead to spontaneity."

She giggled. "You're mad."

"So you have said."

"You make no sense," she said, munching on an apple. "How may planning lead to things which are unplanned?"

108

"Let me see, how shall I explain it? An example. I was in Italy. I laid out a careful plot to meet a certain lady—" He caught her sharp glance. "Not a good example. I'll try again." He leaned back on one elbow and thought. "No, can't use that example, either, the countess would be too angry." He studied the sky, as if racking his brain for that rare example that did not involve amorous adventures.

An apple core bounced off his shoulder and flew into the grass. Morgana's look was all innocence when he glanced at her in surprise. "Never mind the explanation," she said dryly.

He shifted nearer to where she sat. "I suppose you shall just have to try some planning and find out for yourself." His voice was warm and his eyes danced wickedly.

"Perhaps I shall. Someday."

"Mm. And would your plans include me?"

She looked away, smiling to herself. "You may never know."

"You pierce my heart, Blackbird." He toppled over into the grass.

"Eat, my lord," she said, handing him a piece of bread. "You'll soon recover."

"Thank you." He ate the soft bread with gusto, looking up into the sky. "Look at the clouds, Morgana. They are like big white ships, sailing in the channel on a sunny day."

She looked up, curious. He sat up quickly and kissed her soundly. She didn't pull away, didn't stiffen, and didn't try to hit him for once. Instead, her eyes closed and her hands stayed folded in her lap.

"Why did you do that?" she asked when she could get her breath.

"Because you are so lovely," he replied, toying with one of her short curls.

"You shouldn't say that."

"Why not?"

"It isn't true." She looked away, embarrassed by his open praise of her.

"I say it is."

"You are a lunatic," she muttered. "How would you know?"

"Lunatics are the wisest of men, didn't you know that?" He was very close now, his fingers just touching her temple.

"I'm not lovely. I'm small and plain and I look so damn much like a boy that I can pass for one even at noonday."

"Those sound like your stepfather's words." His forefinger was now following the line of her jaw.

Her head came up in surprise. She met his gaze wonderingly. "How do you know?"

He took her hands in his. "I know because I trust my own eyes. Just as you should trust yours. Someone has told you that you are ugly and worthless, and I would guess that that someone is your stepfather, whatever his name may be. Trust my eyes for now, Blackbird. See Morgana through my eyes."

"I—I don't know what you mean."

"Here is what I see." His voice was rich and as warming as the sun on the grass. "I see a face like a dream, with eyes so tender that no man or boy could ever own them. I see a woman's body—have felt a woman's body—so sweetly soft, so desirable that I have trouble thinking clearly when you are near me. I see lips that smile at me and cheer my heart, and when I place my lips to them I am drunk with pleasure."

She felt her cheeks color at his words. She tried to look away but he reached up and held her chin still. "I am not so beautiful as Lady Winston," she murmured.

He drew back as if he had been stung. "Why would you wish to be like her?"

110

"She is your lady, isn't she? You will marry her, won't you?"

"Who told you this?" His eyes were suddenly clouded.

"I heard some ladies talking at the house where you found me. And Sarah says that you are always with her in London."

He relaxed again. "And did Sarah also tell you that Lady Winston has never been to Cygnet House?"

"Yes."

"Why do you think she has never been here, if she is to be my wife, as you say?"

"I don't know. Sarah said that you only ask ladies of your family . . ." Her voice trailed off as his hand began stroking her arm.

"Sarah spoke the truth, in part. Why do you think you are at Cygnet House while Lady Elizabeth has never been here?"

"I—I suppose because I don't count."

"You don't—?" His hand stopped its stroking. He shook his head in wonder. "If ever I meet your stepfather, I shall set one of my falcons on him and have his tongue torn—never mind, never mind," he soothed, seeing her horrified expression.

"Morgana." His tone was deeply serious as he continued. "You are here precisely because you do count. You count because you are lovely and kind and clever. You are here because I want you here. And I have never wanted any other lady here before."

Morgana met his eyes as he lifted her chin once more. He was in earnest, she saw. This was not more of Phillip's idle banter. To her amazement, he seemed to mean all that he said. It was a wondrous revelation. No one had ever made her feel so special, so wanted. The impulse seized her and she followed her feelings. She kissed him.

It was a shy kiss, light as air, but Phillip felt as if she had somehow set off a cannon nearby. The touch of those soft, curving lips on his sent his senses spiraling off into the sky. It was hardly to be fathomed. Phillip Greyfriars, who had kissed more women than he could recall, was rendered absolutely helpless by this first willing kiss from a woman who had come into his life biting, kicking, and cursing! His breath caught, he was keenly aware of the scent of fresh grasses that seemed to be a part of them both and of the cool, sweet taste of her lips. Lost in the world of his senses, Phillip allowed Morgana to end the kiss. When she pulled back, he looked at her in wonder, unable to stir.

"Oh, Morgana," he breathed. "Oh, love."

She smiled at him, her lips curving slowly upward. He touched her lips with a fingertip and laughed softly.

"Something is funny?"

"No, Morgana. I am just very, very happy."

He did not trust himself to be so near her now. And he knew that if he followed his impulses, he would frighten her to such an extent that she would probably resort to hitting and kicking again. He bounced up from the grass and held out his hand. "Come, Blackbird, let's ride back and take the Wren to visit the swans."

She giggled as she came to her feet. "Did you ever imagine that you would have so many different birds to attend?"

He chuckled. "No. But my home has always been named for the young swans. Mayhap I shall change the name to the Rookery. Good home for a Blackbird, eh?"

"I've a better idea. Why not name it the Tryst? Good home for a rake, eh?"

"I suppose you think I deserved that," he said, shaking his finger at her in mock threat. "Very well, demoiselle, just you wait. I'll pay you out for your abuse of me."

"Not if you cannot catch me!" she cried, lifting her skirts. She raced toward the stream.

He was after her in a flash. She led the way to the water and leaped high, clearing the opposite bank with room to spare. He was right behind her, gaining ground with every second. She began to zigzag crazily through the open meadow, trying to throw him off as he reached for her.

They both began to laugh uncontrollably, staggering over the wildflowers and tall grasses. At last, he caught her about the waist, hauling her through the air like a doll and then swinging her up into his arms. But he was laughing too hard. He stumbled and fell, twisting around to take the impact with his shoulder.

She came to land safely in his arms. She was giggling helplessly, so out of breath that she was gasping for air between bouts of laughter. She rolled to her back, holding her stomach. "Oh, please, I've got to stop."

Phillip made a pitiful attempt to sit up but fell back as a fresh wave of silliness washed over them both. At last, their laughter slowed and they lay gasping up at the sky overhead, her head resting on his chest.

Phillip blinked. A drop of rain hit him on the forehead. He waited. Another landed. Then another.

"Phillip?"

"Yes?" he drawled, making his voice rumble in his chest.

"Phillip, is it raining?"

"I'm afraid it is," he sighed.

They lay there for several moments as the rain continued to fall on their upturned faces.

"Should we go back?" she asked at last.

"I'm afraid we should—agghh!"

The sky opened up then and it began to pour. They dashed for the horses and got them saddled in a twinkling. Then they were off for home, cantering along in the rain.

Morgana stole a glance at Phillip as they drew near the gates. He was drenched, his hair plastered to his neck. His surcoat of dark blue velvet had soaked to a purplish black. Rainwater trickled down his forehead. His hose had been torn when he fell in the meadow and so had his

113

sleeve. There were bits of grass in his hair and all over his clothing.

She sighed. Phillip Greyfriars was the most beautiful man she had ever seen. Absolutely perfect.

Chapter Eight

They spent the evening entertaining the Wren. He was looking stronger now, Morgana noted with satisfaction, and he beat Phillip soundly in a game of cards. That is, until Phillip figured out Wren's special method of cheating and bested him at his own game.

Wren's praise was effusive, for the Wren. "Clever, my lord."

Morgana sat entranced when Phillip lifted a cittern down from the wall and began to play. He sang two songs of brave battles from long ago. Then he turned to her and sang several short ballads in a language she did not understand. Still, their nature was clear. She looked away, suddenly embarrassed by the strength of her reaction to these words of love that she could not translate.

Phillip escorted her to her chamber door after they had said good night to the Wren. He smoothed back a wayward curl that had escaped from the cap she wore.

"It's been a fine day, Blackbird."

"Yes," she said. "Thank you, my lord."

"My lord? Are you putting me in my place again?"

"No. Thank you, Phillip."

"Much better." He bent forward swiftly and took her into his arms.

She melted into his embrace. She raised her head to receive his kiss and felt a glowing warmth ignite deep within her. Tentatively, she reached up and placed her hands on either side of his face, holding him still, to kiss him once again. His lips were so warm and so full of gentle urgings. She found that she could answer those lips with her own, reveling in the way her body seemed to ignite a little more with each passing second. The nearness of Phillip, the strength of his arms, the way she fitted against his chest so neatly—it all felt new and yet so indescribably right. She was lost in a flood of sensations that threatened to carry her off somewhere she had never ventured before.

He clasped her hands and lowered them as he backed away. "Good night, Morgana," he said, his voice somehow sounding tight and strained. "Rest you well."

"Pleasant dreams to you," she replied, a little dazed.

She watched him hurry away into the darkness and then went inside her chamber. She felt disappointed somehow, as if something had been left unsaid or undone.

When she climbed into bed and closed her eyes, she saw the sun and the meadow and Phillip's laughing eyes. She was in danger with him. She knew it as surely as she knew how wonderful it had been to be in his arms. If she wasn't careful, she would be in a trap built of her own making.

She frowned and scrubbed her face into the pillow. She could be careful, she told herself. She could.

The next morning, Phillip was occupied with various duties in his library. Morgana and Wren broke the fast together in Wren's chamber and then took a short walk about the gardens. The last of the summer flowers were in high color and the birds and animals were already making plans for winter, judging from the flurry of activity around the grounds. They strolled down the hedge-lined row and visited Raina and Mars on their shimmering lake.

"Do you think the Kestrel has returned to Cadgwyth, Wren?" Morgana took a seat beside him on a little bench and idly plucked at a clump of tall daisies.

"Likely," Wren nodded. Then he shrugged. "Or France. Scotland."

"I wish I knew. Then we could make plans. As it is, we can only run blindly to one place or another, risking our necks to find that perhaps he's gone elsewhere."

Wren's eyes were keen. "Will you leave?"

"Of course." Morgana studied the swans swimming lazily over the water. She plucked several of the big white daisies and laid them in her lap. "I can't stay here."

"No?"

"What are you driving at?" Morgana gave her friend a sharp glance.

"His lordship."

"What of him?"

"He'd have you stay."

"Oh, bosh, Wren." Her nervous fingers began twisting daisy stems together.

"Truth."

"The man has only pity for me. I was in trouble and he helped. He has a kindly nature but he has no wish to have a thief living in his house, I'm sure."

"And you?"

"What do you mean?"

"You'd stay."

Morgana waved her hand. "You've spent too much time in this easy life, my friend. You are having romantic notions. Hell's devils, Wren, I cut purses for my living.

117

Life in the band is for me. I cannot stay in someplace like this.''

"If he asked it?''

Morgana turned to look at Wren. Her eyes were wary. "You think that he would ask such a thing of me?''

Wren nodded. Morgana looked away, coloring slightly.

"I couldn't stay, Wren. 'Twouldn't be right. Besides, he is betrothed, I hear, to the Lady Winston. I would only disgrace him.'' She shaped the daisies into a circle, binding them round with some sweetgrass.

"Perhaps.''

"I know it, Wren!'' she said fiercely. "And don't try any more of your daft arguments on me. I don't want to hear anymore!''

Wren's eyebrows shot up at this outburst. Then he chuckled as a look of dismay came over Morgana's face.

"Oh, Wren, I'm sorry. Damn! I can't seem to think straight around here. Soft place! The sooner we leave, the better.'' She bounced up off the bench and strode a few paces away, kicking at her skirts as they got in her way.

Her companion grinned to himself as he watched her march off in agitation. Then he commenced a terrible fit of coughing.

Morgana rushed back to him. "Are you all right?'' she asked, full of concern. She gave him her kerchief. "Perhaps you should lie down.''

The Wren nodded and allowed himself to be led into the house and settled into his chamber with a cup of hot herb-water and honey for his cough. She left him to rest and wandered down the hall to her own chamber, still holding the flowers she had picked by the pond. She thought about her conversation with the Wren.

Did Phillip want her to stay? He had been more than kind, she knew. He seemed to enjoy her company. He had held her, kissed her, comforted her, listened to her secrets and fears with a tenderness she had never known before.

And she had loved the past few days, though she would have been hard-pressed to admit it out loud. It had been a long time since she had felt so free of cares, of watchfulness. It had been even longer since she had laughed, run, and played. Being around Phillip had reminded her of the joys of her childhood, running and giggling and pretending.

She smiled as she picked up the toy horse that Phillip had presented to her yesterday. He seemed to know so much about her, so much that she had labored for years to keep secret. He had awakened something in her that even now she could not name. All she could think of was the pleasure of his kisses and the warmth of his smile as he held her.

"So? It is only for a few days more!" she whispered. "I'll enjoy the time with Phillip just as I've enjoyed the dresses and the food and the shelter."

She picked up the garland of daisies, grinning. She was out the door in a twinkling, running down the hall to find Phillip and crown him with flowers. Lifting her skirts, she danced downstairs, the garland swinging at her side. She heard his voice in the library and ran lightly to the open door, a blithe greeting on her lips. She halted when she saw that he was not alone.

"My mistress was most distressed to learn that you had left the city so suddenly, my lord. She bade me inquire if you are well."

The short man in the brown tunic stood before Phillip with his cap in his hand. Phillip's back was to her, but Morgana could see the formality and attentiveness in his posture.

"Tell her ladyship that I am quite well, and thank her for her most generous concern. She is as kind as she is lovely." Phillip's voice was smooth and relaxed, in contrast to his stance.

"I will do as you say, Lord Greyfriars. But Lady Winston also bade me deliver a message to you. She asks that you meet with her as soon as possible regarding the establishment of the charity she wishes to found for orphaned girls." The man's eyes flickered to the door where Morgana stood, garland in hand, then instantly back to Phillip. "She would like to begin building the refuge at once and craves your advice as a designer of buildings."

Phillip's reply came instantly. "I will ride to London at daybreak tomorrow. Tell Lady Elizabeth that her slightest desire is my most fervent prayer."

"Very good, my lord. Now, if I may . . ."

Morgana didn't stay to hear more. Turning on her heel, she raced back to the stairs and took them two at a time. Back in her chamber, she stripped off the yellow gown, throwing it on the chest with a scowl. She pulled out her own gray tunic and quickly dressed in her old clothes. Shoving her feet into her boots, she ran down the stairs, avoiding the withdrawing-room door, and headed outside to the stables.

She took a saddle and bridle and had Saracen ready to go in minutes. Swinging up onto the big horse's back, she guided him out of the stables and headed for the gates. The guard, recognizing his master's guest, looked wonderingly at her attire, but allowed her through the gates with no questions asked.

Morgana set her heels to Saracen's great sides and set off across the long vale toward the woods. She had no real idea where she was going, but the need to be away from Cygnet House drove her to urge Saracen to greater speeds, until her mind and body were fully occupied with guiding the horse and staying astride. Saracen seemed to sense the tempest of her feelings, and he drove hard for the woodlands, stretching out his great neck and pounding over the turf. At the edge of the woods, Morgana slowed the stallion and traced the forest edge for a path into the trees. She located a narrow track and rode inside.

The forest closed around her after a time, quieting the horse's hoofbeats and seeming to deaden all other sounds. Here and there, shafts of sunlight pierced the canopy of leaves overhead, illuminating the tiny motes of dust in the air to form golden bars of light in her path. The track began to dwindle away to nothing, and branches threatened to snag her off Saracen's back if they went much further. Saracen pushed ahead, though, and they came into a little glade, sun-filled and green with bracken and mosses.

Morgana reined in the horse and dismounted. Tying the reins to a branch, she rubbed down the stallion's sweaty sides with some grass and let him graze. Tired, her arms and legs shaking from her exhausting ride, Morgana flung herself down by a mossy log and laid her head back against its velvety surface.

"Hell's sweet devils," she muttered. "Damn!"

She realized only too well what had happened. She had invested her trust in Phillip, however small and tentative, and he had destroyed it. She should have known better! He was a noble, the rich, cosseted son of a wealthy man. And Lady Elizabeth Winston was everything a man like that could want: beautiful, angelically fair, wealthy, titled, and graceful. He would of course choose Elizabeth over a dark, skinny, short little thief who was only the recipient of his charity! And if he knew the whole scandal of her life, he would probably not even offer her his mercy, let alone his love.

"Love, Morgana?" she scoffed. "Are you simple-minded?" She picked up a rock and hurled it into the trees beyond the edge of the glade. Saracen looked up with a startled snort. "Sorry, my fellow," she told him. "It's only stupid me."

Stupid, she berated herself, for believing that she could pretend to be at home at Cygnet House, even for a little while. Stupid for believing Phillip's smooth words of admiration and affection. Stupid for submitting to his embrace, when he was only amusing himself with her until he could get back to Lady Winston. Stupid!

Her humiliation fueled her anger, and she hopped up again. Stomping about the clearing, she recited a litany of self-recrimination for allowing herself to be tricked by Phillip Greyfriars.

"God's wounds, but he'll not have me to boast about to his fellows when he joins them in London!" she exclaimed, marching about the clearing. "I won't have it! I'll be gone from his house by daylight tomorrow, before he's on his way to his lady-love. I'll—"

She halted, her shoulders drooping. She was suddenly tired, and sad. She went back to the mossy log and sat down once more.

Why was she railing so? she asked herself. Hadn't she always known that this was the truth of her situation? Phillip wasn't in love with her. He was only playing a game, amusing himself. She'd known about Lady Winston from the very first.

And hadn't she been amusing herself with Phillip? Each day, as each comfort or luxury or courtesy came her way, she had reminded herself that it was just for a short time, and that as soon as the Wren was well again, she would be riding away from Phillip forever. She was making use of him and all his wealth for a bit of a holiday, that was all.

She tapped at her knees. She had failed to keep her wits about her, that was all. She had almost begun to believe that she and Phillip could be lovers, could share a world or a life together. His choice to fly to London and Elizabeth Winston was just a reminder of what she already knew.

She would go back, she told herself. One more evening of food and drink and comfort. And then, when Phillip was gone in the morning, so would she be gone, riding to find Kestrel and Cadgwyth.

The Wren might be a sticking-point, though, she thought. If he was not well enough to travel, she couldn't leave at once. And the idea of remaining in Phillip Greyfriars's house one moment more than necessary made her uneasy. She needed to be gone before she forgot herself again.

Wren would have to remain. He knew where to find her when he was well enough to ride. He would be clever enough not to lead anyone else to her hiding place, either.

It was decided. She jumped up and strode around the clearing again, planning out the details for herself. When she was sure that she had covered every contingency, she mounted Saracen and went back to Cygnet House.

She arrived home just after darkness fell. Phillip met her on horseback, not far from the gates, a torch in his hand.

"Thank God," he cried, looking astonishingly sincere. "I feared you were lost or captured! Where the devil did you go?"

"I but went for a ride. I wanted to be alone."

"Don't do that again, please!" He gave a loud whistle, and in a few moments several men came riding around from the far side of the house, carrying torches. "I know you can take care of yourself, but I would have you safely here inside the walls of home when sun sets."

She gave him a sour look. "You're not my father. Nor my keeper." She nudged Saracen into a trot. "More likely you feared I had stolen your horse, my lord."

He didn't answer for a moment. "My horses are yours for the taking."

Morgana felt a pang of guilt. But she still felt anger now that she saw Phillip and she couldn't help putting out her defenses. "Many thanks for your courtesy. Now, I want to go see the Wren."

* * *

"I must go to London in the morning," Phillip announced as they finished a quiet dinner in Wren's room. Wren had already fallen asleep in his chair.

"Oh?" Morgana kept her voice cool.

"Aye. I have a business matter that cannot be put off. I hope to be back before the week's end. Sooner, if possible." He rose and offered his arm to her. "You must be sure to let Gilbert know if you want anything, anything at all. I've left orders that you and Wren are to be as cosseted as family."

"You are too kind."

They left the room arm in arm, Morgana's cool exterior belying the fact that she wanted to run from the house that very moment. They strolled down the hall as Phillip outlined all the special provisions he'd made for her and the Wren in his absence.

Damn the man, she thought. Why the hell did he have to be so devilishly kind and courteous? Why couldn't he just come right out and say he was off to his true love and she could go take a leap into the pond for all he cared? Things would be ever so much easier. This way, she was almost fooled again into believing she mattered to him.

They came to Morgana's door, and Phillip paused. Silently, he took her into his arms, and his kiss was hard and fierce. Morgana felt the undercurrent of desperation in them both and, despite her misgivings and anger, she responded with equal hunger.

"God, how can I leave you now?" Phillip groaned.

"You must," she said, as lightly as she could manage. She pushed back from him a bit. "Duty calls."

"I will return by midnight tomorrow. I swear it on my soul."

"Don't worry about me. Tend to your business."

He pulled her close to him again, and this time his kisses set up such a painful need within her that she felt almost weak in his arms. She fought to stay in control. She couldn't let this get the better of her.

"I have to prepare," he said, releasing her at last. "I'll bid you good night now, Blackbird. I intend to leave before it's light."

"I understand," she murmured, trying to conceal the puzzling disappointment she felt as he set her away from him, just as she had the previous night. "Will I see you in the morning?"

"Only if you rise with the sun's first ray, sweetest, and I don't wish for you to do that. I will take my gray to London, so you may ride Saracen to his heart's content. I will see you when I return."

"Good-bye."

"Pleasant dreams attend you, sweeting." He took her face and kissed her tenderly, then turned and left.

Morgana watched him stride rapidly down the hall until he was lost in the shadows. Then she went into her little chamber and undressed for bed. She crawled into the high bed and drew the curtains about her, but she couldn't sleep.

She stayed up for a while, running over her plans for the next day. When at last she did fall asleep, she tossed until the soft satin pillows felt like raw wool and the bed seemed full of briers.

"What is wrong with me?" she muttered into the darkness of midnight. No answer came. If it had, she would scarcely have believed it. So she drifted at last into a fitful, dreamless sleep, unaware that her restlessness was no less than a name cried out in the dark, a name that was about to carry away with it all her hopes and desires. That name was Phillip.

Chapter Nine

The many glimmering candles in the room made Phillip feel as if he were in church, but he knew he was as far from the sacred as any man could get. Elizabeth sat beside him before the fire, her lovely, slender hands caressing the small dog in her lap. She turned a shy smile toward Phillip.

"I'm grateful you came so quickly. I know I'm a terrible bother and a fluff-brained nuisance to you, but I didn't know which way to turn. Spenser was urging me to spend my money on the refuge, and at the same time Tarkington was saying I should invest it again in a new business. I needed someone who could advise me and be my champion rather than serving his own interests."

Phillip returned her smile. "You have but to say a word and I will come at once, you know that. Your interests are mine."

"I'm glad." She hesitated. "I was surprised to learn that you were not in London but in Aylesbury at your

126

country home. Is it true that you sold your house here to Lord Elyot?''

Phillip knew that she not only knew it was true, but probably also knew the hour of the sale, the price exchanged, and the inventory of the house's contents. Still, he played along.

"I did."

"Why? It's such a beautiful house and so well-appointed."

"I grew weary of it. I feel the need for something grander. Something similar to Lord Sefton's, perhaps."

"Ah, yes, that would be most advantageous. And so fashionable. Leave it to you to know just when and where to find the very best."

Phillip wanted to jump up and down and squawk like a chicken or stand on his head, anything to break this horrid game of polite coyness. An hour with Elizabeth was suddenly like an eternity and he had already spent twenty-four of them with her. He ached to be away, to Cygnet House and Morgana.

He decided he had to do something now, lest she decide to take him to her bed. In the past, he would have gone. In the early days of their affair, it was all he could think of, day and night. More recently, he would have gone as a duty to her and to his pretense of loving her. But he had no stomach for it tonight. There was only one woman he wanted wrapped in his arms, sharing his lovemaking. Morgana.

The intensity of that desire startled him, but he didn't fight against it. That was why he'd brought her to Cygnet House, wasn't it? To win her? And given what he knew Elizabeth to be, he'd be a certain fool to prefer her over Morgana.

He rose and stretched. "Oh, my pet, I am weary. Sorting out your finances was harder work than I've done in many a long day. I believe I shall wander back to Peter

Elyot's and fall into one of my old beds, lest I bore you any longer with my dull company.''

Elizabeth dropped the dog with a thud. The little animal, fearful that it had transgressed in some way, skittered away under the huge bed that dominated the room.

"Phillip," she purred. "You can't mean it. I've never, ever found you dull." She reached up and caressed his chest, tugging at the buttons of his surcoat.

"You are too kind to say it," he said, disengaging her hand before it could work the top button free. "But I—" He yawned widely. "I can't bear to disappoint you tonight. I must go and rest. Another time I will be more fit for play."

"I'll be more disappointed if you don't stay."

He gathered her to him and kissed her, hard. He felt her writhe against him, urging her desire upon him. He wasn't made of stone; his body wakened and considered the prospect of coupling with some enthusiasm. But his heart and mind wouldn't disengage, as they usually did. They remained firmly aware and insisted upon calling Morgana's name and image to his mind.

He put Elizabeth away gently. "I've not even bathed yet today, and I know that you dislike uncleanliness. Another time, love, and we'll have such a time together that the bed will shake loose of its pinnings."

"Promises, promises." She smiled, but he could hear the frost at the edges of her words.

"I'll send word to you tomorrow, first thing."

"You'd better."

She escorted him to the door of her chamber, a pout on her perfect, rose mouth. Phillip felt relieved. She was angry, but she wasn't going to press him. A thought stopped him cold. Was she meeting someone else?

That would be something to know about, he realized. Weary or not, Morgana or not, he'd stay behind to see just what transpired in his absence.

He kissed her again, pressing as much passion as he could muster into the act. When he released her, she was breathing fast and flushed. Good. He hadn't lost his touch, nor was she utterly immune to him. He needed that advantage in this most dangerous game.

"Good night, my love," he said, cupping her chin in his hand. "I'll return a new man."

"I shall be waiting."

He left her in her chamber and went out the front door, taking his cloak from a waiting servant. He clasped it around him as he went, striding with great purpose toward his old house, now Lord Peter Elyot's. He sensed he was being followed, and stopped a couple of times to make sure. The man was a good shadow, but he was not a match for Phillip's knowledge of all the little side streets and alleyways of this area. Phillip lost him within minutes, then doubled back to Elizabeth's house.

He hadn't been wrong. There was a cart and a good horse by the side door, and someone was climbing down by the light of a servant's lamp. The fellow lifted his head to the light, just once, but Phillip guessed at once who he was.

"Sweet Jesu, the witch has her sights set high indeed," he murmured.

He watched until the man was inside the house and the lights were showing from Elizabeth's bedchamber. Then, whistling softly, he resumed his walk to Elyot's.

Elizabeth and Lord William Fray. A duke, no less. Not the most powerful man at court, but high enough for Elizabeth to gain a solid post at court and a foothold on the ladder of succession, should she ever manage to breed.

On reaching Elyot's, Phillip was let in by a familiar servant and went quietly to his former bedchamber. Peter was at a party at some lord's house this evening and wouldn't be home till cock-crow, no doubt. Phillip pulled off his surcoat and poured himself a cup of wine.

He might not mind if Elizabeth wanted a duke of her very own. Certainly, he didn't want her. But the duke was a married man, and his duchess had blood ties to the king, as well as two young daughters. Elizabeth was up to her old game, and he was bound to stop her.

He drained his cup, set it on the table, and stretched out on the bed. His jaw worked with anger at the memories that rose up when he considered Elizabeth's rise to her current position as Lady Winston.

He had been her pawn in that game, and it had very nearly cost him his soul. He had helped her, albeit unwittingly, to attempt to climb still higher in power and status through the death of an innocent man. She had had her husband, James Winston, murdered, and he had been her aide and accomplice in that vile gambit.

When he had learned of her deed, how she had used him to cover her handiwork, and how she imagined that she was soon to be Viscountess Greyfriars, he had been sickened to the heart. He'd been the biggest fool ever born! He'd left her at once, stealing off in the night in his shame. He'd gone to Europe and spent months there, moping at first. But his sadness soon turned to rage. He let it build and take shape. Then he had made a plan. A plan to ruin Elizabeth Winston forever. A plan that would at least salve the shame he carried and render her powerless to dupe another.

That was why he was in London tonight and not at home, at Cygnet House. With Morgana.

The thought of Morgana waiting for him at his home made him smile. He wished he could take her to meet his sister, Judith. If there was any soul in this whole world who could win Morgana's trust, it was Judith, with her imperious ways and her heart of sweet gold. He wanted Morgana to have people in this world she could trust, who could teach her that not everyone was a betrayer.

She was beginning to trust him, Phillip felt. The way she had responded to his kisses had proved that. He had felt such pride and pleasure when she had clung to him the night before he left. He had sworn upon his soul that he would return by midnight.

"And if I do not perish in that endeavor," he muttered, "she may yet kill me with desire."

He had slept only a little last night. Visions of Morgana, naked and warm in his arms, had haunted him every time he closed his eyes. He could almost taste the cool treasures of her mouth, and feel her small hands trailing down his chest. Three times he rose and bathed his head and chest in cold water from the basin. The fourth time, he gave up on sleep and had gone downstairs to prepare for the journey to London.

No woman, not even Elizabeth, had driven him to such heights of desire. Lady Winston had been well tutored in the ways of love and the power of her sexuality. Morgana was utterly unschooled, except for the cruel advances of her stepfather. Yet her instinctive responses, her heartfelt giving of herself to him, had meant more than any encounter with Elizabeth. Morgana, for all her rough ways, was as shy as a young deer and as guileless. When she offered herself to him, it would be out of love and faith alone, not out of greed or even lust.

If Morgana drove him to new heights of desire, it was also true that she inspired in him remarkable restraint. For the first time in his life, Phillip hesitated at the thought of making love. Morgana's love was a precious thing, he realized. Would he be worthy of such a gift?

He jumped up from the bed and went to take another drink of wine. He was torn. He needed to be home, to be with Morgana. He had sworn to go back this very night.

But Elizabeth was up to something that could turn deadly, if he knew her at all. He had to step up the progress of his plan. He had to make sure that she didn't ruin anyone else's life.

He had to stay in London.

"One more day, sweet Blackbird," he said, raising a toast to her in the firelight. "One more day and we'll be together again."

It wasn't easy to reach the stables undetected, so she decided that the open approach was wisest. She would have to steal a horse; there was no way to get far enough from Cygnet House without one.

She sauntered into the stables past the grooms, who were by now accustomed to seeing her, even in her boy's garb. She saddled a fleet-footed mare and led her out. She mounted the mare and rode straight for the front gates.

The sentinel waved her through with a cheerful salute. She raised her arm and returned his greeting, restraining her urge to kick the mare into a gallop and race away. She wanted them to think she had merely gone for another of her casual rides. They wouldn't give her a second thought until late afternoon, or even sundown. By that time, she would be miles to the north, on her way to Cadgwyth Forest and, she hoped, the Kestrel.

She heard the gates being drawn closed behind her. "Farewell, Cygnet House," she murmured.

She felt a pang at the words. She had come to favor the place in the few days she had spent within its boundaries. Phillip had created a haven here.

"Balderdash," she muttered. "Sentimental rot." Phillip was a trickster and a liar. She was well rid of him. She set her heels lightly to the mare and moved into a canter. She was free, she told herself. Free and easy.

She repeated the words to herself over and over on the road north. At last, she grew weary of them and was able to slip into common daydreams and old plans. She wasn't paying much attention, then, when, just before sunset, a man came riding out of the woods, heading straight for her.

"Ah, no! Dammit! The ninny-pated, stubborn fool!" she cried.

Wren rode up on another of Phillip's horses. He came to a halt and gave her a cheerful salute with his cap.

"Wren, what the devil do you think you're doing? You're still weak! You should have stayed at Greyfriars's house."

Wren gave a shrug. "Too dull."

She glared. "Too dull? You want dull? Try the grave, my friend. There's nothing quite so boring as spending eternity staring at the ceiling of a tomb!"

He rolled his eyes. "I'm better."

"Oh? You could hardly stay awake through dinner last night."

He grinned. "So you thought."

She swore, long and thoroughly. "You mean to tell me you were feigning, you worthless rogue?"

He shrugged again, then nodded.

"I ought to wring your—why the hell were you pretending to be ill? We could have been out of that house days ago, instead of—" Her mouth dropped open and then snapped shut. "You didn't? You couldn't have—"

She spurred her horse again and rode off, fuming. Wren caught up with her easily and rode alongside in silence. She would look at him from time to time, begin to sputter, then turn back to face the road, teeth grinding.

Darkness forced them to halt and make camp. Morgana stomped about, gathering wood and fetching soft branches to make her bed. They shared a good meal, taken from the Cygnet House larders, and then sat, silent, by the small fire they'd built.

Morgana looked at her old friend. "I can't believe you did that. You pretended to be ill because you thought I wanted to stay around Phillip Greyfriars."

"Didn't you?"

"No!"

He was silent for several long moments, looking at her. "Sorry," he said at last.

"It's all right," she growled. "It's done with now. Let's get some sleep. We should be able to make Cadgwyth day after tomorrow, weather permitting."

Morgana had plenty of time to think on the road with her quiet companion. She knew she was right in leaving. She had almost fallen for Phillip's charm, but she had escaped in time. She wouldn't be hurt again, not by any man, king or commoner. She'd had enough betrayals in her life.

She had adored her father and he had died. She had let Cedric come close to her and he had hurt her in every way he could manage. She had seen what men could do in her days with the Kestrel's band. She'd witnessed so much pain. Staying with Phillip, even if he hadn't been in love with Lady Winston, was just asking for more.

She had been close with Phillip and it had been delightful, she admitted. But how long could that last? How long before she was hurt or he disappeared or he turned on her because of all the things she was or had been? Better to leave now. Better to know what she faced.

She stole a glance at the Wren, riding along beside her. He looked her way and smiled. She felt relief. It was all right, then. The Wren was still her good friend and ally. They'd do fine on their own.

Old Fletcher of the White Stag eyed the dark stranger with glum suspicion. He'd seen many a man come into his establishment demanding this or that, but rarely had he seen a man who looked like this one. Where most of the others had had that hot look of reckless greed or temper, this man was as cool as the ale in the cellar below his feet.

"Can't say," Fletcher grunted. "I ain't seen anyone like you said 'round here for a year and more."

"You're lying," Phillip told him blandly.

"As you wish, sir. But I still can't say that there's been anyone in my inn that fits that description. No young lads, no silent fellows, no pretty young lasses with hair like unto a boy's. This mayn't be the finest inn in all o' London, but I do know who comes an' goes about my place." Fletcher moved away, gathering up rough mugs from the tables about the common room.

"I'm sure you do. But I know of someone else who's come and gone from this place in the past weeks and that's the constables. They swarmed all over this place not long ago, didn't they, old man?" Phillip put his foot up on a bench, halting the man's progress.

Fletcher glowered at him. "I daresay they might've. But they found naught, just as you're findin' now." He shoved Phillip's leg aside and went on with his work.

Phillip watched him for a few moments, his face thoughtful. Then he brightened and crossed the room to help the man with his task.

"Here, here, what're you doin'? Leave off, man, I ain't in my dotage, not yet." Fletcher snatched a mug from Phillip's hands.

"It's all right, Master Fletcher," Phillip said, holding back the mug. "You needn't be proud with me. I know how these things are. My grandam was like that when she got of an age with you, as well."

"What d'you mean?"

"Well, a trifle forgetful, shall we say? Couldn't always recall the names of her own sons and daughters, wasn't always certain that she knew what day it was. You know."

135

"No, I don't know, and I'll thank you, young pup, to get out—"

"Oh, it's all quite ordinary, her physician told us, given her age and infirmity and all." Phillip leaned against one of the heavy tables and shook his head sadly. "Some days she wasn't sure if it was the priest from St. Thomas's who had been to visit or the man who sells chickens in the lane."

"Look here, young trouble!" Fletcher bristled. "I've as good a memory as any stripling boy and better! Don't you go sayin' I ain't!"

Phillip's bright eyes were half-lidded as he lounged against the table and examined his heavy gold ring. "I'll wager you can't recall what you had for dinner last eve."

"Mutton. Good it was, too." Fletcher raised his chin in triumph.

"I'd wager you can't recall your mother's name."

"Rosamond."

"Not bad. But too easy. I've no way of knowing your mother's true name. Who is the king?"

"King Henry, God save 'im."

"What's the name of the street outside?"

"Ash End, 'count of the fires."

"The number of rooms in your house?"

"Nine, with cellar."

"The number of stalls in your stable?"

"Six."

"And the color of your horse?"

"Brown!"

"And the color of Tom Black's horse?"

"Gray!"

"So he was here!" Phillip stood upright and seized the man by the sleeve. "Tell me now, old man, and I'll make it worth your trouble. Has he been here lately? In the last day or so? I know he stops here often and I know his friend, so tell me. Now!"

136

Old Fletcher looked at him warily. "How much?"

"Oh-ho, so your tune has changed, has it? When I came in here you wouldn't take even a silver piece for that bit of news."

"Well," the old man said, a smile playing at the corners of his mouth, "I see you have no plans to leave me in peace until you know what you come for, so I might as well make it shorter and sweeter for m'self."

"Good man. Tell me all you know of Tom Black and his friend and I will make it more than worth your while."

"Damn right you will." Fletcher wet his lips and held out his hand.

"Tell, first."

Fletcher shook his head. "I knew you was trouble when I laid eyes on those fancy boots o' yours, I did. All right, here's all I know."

He sat down on one of the benches and Phillip dropped down beside him. After a few minutes of whispered conference, Phillip rose, paid out three silver coins from his pouch, and left the inn. He hurried to the corner and turned north, headed for the Unicorn Tavern.

As he went, his thoughts returned to the night he had left Cygnet House and Morgana. He had been so blind! So stupid! He had imagined that he had bound her to him with a kiss or two and that she would be waiting for him. His surprise was great, then, when he had arrived home to learn that she and the Wren had both ridden out two days before, taking food and horses with them.

He had hardly waited to change clothes and horses before he set out to search for her. He'd had no idea where she would have gone. It was only at the last moment, as he was leaving the gates of Cygnet House, that he recalled that night on the steps of St. Dunstan's and the man she had called the Robin. If he could find Robin, perhaps he could find his Blackbird.

If Robin hadn't found her first. The belligerent thief had been especially venomous in his treatment of Morgana. Was there more to his anger than the eagerness to have someone else in the same fix as he?

Phillip speeded his course to the Unicorn. A very bad feeling was growing within him.

The Robin leaned back against the rough wall of the tavern, his mug in his hand. His rusty red tunic gave proof of his nickname, tattered and greasy though it was, and the grimy fingers that gripped his ale mug were surprisingly tapered and strong. He gave the newcomer an oily smile and swept his gaze over the man's dusty clothing. He sucked on his teeth for a moment and then motioned to a bench close by.

"Sit, then, man. What did you say your name was?"

"I didn't say." Phillip took a seat on the bench and lifted his own mug of ale in salute. "I was told you once worked for the Kestrel."

"Used to is right enough. I'm on me own, now." The Robin's eyes slid to the right, where two more men sat talking, their heads together over the battered table.

"You've left the Kestrel?"

"More like he left everybody. He's not been seen since . . ." The Robin broke off, as if aware that he was speaking too much.

"Since the night you were caught in Lady Winston's house?" Phillip asked smoothly.

"Aye. So you know of that, do you?"

"Word travels fast along this street."

"John the tavern keeper here says you asked special for me. I don't know you."

"I'm called Raven. I worked for Kestrel up north on the borderlands."

"Maybe you did and maybe you didn't." Robin took a deep drink of his ale. "What's it to me?" He lowered

138

his mug slowly, eyes narrowed. "You aren't from Kestrel himself, are you?"

"Maybe I am and maybe I'm not." Phillip gave him a bland smile.

"If you are Kestrel's man," Robin said, leaning forward, "you can tell him that he's finished here. And in the woods, as well. No one'll follow him after this last bit of folderol with the sheriffs and all. He's done." His dark eyes glittered in the dim candlelight.

Phillip nodded. Raising his hand, he signaled to the tavern keeper to bring more ale for his companion. Judging from the Robin's red face and crooked smile, he guessed the man had been well into his cups before he had arrived at the Unicorn. A bit more ale might loosen the Robin's tongue.

A server refilled the mug and Robin raised it immediately to take a long draught. When he set it down, Phillip gave him a cool nod of approval.

"You look like a man who knows his own mind," Phillip said. "I'm surprised a man like you would take orders from someone like the Kestrel. After all, he botched enough jobs, didn't he?"

"That he did. He never would listen when any of us told him an idea was daft. Always said he was in charge and we'd take orders from him or we'd be back on our own, with no help comin' from him. And if we was actin' on our own and it interfered with his doings, then we'd best look out or he'd take us out for good."

"And you didn't care for that, I imagine?" Phillip took another sip of ale.

The Robin leaned forward, breathing ale fumes into Phillip's face. "He wouldn't listen to me nor anyone else, save Wren and Blackbird. And look where it got us."

"Aye. Just look." Phillip lounged back on the bench. "So the Wren and the Blackbird are in charge of Kestrel's men now?" he asked casually.

139

"Who knows? Them two slipped away on the night we all went to jail. Same as Kestrel." He spat into the corner in disgust.

"And you're starting..." Phillip broke off and signaled to the server to bring another drink for the Robin. The server scurried over with the pitcher and refilled the Robin's mug. Phillip took only a bit more in his own mug, but the Robin didn't seem to notice.

"Where was I?" Phillip asked, after lifting his mug in another salute.

"Wren and Blackbird," Robin volunteered. "The Wren, now, he's a bit soft in the head. Never talks. Just gives you them looks like he can see right through you, but I know he's just daft. But the Blackbird—now there's one I'll be havin' back in my band."

"A good man, is he?" Phillip asked quietly.

The Robin gave an unpleasant chuckle. "Not so good a man as some might think. Blackbird's a lass, is what. Kept it a secret from all outside the band and most that was in, as well. Dresses like a boy, she does. But I seen her some mornings when she thought no one was looking, down at the stream. Sweetest little apple-tits on her you ever seen and a behind like—"

"And she's still in London with you?" Phillip kept his voice cool and steady, though his fingers itched to strangle the man where he sat. Morgana, with her experience of Cedric's brutality, would have been terrified had she known of this man's ugly spying. No wonder she kept her knife near at all times.

"Nay." Robin scowled. He drank deep of the cold ale. "I'll find her, though. She was Kestrel's when he was in charge, though they thought to keep it secret. She'll be mine when I take the band again." His eyes narrowed in speculation. "Cor, but I'll wager she's a lively bit when she's spread out upon her back. And I'm just the lad who can put it to her so's she won't forget who's the man and who's the maid. I'll have her begging for mercy, and won't I just grant it, though? I'll grant it 'til the smart little witch can't stand, I will.''

Phillip felt rage boiling up inside him. Through a supreme act of self-control he got himself back into a state of outward calm by sipping at his mug again. He could not let on what he was after. He had to find out where Morgana was and keep this two-legged dung-heap away from her.

''Aye, I'll bet you could show her a thing or two.'' Phillip gave the Robin a conspiratorial grin. ''And let me say that if you're to be taking the Kestrel's place, then I'm for you. You'll be in London for now?''

''Aye, for a week. Then we go to Cadgwyth.''

''Cadgwyth?''

''Aye. You know. The woods.''

Phillip cursed himself inwardly. What the hell was the man talking about? How was he to pass as one of Kestrel's men if he didn't know all of the robbers' hideaways?

''Ah, yes, the woods. Cadgwyth.'' Phillip smiled and waved a hand. ''I thought I might head there tomorrow. Go by way of Cambridge.''

''You could,'' Robin said, belching roundly. ''But we'd get there afore you. We go by way of Worcester and Shrewsbury, generally. Your way'd take you a full week and more.''

''True,'' Phillip conceded, smiling. ''I just thought, open roads, the sheriff's men and all. Cannot be too careful.''

''Aw, hell, that! They're all a-weary of that game by now. And goin' all the way up to the western borderlands is more work than they care to take on. You'd do best to go by straight ways.''

''Right.'' Phillip rose and set down his mug. ''Robin, I'm proud to know you're in charge now. Yours to command,'' he said, offering his hand.

"Right. Good to have you with us, Raven. You won't regret getting hooked on with the Robin, I swear to you." The Robin sniffed and shook Phillip's hand vigorously.

"I'm sure I won't." Phillip nodded to Robin's companions at the table and strode off to find the server and press a few extra coins into his hand.

"Thank you ever so," the boy said, gaping at the heavy silver in his palm. "If there's anything else I can do for you, sir, just you name it."

"I'm well satisfied, my lad. But I'd tell your master to be more careful about who he lets inside his tavern."

"Beg pardon, sir?"

Phillip nodded his head in Robin's direction. "I'm no physician, but yonder fellow seems to have all the signs of—" He dropped his voice to a whisper. "Of the rosy."

"Oh, Lord," the boy moaned. "You don't mean—"

"I do. His tongue seemed a bit colored to me, bruises, thickness at the throat—you know the signs. I'd not have him in my place, if I were you." Phillip straightened and clapped the boy on the shoulder. "Just don't get too close."

The boy's face had gone chalky. "I'll fetch my master right away, sir."

"Good lad."

Phillip strolled out the door, whistling tunefully. He quickened his pace as he entered the road and headed for the White Stag, where his horse was stabled. Behind him a commotion erupted in the Unicorn and in moments a contingent of men was herding the Robin, roaring in protest, toward the docks on the Thames. Phillip smiled with cold satisfaction, knowing that the drunken Robin would be shackled into the next boat leaving port and shipped away from England forever. When it came to the plague, Londoners asked no questions and offered no reprieves.

"Now to find Cadgwyth."

*   *   *

Wren held up his hand as they rounded the curve in the road and came to the entrance of the forest. He reined in his horse and looked around at the ground.

"What is it?" Morgana asked softly.

Wren pointed downward. The ground had been churned up in a path that led into the woods. Many horses had been through this area recently, riding with abandon. The robbers of Kestrel's band would not ride so—they would have come in one at a time, or in pairs, riding into the woods by various routes so as not to leave an obvious path to the retreat.

Morgana bit her lip as she looked at her friend. "Not the prettiest welcome."

Wren cast a glance about the area. Everything seemed quiet and peaceful. The animals were busy in the meadows behind them and in the trees overhead, making ready for winter. He looked back to Morgana.

"I have to know," she told him. She reached out and placed a hand on his shoulder. "And you would know, too, wouldn't you? We've had many a fine time in these woods."

Wren sighed and set his jaw. Without a word, he and Morgana lifted their reins and guided their horses into the archway formed by the trees.

They had not gone far in when Morgana jerked her horse to halt with a cry. "Ah, God, Wren, look what the butchers have done!"

The sight that greeted them in the silent forest was so grisly that it seemed impossible to comprehend. Two bodies, their faces blackened and swollen, swung from the branches of two great oaks like twin guardians of some hellish gates. Morgana felt her throat tighten convulsively, and she swung her horse about to keep from emptying her stomach at the sight. She listened as Wren rode forward, then heard two terrible thuds as his quick knife cut the bodies from the branches. She held herself sternly, resisting the impulse to cover her ears and scream to drown out the echoing of those sounds. She heard Wren dismount and kneel down beside one of the hanged men. She came about once more.

"Who, Wren?"

"Merlyn," Wren muttered. "And Tom Throstle."

"It had to be sheriff's men."

"Aye." The Wren rolled the two men together and began to cover them with fallen leaves.

Morgana got down from her horse and went to help. Wren tried to wave her away, but she knelt down beside him and began to sweep armloads of leaves toward the bodies.

"We'll come back to bury them when we've reached camp. I smell smoke, don't you? Someone's been in here burning as well as murdering."

Wren sniffed the air and nodded. They pushed more leaves onto the bodies and got up, brushing the dirt and leaves from their hands. They mounted up in silence and went deeper into the woods, keeping sharp eyes out for any signs of movement and listening for the slightest sounds.

They heard the band before they saw them. Hugh Penny and Edward the Sparrow were nose-to-nose, wrangling over a fresh-caught hare while five or six others looked on.

"You'll do as I say or you'll taste my fist afore you'll taste this coney!" bellowed Sparrow.

"And I say to hell with you!" shrieked Hugh. "It's mine by rights and you can bloody well get your own!"

Sparrow, whose chunky form belied his delicate namesake, drew back one arm, taking aim for Hugh's jaw. The taller man sidestepped the blow and landed a kick to his opponent's side, knocking him off balance. The hare flew from their grasp and landed in a clump of scorched bracken. Heedless of their loss, the two men hurled themselves into battle.

Morgana was off her horse in a flash. Darting behind Hugh, she stuck a small foot in between his gangling legs. He toppled to the ground with a surprised yelp as Morgana's knife flickered in his face.

" 'At's right!" Sparrow grunted. "Give it to 'im good, Blackbird!"

"Shut your mouth!" Morgana snapped, turning the sharp blade his way. "I'd just as soon slit the pair of you as one. What the devil is this? You two have worked together for years, and now I find you come to blows over a bit of meat!"

Hugh rubbed his injured knee as he glared at his partner. " 'Twasn't me. I caught it, it's mine to eat as I see fit."

"And I say it's mine too. We always go by halves. I want what's comin' to me!" Sparrow made a move for Hugh again.

"You'll not get even a bite after you tried to steal my half of that bird last week!"

"Why, you pimple-faced lout, I'll—"

"Hold!"

The two men froze as Morgana's shout echoed through the campsite. She stood, knife upraised, ready to take on anyone who moved. Silently, her dark eyes took in the condition of the camp and of the two men before her. It was clear that the men were hungry and the camp had been all but destroyed. She took a step back and sheathed her knife.

"Get up, Hugh," she ordered. "Go get your kill from the weeds and bring it here to me."

Hugh started to protest but he saw her hand go to her knife and he blanched. He'd seen that knife at work before, cleaning a pheasant for the pot. He had no interest in seeing how those precise, clean strokes worked on a man. Scrambling to his feet, he went searching for his rabbit.

"You, Sparrow, get the bags from my saddle and set them near the fire. Mind," she said crisply, "no one is to touch their contents or he'll be eating one-handed from now on."

Sparrow nodded and went to do his errand. Wren handed over his own saddlebags and climbed down from his horse. He came to stand beside Morgana.

"What in the name of all that's holy happened here, Geordie?" Morgana turned to a boy who stood nearby.

"It was daybreak, or nearly. They come on us like riders from hell. They had torches and ropes and they was constables or somesuch, they said. They killed near half of us and wounded others. It was all we could do to get away from the fires. We ain't been from here since, Blackbird."

"No one's even tried the village?"

"Nay, they said if any one of us was caught there, they'd come back and finish the job." The boy twisted his bony hands. "They kept watch on the edge of the woods. That's how they got Throstle and Merlyn. We dared not even go cut 'em free."

"And the Kestrel? Was he here, then?"

"Nay. No one's seen him for a month an' more. We been hopin' he'd come, but there's been no sign of 'im." The boy looked at her wistfully. "We was hopin' you'd bring 'im."

Morgana scuffed the blackened earth with the toe of her boot. "Kestrel has vanished. No one knows where he's gone." She looked up again, her expression firm. "But I'm sure he'll come here, soon or late. Meanwhile, we'll tend to business. Blow up the fire a bit, Geordie. Mustard, get out some of the food in the saddlebags and start cooking for the lot. Wren, Sparrow, Hugh, and Jonathan, go you into the woods near the stream and set some snares for game. Tonight, at least, we eat like lords.''

There was some grumbling, of course, and some black looks cast her way. But Wren and Geordie acted at once upon her orders and the others soon followed suit. In a matter of hours, the camp was organized around the fire ring and fresh meat was cooking on spits.

Morgana and Wren sat together in the firelight, sipping wine from the skins they'd taken from Cygnet House. Darkness was soon upon them as they watched the rest of the band eating their meal and talking quietly among themselves.

''Time was when this lot would have been roaring out the chorus of 'A Lad and His Lass' or cutting capers about the clearing.'' Morgana rubbed her hands over her knees, feeling the cold of the settling night. ''Now look at them, Wren. It looks like a gathering of dirty novitiates at the priory.''

''You planning on leaving?'' Wren asked.

She leaned forward, resting her chin on her fists. ''Where would I go?''

''Alderbrydge.''

''That's not my home. My cousin Ariane has more than her share to do and no need for the likes of me about, undoing all the repairs she's made to the name of Langland.''

''Cygnet House.''

Morgana's mouth twisted into a frown. ''Hardly there. And you know why,'' she said, turning to him quickly. ''So don't start all that nattering again.''

Wren was silent, waiting. Morgana sighed deeply as she turned back to the sight of the ragtag remains of Kestrel's band.

''It's here, Wren. For now. The Kestrel's bound to come sometime soon. If we can pull this mob together until he returns, then we'll have a home again. And work. You and I can start putting money aside for that inn we were planning to buy.'' She nodded toward the ten men seated about the fire. ''We can't turn our backs on them now. Will you help?''

Her old friend nodded and offered his hand. They shook hands in the dim firelight, the shadows of Cadgwyth forest looming about them as they pledged their word.

Clouds rolled in during the night, and before morning the whole camp was drenched and muddy. Morgana unrolled herself from her blankets with a groan. She had slept in her clothing and she felt as rumpled and stiff as the old bit of oiled canvas she had dragged out to cover herself with in the night. ''La, Blackbird. That's what you get for living the soft life at Alderbrydge and Cyg—''

She left off scolding herself, unable to pronounce the name of Phillip's home without evoking an image of Phillip himself. If she was to forget him, it was best she begin now and be firm about it.

The other members of the band were straggling toward the meager fire that had been started in the pit. Their moods were as black as the mud that clung to their clothing, and they regarded her with baleful expressions as she made her way to the fire. She bent to warm her hands, then looked about for more firewood.

She sighed inwardly as she straightened up, setting her lips tightly. ''No wood, no fire, no warmth, no cooking. You are a sorry lot. You, Geordie, show your worth, lad. Gather me all the dry wood you can lay hand to. Sparrow—where is Sparrow?''

''He's still abed.'' Hugh Penny rubbed his grimy beard.

''Go fetch him. The pair of you can share out what is left of the supplies that Wren and I brought. The rest of you, come with me. We bury our dead. Then we need shelter and food. That's first. Then we shall see about setting to work again.''

"Oh, get on," groaned Hugh. "There's no use in it. Kestrel's gone. What can we do without him?"

"What did *you* ever do with him, Hugh?" Morgana drawled.

This produced a brief chuckle among the other thieves. Hugh shot them a wrathful glance. "I did my share!" he protested.

"No one more than you, Hugh," Morgana soothed, winking at the others. "None so much as you."

"I did," Hugh grumbled.

"Then you won't mind doing your share now. Same rules as when Kestrel was here. Get going, Hugh."

"Who says?"

Morgana's eyes glittered dangerously. "I say."

Wren moved in behind her. The others fell silent, watching Hugh as he stood to confront the small woman who stood before him.

"Who says you're to be leadin' us, then?" he growled.

"No one said. But I'm doing it all the same. You lot couldn't steal an egg from a blind hen, left on your own. You'd likely be fighting over who got to eat the egg before you even found the nest." Morgana hooked her thumbs in her belt and rocked back on her heels. Her tone was even and her face showed no fear of the man who challenged her.

Hugh stared at her, stiff-jawed, for many long moments. Then he began to grin. "Hell, Blackbird, as well you as anyone else, I suppose. I don't want the lot of 'em trailing me, naggin' for this and that."

"Good, then go get the Sparrow and get to work."

"I'm goin'."

"And be quick about it. The day grows shorter while my hunger stretches long."

"Aye, I said I was goin'. Sluggard Sparrow'd benefit more from your naggin'," Hugh muttered.

Still, he shuffled off to the edge of the clearing to rouse his partner. He was back in a moment, pale beneath the layer of dirt that grimed his features.

"What is it, Hugh?" Morgana asked sharply.

"It's Sparrow. He's taken bad. Talkin' out of his head and burnin' with fever."

Morgana dropped the stick she was using to poke up the fire. Leaping nimbly over the corner of the fire pit, she crossed to a bundle of ragged blankets against a fallen log. Hugh and Wren ran after her.

She knelt down and felt the Sparrow's forehead. The big man shifted in his half-conscious state and his arm flew up, striking her squarely on the chin. Morgana tumbled backward and sat down hard in the mud.

"Damn and blast!" she muttered. "Hugh, hold him. Wren, take his other side. I can't tell a thing with him thrashing about like that."

The two men pinned the Sparrow's arms and each held a leg. Morgana felt his forehead again and probed at the tender area just below his jawbone. She bent her head to his chest and listened to the Sparrow's labored breathing.

"His lungs are thickened and he is swollen about the throat," she announced, sitting back on her heels. "I'll need herbs and water. Bring my blankets and build a pallet before the fire. Let no others come around him—I don't need the whole lot of you sick."

She got to her feet as the men hurried away to fulfill her orders. Sickness, hunger, loss, bickering, and oncoming winter; there was plenty to do here, she could see. Perhaps it would serve to keep her mind from straying to thoughts of Phillip and the memory of the few lovely days they'd shared.

Chapter Ten

Morgana crumbled a handful of the fresh, aromatic herbs and cast them into the little pot of boiling water. Stirring them with a willow stick, she then poured the liquid into a wooden cup and carried it carefully over to the sick man by the fire.

Five more men had been taken with the fever and lung ailment that the Sparrow had ushered into the camp. Those left standing, including the Wren and herself, were dead on their feet from nursing the sick and taking the watch by night lest the sheriff's men come riding in again with their ropes and torches.

Wren came and stood beside her as she got up from the man's side. He offered her a cup of thin broth which she gratefully accepted. They walked away from the fire and sat down on a log.

"That's the last of them, I hope, Wren. I can't face another. Where the hell is the Kestrel?" She set her cup down with a thump.

Wren touched her shoulder as she rested her chin on her hand.

"I can't believe this mess. I can't believe what I'm doing here. I should have stayed in London." She pounded her thigh.

Wren shrugged. "And these?"

"They'd get by. I know I said they wouldn't, but I was fooling myself, Wren. They're only following me now because I know something of healing and because I stood up to them for a moment. They're too weak to resist or to challenge me now. When they are well again I'll be back to being little Tom Black, the cutpurse. There'll be a fight for power that I couldn't hope to win."

"Mayhap."

"It will be so, if Kestrel doesn't come soon. I know it. But I'll stay, don't worry. There's no sense in leaving now." She looked at her friend. "Don't give me that look again, Wren. I know what you're doing and it won't work. You may go back to Cygnet House, if you want it so much, but I'll not be with you."

Wren was silent. Morgana shifted on the log.

"I have a plan, if the others will listen. When enough of the flock are well, we'll take a trip into Kerstone, I think. Alder village is too close to Ariane, so we can't go there. She has worries enough of her own without adding an outlaw relative who steals from her own village."

She went on outlining her plan to the Wren. It would be her first venture into thievery since she had fled Lady Winston's house, she recalled later, as she lay rolled in blankets in the dark.

No, that wasn't true, she thought, frowning. She had stolen after that night, including a white rose, fresh from the London marketplace. That was when her troubles had really begun, with Phillip Greyfriars and his pranks. All for the theft of a rose! If that wasn't an omen of some sort, she didn't know what was.

That wasn't completely true, either, she thought. If she was looking to lay blame, she had but to look back at that eve in the woods when the boar had trapped Wren and he'd been injured. Or farther back to Cedric, and farther still, to the ascension of Henry IV over Richard II. All blame was useless, she had learned that years ago. Life was not fair, and to dream that it ever would be fair was to invite pain and disappointment. She was on her own in this world.

She gave a sigh and slid her hand beneath the tunic that cradled her head. Her fingers closed over her knife, and she drifted into restless sleep.

The days in the camp continued, rainy and dark. Morgana and Wren took turns watching and nursing and hunting with whoever in the band was well enough to work. Morgana watched Wren with some anxiety at first, knowing that he had only just recovered from his injuries and the illness they had brought on. After a day or two, though, she saw that he was well and strong, with no traces of the coughing and drowsiness he had displayed at Cygnet House.

The thought of Phillip and his home brought a swift pain to her mind and heart. She moved hastily to the next task and immersed herself in her work, trying, almost successfully, to banish the sound of Phillip's voice singing to her on those lamplit evenings. She worked for hours, until her head ached and her face was flushed with her efforts.

Would this sickness never abate? she wondered as she bathed Hugh's face and neck for the fifth time that day. It seemed as if there was nothing in the world but sick men, groaning and spitting up around her as she tended them. She pushed herself on, knowing that there was nothing else she could do.

153

By the time darkness began to fall, she was shaking with weariness and her stomach was cramping from hunger. She staggered to the fire, where Wren was cooking still more of the broth she'd been forcing down her patients' throats for days. He looked at her sharply, then scooped up a cup of the broth and brought it to her.

"No, Wren. I can't drink it. I can't even look at it." She covered her stomach with her hands, her head and belly reeling at the prospect of food, despite her hunger.

Wren took off one of his mitts and felt her forehead. He grunted and took her hands in his, wrapping them about the bowl. "Drink."

"Dammit, Wren, I said I don't want it!" Morgana felt as if she were near to tears. What the devil was the matter with her?

Wren forced the cup toward her lips. "You're sick."

"I am not!"

He looked at her with mild annoyance. "Drink," he repeated. "Or die."

She slumped and held her head in her hand. "I'd be better off."

"Codswallop. Drink."

Morgana felt her forehead. It did indeed feel flushed, but then, she'd been working hard all day and now she was seated right by the fire. She could feel how hot the blaze was because it was like a flame on her face while her back and legs felt so icy from the cool air behind her that she was shivering.

"Oh, all right, grandmother," she grumbled, taking the cup. The warm broth felt wonderful going down her sore, aching throat. Sweet Jesu, what a day this had been.

She finished the soup and looked at Wren. "There. Are you satisfied?"

He nodded. She rose and looked up at the sky. The clouds were clearing. The stars were glittering with cruel brightness. She blinked and rubbed her hot, sore eyes. She thought she saw all the stars suddenly shift and change places in the heavens, like partners in a dance.

"What madness is this?" she muttered, swaying. "Wren, did you see—"

The sky turned a somersault over and under the forest. She heard a loud rush of wind in her ears, and then the world went utterly blank.

"Nay, nay, don't—" She slapped at the hands that were trying to remove her clothing. "No, leave me be," she begged piteously. Would Cedric never stop pawing her? How was she to get away from him this time?

"Peace. Peace, angel. It's only me."

"Oh, it's only you."

Only who?

Phillip?

She struggled to open her eyes, to sit up, but there were terrible weights on her chest. She burst into a rage of coughing, feeling as if her very ribs might explode outward with the pressure.

"Lie back. Rest yourself. All's well."

Phillip. Oh, how lovely to hear his deep, velvety voice, to feel his hands on her again.

"Phillip?"

"Yes, angel?"

"I love your horse."

"Better that than no love at all."

"Better a horse than a parsnip, madman."

"Absolutely. Now, get some rest."

She sank down into a cloud of warmth and softness and drifted along the dim skies. She certainly liked it here in heaven. Phillip was here. She was here. Maybe in heaven they could be as they wished, with no thoughts of the past or of Cedric or Elizabeth or even of white roses that seemed to get larger and then smaller before her eyes, then larger, then smaller . . .

155

"He's still out of his head with fever."

"Aye, master, but he's breathing easier. Wren says you got here just in time."

"He's worked himself half to death, hasn't he?"

"Aye. He's been nurse an' cook an' guard an' all for days and days."

Who was this fellow they spoke of? Morgana wondered.

"Well, he's resting now. Go get yourself some sleep, lad. You've done right by the Blackbird."

Blackbird. That name was familiar.

"He'll—he'll get better, won't he?"

"He will, if I have anything to say about it. And I always get what I want."

"I just bet you do."

Morgana wondered how angels could be so chatty. She thought they all went floating about and singing. Oh well, she was in heaven and one of them. Perhaps it was best not to question things until she'd figured out the rules of their game.

She decided she needed a look at this heaven. She tried lifting her head, but realized it was too much trouble. She settled for fluttering open her eyelids, just a bit. That wasn't so hard.

"Phillip?"

"I'm here."

"Oh, Phillip, I'm so sorry you died."

"Are you, sweet?" His voice was warm and his smile was wonderful to see.

"Yes. You were so young. But I'm glad we're together. No worries, now."

"Uh-huh. You shouldn't try to talk. Just rest."

"Oh, we'll be resting for a long, long time."

"That's nice to know. Are you thirsty?"

"Oh, yes!" She frowned and closed her eyes. "But I shouldn't be thirsty in heaven, should I?" She started, her eyes flying open again. "Phillip!"

"What, sweet?"

"Was I—did I? Phillip, I don't recall a priest!"

"Shh," he said gently, cradling her head in his hand. "Let me worry about the formalities. You just have a drink and rest."

Morgana sipped at the cup he placed to her lips. The cool liquid soothed her cracked lips and parched throat. She smiled. "Yes, you'd be better at seeing to protocol. I know you wouldn't let me die without a priest."

"I'll look after you, body and soul," he said. "Now, close your eyes."

"All right. But, you know, Phillip, I don't recall dy—"

Phillip set the cup aside. She was asleep again. Good. When he had stepped into camp three nights ago, she looked as if she had been kept awake for weeks and then beaten. She had been silent and still, and so hot in his arms he thought she might scorch his clothing. Now at least she was talking, however incoherently, and she was moving a bit.

He sighed and settled back down to watch over his charge. When he had first arrived at this dreary camp in the middle of nowhere, he had been surprised at how easy it had been to walk right in and step up to their fire. That had at last brought out the knives and clubs, but Wren had arrived to stay the hands of the three who held him captive.

He soon learned why it had been so easy to steal up on them. Everyone save those four—one of them a lad of no more than ten—was ill or dying. When Wren took him to Morgana, he'd wanted to sweep her up and carry her out of this deadly place. But Wren convinced him she couldn't be moved and that she would be outraged if she found he'd taken her away. Reluctantly, he'd acquiesced and set about nursing her with an energy that was matched only by his fear for her life.

He had seen this fever before. It had attacked his father's household at Wildhurst years ago and had carried off five people, none of them of his immediate family, thankfully, but among them some of their most trusted and beloved servants. He had searched his memory over the past days, trying to recall the methods and medicines they had used against this illness then. He had had a small tent built around Morgana and pots of steaming hot water brought in to help loosen the humors in her chest. He'd stripped her of the dirty clothes she'd been wearing and bathed her overheated body with cool cloths freshened with crushed mint. He'd urged her to drink—broth, wine, weak ale—and when she wouldn't or couldn't manage on her own, he'd borrowed Hugh's pipe, scoured it out, and poured trickles of the healing foods down her throat.

But would it be enough? Wren had told him how she'd been leading the band and how she'd devoted herself to nursing them all, day and night. She had exhausted herself and now she was paying the price. Had he come too late?

He cursed himself again for his stupidity. If he hadn't been so hell-bent on laying a claim to her, Morgana wouldn't have run away.

What was it about her that made her so loving and eager for him one moment and so desperate to be rid of him the next? He shook his head in puzzlement. She was the most complicated woman—nay, human being—he'd ever encountered.

She turned over on the makeshift bed he'd created for her of dried leaves and pine needles covered with cloaks and blankets. Her breathing was still raspy, though not as wet-sounding as yesterday. He felt fear grip his heart once again. She mustn't die. She mustn't. He'd only just found her and there was so much more he wanted to know of her, about her. She had to pull through this.

She was strong and fierce, he reminded himself. And she had lived in the wilds and endured hardships he could only imagine. If anyone could fight this illness, she could.

But she was also so small, he thought, touching her slender hand where it lay on the rough blanket. And so vulnerable in some things. Like her fears and her sorrows over her past. How could she manage to beat so virulent an enemy as this? She mustn't die!

He bowed his head to his knees. God help him. He loved her.

The very notion terrified him almost as much as the thought of losing her. He'd been in love before, he'd thought, and that had led him into the worst folly of his life, with Elizabeth. A man had died because of his infatuation with that woman.

Would he bring the same curse to Morgana? And was he even worthy to love such a rare and extraordinary woman? Would his love be more burden than blessing for them both?

He sat still, his head on his knees for a long, long time, his heart too full of love and pain to find expression in words.

Morgana stirred. Her skin felt cool, but irritated by the rough wool in which she was wrapped. She drew a breath and felt a sense of well-being when the air traveled easily in and then out of her chest. She sighed and opened her eyes.

Where was she? She seemed to be in some sort of ragged, wooly cave. Stray beams of light came through the rents in the fabric over her head, illuminating her surroundings. She frowned. What was this place? She had no recollection of coming here, or of bundling herself up in these blankets, or of . . . taking off all her clothes . . .

"What the devil is going on?" She sat up with a start.

"Hush, Blackbird. Don't worry. Just rest."

"Phillip? How did you—why am I—?"

"It's all right. You've been sick. Your fever broke only this morning."

"Where am I?"

"In your thieves' camp. In a tent Wren and I rigged up for you. You needed shelter and a place to have vapors all around you."

"Phillip. I have no clothes on."

"I had to take them off you. They were damp and dirty, and you needed to be bathed."

"You bathed me?" She felt hot color coming to her cheeks at the idea of Phillip holding her nude body, pouring water over it and washing her. "Oh, God! Phillip! You did this by yourself? Tell me you did! No other saw me?"

"No other. Not even Wren." His tone was soothing. "I know that the rest of the band believes you're a lad. Your secret is still safe."

"Thank the saints. Oh. But you saw me."

"Yes, angel. And sweet and tempting though you were and are, I was far more concerned about your fever and coughing than my own desires. I've never been one to care much for unconscious bed partners, anyway."

"Ah." She paused, resting her head back down on the makeshift pillow. "Then you've been caring for me? Was I so very sick?"

"Very." His voice was strangely gruff.

She looked at him sharply. "As sick as unto death?"

"I don't know. I feared so. It's been near five days since I carried you in here."

"How did you find us—no, never mind. I'm too tired. Tell me another time." She closed her eyes and began to drift off.

She heard him rise to go out the doorway of the tent. "Thank you," she said.

He paused. "Just rest," was all the reply he made.

Two days later, Morgana was ready to get dressed and go out into the camp. She was shocked at how weak she felt and how much thinner she'd grown. She had to regain her strength or she'd never survive the coming winter.

Phillip was seated just outside her tent as she emerged. He was hunched up on a blanket, his heavy black cloak wrapped about him.

"Wake up, Sir Raven," she said softly, touching his shoulder.

Startled, he jumped to his feet. She held up a hand. "It's all right. 'Tis only me."

He looked at her with astonishment; then a broad smile lit his face. "So you're finally ready to stop sloughing about, are you?"

"I thought I'd better get up and see what sort of havoc you've wreaked on this place in my absence. Is there anyone left alive or well?"

"Come and see."

He led the way to the fire, his eyes seldom leaving her. She felt a bit uncomfortable under his hungry, wary gaze, but she said nothing, not wishing to draw attention to their relationship in front of the other men.

"Well," Wren said, rising from his seat on a stump by the fire. He crossed to her and placed his hands on her shoulders.

"Here I am, you worthless lout," Morgana said with a fond smile. "And I suppose it was you that let this scoundrel into our camp?" She nodded toward Phillip.

"Aye." Wren's keen look challenged her to do or say anything against it.

"You're pardoned this time. But see that you keep a closer watch from now on. If you let in his like, no telling who'll stumble in here next."

"This fellow has nursed you night and day, Master Tom," Geordie put in. "He hardly took food or rest."

"More fool he," Morgana drawled, but her smile held no rancor.

Phillip grinned. "I couldn't let you die. They would have torn me to bits."

"And you think they won't now?"

Phillip's mouth fell open, then closed. "They might, but then they'd be left alone with you as their leader again, and I'm not sure they're ready for that."

"Why, you—"

Wren intervened. "Come. Eat."

They sat down and broke the fast. Morgana listened as the men related all the events in the week since she had taken ill. Most of the men had recovered, a few had died. Phillip had evidently sent Wren out with money to buy provisions in the nearest village; then Wren had taken over Morgana's role as leader and chief nurse of the men. The rains had dried off, and though it was cooler now, at least they weren't ankle-deep in mud.

"A week or so and we should be ready to venture out," Morgana said to Wren.

"Aye."

"You and I can work the road between Kerstone and Wroxeter. Hugh and Tom can work with Peter in the village. That'll give us enough to hold us a while. We still need to figure out what we're going to do about Kestrel."

"And what we're going to do with 'im?" Hugh nodded to Phillip.

Morgana looked at Phillip. "He'll be leaving today."

Phillip started to speak, but Wren interrupted. " 'Tisn't safe," he said.

"He's a grown man. He got here by himself, he'll get out by himself," she said.

Wren shook his head. "He knows."

Morgana batted the idea away. "Oh, bosh. He'll not betray us."

"Oh?" Wren cocked a brow at Phillip.

Phillip lifted his cup. "I'd give you all up in a heart-beat."

"What?" Morgana exclaimed.

"It's just as I said. Make me leave and I'll go directly to the sheriffs."

"Why, you, dirty, low—"

"Ah-ah, don't say it. I might take it into my head to leave and tell them anyway. Perhaps you had better be sure that I do *not* leave."

Morgana sputtered in vain. She turned on Wren, glaring. He only shrugged. She turned back to Phillip, light dawning in her eyes. "You two are in this together! It's a conspiracy! Just because I left your—"

Wren cleared his throat loudly. Morgana paused and reddened, thinking of what she had almost let slip in front of the men. She muttered a vivid curse under her breath.

"I'll thank you not to bring my parentage into this," Phillip said mildly. "Now, where shall we start? If I'm to be one of you, I'll need instruction. Will you be my tutor, Sir Blackbird?"

Morgana wished devoutly that looks could kill. The man was too vile for words. How was it that he managed to trick her time and again?

She shook her head. "Nay, Sir Raven. I can't be bothered. The flock needs me as a leader more than you need me as your nursery-teacher. You'll have to learn as you go, or better yet, stay here when we go out to ply our trade."

"Oh, but that wouldn't be prudent, would it? What if I escaped?"

Morgana leaned toward him. "I'd see that you were tied hand and foot to yon tree and gagged besides, with at least two men to stand guard. You'll not betray us and you'll not hinder me, do you understand?"

"Is this the thanks I get for nursing you back from the dead?"

163

Morgana was livid. How dare he use that against her? Of course, she was deeply grateful. He had indeed saved her life, and perhaps many of the others, as well. And she was grateful. But to throw it back in her face, to use it as a way to get what he wanted out of her—it was criminal!

She stared at him, her outrage making her quiver. "I thank you, sir, for all your aid. I am in your debt. But you may not endanger us all for payment of that debt."

"But you will repay me."

It wasn't a question. Morgana felt a shiver of excitement and fear at his demand. "You shall have some recompense, yea."

"Good. The payment I choose is for you to teach me your trade."

Morgana wanted to scream. The man was impossible! It wasn't fair! How had she come to be saddled with this devilishly persistent, all-too-clever madman?

"All right!" she shouted. She glanced around and saw the other men watching them with undisguised interest. "All right," she said, summoning her composure once more. "You follow me and watch what I do. Wren will help you if you have questions. But do not get in my way, do you understand? We are not playing here. This is our livelihood, however precarious."

So it was settled. Phillip shadowed her night and day, following her actions, working with a will at all tasks, large and small, in the camp. He came to the fires at night, obviously weary, but still he managed to entertain the men each evening with either some ribald story or a tale in song. The men took to him as if he were born to their situation, though it was plain he was not. They called him Raven and soon included him in practicing their techniques of picking pockets, coshing heads to give just a brief stun to the victim, the art of distraction, the craft of stealth.

And, to Morgana's chagrin, he was good at it all. His natural strength and grace, his quick mind, his love of a challenge, all combined to make him a most excellent thief, at least in the camp. But she wondered how he would feel about robbing one of his own kind when the time came for him to take part in a real theft. Would he balk? Turn moral? Turn telltale and bring the wrath of the law down on them all?

Her insides churned at the possibility that she might be responsible for bringing destruction to the flock through Phillip. What would Kestrel have done? she wondered. But then, it was unlikely that Kestrel would have been in such a fix. He was too smart to get himself into an entanglement with the likes of Phillip Greyfriars.

And then there were the moments when she and Phillip found themselves alone. He somehow managed to appear when she crept back to the fire at night after the others had gone to their beds. She encountered him at the stream when she went down to have a solitary wash. It was uncanny the way he seemed to know just where she was at all times, even when she would have sworn he was elsewhere in the camp. Finally, she gave up and began to expect him everywhere.

But there was more to her annoyance than merely his following her. Each time she found herself alone with him, she recalled all those times they'd been together at Cygnet House. He never touched her, but she was as aware of his body, his hands, his lips in those times as if he were constantly embracing her. Her own body, traitor that it was, would warm in his presence, and tingle with sensations that couldn't be possible. Her eyes seemed to want to rest on him at the most inopportune moments. Her hands wanted to reach out and caress back a lock of dark hair from his forehead. Her lips seemed to swell and heat at the mere thought of kissing him, as if he were in reality pressing her to him and covering her lips with his.

165

At night, in her bed, she could feel him nearby in the darkness and she tossed and turned as if her bed were lined with nettles.

It was madness. She wanted him as far away from her as possible, yet she longed to have him so near that they would melt into one another, eliminating all boundaries, dismissing all thoughts except desire.

She decided she had to do something soon or leave the camp herself. And with her luck so far, he'd be certain to follow her and make matters worse than ever. She had to find a way to show him that he was not fit for this life, or for her.

"Tomorrow night will be your initiation," she announced to Phillip at the fire that night. "I've found the place. Wren and I will take you there, but you'll be on your own to rob the house."

Hugh scowled. "Oh, now, I don't think that's right, Blackbird. He's never so much as picked a pocket with a pal, he ain't. How's he gonna manage?"

"He's clever enough." Morgana looked at Phillip. "Unless, that is, you'd rather be left here tied to a tree every time we go out?"

Phillip gave her a calm stare. "I'm ready anytime. Show me the place."

" 'Tis well," Morgana said gruffly, wishing he hadn't worn the collar of his cotehardie open at the neck. He'd been wrestling with some of the men and had unbuttoned it, revealing not only his strong collarbone, but a hint of glossy black chest hair. It was ridiculous for her to notice it, but she just couldn't help herself. Lord, what the men must think to see her! She didn't know which was worse anymore, the truth or the pretense.

If he failed at his task tomorrow night, she told herself, he'd have to leave the flock. No one was kept who couldn't pass the test. The circumstances this time were different from all the others, though, for no one had ever

166

before seen the camp until they had passed their initiation. Phillip, in his own inimitable way, had managed to break almost every rule so far and gotten away with it. But she would be adamant about this. If he couldn't prove himself, he had to go. And Phillip had agreed to her terms.

She felt a twinge of guilt at Hugh's protests. He was right, she had set the harshest possible task for Phillip she could devise. He would have to go into a house in the middle of the nearby village, a village that was walled and locked at night. He was to bring out as many valuables as possible, without waking either the members of the household, their servants, or the large mastiff that guarded the place. And he was to do it within the time she allotted, else she and Wren would depart and leave him to his fate.

It would be terribly dangerous and difficult. But she knew that no ordinary task would foil the resources and wits of Phillip Greyfriars. Who knew what trick he might devise, even in this situation? She wasn't going to take that chance. If she wanted him out of her life, this was the only way to do it.

Chapter Eleven

The next night boasted a moon that was almost at the full and a cloudless sky. Morgana cursed Phillip's luck, for now he could find his way in the dark with greater ease. The three of them, Morgana, Wren, and Phillip, set out for the village just before midnight.

"Here is the place," Morgana said as they drew up to the wall of the village. "The house is in the high street, next to the chandler's shop. You have until you hear me whistle."

Phillip nodded and swung down off Saracen. "I'll see you anon," he said with a jaunty salute as he began to climb the wall.

"Mayhap."

Morgana and Wren stealthily followed Phillip over the wall, staying in the shadows well behind him as he made his way into the center of the sleeping village.

Her heart thumped as she thought of all the dangers he faced. And she had sent him there! If he was harmed, she would never forgive herself.

But she couldn't bring herself to stop him. She had set the wheels in motion; now she had to wait to see what would happen.

She was about to whistle when he came around the corner where they were hiding, carrying a bulging sack and humming under his breath as if he were out on a stroll in his gardens. She wanted to throttle him. She and Wren hurried around a back way to get over the wall before Phillip could see them.

He was sitting on Saracen, smiling with smug satisfaction, by the time they returned to their starting point. She was so incensed by his arrogance, and so relieved at his safe return, that she was speechless. She mounted up and rode into the woods without a word. On reaching camp, she handed Sela, the mare, to Geordie to tend and stomped off to her bed, jaws and fists clenched in anger.

He'd done it! He'd passed the impossible test as easily as taking sweets from a babe. Damn him! Was there no end to his cheek? Didn't he understand the dangers? The difficulties? Had the man no nerves as well as no scruples?

Now she had no reason to cast him out of the camp. He was a member of Kestrel's flock, as surely as any of the rest of them. She would have to see him each and every day. She would know he was there, each and every night. This torture and madness would have no end. Or else it would explode into something she couldn't even name but knew would be far more dangerous than any other trial she'd ever faced.

The Raven of Kestrel's flock. It was too much, she thought as she threw herself down onto her bed. What would the Kestrel say if he returned and found she'd let the Viscount Greyfriars, of all people, into the flock?

The Kestrel. That was it!

Morgana stared up at the huge moon, just setting over the edge of the trees around the camp. The Kestrel was the key. She had to find him. He'd know what to do. His word was the final law of the flock. She would leave tomorrow and search for him. She'd bring him back and turn Phillip over to him. Then she'd be free.

But first she had an errand to perform.

Phillip's eyes were quick to adjust to the fading light of the forest. Following Morgana's horse was just a matter of seeking out the blacker, moving shadow against the trees. He kept his distance, paying attention to staying on the snaking path out of the wood. Once they were out on the open road, however, he could see her clearly in the light of the waning moon. And he knew exactly where she was headed.

He watched as she slipped to the ground, tied her horse to a low-hanging branch, and crept toward the village where they had been only two nights before, keeping to the shadows as she went. She was a wonder, he thought once again. So lithe and stealthy in her mission.

The house was dark as a pocket when Phillip arrived. He wondered how the folk inside, having been relieved of all their valuables two nights previous, could be sleeping so soundly. If it had been his house, he would have been up at all hours, keeping a watch over his home and family. But then, he reasoned, he might not bother to lock his doors and go off to sleep like a babe if he had nothing of value left to steal. He smiled to himself. He certainly wouldn't be looking for the thieves to return, not this way and not this soon.

He was waiting in the shadows near the house when Morgana slipped back out the dark hole of a window. He followed her through the narrow village street and over the wall. When she reached her horse, he was right behind her.

"Couldn't resist going back for a bit more?" he asked softly.

He could hear her stifle a gasp as she whirled about. "Phillip! What the devil—"

"Shh." He put his fingers against her lips. "And put the knife away."

Her hand had drawn the knife from its sheath even before she had turned. Now she brandished it under his chin. "You're lucky I don't divide your head from your neck!" she whispered. "Get out of my way. I have nothing to say to you."

"Oh no? I thought that I was your partner now, same as Wren. I get a piece of whatever you've taken this night."

She gave him a shove and mounted up. "You didn't take the risk. You won't get a ha'penny."

He seized her tunic. "No? Perhaps what you mean to say is that I won't get a ha'penny because you don't have so much as a ha'penny."

She glowered at him. "Are you saying I failed at my game? Some talk from a man who but days ago couldn't steal the pennies off a dead man's eyes."

"You're not fooling me, Blackbird." He glanced over his shoulder at the house, untied her horse, and led it further away. She sputtered with outrage but didn't try to stop him.

He called softly to Saracen, who came obediently. Still, he held Morgana's horse by the bridle. "You weren't in there stealing, angel. You were returning." He tugged under the hem of her tunic, and out slipped an empty sack. "No swag at all."

She snatched the bag from his fingers. "I was returning all right. Returning for a few items that you left behind in your first pass. I knew that you haven't the skill to know where such folk keep their real valuables."

"And where are these valuables?"

"Hidden. They were obviously twice wary after being robbed once."

"Ah. I see. And you wouldn't have guessed that before you came here tonight? I would have laid good money that you did have the skill and experience to know that. You could have saved yourself a trip."

"You can't be sure. Some people are not possessed of good sense and don't take precautions even—" Phillip was shaking his head slowly from side to side. "Damnation, it is even so! Ask Kestrel!"

"I shall. But in the meantime, perhaps you can explain to me why your tunic bulged like Edward Sparrow's belly when you went into that house tonight, and why now your waist is as slim as ever."

Morgana opened her mouth, then snapped her jaw shut tight. She gathered up the reins and kicked Sela into motion, tearing the bridle out of Phillip's hand. She was off toward the road, heedless of noise or detection.

Phillip mounted Saracen and tore after her. She was already at the road and in full gallop, her figure bent over Sela's neck, urging her on. He spoke to Saracen. The stallion jumped ahead, eager to chase the mare. In and out of the shadows of overhanging trees they raced, now lit by the moon, now swallowed in blackness. It wasn't long before the gap between them began to close. Saracen was in his element, carrying his master as swiftly as thought. Morgana glanced back over her shoulder, saw them approaching, and took a sudden swerve off the road and into the trees.

Phillip didn't hesitate to follow. He knew that Morgana had unerring skills as a pathfinder and that she would never send Sela into a place where the mare might be hurt.

He was able to keep up most of the way, but Morgana made another swift, sharp turn and was lost to sight in the dark. Unfamiliar with the terrain and handicapped by the dim light filtering through the leaves, Phillip had to slow his pace and take Saracen cautiously over the forest path.

172

The trees parted at last and he was able to see a clearing just ahead. An old cottage stood there, half in ruins, lonely and long-neglected. Its thatched roof looked as if it had been gnawed by Promethean mice, and the doors and window shutters hung all askew. Morgana was nowhere to be seen.

He circled the house, listening for the sound of hoofbeats in the surrounding woods. He heard none, but that didn't necessarily mean that she hadn't gone on, slowing Sela down to a silent walk over the deep beds of leaves and pine needles.

He stilled his horse and sat, looking at the house. A moment later, he swung himself down and crossed the little yard to the front door.

His boots echoed hollowly on the wood floor. Inside, all was dark, except for a few slivers of moonlight leaking in through windows and cracks. He stood and listened.

Morgana tried to hold her breath, but her heart was pounding out its own betraying rhythm. She willed herself to melt into the shadows of the dusty corner. He couldn't possibly see her. She had found her way over here by groping in the blackness. He'd soon give up and go back out to hunt for her in the woods. Or he'd head back to Cadgwyth, thinking she would logically return there. And so she would. But not tonight. She couldn't face him or the others tonight. Especially if he let it slip that she had gone back and returned everything she had ordered him to steal.

Damn him! She could see him, outlined by the pale light of the doorway. Why didn't he just give this up? Why couldn't he mind his own business and go back to London where he belonged? She was getting deeper and deeper into trouble every minute he stayed near her.

To her horror and outrage, he swept his cloak around him and sat down, right there on the floor. What the devil

173

did he imagine he was going to do in an abandoned old woodsman's hut in the middle of a forest at night? She jumped as he spoke.

"It's no shame, angel," he said softly.

She held still and silent, hoping against hope that he would think he had made an error in supposing she was in the cottage. When he continued, she knew the trick wasn't going to work.

"You knew that that family had little to spare and that they have an ailing son. You came tonight to give them back their belongings. 'Twas an act of kindness. You have a tender heart beneath your valiant armor."

"If you ever tell anyone of what I did this night," she whispered fiercely from her corner, "I'll split you in two and roast you like a coney on a spit!"

His laughter was soft, like the shadows. "Never fear, sweet. Your secret softness is locked away with me. But never try to fool me again about your fierce and wicked ways. I know you. I know all about you."

She stood and stepped out of the corner. "No. You do not."

He only looked at her. "What is it that I do not know?"

"Oh no, you don't. You won't trick me that way, Grey-friars."

"No?"

"No!"

"You know that all your secrets are safe with me."

"No, I don't know that. You're a liar and a trickster and a cheat!"

"All traits which should endear me to one such as you, love."

"Don't flatter yourself. You're no more or less than any other of your sort. Your wealth and your birth give you your power, and you use it as you wish!"

He was silent for a moment. "And I am to blame for the circumstances of my birth?"

"You are to be held responsible for the way you use those circumstances. You are so proud and self-righteous in your position, but let that wealth be taken from you, let the titles you claim be stripped from you and all your heirs, and then see how you strut!"

She stood in the shadows, feet braced, fists clenched. She wished she could see his face, yet she was glad of the dark that gave her protection.

"What has my title to do with your act of kindness tonight?" he asked.

"Ah. I should have known you'd be too arrogant to see it. It's so easy for you. So easy to play at being a thief. So easy to play at being an outlaw. So easy to pretend to be one of us. But you can go back to your pleasant life and your glorious house and your dainty swans anytime you wish. And yet what will tomorrow bring for those you leave behind? And what of the people you rob, who have far less than you?"

Phillip rose. "It is easy enough, aye. Easy enough for someone who has the wit to learn your craft. I won't say I'd make my mark as a highwayman. But you know that I risked my neck the other night when I robbed that house. I could have been killed or caught. The law will hang a nobleman as easily as it will a commoner." He stepped nearer. "Or didn't you know that?"

She swallowed hard. What did he mean? Had someone told him about her family? "Yes, the law does hang the noble as well as the commoner. But one such as you, one who has great wealth and the ear and favor of the king, one who is on the side of the angels in everyone's eyes, your neck will never be stretched so long as you can talk, buy, bribe, or extort your way out of the noose!"

Phillip began to circle around her. Her eyes were well used to the dark by now, and she could catch the glint of his eyes and the set of his mouth as he moved. She held her ground, refusing to follow his progress or meet his gaze.

"Such prejudice," he murmured. "I never thought it of you, Blackbird. And you have your own self-righteousness, I'd say. It seems that in your code it is a sin for the rich to rob but merely trade when the poor cut the purses."

"The rich have no need to steal—"

"And the poor have? Since when have the laws of God or the laws of man viewed stealing as a conditional enterprise? For the poor to rob the poor, when they know better than anyone the suffering of poverty—why is this not a greater sin than that committed by the ignorant rich?"

"Saints and devils, the man's a lawyer, too!" Morgana made her words drip with disgust.

"If you wish." His circles were growing smaller, tighter about her. "But who is it that's on trial here?"

She felt him behind her, his body so near. She held herself even more sternly, fighting off the tremors that coursed down her spine at the gentle brush of his breath against the back of her neck.

"This is no court of law," she said evenly. "And you are neither judge nor jury nor counselor."

"No. I am none of those things. But as I said, I am shocked by such prejudice. You are so contemptuous of my status. What is it that sets us apart, pray? I have not asked you to tell me much of your past. I have let you tell me in your own way and time. Yet, you must know that even an arrogant viscount would recognize your speech and habits as belonging to the privileged class. I have my own ideas of who you truly are and how you came to be the Blackbird of the Kestrel's flock.

But perhaps you would prefer to educate me in that matter, too? You seem in a mood to instruct tonight."

"I shall do nothing of the sort! I'll tell you nothing!" she whispered, jaws clenched. "You've stolen enough from me. You won't have that, too."

"Have what?"

"My n—" She halted.

"Your name?"

"I didn't say that."

"True." He began to circle round her again, his body, warm, powerful, merely inches from her own rigid form. "I don't need your name. I've told you that."

"Then why are you here? Why do you persist in following me?" His path around her began to dizzy her, as if she were being pulled with him, around and around.

"Haven't you guessed, Blackbird? A clever one such as you should have summed it all by now."

"I only know that you have imposed yourself upon me in every way possible."

"Then why have you allowed me to stay? Why didn't you have your friends drive me away? Why all this bother to teach me your ways, keep me in your camp?" He was behind her again, this time so close she could feel his cloak brush against her legs.

She was silent. She wished she had an answer, a sound and scathing one for him, but she hadn't. She wasn't sure herself why she had agreed that he could stay in the camp, why she had taken pains to teach him how to ply her trade. "I knew you wouldn't leave. You'd stay and bungle things and put us all in jeopardy. You threatened to turn us in. I had to at least protect myself and the flock."

"Then why not have me taken away? You have the force of men and arms to do it."

His voice was quiet, floating in the dark just beside her ear. Her body was heating, shaking, undercutting her firm resolve to remain cold and distant with him. She struggled to answer.

"You might have gone straight to the sheriffs and told them where to find us. It was better to keep you where we could see you than run that risk."

"Why not have me killed?"

"We're thieves, not murderers. I won't burden my soul with the likes of you."

His mouth was now so close that his words were scarcely more than a breath, stirring the curls against her cheek. "You've thought of everything, haven't you?"

She didn't answer. Her mind was whirling and tumbling, memories of kisses and whispered endearments twining with her fear. Her breath caught in her chest, and she couldn't seem to calm her racing heart. She wanted him to move away, give her space to breathe and move, and yet she couldn't bring her hands up to push him away, couldn't make her feet move to carry her out of his reach.

"All your answers may be true," he said. "But you've left one unspoken."

"There is no other, pestilence," she said, her voice tight with the effort to conceal her breathlessness.

"Oh, but there is. You took me in and took me on because you want what I want." He didn't touch her, didn't move, just stood there, so close that she felt she was going to melt from the warmth of him.

"You want amusement," she muttered. "You want novelty. That's the only reason you are here. You're bored with your pampered life and want a bit of excitement."

"Excitement, yes. Novelty? I won't deny it. Relief from boredom? I think not. I've never lacked for interest. But there is one thing more that I want."

"Another rose, my lord?" Sarcasm edged her words.

"Aye."

The word fell into the darkness like the peal of a church bell, yet he had uttered it with no more force than a butterfly's breath. Morgana closed her eyes. She wanted to retort, but she couldn't. She knew what he meant. She

178

knew he was speaking the truth. She was the rose he wanted.

"I can't," she whispered.

"Oh, sweet, you can." He lifted a finger and caressed her cheek.

"It's all wrong. It can only lead to trouble and more—"

"It can lead to heaven, too."

"That's not a place for the likes of me."

"Let me take you there and then decide."

"Phillip," she moaned softly. "Please—"

"Please what, angel?" His finger traced the curve of her jaw, smoothed her trembling lips.

"You don't want me. You need someone else."

"Let me show you who I want. Who I need. And how much." He moved to stand before her, took her face between his hands. She gazed up at him, anguished in her fear and desire.

"Oh, God, forgive me." She reached up with both of her hands then and drew his face down for a kiss.

The sensation rocked her, made her even dizzier. His mouth was so firm, so warm. She knew she was drowning and she didn't care. Let this wild current take her, she thought. If she paid for it for the rest of her days, she would have this one taste of paradise.

They moved in perfect accord with one another. A button or lace undone here, a caress echoed there, mouths that met with matching intensity. Only when the two of them bent to remove their boots was there a break in the rhythm. As soon as the annoying impediments were tossed aside, they resumed their dance, touching and smoothing and tasting and sighing.

Morgana had never imagined such joy. She had had many thoughts of Phillip, of touching him and kissing him, but she'd had no notion of the sheer force supplied by her feelings once they were set free. She knew she was awkward and inexperienced, but when they were unclothed at last, and Phillip had swirled his heavy cloak to the floor as their bed, she couldn't wait to join him there. And the sweet, hot strength of his body against hers as he gathered her close in his embrace was like the breaking of chains that had held something long imprisoned within her.

He let her lead the way in all things, allowing her free play and exploration of him. Her fears had long since fled—this was Phillip and she knew, with heart-certainty, that she was desired, and wanted, and protected in his arms. And as that certainty dawned on her, she almost laughed with delight, her mouth pressed against the pulsing of his throat. For this moment, for this hour of moonlight, she was free to learn and test the uttermost limits of feeling. For the first time in many long years, she would take her time with life and have her fill.

"So much," she murmured, her hands running over his chest and shoulders. "There is so much to know."

"I'm your willing subject, student, and teacher," Phillip said, kissing her eyes. "Let's form our own university."

She giggled and rubbed her cheek against his. "Educating a woman is a dangerous practice."

"Not in my school."

"Madman," she said tenderly.

"Let me never grow sane."

Her only reply was a gasp of delight. Then all words were vanquished and sensation and feeling reigned. The moon, peering in at the window, was the only witness to their joy.

Phillip reached out for his tunic and tucked it under his head. In his arms, curled warm and loose, was Morgana, his Morgana. He smoothed his cloak around them both and rested his chin on her ruffled, dark head.

What had possessed him? he wondered. Never in all his life had he felt such utter peace and yet such fiery passion mixed within himself during the act of love. It was as if he were dying in her embrace and yet more alive than ever before.

It wasn't just her body, though God knew her smooth, satiny skin and supple, strong limbs were pure pleasure. The spicy-sweet smell of her, the taut thrust of her nipples, the perfect curves of waist, hip, thigh, the tender giving of her breasts—all of these had been as heady and enticing as any man could desire.

It wasn't just the ages-old magic of their joining. Or was it? He had gone as slowly and as gently as he could manage, especially when he met with the natural barrier her body held against his entry. How had he known she was yet a maid? He just had. Her bastard stepfather had not taken that from her.

Perhaps that was what had stirred him so. His dark-haired, dark-eyed, salty-tongued little thief was as innocent as a convent-raised maid. His exultation at the moment when he was finally joined with her completely was so unbounded that hot tears had sprung to his eyes. She was his, in truth. He knew now, afterward, that it was as tenuous a claim as ever was made, but in that moment, when he had kissed away her own tears of pain and soothed her ragged breathing, he had felt a sensation of such pride and tenderness and fierce possessiveness that he shook now, even at the memory.

And when they had joined together in the exquisite, dancing rhythms of lovemaking, he had never felt so free and yet so connected to another soul. The sweet arching of her body beneath his, the joyous movement of surging forward to bury himself deep within her, the wrenching, agonizing pleasure as he held himself still for her trembling climax, the final, exultant fulfillment of his own release had shattered him, and yet he felt more whole now than ever in his life. And the tender aftermath, of being cradled together in the darkness that was full of light, that had been the seal placed on his heart. He had claimed her, and in the same instant, he had lost himself.

"Thief," he murmured.

"Mm?" Morgana sighed in her sleep.

His only reply was to gather her closer and drift off, unable to fathom the depths of this new experience and not caring to trouble himself while Morgana was here, in his arms.

She awoke to the feel of Phillip's hand, stroking lazily up and down her body. She moaned softly with pleasure and arched up to greet the hand that so gently cupped her breast. She wondered if she would ever again feel the same passion she had felt last night. In truth, she didn't feel quite the same tension or urgency. But the memory of all those exquisite pleasures returned in a warm rush, and she rolled over to rub herself against his naked form.

"Good morrow," she murmured against his mouth.

"Good morrow," he replied, and with one expert motion slid up to join himself with her.

"Oh, Phillip," she gasped as she wound her arms about his neck. "This can't be possible."

"I assure you, it is."

She held still in a moment of pure, animal delight, reveling in the feeling of his fullness within her, in the way her muscles clasped and held him in their own eager embrace. No wonder people were mad for this, she thought. She had imagined pain and humiliation in this act. But Phillip had shown her that what Cedric had done to her was doubly wrong—not only had it been cruel, but it also had been utterly contrary to the natural sweetness and truth of the word: lovemaking.

She rolled onto her back, pulling Phillip with her. He braced himself on his arms, looking at her with smoky

182

eyes. She smiled, closed her eyes, and began to move against him, slowly, slowly.

"That's right, angel." Phillip's words were crooning, seductive. "Take your pleasure."

"But I don't know if I can—"

"Yes, you can. You can take it all, have it all."

Her hands slid to his hips and she drew him down into her slow, melting upthrust. This was heaven, she thought. For surely she had died.

No, on second thought, she was dying now—now!

It was a long time before she came to herself again. Phillip was still in her arms, his triumphant shout following seconds behind her own rapturous cries. They lay together, tangled, sweat-sheened, and utterly sated.

Full daylight was streaming in through the window and the cracks in the walls. A beam of sunlight fell across Phillip's eyes and he shifted away from her, blinking. She felt the chill morning air slip between them.

"It's morning," she said, knowing as she said it how idiotic it sounded.

"It is." He sat up and stretched. "It looks to be a fine day, too." He looked at her with a smile. "I'm afraid I haven't brought anything to break our fast."

She sat up and gathered her tunic to her front, suddenly shy. "Not to worry. There'll be food at the camp."

"Are you well?" he asked, his voice gentle.

She pulled her tunic over her head. "I'm fine."

He sat up and retrieved his hose and shirt. He slipped them on and rose to stand behind her as she stared out through one of the half-shuttered windows.

"If I hurt you . . ." he began.

"You didn't." She shrugged away from his hands as they reached for her. "But it's time to get back. I don't like leaving that lot for too long on their own. They're likely to set fire to their beards."

"Mm. Perhaps you're right."

Morgana resumed her dressing, averting her eyes from Phillip's. In truth, she didn't know what she felt or thought. Up until a short time ago, she had been in some lovely dreamland, another place. She had been another person. One she hardly recognized. She had given herself so utterly to Phillip and had even been bold enough to pursue her own pleasures with him. She had been happy, yes, but as a result, she was also more vulnerable than ever to him. What would he expect from her now? How could she go on with her life? In one, breathtaking night, her world had been changed.

She stepped outside while Phillip finished dressing. She was mounted up when he came out of the old cottage.

"I'm famished," she said, feeling more awkward than ever. "Let's be off."

"Very well." He came to stand by her horse. "Morgana." She refused to speak. She stared off into the forest. "I have no regrets about what we've done. 'Twas the most right and natural thing we could have done. And I couldn't be happier."

She shook her head. "I never have regrets. They're a waste of time. But I want to get back to camp."

She felt his eyes on her, dark and powerful, but she resisted the urge to turn and face him. If she did, she was afraid—of what she didn't know. All she knew was that she felt as if her life was a basket of grains that had suddenly been tossed up into the air. All was in confusion. She had to get back to something familiar, to her old ways and her old world so that she could sort things out for herself.

They rode back to the camp in silence. But she found no relief from her confusion when they arrived.

"Ho! Blackbird! Raven!" Edward bellowed as they entered the clearing. He was waving a mug and was obviously well on his way to a fully slaked thirst. "Hey-o, lads, look who's back!'' he shouted.

"Well a day. Tom Black and the Raven, indeed.'' The Robin hitched up his breeches and grinned at them from across the fire.

Chapter Twelve

It was a bad dream. Robin was back. When she had first heard the commotion and seen Edward Sparrow's happy face, she had held a fleeting hope that it was the Kestrel who had returned. But the Robin—God's wounds, it was like welcoming the very devil himself back into her home.

Morgana wet her lips. "Robin," she said with a cool nod.

"Blackbird." Robin's greeting was just as measured. His eyes turned to Phillip. "I see you took my advice and came up by short ways, indeed," he said.

Phillip gave a brief smile and slid from his horse. "Excellent directions and a clear road from London all the way. I trust your journey was the same?"

Robin grinned at Morgana but his eyes held no mirth. "Don't he talk fine, though? I knew you'd take to him, Tom me lad. You always liked the fine ways on the Kestrel, you did."

Morgana dismounted. "I see you brought provisions," she said.

"Oh, aye. I didn't have such a clear road as all that," Robin replied, with a darting glance at Phillip. "But it turned out to be a profitable one. Thought you lads could use a bit of cheer and a bite or two of good mutton. Seems I was right, as Sparrow here tells me."

"Where's Wren?"

"Oh, him. He had a drink or two and then said he'd go on watch while the rest of us had a bite and a sup."

"I'm glad somebody was watching. We've been too lax about such measures." Morgana pulled her saddle off Sela and led her away to be staked with the other beasts. Phillip followed.

"You know him?" she asked.

"I met him in London. When I was trying to find you. I thought I had disposed of him for good and all, but the man is more slippery than I imagined."

"Slippery isn't the half of it." Morgana rubbed Sela down with a woolen cloth.

Phillip tended to Saracen. "He knows about you."

"I know. He and Wren and Kestrel are the only ones that know."

"He's dangerous."

"Tell me what I don't know."

"I don't want him near you. I don't want you near him."

She walked around Sela and began rubbing down the horse's other side. "I can take care of myself."

"Not with him. You're out of your depth with him."

"Oh, and you aren't?"

"I am. I admit it. But I have less to lose than you."

"Bah."

"Blackbird."

She glared at him. "I don't need a nursemaid. I've been around the Robin. I know what he's capable of. He's done me no harm, and I don't intend that he should now."

"But then you had the Kestrel to protect you. You should leave, soon."

She went red. "What can—"

"The man's right," a new voice interjected.

She turned her furious gaze on Wren as he stepped quietly up behind them. "Oh, no. Not you now, too," she said.

"Kestrel's gone," Wren said.

"I know that. But I can handle Robin. I'll keep clear of him. And if he tries anything, I have my knife."

"What if he exposes you to the others?" Phillip demanded.

She shrugged. "He hasn't yet."

"He'll be leader," Wren observed.

Morgana felt uneasiness rising within her. Robin would want to be the leader, would believe himself entitled to be. She doubted that he'd ever give up that power without a bloody struggle. "I can't believe they had him back," she said, "after the way he turned the dogs on all of us back in London."

Phillip nodded to where the men were still loudly celebrating by the fire. "These fellows haven't had much of good wine or meat in months, I'll wager. No doubt his provisions greased his way into their hearts once more." He gave her a bitter smile. "And you must admit, honor among thieves is a rare commodity."

Morgana bit her lip. Phillip was probably right. By the time the men had a taste of mutton and a good bit to drink, they no doubt would have forgiven him his trespasses. After all, they were still alive, weren't they? And who was to say that they wouldn't have done the same were they in his shoes?

But Robin as leader would be hell for them all, but most of all for her. His jealousy, unchecked by Kestrel's authority, and his innate meanness would compel him to make her life with the flock a miserable, nasty affair. It would be better for her to leave at once and avoid the fight that was sure to come.

Still, she couldn't simply abandon the men to him. She

couldn't run. These were Kestrel's men and she owed Kestrel at least that much allegiance, to see that his men weren't lost to a petty tyrant like Robin.

She tossed her rag over a branch and faced Phillip and Wren. "I can deal with this man. And that's all I will hear of it."

"Blackbird."

"No!" She lowered her voice. "That's all. I won't have you filling my mind with doubts. I've handled Robin in the past and I'll handle him now. It's settled."

"Watch your back." Wren's look was resigned, but wary.

"And your front," Phillip added. "And like it or not, I will be watching all parts of you and him as well. I trust him as far as I can throw Saracen."

"Do as you like. But stay out of my way."

Morgana strode back to the campfire. She accepted food and drink from Hugh and sat on her cloak while the others continued their merrymaking. When the revels grew sour and the bonhomie of the celebrants turned to belligerence, she stood and slipped away to her bed, making sure that her knife was sharpened and at the ready before she rolled herself in her blankets.

What now? she asked herself. Only a few hours ago, she was in bliss, lying in Phillip's arms, with just the two of them in all the world, it had seemed. Robin's appearance had certainly shattered all of those illusions, if she hadn't already known that they were the merest of dreams.

She was in for a fight. A bad one.

And it wasn't only the fight with Robin she was facing. She was in for a battle with herself as she struggled each day with the tantalizing memories of love shared with Phillip and all that act had meant to her. She had to let those memories go and get back to being the rough-and-tumble Tom Black. There was no future for her and Phillip. He had said she was out of her depth with the Robin. Well, Phillip was out of his depth with her. Now, more than ever, she had to remain steadfast in her vow to stay free and beholden to no man.

She reached over and pulled her cloak over her blankets, shivering against the sudden gust of chill wind that cut through the glade. Dry leaves danced over the ground and came to rest against her bedroll. Autumn was upon them. It was time to harvest what they could against the cold ravages of the winter.

Elizabeth paced the length of her hall. "Where the devil is he?" she demanded of the servant who stood before her.

"As I said, my lady, no one could tell me. All they could say was that Lord Phillip had departed suddenly in the night, saying he was off to London. No one has seen or heard from him since."

The servant cringed as Elizabeth advanced. "And have you looked in London, Durel?" she murmured.

"Yes. I mean, no, my lady. Not since I went to Aylesbury—"

"Then get out there and search every alley, cot, and corner of this city!" she hissed. "I want him!"

"Yes, my lady. It shall be as you say." Gerald Durel was on his way to the door before the words were past his lips.

"See that it is!"

He heard the crash of pottery against the door just as he closed it behind him. Mopping his brow, he scuttled for the front door and the relative peace and safety of London's busy streets.

Back in her chamber, Elizabeth vented her rage on the furnishings for a few moments, then, recovering herself with remarkable ease and speed, went to her dressing table and picked up an intricately carved wooden comb. Releasing her hair from its coils, she slowly began to comb out the pale, silver-gold tresses. She lifted a polished silver hand-mirror and contemplated the results.

"So he's vanished," she told her reflection. "And no

word to me in weeks. This is not the way to treat his lady-love.''

She set aside the mirror and took up a jar of scented cream. Slowly, carefully, she rubbed the precious unguent into her hands and over her throat. ''I shall have to show him the way to behave,'' she said softly. ''I need him. At least until I have achieved my ends.'' She paused and smiled. ''And perhaps, even after that. It would be foolhardy to give up such pleasure as he gives me just for the sake of a marriage vow.'' There was a knock at the door. ''Come.''

''My lady.'' Her steward bowed low in the doorway. ''It is Master Threadgill.''

''I'll meet him in the library.''

After a leisurely check of her person, Elizabeth covered her hair with a scarf and donned a simple gold circlet to hold it in place. She smiled at the effect in her hand-mirror. So simple and yet so elegant. So like a true crown.

She sailed down the hall to the library and entered with a blithe greeting on her lips. ''Master Threadgill. How good of you to come and see me. You know how I dislike going out into the hurly-burly of the counting-houses and such.

Threadgill, a stout man in distinguished gray and black, bowed over Elizabeth's hand. But his eyes, when they met hers, were troubled and more than a bit fearful.

''What is it?'' Elizabeth murmured. ''Surely, Charles, you haven't bad news to relate?''

The man was positively quaking. ''My dear Lady Winston, I fear I have.''

Elizabeth's smile faltered only slightly. ''Tell me your news,'' she said in a voice as smooth and cool as new cream.

''As you know, my lady, on good advice I have invested a substantial sum of your money in trade with various merchants in Florence. Money, I fear I must add, that was made available to you, in large part, by a loan I secured from a lender here in London.''

''I am with you so far.''

191

"I have had a letter from the Florentine gentleman who was to ship the goods purchased before the winter. He regrets to say that the ships, fully laden, were lost off the coast of Italy, not more than a few days after they set out for England." Threadgill twisted his hat in his hands, swallowing hard before he continued. "Pirates, my lady. All was lost. Only two men, common sailors, survived, as I understand it. The loss to us both is . . ."

"Yes? How much?"

"Total, my lady."

"What? What the devil does that mean?"

"Every bit of our investment was aboard those three ships. I was so sure, Signor Mantalini was so reassuring, my contacts in Florence gave me such good report, that I invested it all."

Elizabeth raised her hand and gave the man a powerful slap across the face. "You were sure? Signor Mantalini was reassuring? And for your stupidity I have lost all hope of any profit from this venture?"

Threadgill nodded and stepped back, out of her reach, rubbing his cheek.

Elizabeth raged on. "How am I to pay my creditors?" she railed. "God, the cost of maintaining this house alone—the parties I've had to hold—my clothing! You imbecile! It will take me another year and more to make good on the bills I have already!"

Threadgill was backing toward the wall. "There is more, I fear, my lady."

"More?"

He nodded, cringing.

"Out with it, worm."

"The loan, my lady. The sums I borrowed for us both from my lender friend."

"What about them?"

"They were due upon arrival of the ships from Italy."

"Yes, but now there will be no ships."

192

"Exactly. The terms of the loan were such that if the agreement with Florence failed, the principal of the loan was to be repaid within the fortnight."

Elizabeth stared at him, her pale face going even whiter with rage. "And you expect me to produce such a sum? After you have ruined me with your foolish sureties?"

" 'Twas unforeseen! It was a most secure investment but for the pirates—"

"I don't care if God himself snatched those ships out of the water!" Elizabeth shrieked. "I will not pay!"

"But, my lady, you signed the papers. It is a legally bound agreement. The lender will have us both into court."

"So? Let him!"

"My lady! It would mean debtor's prison for us both."

Elizabeth choked in fury. Debtor's prison? God's wounds, but she wouldn't go there. Not while there was life in her body. She had too much to do, too many plans. She began to think.

"Threadgill," she said after a moment, her voice softening to something more like its usual musical tone. "You must go to this money-lender. You must plead our case for us. Beg him, if you must, to give us more time, to find a way to make this profitable for us all—him, as well."

"But, my lady, he is most adamant."

"I don't care!" Elizabeth snapped. More calmly, she continued. "Go to him. Tell him that you have another shipment readying in Florence."

"But I haven't!"

"Sweet Jesu, is there nothing between those ears of yours? Tell him! Then go you at once and start making that trade with Florence. Go to Mantalini yourself! But get it done. I won't be ruined in this. I will not!"

Threadgill left the house at a trot. He nearly forgot he had his horse with him, he was in such a hurry to depart, and had to go back and fetch it, looking over his shoulder the whole time and jumping at the sound of objects breaking inside the house.

Morgana had not underestimated the Robin's intentions. From that first day, he began a steady, none-too-subtle campaign to gain mastery over the flock. He started with gifts, such as the mutton and ale he had brought that first day. He let it be known that he had been tortured and starved in prison and thereby compelled against his will to bear tales against his fellow thieves. He went on to challenge every decision that Morgana made. Now, little more than a week since his arrival, he was at work dividing the men against themselves, and, ultimately, against her.

"Here, Hugh, what's a man doing, hauling water like a common drudge?" he asked one morning as Hugh lugged the bucket into camp from the nearby stream.

"Blackbird says we all got to eat, so we all got to work," Hugh puffed as he carried the water to the fireside.

"Ah, he would, wouldn't he?" Robin set one booted foot up on a stump and began to pare his nails with his knife-blade.

"What d'you mean?"

"I'm only sayin' that you don't see him carrying no water nor splitting no firewood. He talks like we's all one, but you notice that him and his favorites will always get the best of it all, with the least of the work."

Hugh scowled as he pondered this. "Yea, I suppose that's true. But Blackbird does all the plannin' and he tended us all when the fever came through here and he's always the first to offer to stand the watch."

"Oh, aye. He's the one for the easy work. Nursin'! What kind of a skill is that for a man? For a thief?"

"Well . . ."

"Well's a pretty deep subject, Hugh, me lad. But you

just think on what I say. I'll wager you'll not see Blackbird sully his hands with anything save the fat of the meat
from one day to the next.''

Hugh did the best he could to ponder this as he went
about his work. And Robin continued to sow discontent
among the birds of the flock.

''Say, Raven,'' the Sparrow said one day. ''Did you
ever notice how Robin is always right in there, helping
the lads with all the work about the camp?''

Phillip shrugged. ''I suppose he does his share, Edward.''

Edward the Sparrow leaned on his ax-handle. ''Blackbird don't do none o' that. Don't seem right, somehow.''

Phillip nodded to where Morgana and Wren were
counting the stores of the camp and readying to hunt.
''He's never let you go hungry.''

''No, that's true. But how come he does all the soft
duty? And how did he come to know so much about nursin' the sick and all? What kind of a man is he?''

''In truth, Sparrow, I've known many men in my time,
but I've never known one that was his equal.''

''Hmm. I don't know. I always thought it'd be the
Robin takin' charge if anything was to happen to Kestrel.''

Phillip glanced at the man. ''Is that what Robin
wants?''

''I dunno. Just seems like that was what was meant to
be.''

''Have you complaints against the Blackbird?''

''Well, not complaints, as it were, but—''

''If you have any, go to him with them. I've never
known him to deal unfairly with any of you. Any of us.''

Sparrow hefted his ax once more. ''That's true enough.
You can't beat Tom Black for his even hand.''

Later that night, while Morgana was on the watch at
the edge of the forest, Phillip joined her.

"What the devil are you doing here?" she demanded. "Are you mad? There's enough bad feeling around this camp without you bringing up more stupid questions."

"I won't stay long. But I just want to be sure that you're aware of what's going on. The men are grumbling over every little task you set for them and quarreling over who's entitled to what. Robin works fast, I'll give him that."

"I'm not leaving."

"I didn't say you should. But you had better be prepared. There's a fight spoiling, and it won't be a pretty one."

Morgana pursed her lips. "I know it," she admitted at last. "I actually didn't give Robin enough credit. I thought he'd just barge in here and demand to be named the prince of thieves. But he's been more than civil to me and he's gone about his work with more cunning than force."

"He's winning their loyalties. He hopes they'll do the job for him."

"And well they might. One thing troubles me, though."

"Why hasn't he used your true sex against you?"

"Aye. He hasn't breathed a word about it." She shook her head and squinted out into the darkness. "I don't understand it."

"He's saving it for his trump card."

"What do you mean?"

"I mean that Robin is a fairly clever general, and more than half a politician. He's laying the groundwork, turning the men against you for any reason he can create. But the time will come when he will challenge you openly. And for all those who still side with you, he will bring out your ultimate, and final, calumny. Your sex. How can they follow someone who is not only a woman, but who has lied to them all about it since the day she first entered their midst?"

Morgana looked at him, horror-struck. "He will expose me."

Phillip nodded. "And I do not think they will think first of Christian charity."

"God."

Phillip reached out and turned her face to his. "You can't go on thus. You can't stay here and let them rip you to pieces."

"But the Kestrel—I promised!"

"Your vow does not extend to your life."

Morgana pulled away from him. "You make it worse by being here. You're the one who should leave."

"I will not."

"You must! If I am exposed, so will you be! And if they despise a woman, what will they think of a nobleman in their midst?"

"I will not leave."

"Stay then. But leave me now. If Robin or one of his spies should hear us or see us, he would have more than a mouthful to tell."

Phillip sat silently at her side for a moment more, then with hardly a sound he was gone, and Morgana was alone at her cold station once more. She blew out a cloudy breath and wrapped her cloak more tightly about her.

How far did her vow to Kestrel, her debt to him, extend? Phillip said that she did not owe him her life. But Kestrel had taken her in, trained her, protected her, given her his trust. When all other folk would have reviled her or used her ill, he had simply accepted her and given her a place in his flock. And she had given her oath of loyalty to him. The flock had been her only home for so many years. How could she turn aside now?

She couldn't allow Robin to take over the flock. Not without a fight. That much she did owe to Kestrel. And if it was Robin that won out, so be it. She would remain and make the best of it. She was a tried-and-true soldier of the Kestrel's troops. That was who she was.

Robin licked his lips and wiped his chin on his sleeve. This was the last of the ale. It had lasted just long enough to serve his purpose. When it was gone, and they were reduced to drinking water with a bit of sour wine in it to kill the poisons, they'd be in an even more rebellious mood.

Then, he'd make his move. He had cast his nets with care and it was time to haul them in and see what fishes he'd caught. There were only one or two of the flock that troubled him.

One was that halfwit, the Wren. The man had always been a loner, keeping to himself when he wasn't with the Blackbird or the Kestrel. But he never talked. Robin never could tell where he stood. He'd wager that the old crackbrain was still loyal to the Blackbird, though. It wouldn't be prudent to think otherwise. But how far did that loyalty reach?

The old man knew the secret of Tom Black's identity. Had he been the beneficiary of her favors all this time? Robin spat into the fire at the thought. The old fool didn't have sense enough to take advantage of what was right under his nose.

But surely the Kestrel had had her. The man was no monk, and he had favored the smart little bitch above almost all others. Jesu, it was a wonder the girl hadn't already borne him a bastard or two by now. Ho, but maybe the clever hawk wasn't up to the task. The Kestrel not man enough to father a child on a ripe little chit like that? It was too delicious!

"What's so funny, mate?" Hugh said.

"Oh, nothing. Nothing. I was just rememberin' what a chap Kestrel was with the ladies, is all."

"Oh, aye. That he was. Had but to wink an eye and

they'd be wettin' theirselves for 'im, it seemed."

"Yeah, well," Robin growled, "you and I could 'ave had 'em all too, if we was in his position."

"Mayhap." Hugh returned to gnawing on his mutton bone.

Robin returned to his musings. The other thorn in his side was this Raven. He didn't like him and he didn't trust him. The man was too well-spoken and too handsome for a thief. He had none of the look of a man who'd been in danger or who even had need to steal, come to that. And no one, not even Robin himself, could figure out where his loyalties lay.

Back in London at the Unicorn, the man had said he'd be happy to serve under Robin rather than Kestrel. But Robin could see nothing in his behavior or his speech that indicated that he cared one way or another who led the band. He was a man who would go his own way and hang the rest.

And that made him dangerous.

Robin thought back to the morning when he'd arrived in camp, and how Blackbird and the Raven had come riding into camp together. They'd given no account of where they'd been or what they'd been doing. . . . Robin sat up straight. "Well, damn me," he muttered.

"What say?" asked Hugh.

"Nothin'," Robin growled. "Nothin' that matters to you."

He bounded up and left the fire, stepping over men as he went, cuffing any who got in his way. He crossed the clearing in a few strides and came to where the horses were tethered.

He went up to the big black that he knew belonged to Raven. Saracen whinnied and shied away from the heavy hands that patted him down. "Deep girth," Robin muttered, "and legs neither too long nor short. Good coat an' muscles. He's as blue-blooded as any king, he is."

He stepped back from the stallion. "Now, what's a thief a-doin' with a horse fit for a prince, eh?"

"What's a thief do with anything?"

Phillip stepped out of the shadows beyond the horses. Robin gave him a grin.

"I was just admirin' him," he said easily. "He's a fine one, he is."

"The finest," Phillip said, coming to stand at Saracen's head. He said nothing, only eyed the Robin, waiting.

Robin shifted on his feet. "No doubt from one of the best stables goin', eh?"

"He is."

"Chatty fella, ain't you?"

Phillip shrugged. "When there's need, I speak. What is it you'd have me say?"

"Just out of curiosity, where'd you find this beast?"

"Aylesbury. Ever been there?"

"No, no reason. Too easy to get pinched for poaching on royal grounds thereabouts."

"True enough. Anything else you'd like to know?" Phillip's tone was affable.

"There might be. I might be wantin' to know where you met up with the Kestrel. I been with him five year and more now, and I ain't never seen you around before."

"It's as I told you in London. I worked with him up north, in the borderlands."

"When?"

"Two years ago. You lot were here, he told me, in Cadgwyth."

"Two year ago, eh?"

"Aye."

"Well a day. I allus wondered where he went on those trips off by hisself."

"Now you know."

"Aye. Now I know."

"Well then, if that's all, I'm going to my bed." Phillip

gave Saracen a final pat and strode off into the dark once more.

Robin stood staring after him with narrowed eyes. "Two year ago, eh?" he muttered. "Two year ago my arse."

The next day, several of the men went out with Robin to visit the market fair in a nearby town. Wren and Phillip rode with them, to keep an eye out for any treachery on Robin's part. The men returned to camp late that night, roaring and stumbling, toting casks of ale, many of which had been freely sampled.

Morgana came to sit by Wren, just outside the circle of the firelight. "They're absolutely sodden," she said, half-amused, half-disgusted.

Wren nodded and smiled. He had had a few tankards of the new catch himself.

"Well, as I'm the only one here who's sober enough to keep eyes and wits working together, I'll take the watch. Don't put on too big a head," she said, slapping Wren on the back.

"Careful," Wren said, raising his cup to her.

"Always."

She passed through the camp toward the forest, noticing that Phillip was seated with Hugh and Edward, drinking and regaling them with songs. She sighed. If only the man wasn't so damned stubborn, she grumbled to herself once again. If only he would go back where he belonged.

She waited just inside the forest edge, allowing her eyes to adjust to the darkness. If only . . . She shook her head. It was useless. She couldn't shake her thoughts of Phillip for one waking moment. And her dreams at night were no help, either. She was shocked and amazed when she roused from these night visions, flushed and panting as if they had been real. And always, always, at the center of every dream was Phillip, and Phillip's hands, and Phillip's mouth, and Phillip's arms pulling her into a sweet, hot embrace.

201

She made her way slowly to the cover of a gorse bush, and took up her place for the night. From here she could see the path, what there was of it, the edge of the woods, and she could hear clearly on all sides. No one would enter this area without her knowledge.

She pulled her mitts from her belt and drew them on over her chilly hands. The nights were growing bitter. By month's end the rains would begin in earnest, and following that, the snow. It was time to think about going south once more. But would London be safe for them? After the fiasco at Lady Winston's house, and the way the Robin turned the law on them all to save himself, would they still be looking for members of the flock?

She winced at the thought of Elizabeth Winston's name. Phillip's connection to her was still a puzzle, but she couldn't help the jealousy she felt at the idea of Phillip rushing off to be with her, declaring his undying service to her. Why the devil was he here, in this godforsaken mire, hanging about a guttersnipe like herself?

Thoughts of the night they'd spent together in the abandoned cottage rose again, like smoke that could not be contained. She'd relived every moment there, in Phillip's arms, since that night. It took all her strength not to go to him, when all the others were asleep, and beg him to share with her again the sweet secrets he had revealed to her. The awareness of him sleeping across the clearing from her was torture. But she had steeled herself against all those feelings, knowing that they could go nowhere and that to reenact that night would only make things worse.

What was more, Phillip had not come to her. He had made no move to touch her or to speak to her of love since that night. Had that been enough to satisfy him? Had he been so disappointed, so repulsed that he wanted no more of her? Then why—

Her next thought was lost as a hand came around from behind her and she was quickly pinned to the ground.

Chapter Thirteen

Phillip tossed on his bedroll, the taste of ale sour in his mouth and his head pounding. Something wasn't right. He could sense it. And it wasn't just the effects of too much drink.

It was Morgana, as usual. Sweet Jesu, but he was like a pup in his lust for her sweet little body. The merest thought of her, lying on her bed, so near and yet so unreachable, caused his body untold suffering, night after night. He'd never been so besotted, not even in those early days with Elizabeth. In those days, his thoughts had all been on himself, his pleasure in her, and how he could get that pleasure once again.

But with Morgana, he not only wanted the ecstasy of coupling with her, but he wanted her mind, and her spirit and her soul, as well. He wanted, above all, for her to be safe. And each day, in this place, that concern became more urgent.

Was he a fool or a madman? Morgana would look at him with sour humor and tell him he was both. He chuckled softly at the thought. What a brier patch she made of love! And how he enjoyed it. But was it madness to love a hot-tempered little thief who cared more for a band of rogues and outlaws than for her own safety or future?

He tossed to the left. Perhaps he should take his leave. It was undeniable that he and she both were in danger here if his identity were discovered by the band. None of these men would ever believe that a landed, wealthy nobleman wanted only to be included in their ranks. He would be lucky to escape these woods alive, but more likely he'd be ransomed first, and then killed upon delivery of the fees.

He tossed right. But Morgana was in danger, too. Not only for not denouncing him at the first, but because at any moment now, Robin would play his hand, and her own true identity would be revealed. The prospects of what punishments those revelations might bring were horrifying to his mind.

He flopped onto his back. What the devil was he to do? Robin was getting too close to the truth. And the time was coming, he could feel it in the air about the camp, when Robin must confront Morgana for control of the flock.

Was she strong enough to withstand him?

He didn't like to think about that. She was strong. Aye, and clever. And she had allies.

But was it enough?

Unbidden, a vision of Morgana writhing at Robin's feet came to his mind. Strong or not, she was not a match for his treachery. The image grew, and he saw Robin reach for her, tearing her clothes. The tender, pale skin that he, Phillip, had touched and loved was bruising beneath Robin's filthy hands.

"No!" he whispered, jumping to his feet.

He scrambled into his tunic and boots and headed off through the sleeping camp to Morgana's bed.

*　　*　　*

Morgana fought back the panic that was coming in waves, swamping her. Robin held her down by the throat with one hand and, grinning, slit the fastener on her cloak with her own knife.

"Well a day," he growled. "Your time's come, Tommy, me lad. Or should I say—" He slit her tunic from neckline to hem. "Or should I say lass?"

Morgana tried to kick out, but Robin slammed his knee across her thighs, painfully halting her efforts. He cast aside the knife, and his hand groped at the neckline of her shirt. She writhed and tried to scream but couldn't get the air needed to push the sound forth.

"Did you think I was goin' to just hand over the flock to you? Now, did you, little bitch?" Morgana tried to shake her head, but Robin held her fast.

Phillip had been wrong, so had the Wren. Robin had been waiting to play his card, but not in some blazing revelation in front of the men. He had chosen a private field of battle instead, one in which he had all the advantage. And it was here that he was revealing his knowledge and just how he planned to use it.

"I been waitin' to get my hands on these little apples of yours for many a long month. Right patient I've been. But now—" His hand gathered the cloth and ripped it away. "Now, I'm out of patience. And you're out of luck, little bitch."

His hand pinched and prodded at her breasts, bruising and scratching. It was the old nightmare. Cedric again. The hands everywhere, hurting her. The vile names, the breath stinking of ale. Morgana fought for control, for her sanity, but the nightmare just went on. She thought she saw lightning, heard thunder, and cringed, wishing she could just withdraw up into herself.

"Now, just so's we don't have you cryin' out and disturbin' the others," he panted, forcing a kerchief into her mouth. "And just so's I can get me soldier into his place without you troublin' us—"

He yanked her hands above her head and quickly tied them with cord. She tried again to kick him, but he dodged away. With a grunt, he backhanded her across the face, bringing tears to her eyes and the taste of blood in her mouth.

"Don't fight it, wench. You knew this was comin'. I aim to have my fill of you. And maybe give you a bit of something to fill you up, as well, eh? Won't be so easy to stand up to a real man when your belly's gone out to here with a brat, will it?"

She could feel her fear deep within her, like a cold, terrified animal, scrabbling in a trap, growing more and more desperate. She couldn't stand this. She had vowed this would never happen to her again, but this time she was more helpless than ever before. She didn't know what to do. His hands were on her breeches, tearing at them. She could hear him panting and grunting and chuckling over his triumph.

But then, blessedly, the sounds were softer now, getting farther and farther away. The chill air on her exposed skin reminded her of days at Rushdoune when she and Ariane had played in the snow. She could see Ariane's bright red-blonde hair flying loose on the wind and she concentrated on that. The bright hair and the bright snow and the bright sound of laughter on the winter air . . .

Phillip crashed through the brush, heedless of thorns or twigs that tore at his clothes. He couldn't see the path on this moonless night but he knew he was heading in the right direction. Something was wrong. Something was wrong with Morgana.

She hadn't been in her bed. She was on watch, he'd remembered. She'd done it often enough.

But something was wrong this time. It was a feeling he couldn't shake. He'd run to the Robin's bed and found it unoccupied as well.

Nothing could compare with the sudden emptiness in his gut when he'd seen that flat bedroll. And nothing ever again would compare with the rage that just as suddenly rushed in to fill that emptiness. Now he was running in the dark, and what should have been a few minutes' journey seemed to turn into an eon.

He couldn't see, dammit! He smacked up against a fallen tree, and limped for a few strides, but he didn't pause. He had to get to her. He had to—There, his eyes were getting used to the dark. He could see the outlines of the trees at the edge of the woods now. Morgana's watch-post wasn't far. He halted as he heard someone speak nearby.

". . . and now, bitch, get ready. Here comes the likes of which no man's ever put to you before, I'll warrant. Just let me get my soldier into his place—dammit, stop yer squirmin' or I'll knock you silly!''

Phillip, thoughtless of anything save red rage, launched himself into the darkness. He seized a handful of greasy hair and yanked, almost falling backward as he pulled the Robin off his prey. With a motion swifter than thought, he rammed his fist into Robin's exposed parts, sending the man into a screaming, gurgling fit of pain. Phillip stood up, panting. Robin struggled to get to his knees. Phillip raised his boot and with one kick sent him flying back into the gorse, unconscious.

"Morgana." He quickly removed the gag from her mouth. "Don't try to talk. Let me get you up and back to camp."

She lay there quietly as he unfastened the cord at her wrists and chafed them to get them warm again. He slid his arm beneath her shoulders and lifted her to a sitting position. "There. Can you sit?" She gave a nod.

His heart still hammering, he yanked off his tunic and wrapped it around her like a blanket. Footsteps were now pounding toward them from the camp, and he could hear men calling to each other among the trees. Morgana sat, gazing off into the trees, her dark eyes dulled and unseeing.

Wren was the first to reach them. He had a torch. He took in the scene and went at once to Morgana. Kneeling down beside her, he whispered something in her ear. She nodded, and then he nodded to Phillip. Phillip scooped her up into his arms, and she felt so light and so lifeless he wanted to howl at the sky with grief. But he caught the Wren's steadying glance and only cuddled her closer to his chest.

Hugh, Edward, Geordie, and several of the others crowded into the little clearing in the thicket. Their mouths fell open when they saw Robin laid out in the briers, but their jaws nearly came unhinged when Phillip's tunic slipped and there, surer than any word, was the proof of Blackbird's real identity.

Wren pulled the cloth back over her chest and stood between her and the men, as if daring them to speak or move. No one stirred.

Phillip went forward, with Wren leading on with the torch. The silence of the forest night was crushing.

"She's so damned quiet," Phillip said to Wren several hours later. "She's been hurt, but I don't think in any way that would render her mute."

Wren shook his head. "Shock."

Phillip raked his hands through his hair. "Then you think he did rape her?" he asked, his voice low and rough.

The older man shrugged. "Or as good as."

Phillip swallowed the bile that rose up in his throat. "I should have killed him. I wanted to. He disappeared fast enough."

"He'll be back."

"I know it. And he won't be bringing casks of ale and joints of mutton. She needs to get out of here. But in this state . . ." He tossed the last of his ale at the fire, where it was consumed with a hiss.

"Take her away."

Phillip stared at him. "Against her will? I promised her I'd never do that."

"Her will's not home."

Phillip looked over at the mass of blankets that was Morgana, sleeping at last after hours of silent staring. Wren was right. Her will was not with her just now. She'd been robbed of it, along with her senses.

And Robin would be back. The other men were tiptoeing around, in shock and wonderment themselves. No matter how loyal this band of outlaws might prove toward one of their own, they wouldn't follow a woman, especially one who had been revealed at her most vulnerable. He didn't know if they'd follow the Robin, either, but he knew Morgana's days as the leader of the flock were over.

"He'll be after you, too," Wren said.

Phillip almost smiled. The man was positively chatty tonight. No doubt out of concern for his friend. "Yes. I'm as much of a hazard to her as she is to herself. A fine pair we make, eh?" He scowled at the fire. "What will you do?"

"Go."

"Just like that?"

"Aye. Naught for me here."

"Then you should take her away. She'll be safer with you. Robin will have a harder time finding her if we split up."

Wren shook his head. "No."

Phillip frowned. "Why not? You can't tell me you don't care for her."

"She belongs with you."

"Oh, that's rich. She'll spit in your eye for that one. That is . . ." He couldn't bring himself to say the rest, but the thought was there: that is, if she ever recovered her senses.

"She's yours." Wren gave him a knowing stare. "All yours. I've seen it. Take her. Let her be happy for as long as may be."

It was an oration, by Wren's normal standards. Phillip couldn't have felt more convinced if any other man had worked his tongue for hours to persuade him. He clapped his hand on Wren's shoulder. He knew Morgana's friend wasn't abandoning her. He was making sure she was cared for, that she had the best.

"I'll do it. For as long as she'll allow it."

Wren gave him a grin and offered his hand. The two men shook hands solemnly, and then, without another word, Wren stood and walked off into the night.

Phillip gazed at the fire for a moment more, then slapped his knees, rose to his feet, and went to saddle the horses. He noticed that Wren's sturdy pony was already gone.

"Blackbird," he said softly, after he had made everything ready. "Angel, we have to leave here."

Morgana sat up, like an obedient child. The simple eloquence of it was not lost on Phillip. He felt his chest tightening at the sight of his peppery Morgana as docile as a doll.

"Come, sweet. Put on your cloak. We have to go now. Everything's ready."

She tried to fasten her cloak, but the ties dangled to one side, slit by Robin's hand. She let her hands fall listlessly to her sides.

Phillip took up a rag, ran it under the broad collar of her cloak, and made a makeshift tie of it. Then he quickly rolled her bedroll tight, took her by the hand, and led her to the waiting horses.

She mounted up and gathered the reins. Phillip tied her saddlebags and then mounted Saracen. She didn't even look back at the camp as they moved off, into the forest and away from Cadgwyth.

At least the lightning was gone, Morgana thought. And all that thunder.

She sat on her horse and looked at the snowy landscape. Christmas must be soon, she thought, looking at the bright red holly berries on the bushes that grew in profusion at Rushdoune. She should come out and pick some soon, to decorate the hall. It was already such a bitter winter, she thought. Her skin felt raw and chafed in the cold. But it was good to be home.

"Angel?"

She startled. Who was this? A dark man, a stranger. She drew back in fear.

"It's all right, sweet. It's only me. We need to water the horses. They've been traveling a long while and need tending."

She blinked. Phillip. Yes, she knew him. But it was too much trouble to speak. She only nodded and turned her horse to follow his to a stream just off the road a few yards.

Charles Threadgill was not a well man. This was evident to all who saw him that morning on his way out of Watling Street. His color was the same vile shade as raw wheat paste, and his expression was that of a man who has been forced to eat a bowlful of said paste, cold.

He was on his way to Lady Winston's house and he was bearing bad tidings. Mantalini had cried bankrupt, folded his shop, and retired to the rural mountain home of his ancestors. There would be no more ships, no way to make up the loss of the stolen three. Everywhere Threadgill's Italian friend had gone, everyone he had importuned, had but shaken their heads and shrugged. It was a bad omen, they said. There were better offers, many of them, coming from France and the Netherlands. It was a pity, they all said, but they could not be moved to reconsider.

And now, this morning, Blakelowe, his money-lender, had all but thrown him out of his shop when Charles had gone to him to beg for yet another extension on his debt. It was an insult not to be brooked, the lender had railed at Charles. He was an honest man of business, with the right to expect fair and timely payment for services rendered. Charles would have the money for him, in full, by the end of the week, or he would be visited by the sheriffs forthwith.

And while that was bad enough, Charles now had to face Lady Elizabeth with the news. Lady Elizabeth Winston, of the fairest, sweetest face and the most musical voice and the most delicate of forms—and the most fearful temper in Christendom. He'd heard of a tailor who'd once dared to substitute mink for sable on one of her cloaks, thinking she'd never notice the difference. The tailor had been assaulted with his own shears and soon after, he'd left London for Glasgow, of all places, saying that it was a far more congenial climate for his health.

So it was with terror in his heart that Charles Threadgill was admitted into Elizabeth's sitting room once again. And when he emerged, half an hour later, it was to go straightway to the Moor gate and out of the city, at a speed unparalleled by another soul walking on that road that afternoon.

The neighbors wondered at the screams from within Lady Winston's house soon thereafter, but when she came out to ride to Lord Fray's house a short while later, her face was as composed and as lovely as ever, and she laid her hand so gracefully on the arm of her limping steward.

* * *

Phillip led Morgana southward by a sinuous route, avoiding the main roads and shunning any inns or taverns on the way. He wasn't sure if Robin would follow them or go back to Cadgwyth, but sooner or later he would seek them out. Robin wasn't the sort to forget a humiliation such as the one he'd suffered, and Phillip wasn't about to permit him a second chance at Morgana.

Morgana. He looked at her, sitting slumped near the smoky, pathetic fire he'd cobbled together, mechanically eating the dinner he'd managed to scrape up. She was aware enough to eat, sleep, ride a horse, and she seemed to understand most of what he said to her, but it was with a vacancy, an air of absence, that chilled him. He didn't know what to do for her. He wasn't even sure how badly Robin had hurt her. She permitted him to examine the splits in her lip and cheek where she'd been struck, and to bathe them, but she pulled back, cringing piteously when he reached to see if she was hurt anywhere else. She didn't seem to be suffering—she'd ridden steadily and without complaint for days.

Yet the question still raced around in Phillip's brain: had she been truly raped? He knew she had been foully violated, but had Robin completed the act? Did she have to fear that she might be forced to carry that villain's bastard? Was that why she was so fearful and withdrawn?

He knew of her history with her stepfather, and knew that those memories had made her wary and frightened of all men and the intimacy between men and women. But she had not withdrawn into herself this way, not according to what Wren related of how he'd found her those years ago. When he himself had lain with her, she had seemed pleasured, loving, reassured in the act, a willing partner. And while she had not thrown herself at him in lovelorn excesses afterward, neither had she been shattered in this way. Indeed, she had seemed to be her ordinary, thorny self.

213

He nursed his last bit of wine, heated over the fire. What had he gotten himself into? Here he was, the Viscount Greyfriars, "lazy lout of a noble," lover of luxury, pursuer of whims, raised with a golden spoon—out in the woods God knew where, with the season turning colder and damper by the night, with a woman who had been tortured almost to the point of speechlessness. A woman who, for all he truly knew, cared not one whit for him.

He pondered this for a moment. Did he believe she cared for him?

He looked over at her, sitting so still, the remains of a breadcrust in one limp hand. Something turned over in his heart.

He wasn't sure.

But in the following instant he knew it didn't matter. He cared.

He quickly packed up the meager remains of their dinner and stored them in the saddlebags, taking the last of the bread out of Morgana's unresisting hand. Then he went to her and sat beside her, and began to talk.

"You shall have to go to Italy with me. I have seen houses there that are built squarely around a garden. Almost every room looks not outward to the streets or the grounds, but faces inward to this garden, which is tended and paved and even fitted with tables and benches for eating out of doors."

Morgana didn't speak, but her hands moved to her lap. Phillip went on.

"And such fruit trees. Oranges and lemons. And salty black fruits they cure in brine and call olives. You'd like it there, I think. They have good horses and high hills and pretty valleys to ride through."

Phillip continued to talk to Morgana, about anything, everything. He told her about Italy, including detailed descriptions of the clothes, the habits, the weather, and the architecture. What he couldn't recall, he made up. All he wanted to do was reach her—reach into that cold, bleak place where she was hiding and somehow, some way, coax her out into the light once more.

He went to his bed exhausted and hoarse, not knowing what effect his efforts were having, if any. When they arose the next morning and started out on the southern road once more, he started to sing. He sang every ballad and ditty he'd ever heard, every verse and chorus.

When they halted for the night and made their camp, he was weary, but he continued to talk to Morgana as if she were fully cognizant and participating in his discourse. But there was no rewarding light in her beautiful deep eyes and no motion or sound that showed she was aware of the world around her.

The third day, he recited all the poetry he could recall, a treatise on the construction of a water-clock, and in a moment of sheer exhaustion and desperation, lapsed into his old prayers. He was rattling along, carelessly mangling the Latin at will, when he heard a sound that almost stopped his heart.

It was the softest, faintest sound, but he was certain his ears had apprehended it. It was a chuckle. One of Morgana's throaty, delicious chuckles, such as he'd heard so often before when he managed to penetrate her scoffing exterior and actually amuse her.

He went on with his recitation, fearing that to stop might send her back into herself again. An hour or so later, he was rewarded with a sigh.

"Am I talking too much, sweet?"

She merely looked at him, but it was enough to make him want to whoop in delight. For that brief, fleeting second, a tiny spark had shown out from the shuttered windows of her eyes.

He grinned. "You'll have to do better than that, angel, to stop me."

She turned back to face the road, but Phillip was satisfied. He moved on from his catechism to a spirited, one-sided discussion on the best way to choose a saddle. If he couldn't charm her from her somnolence, he thought grimly, perhaps he could provoke her into screaming for mercy out of sheer boredom.

Morgana was puzzled. The house was gone.

It had vanished and Ariane had gone with it. She was left alone on the grounds, which were still frozen, silent and snowy. The safety she had felt here was waning. She wanted to leave, to go someplace warm.

But she was afraid. If she left, she might never get back. And there were things out there, beyond, that she didn't want to think about or hear.

What the devil was that constant droning? She had no recollection of when it had started, but it was getting annoying. It was like being with her tutor, on days when he read to her, going on and on and on until she felt she must either fly out of her seat screaming or drop to the floor, fast asleep.

How was she to get the man to stop? Didn't the old fool have an ounce of warm blood in his veins? She didn't care a fig what Cicero had said about how the infidels of the Holy Lands cared for their horses. Saints preserve her, she didn't think the man would look up from his book for anything less than a sudden shower of tadpoles.

She chuckled at the image of Brother Dumfries gaping through a cloudburst of squirming frog offspring. It would serve him right after he had frightened Ariane with those Bible tales of pestilence and blood.

"Am I talking too much, sweet?"

She almost cried *yes*. But even as the word was forming, she let it die. She wasn't ready to leave. She needed to stay where she was.

She contemplated the snowy landscape once more. Who the devil was that man and why was he smiling at her with such maddening amusement?

She wouldn't think about him now. She'd go see how the rabbits were faring this winter . . .

"I've never told you about my sister, Judith, have I, Blackbird?"

Morgana scowled. She was seated before a fire in the woods somewhere. That man was there again, right beside her, smiling and talking. He was familiar. She should be wary, but she just didn't feel afraid.

"Who?" she whispered.

"Judith. Or I suppose I should say, Lady Judith Greyfriars Redmayne. She's a woman now, my little sister. A wife and a mother. I remember the day she became betrothed to Gregory Redmayne. She wasn't much more than twelve, if that. It was right after Twelfth Night. Father had engaged a troupe of traveling players for the revels, and there was among them the most exotic lady we had ever set eyes upon. Skin as lovely brown as an oak leaf, with black hair that curled in every direction at once. A Nubian, someone said she was. Well, Judith, the vain little chit, coveted that hair and she came to my room and demanded that I help her make her hair as curly as that. I gave in to her—she's a force to be reckoned with, is Judith—and together we contrived to . . ."

Morgana shook her head. She knew this story. But how could she? And yet she did. Why was he repeating it?

"You burnt her bald-headed," she blurted out.

There was a pause that was long, wide, and deep. Morgana opened her eyes, only they were already open. She looked over, and saw . . .

"Phillip."

"Welcome back, angel."

His voice sounded strange, somehow. Hoarse, and rather constricted, as if he were choking.

217

"Are you all right?" she asked. "Why the devil are you looking at me as if I had two heads?"

He threw his head back and laughed at the stars.

"You say I couldn't speak?" Morgana asked, some time later.

"It's been almost a week." Phillip handed her another bit of cheese.

"But what happened—oh . . ."

She felt it all at once, the horror, the pain, the shame, the terror. Tears welled up and she gasped for breath.

"It's all right," Phillip said. "You're safe now. It's over."

"Is—is he dead?"

"Not yet. But if he comes within a league of you, I'll see that he digs his grave with his bare hands. Just before I kill him."

Morgana shivered at the ice in Phillip's voice. In an instant, he'd changed from the blithe, amusing companion who'd wooed her out of her death-in-life by virtue of endless conversation, into a steel-jawed warrior, bent on revenge at all costs. She could only partly recall the night Robin had assaulted her, but she remembered Phillip's presence and his rage. She knew he was as good as his word.

The fire was dying. The food was gone. Phillip rose and went to make up their beds on the ground. Morgana sat where she was, suddenly weary and sad. She could hardly comprehend that she had been silent for almost a week. She had little or no awareness of time passing. For all she knew, only a few moments had passed between the moment Robin had grabbed her and the moment she heard Phillip mention his sister's fiery coiffure. Yet here she was, obviously far from the camp, alone with Phillip in the wilds.

She looked at him with mingled pain and love. All he had gone through for her, she thought. All the danger. All the worry. And he was still not out of danger. Robin would be just as bent on vengeance against Phillip as against her. She sighed. Truly, she was a millstone about the man's neck.

Her days with the flock were over, that was certain. She had no idea where either the Wren or the Kestrel could be, her only true friends in the band. All the men knew who and what she was and most likely could guess who the Raven was in his other life. They all knew she had been attacked by Robin, laid out mute and helpless. They would despise her, or worse yet, pity her for her victimization. She couldn't face them. Not after they had seen . . .

She moaned and sank her head into her hands. She heard Phillip come to kneel beside her. He touched her shoulder.

"Don't!" she shrieked, jerking away. "Don't touch me!"

She caught the look of sorrow in his dark eyes and wanted to take back her words but couldn't. She hung her head again. "I can't stand it. Not after him. Not after that." Tears, few but scalding, dripped over her cheeks. "I don't even know what happened," she whispered. "I know you came to help me . . . thank you . . . but I don't . . . I couldn't see, couldn't feel. First there was Robin and he was . . . touching me . . . I was fighting . . . and then I was at home and it was snowing and I was with my cousin."

Phillip's voice sounded puzzled. "Home? Snow?"

Morgana shook her head in bewilderment. "I . . . went away. When he touched me. When I knew I couldn't get away from him with my body, I went away in my mind, I believe. I was a child again. At my old home. With my cousin. It was Christmastime. I was just . . . gone home." She raised her eyes to Phillip's at last. "Do you know if . . . when you came upon Robin, was he . . . ah, God, I can't stand this!'' Great, wrenching sobs burst from her. She wrapped her arms about herself and began to rock, keening.

Phillip sat beside her. She didn't know how long she wept, but at last the first flood of grief was released and she could look at him once again. He fixed her with his deep gaze and held her.

''I wish I knew, angel. It was terribly dark in that thicket, that night. All I heard was him attacking someone, and I went for him. I did not see . . . anything clearly.''

Morgana felt sick. But Phillip went on.

''But I could hear,'' he said slowly, as if listening again to the noises of that nightmare time. ''The bastard was cursing you and telling you to hold still—never doubt that you fought for your life, angel. He was saying—Morgana! God save me! He was—'' Phillip started to chuckle.

Morgana stared at him, horrified. ''How can you laugh—'' she began.

''No, love. Hear me out. He was telling you to hold still because he couldn't get his—'' Phillip was laughing now. ''Because he couldn't get his damned little 'soldier' in place!''

Morgana was lost. What was the man talking about? ''Soldier?'' she asked, shaking her head.

Phillip smiled indulgently and made an eloquent gesture toward the region of his codpiece. Morgana stared, then gaped up at him. ''You mean—?''

''Aye, sweet. He never managed it. You wouldn't let him.''

''Oh, praise the saints,'' Morgana gasped weakly. ''And you came just in time. Oh, thank God. Thank you.'' Tears suddenly welled up again. ''Oh, Phillip! I was so afraid!''

Phillip reached out with one finger and caught a tear as it trickled from her eye. This time, she only drew back a little. ''I know, sweet,'' he murmured. ''I know.''

Morgana looked up at the stars, swimming bright dots in the midst of her tears. What had happened to her had been bad. But this time there was a difference. She hadn't been as helpless as she had felt. Once again she had saved her life, and preserved the honor of her body. And this time she had had help. Someone had come to her rescue. That had not been the case all those years ago in Cedric Bracewell's evil house.

She looked at Phillip. He looked tired and worn. Stubble adorned his cheeks and his hair was a mess. His clothes were travel-stained and smelly, and his long, elegant hands were cut and chapped and filthy.

She smiled at him, her heart bursting. He was absolutely perfect.

"You need rest, Greyfriars," she said gruffly. "And a bath. This is no life for a man of silk."

"Better a man of filth than a man of silk with no Morgana."

She chuckled, sniffing through her tears. "Madman."

"Sweetest rose."

She glanced down at her own ragged and dusty self. "You're a poor judge of flowers, my lord."

"I cultivate only the rarest," he said softly.

"Lunatic," was all she could bring herself to say.

"Come, angel. Get you to your bed. It's been a longer week than any I've spent, and so it must have been for you. Let's get our rest and tomorrow we'll go looking for a tub of water."

She nodded, feeling the aching weariness in all the fibers of her being. She rose and went to where he had made a bed for her by the fire. She lay down and rolled herself in her cloak.

Phillip went to check on their horses one last time, then lay down on his own bed across the fire from Morgana's. She watched him as he moved in and out of the shadows, wondering how this man had come into her life and how

221

she was going to manage without him. She decided she'd think about that on the morrow. Right after she showed him how to build a fire that didn't smoke like a stopped-up chimney. . . .

Chapter Fourteen

Phillip was as good as his word. By nightfall the next day, they had come to a prosperous-looking little village, its harvest almost in, the houses snug and ready for the coming of winter. Phillip dismounted at the inn and gave their horses over to be stabled and groomed.

Morgana halted him as he headed inside. "Phillip. We haven't any money. Leastways, I haven't. Have you?"

"Not a farthing, sweet. I didn't bring much when I came looking for you, and you returned my first and only takings, remember?"

"Then how can we—"

"Leave all to me. But keep your wits about you."

Oh, Lord, she thought. Phillip the schemer was about to enact another of his famous plans. How deeply was she going to get into trouble this time? she wondered. Still, she thought, she would dearly love a hot bath—it would help to wash away the taint of the Robin's touch. She gathered up her courage and followed him into the warm, cozy house.

"Hey-ho, here's a pair of weathered travelers, if I've ever seen any such before." A stout, sturdy little man with a head of burning red hair and a broad, freckled face came out to greet them. "And what may I do for you?"

"We need a hot meal, hot water to bathe in, and with those two items fulfilled, all we should need is a bed in some corner," Phillip said, pulling off his cap and turning on his most charming smile.

The man nodded. "All those I have, but you will understand, sir, that I'll need to see the color of your money before I set out my best for two such, ah, well-worn strangers."

"Sir, we haven't a ha'penny between us," Phillip informed him cheerfully.

Morgana saw the innkeeper's smile begin to fade and turned to the door, expecting to feel the sole of the man's boot on her backside, helping her along. Phillip reached out and caught her wrist, holding her still.

"But we have no intention of presuming upon your charity, good sir," he went on. "We are traveling players who can provide your patrons with an evening's entertainment the like of which they will not see this side of London."

"Players?" The man looked suspiciously at their torn and filthy clothes and grimy faces. "What do you do?"

"I sing, sir, and my companion dances."

"That's all?"

"I juggle. She reads fortunes in palms."

The man drew himself up, scowling at Morgana. "She?"

"Aye. Master Humfrey Grey and Mistress Malinda Grey, my wife. You must forgive our appearances, sir, for we were set upon by thieves in the forest and robbed of all we had save our horses. They left us only these meager garments."

The man had a way with the truth, Morgana thought wryly. He could take it or leave it alone. She waited for the innkeeper to begin guffawing.

"You don't plan to perform looking like two rag-bags?" the innkeeper asked.

"Alas, it's all we have. Until we have some money, we cannot buy more. And until we perform, we will have no money, nor food and drink, nor a place to stay. But I can see that we are troubling you, sir. Your good wife is even now beckoning to you from the cooking fire."

Morgana saw that a woman was indeed crooking her finger for the innkeeper to come over. She glanced at Phillip. He left her side and in three long strides was at the fireside, taking the cooking spoon from the woman's hand and stirring the pot, all the while plying her with his most beguiling smiles. As she watched, the woman began to simper and grin, and before long there was a whispered conversation between the innkeeper and his wife, with much gesturing and nodding and shaking of heads.

Not long after that, Morgana and Phillip were shown to a small, private room on the floor above, near the family's quarters. And within the hour, there was food and drink, and a large bathing tub being filled with water heated over the blazing little fireplace. Clothes had been brought, though all of a size to fit either the stout little innkeeper, Ruggles, or his plump little wife.

When they were alone at last, Morgana went to the door and peeped out to make sure that no one was about. Then she closed the door, latched it, and turned to face Phillip, her hands on her hips.

"Never again will I underestimate the Greyfriars charm," she said. "But now that you've gotten us thus far, pray how do you plan to get us out of here?"

"Out of here?" Phillip sprawled across the lumpy little bed and seized a leg of fowl from the tray of food on the

225

chest. "I love it here. I intend to remain here all my days."

"Codswallop. You told those people we were players. We're players, all right, but at a very different sort of game."

"I sing. You've heard me. I'm passing adequate, if I do say so myself."

"Very well. You sing. I don't dance. I've never seen you juggle. And I haven't the faintest idea how to tell fortunes by looking at someone's hand."

"That's all right. Neither do they."

"What?"

"Neither do they, I'll warrant. And I'm willing to wager that not many players pass through here every day. These are simple folk. They'll not be expecting a conjurer from the king's court or mummers from London's best houses. A song or two, a few dance steps, and we'll have them begging for more."

"Which we can't provide!" she retorted.

"Tut, love, you give yourself too little credit. Besides, we could always steal out tonight, under cover of night. Those skills we have aplenty."

"But these people trust us! They've taken us in, given us their food. Their clothes!"

Phillip clucked his tongue and took a drink from the brimming cup at the bedside. "The most moral little thief I've ever met. You're a disgrace to your trade."

"Former trade."

He raised an eyebrow. "Indeed?"

"If I can do anything else at all, I will. I'm tired of the life. Wren and I were planning to have a little inn like this somewhere, just as soon as we'd gathered the wherewithal to begin. But that time never came, and now it never will. I can't go back to stealing."

He sat up. "So? Then why not be a traveling player?"

She wanted to grab handfuls of his hair and yank. "You! You are the damnedest, most conniving, scheming—"

"Do you want the first bath?" His smile was as bland as milk.

"Aiigghh!" She stomped over to the tub and stuck her hand in the water. It was as warm as a fire and more welcome than any food or drink. She began pulling off her boots.

She looked up to see Phillip sitting back on the bed, watching her with calm interest. She felt a flush blossom on her cheeks. She hurried to pull off her tunic and let her long shirt fall. She slipped her stockings off, and taking a stump of a candle off the mantelpiece, she stepped into the tub and drew its curtain closed. She stuck the candle onto a ledge and began unfastening the ties of her shirt.

In the candlelit privacy of that tiny space, she removed the shirt and tossed it over the bar that held the curtain. She sank into the water, an audible moan of pleasure and relief escaping her lips. She heard Phillip humming to himself and settling back onto the bed pillows.

She longed for real soap but there was only a cambric bag of herbs to help wash away the grime. It was enough, she decided, closing her eyes. Slowly, methodically, she began at the top of her head and scrubbed every inch of her body. There were more tears to be shed, she discovered, but not the torrents she expected. She let the cleansing tears wash away more of the stain on her spirit and continued with the ritual of reclaiming her body. She was grateful for this small blessing.

When she opened her eyes, a cup was being slipped in through the edge of the curtain. She grinned. Phillip.

"Thank you."

"You're welcome, sweet."

227

She raised the cup of sweet, clear wine to her lips and drank deeply, letting the warmth of it begin to course through her veins. Another little parting of the curtain permitted only a hand and a fresh addition of hot water to warm the bath.

"Thank you."

"My pleasure."

She grinned. What a silly. Traveling players, indeed.

She sank back into the water and sipped her wine. What a life that would be, she thought, traveling around the countryside with Phillip in a bright little wagon, beating on a tambourine and singing and dancing for their supper. Visiting houses for Twelfth Night and Michaelmas, entertaining at market fairs. And at night retiring to their own little pallet in their wagon, to sleep curled like two twining vines. . . .

She shook her head. Phillip's fancies were contagious, she thought. Now *she* was dreaming of the most impossible things. That wasn't her way. She needed to be clear, to see the world as it was. There could be no life for her with the Viscount Greyfriars. He needed to get back to his family and his business, and she needed to find some honest work, somewhere, that would keep her from the desperation and danger of her life these past few years.

She rose and reached for her shirt. It was a shame to put the dirty thing back on now that she was so clean.

A heavy towel came over the bar. With a grudging chuckle, she rubbed herself down vigorously and then, wrapping the big cloth around her, drew back the curtain and stepped from the tub.

Phillip was back on the bed, eating an apple and watching her, again with that same calm interest, and a sparkle in his eye that told her he could do more. She blushed again and went to the pile of clothes the innkeeper's wife had brought for them. Going behind the high back of the tub, she shed the towel and pulled on the rough, black linen kirtle that was of the proper length but billowed at the sides like a sail. Giggling, she stepped out from behind the tub and stood before Phillip, holding the sides of the gown out wide.

"Bat's wings," he said solemnly.

She laughed. "Indeed. But 'twill do for dancing and fortune-telling, don't you think?" She seized up a head-scarf from the pile and wound it around her waist. The gown now flared out like an inverted mushroom. She whirled, her bare feet flashing out from under the fluttering hem.

Phillip sat up, his smile flashing. "Charming."

She came to a halt, smiling. "So. That's all for my rehearsal. Now, sir, let's see you juggle."

"Ah, I believe I had better have a bath before we run out of fire to heat the water," he said, slipping off the bed.

"Ho!" she cried. "What's this? The brilliant, witty, and resourceful Lord Greyfriars is lacking in some skill? Can it be?"

"Never you mind, mischief. You just brush up on your fortune-telling."

"But whose hand shall I read?" she asked, plopping down on the bed.

"You have hands, haven't you?" Phillip raised his arms and pulled his shirt off over his head. His chest, bare in the firelight, rippled with lean, powerful muscles. Morgana stared for a moment, then, as his hands went to his belt, she bent her head over her palm with studious attention.

"A long life," Phillip intoned. "Many sons and a big cask of ale. Lovers in an endless procession, fainting at your feet."

"Is that your fortune, sir, or mine?" Morgana asked, not daring to look up.

"The patrons', smart wench."

229

She heard him step into the tub and draw the curtain. She blew out a breath of relief. She hadn't expected to feel so much at just the sight of his bare chest, its mat of silky black hair adorning the smoothness of his skin. Terror and delight had coursed through her at once, making her thoughts swim in confusion. She had wanted to touch him. She had wanted to run as far and as fast as she could.

She looked about the room. There was only the one bed. The innkeeper and his wife believed that she and Phillip were married, so of course there would be but one bed. What was she to do?

Don't be an idiot, she scolded herself. You've just spent a week out in the woods alone with Phillip and there was no problem.

She would simply roll herself in her cloak and curl up on the hearth. She was used to it, and it would be warmer and safer than many places she had slept in her life.

But would she be safe?

She looked over at the tub where Phillip was splashing and murmuring little snatches of song. He hadn't touched her since that night they'd spent in the cottage.

She didn't think he'd move to touch her now. The thought made her shiver once again. There was a part of her, she had to acknowledge, that wanted to touch him. To wind her fingers in his hair, to stroke the glorious, warm planes of his body once again.

But it was too soon.

Too soon? she asked herself. There never would be a right time, even if she could ever get over the old horrors of Cedric, and now the Robin. It wasn't right. Nothing could be more foolish.

She stood up and unwound the sash about her waist. She laid her cloak on the hearth and took the top cover from the bed for extra comfort. Quickly and quietly, she lay down, rolled herself up tightly, and closed her eyes.

She heard Phillip rise from the bath and draw the curtain aside. She closed her eyes tighter, as if her eyelids might turn traitor and fly up of their own accord.

She heard him step out and rub himself down with the towel she had laid out to dry. She thought about the drops of water running down his long, strong legs. She flipped over to face the fire.

"Morgana, sweet."

"Mm?" she muttered, feigning sleep.

"You should have the bed. I can sleep there."

"No, I'm fine here."

There was a silence. Then there was a rustle of cloth, a quick draft of air as if something had fallen to the floor, and she heard the sound of Phillip settling down to sleep on the floor as well.

She sat up. "This is foolishness. I'm used to the ground. You're not. Take the bed."

Phillip propped himself up on one elbow. She gulped. He wasn't wearing a shirt, and the blanket was only a little above his waist. "I've been sleeping on the ground for weeks," he said. "I can't allow a lady to sleep on the floor while I take the bed."

"Oh, pish, Greyfriars, I'm no lady. And I'm sleeping right here."

"Fine. Then so am I."

"Dammit! Why do you have to make everything so cursed complicated?"

He shrugged, and started to toss back the blanket that covered him. She gave a gasp and flopped down, eyes closed.

To her shock, he scooped her up, blankets and all, and began to carry her across the room. "Phillip! No!" She struggled in his arms, but stopped as he released her suddenly and she landed with a thump in the middle of the bed. Her eyes flew open and she beheld a naked Phillip, in all his beauty, standing before her with his fists resting on his hips.

"Go to sleep, Morgana," he told her firmly. "Tomorrow you dance."

"You—you—" she sputtered. But he had already turned and was stretching out on the floor, rolling into his blanket and cloak again.

"Good night, sweet," he said.

"Arrgghh!" She gave the lumpy pillow a resounding thump.

"And the same to you, love."

It had to be the silliest thing Morgana had ever done. Phillip had been serious. Come the next afternoon, the inn's common room had been set with tables and soon began to fill with local folk, looking to eat and drink and gossip. They found all that and a show, besides.

And Phillip, curse his arrogant heart, she thought as she was reading her tenth callused and work-worn hand, had been as right as rain about the people not knowing—or perhaps not caring—how skilled they were as performers. The two of them were novel, they were a distraction and a bit of color in the cold of the dying autumn. The locals clapped and shouted for more, despite her awkward dancing, Phillip's hapless juggling, and, the one grace in their repertoire, Phillip's fine singing.

Ruggles the innkeeper beamed on them both, and Lydia, his wife, found every excuse possible to trot her friends up to Phillip and show him off. He was as gracious and charming to each and every farmer's wife and miller's daughter as Morgana knew he'd be with any duchess. She had to smile at the sight of him, so easy with people that most men of his station would scarcely allow into their presences. For all his wild schemes, his power, his wealth, his beauty and his whimsy, Phillip was what her mother would have described as a true nobleman—noble in character, not just by right of birth.

God help her, she thought again for the fortieth time that night, she was falling in love with the man. And there didn't seem to be any help for it. She could no more stop herself than she could prevent the sun from rising and setting.

She finished the last of her fortune-readings and went to sit in a corner by the fire while Phillip sang. Someone had found an old cittern, battered and only half tuneful, but he was managing to coax music from it in accompaniment to his voice. It seemed the man could hardly take a false step. She felt she should be envious of him. Everything about his life was the opposite of hers. Where she had terror and strife, he had comfort and ease. Where she had poverty and ill luck, he had wealth and fair chance. Where she was rough and thorny and awkward, he was charming and handsome and full of graces large and small.

Yet she couldn't fault him. He was generous with all he had, and she had been the beneficiary of his good fortune time and again. She just loved him, in spite of all his perfections.

But there was no place for her in his charmed life. Phillip was powerful and charming, but there was no way he could transform her past or change her into something she was not. His fancy of them traveling as players was just that—a fancy, a dream. He could no more abandon his position, his family, and his estates than she could enter his life and pretend that she was anything other than an outlaw, in every sense. She had to find a way to leave him and make her own way in the world. Nothing else would do.

The fire burned low, the patrons went home to their farms and little shops, and Phillip and Morgana retired once more to their upstairs room. The peace of the room after the noisy, active evening was a welcome balm to Morgana's spirits.

Phillip came to join her by the fire. "Ruggles and his wife want us to stay a week," he said, handing her a bit of bread and cheese from the plate they'd brought up.

"You didn't—"

"No. I told them we had an engagement in Aylesbury."

"Good. I don't think I could fool them for long with my so-called dancing, and as for juggling—"

He nodded sadly. "I know, I know. It is a skill that I aim to see my sons acquire. Clearly, my own education was sadly lacking."

She laughed and chewed her bread. She looked into the fire, the quiet between them growing full with unspoken questions.

"At least we are fed and washed, and clothed and rested," he said. "I think we could make Aylesbury in a day's ride, now that the horses have had a rest."

"That would be good. I know that you're eager to get back to your home."

The silence grew long once more. Morgana wished she weren't quite so aware of his body next to hers, his long legs stretched out before the hearth, his lean form leaning against a heavy chest as he finished his meal. Even in the preposterously short clothes Ruggles had loaned him, he looked delicious to her. And dangerous.

She shifted, suddenly warmer than the little fire warranted. He was looking at her with those smoky-blue eyes, and it was as if his very eyes were caressing her, bringing back a rolling, sinuous wave of memories. She knew how it felt to touch Phillip. And how it felt to be touched by him. The memory of that one sweet night would never leave her. She looked away quickly, back to the flames.

"Morgana."

234

She felt him lean toward her. "Yes?" She kept her eyes on the fire.

He reached out a hand and stroked her cheek. She felt a melting, bittersweet sensation around her heart. She took the hand and held it to her cheek.

He moved closer. "I won't hurt you, sweet."

"I know." The words were scarcely more than a breath of air.

"But I'm not made of stone."

She looked at him. He was wearing a wry smile. She smiled back. "Nor am I," she said softly. "But—" She hung her head.

"I won't press you." His voice dropped low, caressing her with its most velvet tones. "But I want to love you again. I'm serving notice, sweet. I can be most determined. And patient. And I will have my sweet brier rose back in my arms."

Morgana shivered at the nearness of him, the intense heat in his voice as his words sank in. She closed her eyes. His hand cupped her chin and lifted it. She looked up into his eyes, pleading.

"No, sweet. You won't be rid of me. I will be right here, this close, every day, every night, until you are ready."

His mouth was so close, so firm and inviting. She couldn't seem to get her breath. He lowered his lips to hers, ever so gently, ever so slowly, giving her every chance to pull back, but not granting any quarter himself. His kiss was soft and full of such aching tenderness that Morgana felt tears coming to her eyes.

He pulled back and looked at her once more. A look of concern was in his eyes at the sight of her tears. "I didn't mean to frighten you—"

"No." She wiped at the tears. "It's all right. I just seem to be weeping a great deal of late. You did . . . nothing wrong."

He stroked her cheek again. "That was just to remind you."

She nodded, not sure how to answer him. She wanted to touch him in return, but she couldn't make herself move. She looked away at the fire, confused by all the feelings racing around inside her.

"Get some rest now," he said. "It's been a long day and we have a long ride tomorrow."

He rose and put out his hand. He helped her to her feet and then gave her a swift, firm kiss on the forehead. "Sleep well, love. We'll be home this time tomorrow night."

Morgana pulled off her gown and crawled into bed in the outsized shift she'd borrowed. Phillip blew out the candle and began to undress. She turned to the wall, avoiding the sight of everything her imagination had been torturing her with all day.

Home, she thought. What a wonderful word. A word to break your heart on.

They parted from the Ruggleses the following morning with many thanks and kind words and half-promises to return for an encore whenever they were back that way. Their clothes had been cleaned and dried, and Morgana felt a bit more secure in her good old boots and man's tunic.

They rode in silence, each lost in thought. Morgana wondered what new scheme Phillip was hatching, or if he was just thinking of his home and all that would be waiting on his return. She knew she had to have a plan of her own. She had loved her time at Cygnet House, and she knew that if she went there again, it would hurt too much to leave.

Perhaps, now that she was no longer in the flock, she could go to visit her cousin, at least for a short time.

236

Perhaps Ariane would have some idea of what she could do for the rest of her life.

She shook the idea away. Ariane was too soft-hearted. She would ask her to stay. But Ariane had only recently married, and her estates and stores had suffered greatly in the last years since Henry had become king and Ariane's father had died. She didn't need another mouth to feed or a confused cousin dithering on her doorstep. No, there had to be another way. . . .

There had to be another way, Phillip thought to himself. He knew Morgana was prepared to resist him at all points. But dammit! He wanted her and he wasn't going to let her go!

The sudden power of his possessiveness surprised him. He wanted Morgana and no other. He couldn't imagine his life without her. And yet he had spent his whole life in the pursuit of one woman after another, one whim after another, believing that he was just like his father, whose desire for—and indulgences with—many different women had been the bane of Phillip's mother's life. Phillip had never intended to marry and let his fickle tastes be the cause of unhappiness such as he'd seen in his own family.

Yet here he was, dreaming of ways to get Morgana not only into his bed but into his house, his life, his future. He wanted to bind her to him with promises and covenants, with rings and ceremony, with his body and his soul. He wanted to kill at the very idea of anyone else touching her or daring to take her from him.

But there was no rival that he could fight. There was only Morgana herself who barred the way to his goal. And he had no idea how to get around her. He was getting desperate. Not just because his body was in an agony of pent-up desire for her, but because he knew full well that even as he was planning to draw her to him, she was planning to make her escape. In all his contacts with women in his life, never had he encountered a woman so frustratingly resistant or complicated.

The thought of the other women in his life brought him up short. Elizabeth. Damn! There was another trouble he had better solve, and soon. He wanted that chapter of his life closed, locked, and buried in the strongest vault in England. He had a future now. He had Morgana, whose briery exterior hid a heart and spirit so tender and strong that he wanted nothing evil or dark ever to touch her again. He wanted to come to her with a clear future, all his old business finished and set aside forever. He needed to finish with Elizabeth.

Then, *then,* he would make sure Morgana was his.

The green vales of Aylesbury were turning to the grays and browns of autumn. Cygnet House, in the last pale streaks of daylight, looked serene and secure on its low hill. Morgana's heart leapt up at the sight of it, its black and scarlet pennons fluttering bravely on the wind. She wondered at how she had become so attached to one place after so short a stay.

Two of Phillip's men rode out to meet them on the road. They were discreet, but Morgana could tell that they were shocked at their master's disheveled and somewhat haggard appearance, and at the sight of the thief who had ridden out from beneath their very noses.

Phillip only explained that they had been on the road for many days and were in need of rest and food at once. The men turned with crisp salutes and raced away to the house, to fulfill their master's orders as soon as possible.

"Home," Phillip said to Morgana as they rode to the gate.

"Aye. You must be glad to see it."

"And you?"

"It's a fair place, my lord."

Phillip scowled. " 'My lord.' Should I put you on my rolls and list you as a servant of the house, pet? My name is Phillip."

"I'll try to remember that, Greyfriars. And I'm not your pet any more than I'm your servant."

Phillip gave a brief laugh. "As you wish, Blackbird."

"Don't call me that, either." Morgana's tone was sharp. "I'm no longer the Blackbird. I might need to be Tom Black again, but I'll never again be the Blackbird of Kestrel's flock."

Phillip gave her a quick glance, then looked back to where the gates were being pushed open wide to welcome them. "I will remember that."

The household was in an uproar as they entered. Gilbert, the steward, came forward, his hand outstretched, his seamed old face beaming. "My lord. God be praised. We'd almost begun to think you were lost to us."

Phillip clasped the older man's hand in his. "I'm sorry to have worried you so. My business was pressing and I was unable to get a message to you. Thank you for keeping my house so well."

Morgana hung back behind Phillip, but Sarah was soon beside her, clucking and exclaiming. "My lady, we didn't know what had happened to you, either! Stole horses, they said! Not my mistress Morgana, says I. I won't believe a word of it, unless I hear it from her own mouth."

"I fear it is the truth," Morgana told her. "But I have returned the one I stole. Lord Phillip gave the other to my friend Wren."

"See. There. I knew it'd all be solved, somehow, especially after Master Phillip tore out of here as if all the hounds of hell were at his heels, to go look for you. I've never seen him so set upon a thing, and you know my master, he's not a one to be shy about what he wants."

"I know," Morgana sighed. "I know."

"Oh, my lady. You must be fair worn through. And just look at you. You look as though you haven't seen bread nor meat in a six-month."

Between Phillip and Sarah, Morgana found herself propelled upstairs to her old chamber, where Phillip left her with a wink and a nod, to be coddled half to death by the exuberant Sarah. The kindness of everyone, to someone who had stolen from their household—to a guttersnipe of a little thief who was a grimy, dusty mess—it was too much. Morgana almost burst into tears.

She held the tears back, however, and welcomed the chance for another hot bath, this time with rose-scented soap. She accepted the clean garments Sarah laid out for her with gleeful abandon. There was nothing she could do tonight but play the guest and prodigal returned with as much grace as she could muster. Tomorrow there would be time to make her departure.

Phillip came to her door and knocked when it was time to sup. Morgana caught her breath when she saw him, clean-shaven and groomed and dressed in the deep purplish-blue surcoat she loved so well. He gave her his most devilish smile when he saw her, gowned as she was in soft, dark green silk.

"How am I to keep my mind on my victuals?" he demanded. "Don't you know that a man needs to eat, not just stand about gaping at beautiful women?"

"Lunatic," she said, trying to suppress her own smile.

"Fairest lady."

"Stop that."

"Make me."

"What?"

"You heard me. Make me stop."

"I shan't waste my time on such a daft notion."

"Better a waste of time than no time at all."

She stared at him in bewilderment. He shrugged. "It was the best I could summon up in the moment. In truth, Morgana, I am famished."

She laughed and took his arm. "Then let us go to supper, sir. I can't stand a man fainting at my feet."

"So I've noticed."

She whacked him on the arm, and they proceeded down the hall to his solar, where a table was set to groaning with every kind of food and drink imaginable. They looked at the table, looked at each other, and scampered to their seats, laughing.

The meal was almost more than Morgana could stand. Hungry as she was, she had gone so long on so little that she couldn't manage even to taste half of the dishes set out before them, at least not without risking a night of stomachache. Still, they both ate to full repletion and then sat back, sipping sweet mead and nibbling at cheeses.

Phillip smiled at her across the table. "I'd regale you with a song," he said, "but I believe I've had my fill of singing for a while."

"I don't imagine I'll make my living as a dancer, either."

"And whether you recall it or no, I believe that while we were on the road from Cadgwyth, I told you every story I've ever heard."

"I know. Bits of it still come to me now and then. Did you truly recite a treatise on buttresses to me?"

"I may have. It escapes me now." He leaned forward, his elbows on the table. "Are you free of those visions now?" he asked softly. "Do you want to go away in your mind, as you put it?"

She nodded. "Yes, I'm free. I know who I am. And where."

"Home."

"Your home."

"For now, yes." He pushed back his chair and rose from the table. "Come, let us sit by the fire and not sing, dance, juggle, or recite, shall we?"

Morgana smiled and rose to take his arm. "No fortunes, either. If I have to tell another soul that he or she is going to find happiness in the arms of their true love, I shall jump up and scream."

"No fortunes, no screaming. It shall be as you say."

Morgana pulled back as he began to lead her away from the fireplace. "I thought we were to sit by the fire," she said, smiling uncertainly. "Do you plan to build a fire outdoors? If so, then you had better let me instruct you."

He frowned. "What's the matter with my fires?"

"Nothing, if you want to cure meats."

"Impertinent wench!"

"Honest wench."

"Such honesty is hardly to be lauded. You wound me, lady."

"You'll live."

"And coldhearted. Well, let us go make you warm and me well, shall we?"

He led her to a door in the wall opposite the fireplace. She knew it must lead to his personal chamber. His bedchamber.

"I can't."

"I gave you my word, angel. I won't hurt you."

"It isn't right."

"Let me make it right." He tugged at her hand.

She paused. He gazed at her, his eyes warm and sparkling. God, how was she to resist him? She loved him so.

She went with him, warring with herself every step of the way.

She shouldn't do this. It was too dangerous, for too many reasons. She needed to get farther from him, not nearer. She couldn't risk falling any deeper in love with him. She couldn't risk her freedom, her safety.

But she couldn't bear to turn away from him. Her soul and spirit needed his tenderness. Her body craved his touch. She was already in love. If she went to his bed now or not, it wouldn't prevent her from falling deeper in love—she was already well in over her head.

Phillip led her through the door to the bedchamber and closed it softly behind them. She looked about. The room was not large, as she would have expected, but it was elegantly appointed and luxurious in every detail. The walls were hung on every side with heavy tapestries, the floors scattered with clean woven rush mats and small carpets in dark jewel tones. The bed was draped around with scarlet curtains and the coverlet was of the same scarlet, embroidered with Phillip's signature black swans. A fire burned brightly in the hearth and threw its heat well into every corner of the small room.

Morgana felt herself relaxing in its warmth, giving herself up to the pleasure of such complete comfort. She had made her choice; she would make the best of it.

Phillip drew her to the fire, where large fur pelts were spread before the hearth. A table with a pitcher of wine and a platter of bread and fruits waited nearby. He seated himself and poured a goblet of the wine, then patted the spot beside him.

Morgana came to him slowly. She took off the slippers Sarah had given her and sank to her knees in the thick, soft fur, curling her legs beneath her. She accepted the goblet from him and drank.

He poured himself a cup. He gazed at her over the rim of the golden goblet as he drank. The heat in his eyes was a rival to that from the hearth. She wanted to look away but willed herself to hold, to see and to know every nuance and shade of his expression, to experience fully every moment of this brief but precious night.

He reached for the plate of fruits and took a plump, dark cherry. He took a bite of it, set aside the pit, and then held the remaining half out for her to take. She leaned forward, her lips parted, to receive the gift. But instead of placing the cherry in her mouth, he touched it to her lips, tracing their outline with the luscious fruit. Morgana closed her eyes, savoring the slick, gentle caress.

His lips met hers with the same gentleness as the cherry. He held the kiss for a long moment, then his tongue slid between hers, and it seemed as if he were drinking deep of the cherry nectar he found there. Her heart fluttered in her breast at this unique pleasure. There was no turning away now. She had to know more of this joy, if only to carry it with her in the long, lonely days ahead. She wanted a store of him, a bounty that she could keep in her heart.

She moved closer to him, meeting his kiss like for like. He pulled her to him and deepened the embrace, holding her head between his hands and slanting his mouth across hers in a kiss that started a new warmth trailing down her spine.

Deftly, his fingers sought the pins of the scarf on her head and removed them. He tossed the silken scrap aside and took her face into his hands once more. His kisses were like little prayers, blessing first her forehead, then her eyelids, her nose, her cheeks, her jaw, her lips once more. Her heart swelled gently within her as she felt pride in the way he found pleasure in touching her.

Once again, she thought of the evil way Cedric had touched her. And the Robin. There had been no pride then; they had taken a pleasure that was nothing like that of Phillip's with her. She had survived their evil, she thought with wonder; she had come through it with all of her own senses and intuitions intact. She did know love and tenderness when she found it. And she had found it, here, in Phillip's embrace. It was a triumph to know it.

She sighed as he pulled back from her, settling back on the furs to take another sip of wine. She opened her eyes and saw him watching her again, his eyes still lit with those magnificent blue-gray fires.

She smiled and reached for the platter of fruit. She found a round, heavy plum and took a bite. She held it out for Phillip to share. He leaned forward to take a bite, some of the juice escaping from the corners of his mouth. He raised his hand to wipe it away, but Morgana stopped him. Inching closer, she used the tip of her tongue to flick the sweet liquid from his mouth to hers. With a low growl, he pulled her to him and kissed her with a fierceness that was as sweet as any fruit to Morgana's thinking.

"You would tease me, eh?" he whispered.

"Turn and turnabout, my lord."

"Indeed."

His hands slipped under the shoulders of her gown and slid the silk down over her arms. The tight sleeves caught, trapping her arms at her sides. With a wicked smile, he unfastened the buttons that held the high bodice, and smoothed the fabric still lower, baring her breasts to the heat of the fire and of his eyes.

Morgana held her breath, wondering what he planned to do. She knew Phillip. He was always inventing. It would be no different with his lovemaking.

Phillip again took a large, ripe cherry and bit off a portion. With one arm, he drew Morgana to him and held her, kissing her long and thoroughly. Morgana felt her entire body heating and quivering slightly with anticipation. He lifted his head from hers, bent her back over his arm, and smiled once more. With infinite care and precision, he took the cherry and began to rub its bright liquid on the nipple of her breast.

Morgana gasped, but watched, fascinated, as his fingers swirled the rich red fruit round and round, painting the rosy circle a deep, shining red. She went still in his embrace, afraid that any movement might break the spell he was weaving.

Phillip popped the fruit between her parted lips, then bent his head to place his tongue where the cherry had

245

left its mark, tracing the moist circle and cherishing the hard little tip. Then his mouth closed over all, drawing hard on the aroused bud. Morgana arched and clutched at the fabric of her gown, her arms pinned, making her a prisoner to his sweet torture.

At last, he raised his head and asked softly, "Did you like that, sweet?"

"Yesss."

"And shall I care for this one as well?" he whispered, caressing her other breast.

"I might die," she murmured.

"Let us risk it."

The second time was less shocking, but his ministrations compounded the desire that was catching hold inside her. She wanted to touch him, wanted to move, but she couldn't raise her arms and she didn't want to cut short the heady delight of his mouth at her breast.

He returned at length to her lips, sharing the slightly sticky, sweet cherry taste with her. She felt her senses spinning off without her leave. Better to let them go, she thought giddily. She had no idea how to control what was raging around and within her, wasn't sure that she wanted to control it.

Gently, carefully, he raised her to her feet. He unfastened the heavy golden girdle about her hips and let it drop to the floor. While Morgana watched him, treasuring the sight of his dark, handsome face, he slipped the gown from her arms and it swirled into a heap on the furs at her feet.

She stood before him in a shift of fragile white linen, her flushed cheeks and cherry-stained lips glowing in the soft candlelight. Ever so slowly, he lifted the hem of her shift with one hand, and with a practiced movement, undid the ties of her hose on one leg, then the other. Morgana reached down and slipped them off. They joined the pile of silky garments below. The shift followed.

"You are so lovely," he whispered, stepping back to gaze at her, silhouetted by the firelight.

Morgana closed her eyes, suddenly shy, yet she held herself proudly for his observation, pleased at the unmistakable joy and pleasure in his voice and on his face. She wanted so much to be beautiful for him. Under his loving, heated regard, she felt she was, at last, beautiful.

She opened her eyes at last to see Phillip removing his own garments and letting them fall to the floor. She caught her breath as each glorious, masculine part of him was revealed, and this time she didn't look away. Instead, she feasted her eyes on him and permitted the heat in her to rise.

He stepped forward to stand before her. He reached for her hands and placed them on his hips, then placed his own on hers. Morgana could feel the warmth of him; it seemed the air between them was wild and stirring. He pulled her close and held her against him.

"Sweet Morgana," he murmured. "Love, I've been waiting so long for you."

She raised her arms and wound them about his neck, drawing herself up on tiptoes. "I am here. I am ready, now."

Chapter Fifteen

He set her gently away from him and led her to the bed. With one hand on her arm, he reached out with the other to the small table at the bedside. He lifted a red rosebud from its tall vase and held it out to her. She took a long, rapturous sniff of its heady fragrance and felt the coolness of its petals against her flushed cheeks.

Gently, he took the rose from her. He set it aside on the table and bent to lift her into his arms. With infinite tenderness, he placed her on the bed and kissed her. Then he retrieved the rose and stretched out beside her.

Holding it by its stem, he traced over her cheeks and forehead with the cool, heavy blossom. He slipped it down the slope of her nose, caressed her lips. Morgana smiled and kissed the deep red flower. Phillip raised it to his lips, taking the kiss for his own. Then he recommenced his tracings.

She closed her eyes and the rose became a lover, stroking and tickling and smoothing and kissing. It swirled across her breastbone, circled her breasts, touched the sensitive insides of her elbows. It placed a kiss at her navel, trailed cool and soft down her thighs. Tickled her toes. Slid up her calves. It hovered over her thighs, teasing. It returned to her throat, visited again the taut nipples that thrust upward for its caress. At long, long last it slipped down, over her ribs, causing her to squirm with laughter, down, over her abdomen, causing her womb to tighten inside her, down, over the black vee at the juncture of her thighs. Delicately, yet insistently, it tapped at her thighs, asking them, then urging them, to part. And they obeyed.

Morgana gave a tiny moan as her rose-lover stroked her most intimate places. The bud was so cool and firm, smooth, yet ruffled. She parted her legs even further, to give it freer play, concentrating with all her being on the exotic caress.

She didn't even feel Phillip move until he was there, rising over her, replacing the rose with himself. And then he was there, stroking at the tender, swollen center of her, and then he was there, sliding into her more smoothly than a rose petal, and then he was holding her, kissing her, bringing her ecstasy.

Morgana lay still for a while, simply taking, receiving, gathering in Phillip's deep, slow loving. She wanted no other distractions from this potent, honey-slick pleasure. She wanted only to be open to him, accepting, enjoying, being moved.

But soon the coils of pleasure that had loosened within her began to tighten and she wanted more. She reached out for Phillip, twined her arms about his neck, and began to match his rhythms, his kisses, his touches with her own.

What began as a long, slow, leisurely dalliance became a fevered dance. It became a wild twining and twisting, a drumming of skin against skin, a chant of love words, enticements, challenges, praises. It gathered and grew and whirled both of them in its pulsing music, its urgent motion. It built and intensified and expanded and then held them, straining and calling, in its climactic grip. And held them. And held them. And let them slow and sigh and sink back into themselves.

And in that slow, drifting song that drowsed and soothed, Morgana held Phillip's head cradled against her breast and felt her heart open utterly, at last.

> "All night by the rose, the rose I lay,
> all night by the rose I lay;
> and though the rose I dared not steal,
> yet the flower I carried away."

Phillip murmured the song to himself as he lay beside Morgana. She was still asleep, cuddled down into the pillows, her body curled against his. He pondered the events of the past few hours as he idly toyed with one of her soft, dark curls.

He had experienced once again the heart-stopping, heart-widening joy of being coupled with Morgana. It was as heady a sensation, or more so, than the first time. He wanted to stay like this forever. He was a man who liked a challenge, a diversion, and Morgana promised to offer him delights unfolding for years to come. He had no doubt of it.

And what words had she whispered at last in his ear, just as he was drifting into sleep, his body pleasure-heavy and sated?

"My love."

Had he dreamed it?

No, he had no doubt of that, either. She loved him. She had said the words. The rose had been won.

Or had it?

> "All night by the rose, the rose
> All night by the rose I lay . . ."

But had he indeed triumphed? Had he carried the flower away?

It was not so simple as that, this business of love. He wondered, even if her heart was his, could he possess her? He thought not. She would still refuse to be his mate, to come with him, to live with him. Everything had changed, yet nothing had changed.

He growled in frustration. Why couldn't love be like those old ballads he'd learned at his mother's knee? Why didn't things fall into place as soon as the lovers were aware of their mutual love?

He looked again at his lovely little thief, his rose, sleeping so blissfully beside him. Why couldn't she see that he was serious, and that she had nothing to fear from him? Were there more secrets she was keeping from him?

He scowled. He knew there were. There was the mystery of where she had come from and how she got to be who she was. The business with her stepfather, and her life as a thief accounted for only a few years of her life. She had to have a mother, and a father who gave his seed to create her, if nothing else. He knew that she had been gently raised, for she could read and write and speak with clarity and she knew the ways and habits of life in a fine home.

That was what he needed to learn—the rest of her past. It hadn't mattered to him before, but now that he wanted her with all his soul, he needed to know. He needed the key to overcoming her terror of being known, or of going among gentlefolk.

He would embark on his education as soon as possible. If he didn't, she might up and flee from him once again. And that prospect made him feel as if he were being condemned to hell itself.

"There is a messenger here. From Lady Winston."

Gilbert fell into step with Phillip as he came into the hall that morning. "She's sent many these past few weeks of your absence. It seems she is most concerned for your well-being.''

"Yes, I imagine she is. Thank you, Gilbert. Send the messenger to me in the library.''

Phillip went to sit at the massive desk from which he and Gilbert ran most of the affairs of Cygnet House. Elizabeth. His lip curled in disgust. He had very effectively blotted her from his mind of late. All he wanted to attend to right now was Morgana. He knew he still had to deal with Elizabeth; he just hadn't imagined it would be quite this soon. He'd hardly entered the house and here was her flunky, waiting to be heard.

He supposed it was just as well. The sooner he dispatched Elizabeth Winston, the sooner he'd have fulfilled his vow. Then he could concentrate on Morgana.

"Lord Greyfriars.''

"Gerald. What news of my lady?''

"She has been most distraught, sir. Your sudden disappearance, no word from you, no news of your whereabouts—she feared the worst, as you might imagine.''

Phillip summoned a look of deep concern. "I'm sorry to have been the cause of any worry on the part of Lady Winston. If I had been free to do so, she would have been the first to know of my situation.''

The man waited, obviously hoping for more details. Phillip elected to leave him unsatisfied. "But now you see that I am back and well, and I hope you will convey my most heartfelt apologies to your mistress that I should have been the source of any distress to her.'' He eyed the man with a judicious mix of anxiety and goodwill. "My lady is well, is she not?''

"Oh, quite well, sir. But she was most adamant that I convey her desire to see you at once upon your return. If need be, she will come here.''

"I won't hear of Lady Winston troubling herself on my account," Phillip said smoothly. "Tell her I will be delighted to wait upon her tomorrow afternoon, at the very latest."

The man looked deeply relieved. Phillip could imagine the price the man was paying to Elizabeth each time he returned from Cygnet House with news she did not wish to hear. He sent the man off to the kitchens for refreshment before his journey back to London.

"So. You're off to London, then."

Phillip turned slowly to see Morgana leaning in the doorway at the far end of the room. He nodded. "So. You're listening at keyholes, then."

"Old habits die hard."

He approached her. Her eyes were dark with anger and confusion.

"Morgana, I—"

"Don't."

He paused. "Don't what?"

"Don't bother. I'm off today myself. I've a cousin up near Oswestry."

"But you don't understand."

"That's well with me. I don't want to understand." She gave him a rueful smile. "We owe each other no explanations."

"Dammit, Morgana, you can't go!"

She took a step back and placed her fists on her hips. "And who shall prevent me?"

"I shall. And you know I'll find a way to do it."

"You might try," she said evenly. "But you would not succeed, even if you were to find me and bring me back, even if you were to imprison me here in this house."

Phillip swore under his breath. "I don't want to hold you prisoner! I want you safe! Think, love. Robin is out there. God knows what his mind is set on, but you can bet it won't be a game of cards."

"I'll be as safe with my cousin as with you. Safer, perhaps. Robin might just as well come looking for you, Viscount Greyfriars."

"Don't do this."

"I must. I can't stay here. It isn't right and you know it."

"Who is to know?"

She looked shocked, then gave him a glance that would have withered a weaker man. As it was, he immediately knew he had erred. "I didn't mean it that way," he began. "If you'll only let me—"

"No!" She clapped her hands over her ears. "No more of your words. I've made up my mind, and this is what I must do." Her anger became tinged with sorrow. "Don't you know how hard this is for me?"

"Aye," he said, his own anger boiling up. "And you think it a lark for me?"

Morgana's face softened. "I'm sorry. But you have things you must do. So must I."

She whirled about and ran for the stairs. Phillip slammed his palm against the door, closing it like a clap of thunder. He stood in the middle of the room for a moment, frozen in anger and desperation. Then he bolted from the room, shouting for Gilbert to come at once.

Elizabeth studied her mirror, checking for any signs that her recent worries might have marred her looks in some way. She breathed a sigh of relief. Her skin was still as tender and dewy-looking as a new rose. No lines or furrows revealed the days she'd spent first raging over the loss of her money to that idiot Threadgill and his speculations, nor the days following, when she learned that Phillip had vanished and could not be found.

What if he had been killed? Or taken by kidnappers? Who could she then turn to for money and security? She might be left destitute.

She smoothed a light, cool cream onto her perfect forehead and laid down the mirror. She drew several deep, calming breaths. She couldn't get upset now. Phillip was on his way. She needed to be at her most beautiful and her most beguiling. She wasn't going to be destitute. She had several options left to her.

She heard him in the corridor and prepared herself to jump from her seat the moment he entered the room. She only hoped she could manage the necessary effect of tears.

And then there was no more time to plan. He was stepping into the room and she was running to him, and yes, the tears came, just as she desired.

"Oh, Phillip!" she cried, throwing her arms about his neck. "I've been frantic!"

Phillip clasped her to him. "Sweet girl, I'm so sorry. I never meant you to know a moment's grief on my account."

"Are you all right? You've not been hurt? Were you robbed?"

"I'll tell you all, soon enough. But tell me of yourself, pet. I scarcely waited at home to change clothes before coming straight to you."

"Let me ring for some refreshment," she said, leading him by the hand into the room. "Then we may talk."

They ate and drank and made idle talk, as if this were an ordinary social call. But Phillip knew Elizabeth had more on her mind than just his absence and the lack of interesting company in London of late. It had taken him some time to learn her true emotions, limited as they were, for Elizabeth either covered all with an expert grace and serenity that suited her delicate beauty to perfection, or she shammed another emotion, more useful to her purposes at the moment. But he saw the telltale little tremors of her hands as they poured wine for him and knew that she was agitated about something—something he would soon hear about, or she wouldn't have been so anxious to

255

see him, or so emotional in her greeting. At last, she came around to the true subject of their meeting.

"How are the plans going for your refuge for orphaned girls?" he asked.

She sighed and looked stricken. "I've had to put a halt to my dream of caring for those poor creatures," she said.

"Oh?"

"Aye. I'm ... it distresses me to say it ... I've had rather a bad change in my finances."

"No. But you are cautious with your money, and clever, pet. And Jamie's estate left you quite well-supported."

"Nonetheless, it is true. I placed a great deal of money into a shipping venture with a Florentine merchant. The ships carrying our goods made it safely to Italy, but on their return they were captured by pirates and all the cargo in payment was lost."

"But surely they can ship again, and make good on their payment?"

She shook her head. "It is not possible. The merchant with whom I was dealing has gone bankrupt and disappeared. No one else in that silly, superstitious country will deal with us. They say it was a bad omen that the ships were taken and won't try it again."

"But that's terrible. Is there no one who will make good the debt they owe you?"

"No." She rose and went to stand by the window, her fair head silhouetted by the afternoon light. "Those who aren't bound by nonsensical beliefs seem all to have been struck with poverty themselves. No one in all of Italy, it seems, is willing to trade with England." She made a small grimace. "I fear I am the victim of bad policies by our government and theirs."

Phillip nodded. "It would appear so." He took a drink to ensure that no hint of his pleasure showed to Elizabeth's keen eyes. But he was pleased. The first step in his scheme to ruin her had been a complete success. He must remember to send his old friend Mantalini and his compatriot, Signor Bruzzi, a generous thank you for their good work. He leaned forward in his chair, his face the picture of genuine concern. "My darling, did you invest quite a lot in this Italian fiasco?"

She let her lashes flutter downward. She nodded. "I fear I did."

He blew out a breath. "Well, then, we must see what we can do to help you recoup your losses. What have you in your coffers now?"

"Scarcely a hundred in gold."

He clicked his tongue. "Not much, but perhaps it is enough. Go you to my man, Nichols, and tell him that you want—no, wait, better that he should come here. You shouldn't have to go about the town, seeking favors. I'll send my man Nichols to you. He will set up something that will help, I'm sure of it. He's always done well by me."

"Oh, but Phillip, if I give him the last of my money, how will I live?"

"Oh, pet, you needn't worry about that. He will find you an income. He's a wizard, is Nichols." He rose and went to stand before her, taking her hands in his. "Never fear, my lady. You'll get all that you so richly deserve."

"Oh, Phillip!" She pulled her hands free and wound her arms about his neck. "I knew you would have the answer! I knew you would look after me, even when I make silly mistakes."

This last was in a voice as sweet and piping as a child's. Phillip could hardly believe that he had once been so besotted with this woman that he had permitted her to embroil him in murder. What an idiot he'd been!

But no more. She was not going to entangle him in her nets another time. And if all went as he had planned thus far, she would founder in those very same nets herself. He would have his revenge.

He submitted to her kisses, and added his own for effect. Then, he unwound her arms from his neck and set her gently away from him.

"This is so pleasant, pet," he said. "But I can't think of anything right now but the losses you have suffered. I am going right now to Nichols and will send him here straightaway. You shan't go another night with such worries in your tender heart."

She gave him a radiant smile. "And will you return with him?"

"I have some business to do here in town. I'll let you two work out all the matters you need to attend to, and then I'll be back this evening. Till then, my love."

"Oh, all right." She gave a most adorable pout. "But 'tis twenty years till then. Remember," she added, "you've been gone ever so long."

"I shan't waste a moment until I return to you!"

And with that, he managed to disengage himself from her and escape the house. He mounted Saracen and rode as slowly as he could to the countinghouse where Robert Nichols spent his days laboring, with outstanding results, for the Greyfriars family and a few of their closest associates. He greeted Phillip with his usual dour cheer. When Phillip told him of his plan for the Lady Winston, he looked at him as if his young master had lost his wits.

"But the Holland Drapers, my lord! The Guild of Drapers here in London is all but set to put them out of business and send them home. They are most likely sending their stores to the Netherlands at this very moment. Were I to put her money there, it would be lost completely and in short order. It would be sheerest folly!"

"I don't pay you to question my wishes," Phillip chided. "This is what my lady wants and what I want. She is waiting on you at her home in the Strand even now. Go to her and see that you don't distress her with any such dark warnings and predictions. I want her to be fully confident. And I know that you can make it so, eh, Nichols?''

The man shook his head and scrubbed a hand over his narrow chin. This was unlike any request he'd ever received from Phillip. It was more in line with Thomas, the viscount's late brother. As a rule, the Greyfriars were the most shrewd of investors, and seldom went against his advice unless it was a matter of special interest. He decided that this was one of those matters and that it would behoove him to follow along with the plan. Either way, he made his living, and handsomely, too.

"It shall all be as you say, my lord," Nichols said. "The lady shall be most peaceful in her mind when I leave her."

"Thank you, Robert. I knew that I could rely on you."

Phillip left the countinghouse, after paying Nichols a handsome gratuity, and went on to Peter Elyot's. He was welcomed in like a prodigal son and was soon seated in Elyot's solar across from his host, who was dining late that day.

"A late night, my lord?" Phillip asked with a grin.

"Rather," Elyot said, serving up some fritters. "Lord Fray's party. Most amusing. Many beauties. A multitude of food and drink."

"Just your style."

"And yours, I should say. Lady Winston was there, looking such a forlorn little waif without you that every man in the house did his utmost to cheer her. Lord Fray, especially."

"A most Christian act."

"A most agreeable one, I'd say. Where the devil have you been, Greyfriars? If she were mine, I'd not let her out of my sight. Why she puts up with you, I can't imagine."

"Can't you?"

Elyot looked at him. "Don't tell me you've found a lady that exceeds the Lady Winston's charms? Damme, I won't believe it's possible."

Phillip shrugged and tasted his food. "I won't trouble you to stretch your imagination, old friend. But I have been occupied elsewhere. I'll tell you all about it sometime soon."

"Occupied?"

"Mm. Let's just say that I have been traveling in the north on a personal matter. But tell me, Elyot, how are you fixed with Lord Fray? Still on good terms?"

"As good as gold. He's a cousin of sorts, you know. At least by marriage."

"And you say he was most attentive to Elizabeth in my absence?"

"Aye. Quite the swain he was, though, of course, he had to dance attendance on his lady wife, as well."

"And Elizabeth? Did she seem to welcome his attentions?"

Elyot sat back in his chair and stared. "Strike me! Phillip Greyfriars—jealous? I never thought I'd live to see the day." He frowned. "What is this? First you act as if you don't give a damn for Lady Elizabeth and now you're worried that some other fellow is taking your place? Come now, even you can't have it both ways."

"Can't I?"

"Don't play the fool with me. I've known you too long."

"I'm only asking who has been warming my place in Lady Winston's bed since my absence."

"Oh, well, that. Don't know anything for sure, but— say, are you certain about this? If I tell you, you won't try to demand retribution, will you?"

"No. I can assure you I will do nothing to harm the man."

"Very well. I'm a bit muddled as to where my loyalties should lie, but it is strongly rumored that my cousin Lord Fray has indeed been tasting her favors, as it were." Elyot drummed his fingers on the table. "They've been discreet, but Fray isn't the subtlest of lovers. My lady-cousin, Alys, did not look overmuch amused at the party last eve."

"I can imagine." Phillip braced his elbows on the table and leaned toward his friend. "Your cousin is of a most powerful family, is she not?"

"She is. And a favorite lady-in-waiting to the queen."

"And Lord William is in service to Henry at court, is he not?"

"Since the coronation. Before, even."

"And many lands and properties belong to them both?"

"Aye. But what are you leading to, Greyfriars? How can this possibly matter to you? You're as rich as they, more so, and your family near as powerful. The only difference is they are closer in blood relation to the king."

Phillip leaned back in his seat. "I'm leading nowhere, just now. But I may need your help in a matter of some delicacy."

"Oh-ho. There's a female in this, I smell rose water and lilies."

"Smell away. Here's what I need you to do."

Phillip got up and went to close and latch the door. When he returned, he dragged his chair around closer to Elyot's and sat down. In a low voice, he laid out his plans in careful detail. When he had finished, Elyot was gaping at him open-mouthed. Phillip leaned back in his chair and steepled his hands before his chest. "Well, friend? Can I depend upon you?"

Peter Elyot shook his head in wonder. "I had no idea. Of course, I'll help. Damme, I'll go right now and see my cousins!" He started to leap from his chair.

Phillip restrained him. "No, no," he said calmly. "We must take our time. Keep cool heads. Tomorrow will be soon enough to begin our task."

Elyot nodded. "Yes. You're right." He summoned his composure, lifted a cup, and raised it in salute to Phillip. "Here's to it, then."

"To *it*." Phillip grinned and clanked his cup against Elyot's.

Elizabeth shifted impatiently. The tailor, kneeling at her feet, flinched but said nothing, only went to work to remark the garment he was fitting to her.

"How much longer?"

"But a moment, my lady. The hem is the last."

"I want this made up by week's end. Understood?"

"It will be as you say, mistress."

Elizabeth heaved a pained sigh as the tailor finally scuttled back and motioned for her maid to help her lift off the heavy velvet gown. It was an extravagance, she knew, but as soon as the investments she had made with Phillip's advisor paid off, she'd have more than enough to meet the bill. Right now, she needed a lift to her spirits, and a new gown was the best way she knew to fulfill that need.

The tailor and his helpers scurried away to work night and day on the project as her maid helped her to get dressed again. "Gwen, send Gerald Durel to me as soon as you've finished here," she commanded. "I have a message to send."

"Just as you say, m'lady."

The maid left, a pile of garments for the laundry in her arms. It was grumbled in the servant's quarters that the lady of the house changed her clothes as often as the hours, but, of course, it was never grumbled loudly enough to reach their mistress's ears.

There was a knock on Elizabeth's solar door and Gerald Durel stepped inside when she beckoned. "Gerald. Thank you for coming so quickly."

"My pleasure, my lady," he said, bowing.

"I need you to carry a message to the Lord Robert Fray at court." She handed him a paper carefully folded and sealed tight. "See that it is laid in his hands alone, do you understand?"

"I will do so, Lady Winston."

She looked thoughtful for a moment. "Tell me, Gerald. Did anything seem amiss to you at Cygnet House when last you were there?"

"Amiss?"

"Aye. Was there any sign of trouble, or any visitors or strangers there?"

"No, my lady, not that I could see. All seemed as pleasant as ever."

"Very well. Be off, then. I need that message delivered at once."

"As you say, my lady." Gerald bowed, ready to depart. "Oh, there was one thing I noticed."

"At Cygnet House?"

"Aye."

"Well?"

"When I was going out to the stables to see that my horse would be ready for the ride back, I heard a door slam like to splinter and come off its hinges. I looked around and I saw her again."

"Her?" Elizabeth's voice was feather-soft.

"Her, aye. She was running up the stairs and I only caught a glimpse of her, but I'm sure it was the same lady. The one that was at Lord Phillip's house when I went there last time. The time before he last visited you."

Elizabeth's face went whiter than milk. Her violet eyes were like purple storm clouds. "And who is this lady?" she asked, her voice even lighter and softer.

"I can't say, my lady." Gerald was twisting his cap nervously in his hands. "I've never seen her before or since, nor in any other place."

"Perhaps it was Lady Redmayne, Lord Phillip's sister," Elizabeth said. "Describe her. Was she dark-haired, like Phillip?"

"Aye, she was." Gerald nodded and smiled, glad to have an agreeable answer for his mistress. "But small and dainty, of course. Of a height no taller than my chest, I'd say. Her hair was loose, too, and I saw it was short as any man's. Perhaps that's the fashion for married ladies now?"

Elizabeth's voice was ice-rimmed. "Lady Judith is tall. Taller than I. Near as tall as Phillip himself. And she is known for her long, abundant dark hair."

"Oh. Well, then I suppose it was another lady—" Gerald broke off, realizing his error at once. But it was too late.

"Of course it was another lady, you imbecile!" Elizabeth shrieked. "And you waited until now to tell me about her! It's been months! Devil take you, Durel, if there's been . . . if she's . . ." She brought herself up short and composed herself coldly. "Go to the court. Give the duke my message. Then, straightaway, get you to Cygnet House and find out who she is. As you value your skin, don't fail me."

"I won't, my lady. I'm going now." Gerald backed out the door, bowing, and raced for his horse.

Morgana was glad to be back in London, whatever the circumstances. She had made a little money on the sale of her horse and now she was set up in quarters above a baker's shop in Vanner Lane, not far from the White Stag, her old home when in London. It was a shabby little hole of a room with no window and only a pallet on the floor for a bed, but with winter coming on, it was blissfully warm from the bakery ovens below.

She had been looking for work about the district, but with little luck. In many places where she would have asked for employment, she was afraid to go in, for fear of being recognized as a thief. In others, she was too small. In others, they wanted only someone with skills. Still others wanted only guild-approved apprentices. She was becoming more discouraged by the day. But it was better than living beholden to anyone, and so far, it was safer than stealing.

She missed Wren. He had been her mainstay for so long, especially in their London days. She wondered where he was and if he, too, was safe from Robin and other such dangers. Phillip had said that Wren had left the camp even before he had, and so it was likely that the sly, quiet fellow had gotten clear away before Robin's rage could be visited on him.

If only Wren were here, she thought. He would know what to do. They could make their way together.

She trudged along through the marketplace, pulling her cloak tighter against the chill wind that was blowing in off the river, promising to bring an icy rain within the hour. It was time to sit down and think out a plan, she thought. She needed a scheme to somehow procure a job that would keep her in bread and shoe leather.

The thought brought a fresh pang to her heart, this one more bitter than thoughts of Wren. Phillip would have a scheme. He was never out of ideas or tricks.

She wanted to groan aloud in frustration. How many times in every hour of every day had she thought of him? And how many times had she scolded herself for a fool? It was ended. Phillip was no longer a part of her life. She had to stop torturing herself with thoughts of him.

But everything about her seemed to conjure up some new association with Phillip. The scent of sandalwood from a merchant's wagon, a bit of a song wafting out of a tavern door. The sight of any tall man on a dark horse. A swan on the riverbank. He had insinuated himself into her life and into her very soul. How could she possibly hope to forget him?

"Hey, there, boy, look where you're going!"

She jumped at the shout. In her reverie, she had almost stumbled into a peddler's cart. She backed up and bumped into a woman struggling with a heavy basket of leeks. Several of the vegetables bounced into the dirt.

"Curse you, boy!" the woman cried. "Look what y' made me do!"

"I'm sorry! I—" She bent to help the woman pick up the leeks. Someone seized her arm. Her old instincts rose up at once and she whirled about, snatching her knife from her belt.

"Hold, there, lad. I don't think you want to do that."

Morgana was so startled she almost dropped her knife. "Kestrel," she breathed.

Chapter Sixteen

The inn was cozy and the food and drink had braced Morgana's spirits considerably. But the sight of the Kestrel, looking well and hale and smiling across the table from her, was a feast in itself.

"But where did you go?" she asked. "What men there were left all met up again at Cadgwyth. We waited for you to come."

He shook his head. "It was too dangerous. Robin had seen to that. The songs he sang for the sheriff had many verses, most of them about me and all the places I was known to frequent."

"He came to Cadgwyth," Morgana said, her eyes darkening. "I believe he leads the flock now."

Kestrel nodded. "I expected as much. Though I had hopes that you and Wren—?"

"We tried."

Kestrel's brown eyes studied hers for a long moment. "Wren is all right?"

"I think so. We did not leave together."

"And you, Blackbird?"

Morgana looked away, embarrassed. "He . . . tried to rape me. But he did not succeed."

"I'll kill him for that, if ever I see him again." Kestrel's voice was soft but his tone was deadly.

Morgana heaved a sigh. "I hope you never do."

"Amen. Such scum is best left in the muck of their own creation." Kestrel motioned for another drink of ale. "Where are you staying?" he asked, after the server had brought the pitcher and poured them fresh cups.

Morgana told him. "It's not much, but if I don't find employment soon, I'll have to leave even that."

Kestrel seemed to ponder this for a moment. "I can help."

Morgana's look was guarded. "No, I don't think so. I want no charity."

"I've never offered you charity, Blackbird, and I never will. Do you think I don't know your pride?" Kestrel smiled. "Proud and as prickly as a hedgehog, Wren called you when he first brought you to me."

Morgana grinned. "I've been told as much before. And since."

"And well it serves you. Don't try to be otherwise. But I was saying that I could help you. I make no offer of charity, but I would take you on as my partner."

"Partner?" Morgana lowered her voice. "You mean, back to the business."

"Aye. But just we two. No flock. It's too risky. Two may move more easily, come and go with less fuss."

"I don't know." Morgana turned her cup of ale in her hands. "I had thought to be finished with that trade by now. Wren and I had plans for our own inn, you know."

"It wouldn't be forever. Just until you have enough to set you on your feet and I have enough to carry me to France."

"France?"

He nodded. "England is too hot for me, just now. I think I may go to France and find some little village where I can settle down and be a farmer."

Morgana almost choked on her ale. "A farmer? You?"

Kestrel smiled. "No dishonor in that, is there?"

"No. Of course not. It's just that I thought . . ." Morgana spread her hands, not knowing what else to say. "I always pictured you a thief."

"And so I have been. And so I must be until you and I can get our hands on the pounds and pence. What do you say?"

Morgana chewed at her lower lip. She had sworn to herself that she would put off the outlaw's life. She might be an outcast, but she didn't have to be a criminal as well.

But this was something different. To work with the Kestrel, whose finesse and skill she had witnessed a hundred times and more—it was an opportunity well above that of picking pockets or riding the highways with Wren. And he was of the same mind as she: make just enough money to retire to life inside the law.

She weighed her options. She had already ruled out going to Ariane's house in the north. She certainly couldn't ask Phillip for help. Her mother was lost to her. She wasn't having much luck in securing so-called honest employment. If she didn't find work soon, she *would* be reduced to picking pockets. Beyond that, all that was left was turning harlot or reading fortunes.

"When do we start?"

Kestrel offered his hand across the table. Morgana took it. The deal was struck.

Gerald Durel had scoured every square mile of Oswestry, Shrewsbury, and Wroxeter, and he was thoroughly sick of the whole damp, stony, godforsaken landscape. Like any right-thinking Londoner, he'd been raised to believe that anyone born or bred beyond the limits of Coventry, say, was little short of a barbarian. He saw nothing to disabuse him of this notion as he went about the countryside, asking after a girl or woman or lady by the name of Morgana.

His inquiries at Cygnet House had garnered him only her name and the possible notion that she might have gone north, to Oswestry. Beyond that, every man, woman, and child in that house seemed utterly ignorant.

Still, he knew it was no good to return to Lady Elizabeth and tell her that. He knew it was much safer and wiser to head for Oswestry posthaste and see for himself what he could see. Which was just a lot of rocky hills and forbidding forests and the odd village and country gentleman's house.

He was heading for London when he came to the village of Alder. He stopped at a snug-looking cottage on the outskirts of the town.

A rugged old man came through the rough fence around the vegetable garden, a spade in hand. "What will you be wantin', young sir?" he asked. "This ain't no inn and the tax's not due for another fortnight."

"I only wish a bit of food and drink for myself and my horse," Gerald told him. "I will pay you."

The man eyed him and his horse, and then the good leather purse that hung from his belt. "Aye, I think we got a bit of both for man and beast," he said at last. "But just you wait yonder, by stable. I'll bring some sup to you."

Gerald cared for his horse and glanced around the little cottage yard. It was a nice-enough little place, he supposed, for a poor man's home. This Alder must be prospering.

The old man came back with a wooden bowl of porridge and a rough clay cup of well-watered wine. The porridge was hot, though, and garnished with bits of mutton, and the price Gerald offered seemed more than acceptable to his host.

"London bound, are ye?"

"Aye." Gerald went on with his meal.

"Never been there. Don't aim to. Can't see what all the fuss is about."

"Yes, well. I suppose city life isn't for everyone." Gerald eyed the old man. "I'd guess you see a lot of folks on this road, it being so near your house."

"That I do. That I do." The man spat. "Not so many stops here as before, now that the village is growin' so. But I used to greet a stranger like yourself maybe once a fortnight or so."

"Have you knowledge of the better families of this area?"

"Betters? Oh, that'd be the Langlands. Though now it's Carrowes, o'course."

"Carrowes?"

"Aye. The Lady Ariane Langland. She's gone and married up with Lord Tristan Carrowe, he that's a knight in Henry's service."

"Ariane. Are there any other ladies of that house?"

"Ladies? Oh, no, no ladies. Only the Lady Ariane, but she's good enough for a whole wagonload of ladies, I'd say."

"No sisters? One by the name of Morgana?"

"Morgana?" The old man frowned. "No, there was never any but the one girl-child of the family, and her the last when her father was killed for a rebel some years ago." He grimaced. "But that name is summat familiar, now you say it. Welsh name, ain't it? Bein' on the borderlands here, we get a lot of 'em comin' acrost. Strike me if Lady Ariane's mother wasn't a Welsh lady, and all."

"Lady Langland, this would be?"

271

"Aye. Langlands have sat on this land for generations. Now, o'course, it'll be Carrowes. Heard the other day that her ladyship is bearin' two babes at once! If that ain't proof her man knows what's what, I don't know what is!" The old man cackled and slapped away a fly. "Two babes. It'll be good to have family at Alderbrydge, like the old days."

Gerald was pondering as the old man nattered on about various local landmarks and his views on travelers now as opposed to twenty years ago. A Welshwoman for a mother, Gerald mused. It was probably just the witless chatter of an old man, but he decided to visit this Alderbrydge and see what he could learn. If he gained what he needed, it would save him a world of grief when he returned to London and Lady Elizabeth.

Morgana went back to her little room above the bakery that night with a head full of questions and a heart that was somewhat lighter than it had been since the day she left Cygnet House for London. Kestrel had outlined his plans to her, and they had agreed to meet tomorrow to begin work on the details.

She was still a bit uneasy at the thought of returning to thievery, but Kestrel had assured her that if this one foray was successful, they would both be set for a good many years. And, she had to admit, it did look that way.

Robbing a countinghouse! If anyone else had suggested it, Morgana would have laughed in his face. But Kestrel—that was another matter. She'd known him to gain access to houses that were virtual fortresses, talk misers out of their purses, slip in and out of places as if he were a shadow on the wall. He had been studying this house for weeks, learning all its routines and its regular patrons. It was small but prestigious; wealthy but not exactly equal to the royal coffers. It was well situated at the end of a street, so that on one side there were no other buildings or houses. And best of all, there were rooms to let in the building next door. Tomorrow, she and Kestrel would go there and take those rooms, pretending to be a widowed father and his son. They would soon be a part of the neighborhood, part of the local landscape.

She sighed as she prepared for bed. It wasn't what she had envisioned for herself when she left Phillip's house, but it was something. And if it netted her enough to set up her own inn, then she would be well out of the stealing business.

What would Phillip think if he knew she was in London and working as a thief again? she wondered. She knew he was probably here himself, but his time was all occupied with Lady Winston. He would forget her soon enough in the company of Lady Elizabeth and all his rich and powerful friends. Still, she'd have to be careful. Though she longed for a glimpse of him and her dreams each night were haunted by his voice, his eyes, his touch, the last thing she wanted was for him to see her here. It would be too painful, and she didn't know if she could bear to leave him again.

For now, she'd content herself with dreams.

Phillip and Peter Elyot had spent the past two days at court. Today in particular had been a most productive one, full of amusing chat, music, and gossip. Best of all, gossip. Phillip, so long away from the court, was welcomed back with delight, especially by the ladies-in-waiting to Queen Joanna. He turned his charm on like a sunbeam aimed at each and every one of them, and by the end of the two days' time, had learned much of what he needed to know and had even begun to plant the seeds of his own purpose within that elevated, and most influential, circle of gentlefolk.

He was staying at Elyot's house, and they went there now to change out of their fine day-robes and into more finery for the evening's revels. Phillip was squiring Elizabeth to a party at the house of Lord and Lady Osborne, while Peter had secured the company of one of the ladies of the court as his escort.

Phillip stretched out on the bed in his room and clasped his hands beneath his head, studying the ceiling. How long would this take? he wondered. Already a week had been lost to him, a week he would have far preferred to share with Morgana.

Damn it, where was she? He had sent a man out to follow her when she left Cygnet House, but the little minx had given him the slip somewhere around Oxford. He had then dispatched the man north, to Oswestry, where Morgana had said she might go to visit her cousin. But the fellow had yet to return with any report, and Phillip was growing weary of waiting and worrying. Heading north again, where the Robin might still be roaming, was tantamount to suicide, he had told her. But she had been adamant, and he had been in no position to argue with her, bound as he was for London and Elizabeth Winston.

He wondered if he should have told her the truth about Elizabeth. Would she have stayed? He doubted it. Or, if she wasn't utterly contemptuous of his weakness and how he had been compromised into aiding in the murder of an innocent man, the wild little witch would probably have insisted on helping him in his revenge. He couldn't have borne that, for then she would have been doubly in danger, especially if Elizabeth learned of her existence and how much she meant to Phillip.

He yanked one of the pillows out from beneath his head and flung it at the wall. "Damn Elizabeth!" he swore under his breath. It was as if her hold on him was some sort of creeping vine that threatened to twine itself around all he held dear and slowly choke it out of existence.

But no more. He would end Elizabeth's influence for good and all, and then he would turn the kingdom inside out looking for his Morgana.

He took another pillow and flung it. God in heaven, but the very thought of that sweet, thorny rose made him hard in an instant. Several times now, he'd been in agony at the most inopportune moments, whenever a particularly vivid image of her came upon him—such as today at court, when one of the ladies had offered him a cherry. He'd had to quickly force his thoughts in another direction lest he disgrace himself in the king's own house. But here he was again, as excited as ever, just at the very notion of finding Morgana and holding her close once more.

He leapt off the bed and strode to the window. He shoved it open to let the chill evening air flow in and cool his heated body. But nothing seemed to cool or soothe his spirit. He gave up any hope of rest or peace and went to dress. At least there was some relief in taking action.

Elizabeth was facing a dilemma. Her first reaction to Durel's news about Phillip's little bit on the side had been to go find Phillip and kill him. She discarded that as dangerous and unproductive, and, seeing Durel cringing before her so piteously, she thought she might do the time-honored act and murder the messenger of such bad tidings.

But she resisted that impulse, as well. It would provide her with only a short-lived satisfaction and wouldn't truly hurt the parties involved. No, she needed to see that someone else suffered, someone who had taken part in this scurrilous betrayal.

She wanted to punish Phillip, but she needed him just now. Her affair with the duke was at its most delicate point, and she needed to be sure she had Phillip not only as a cover for her true activities but also as her security against the possibility that her marriage to William Fray didn't come about.

It was the girl she had to find. This little bitch who had dared to touch her property. This one who had been at

Cygnet House, Phillip's personal sanctuary, a place to which she, Elizabeth, had never been invited. She would find her and show her what it meant to go poaching on another woman's property.

Durel, to his credit, had left few stones unturned. She dismissed him now to go to his supper while she planned her next move. When he had left, she pondered all that he'd told her about this Morgana person. Clearly, there was enough scandal there to make it easy to find a multitude of punishments for the chit. All that she lacked was the girl's whereabouts.

Durel had said there were rumors that the girl had turned thief and had been a member of the infamous Kestrel's flock. The name was not unfamiliar to her. She still seethed when she thought of how those brigands had tried to rob her house, of all places!

She tapped her cheek with one slender finger. There had been one who had been willing to talk, she recalled. One of the thieves had been more than eager to give up his fellows in exchange for leniency.

She looked out the window. There was still enough time to start on her new task before Phillip came to escort her to Lord and Lady Osborne's. She skipped lightly over to the bell and rang to summon Durel back to her solar.

Less than an hour later, one of the sheriff's men was leaving her house, a smile on his face at the graciousness and charm he'd been treated to by the lady within. Inside the house, Durel was again being summoned from his meal.

"There is a man you must find," Elizabeth told him without preamble. "He is said to live in a forest camp not far from Shrewsbury. Find him and ask him all he knows about Morgana Langland. If you can, bring him back here with you. Tell him I will make it more than worth his time if he will help me find her."

*   *   *

Morgana looked around the rooms, noting with satisfaction that Kestrel had secured a place with a window that looked onto the countinghouse next door. The place wasn't as warm as her last quarters, but here she had a real bed in her small room and there was even an oil lamp hanging from the ceiling in the larger of the two rooms. Kestrel had seen to everything, including new boots and clothing for her. Men's clothing, to be sure, but new and warm all the same, and of good quality.

"If we're to be a country lawyer and his son, we must look as if we had gouged enough out of our patrons to at least buy good clothes and live in a better district than Vanner Lane," Kestrel had said.

For himself, he had cast off his customary browns and donned well-cut, expensive black wool, with a fine green cloak and hat over all. Morgana smiled when she saw him dressed up for the first time.

"Such a dashing gentleman," she said. "A widower about the town, handsome as you are, shall have the ladies lining up outside our door just for a glimpse of you."

Kestrel gave her an odd look, then smiled. "Methinks they might not see me for the fair face of my young son."

Morgana colored up at this. "I don't know if I should be flattered or disappointed," she said.

"Be flattered, little Blackbird." Kestrel moved swiftly to the table, tossing his cap, cloak, and coat across a chest. "Now, we begin. Get those pens and the paper I brought. We need to draw up a map of the establishment next door."

Morgana went and fetched the supplies and they sat together at the table until it grew so dim in the room that Kestrel had to light the oil lamp overhead. "And you say that the coffers are in this little room?" she asked, pointing to the center of the sketch he had drawn.

"That's our treasure trove, aye." Kestrel went to his saddlebags and brought a loaf of bread and some cold meat to the table. "As you can see, there's only one way into that room, and it's right under the noses of every clerk and flunky in the place."

"And there are two more rooms we must pass through just to reach it." Morgana tapped the table with her pen. "The place is a labyrinth, Kestrel. How can we ever hope to get in and get out, especially laden with gold?"

He sliced off a piece of bread and handed it to her. "That's where you are going to be most helpful." He looked her up and down, eyes bright. "I'm glad to see you haven't filled out overmuch. Still as slim and dainty as ever."

Morgana felt a little flustered at his words. "I am not much the buxom sort, no. But why should that be a help?"

"Because, little one, you will make a most excellent chimney sweep." He laughed at her wide eyes. "Don't worry. I'll be with you. We'll begin your training tonight, as soon as it's fully dark."

The days passed in swift succession. By night, Morgana practiced slipping up and then down the chimney into their rooms. The shop below had long since closed and the fire was cold, so there was only the residual soot and smoke with which to contend. It wasn't long before she could climb up as quick as thought, even with a loaded pack on her back.

By day, she and the Kestrel went out together. Ostensibly, he went to work as a partner in a law office, while Morgana went to be an apprentice clerk in a shipping house. They parted at the end of Kyroun Lane, went their parted ways about the city, and met up again at the end of the day in the same spot, as father and son coming home after a hard day's labor. On some days, Morgana stole back to their rooms in some guise or other and spent hours observing the routines of the countinghouse from her window above. On other days, it was Kestrel, until they both had intimate knowledge of the place, its inhabitants, and the progress of its business.

They each had visited the countinghouse on two separate occasions, using some trivial excuse to borrow some small necessity and return it the following day. The staff there soon came to know them on sight, and they nodded and greeted one another in the mornings and evenings as they passed each other on the street.

One evening, Kestrel ordered a holiday for them both. Morgana put away her sooty work clothes and they went out together to a small tavern in the next street. They sat in a corner and drank their ale and chatted quietly till it was quite late. They left after several hours in the pleasant place and went out into the cold, foggy night.

It was easy, then, for them to be followed.

Elizabeth wrinkled her nose at the man in the greasy red tunic. He smelled most vilely, and she despised the man's smug grin. But he had information for her that she wanted more than anything else in the world.

"Aye, it were her all right. And him, as well." Robin rocked back on his boot heels, nodding his head. "I seen 'em plain as plain and I know where they can be found."

"That is excellent. You will show my man where this girl is hiding. Then you may go back to your . . . people," Elizabeth said.

"Oh, now, I don't think I can do that, mistress."

She bristled. "What do you mean?"

"Well, now, first, there's the matter of my pay—"

"My man Durel will pay you as soon as you have shown him the place where he can find them. My offer is more than generous."

"Oh, aye, that it is, I got no quarrel with you there, mistress. But what I mean is a personal matter, you might say. There's summat that I want from her, as well."

"Well, you shall have to wait until I've done with the girl. You can do what you like with her companion."

Robin rubbed a dirty hand over the stubble on his chin. "Well, now, I don't know if I can do that. See, she's done me ill. Her and that Raven fella. I owe her a lesson."

Elizabeth shook her head. "I don't know any Raven. You were to find this Morgana or Blackbird or whatever she calls herself. You said the man she's with is the Kestrel. As I said, you may have him. But the girl is mine. When I've finished with her, you may have what remains."

Robin opened his mouth to argue, but caught the glint in Elizabeth's eye. He chose the path of prudence and held his tongue. He'd have what he wanted, soon enough.

Nichols fastened down the flaps on his down-lined cap and trudged down Kyroun Lane. The weather was turning damp, a fact that his bones had been announcing for two days. He would have liked to have stayed in the cozy main room of the countinghouse, working at his tall table. But he was setting out to meet Lord Phillip, and his lordship had said it was imperative that he alone come to him, not one of his operatives or clerks.

He nodded to his new neighbors, Master Browne and his young son. The pair seemed sober and well-behaved, he thought. They'd been into the countinghouse a couple of times to ask a question about the neighborhood or to borrow a stick of firewood to light their rooms. The father was a lawyer, Nichols knew, and the boy apprenticed somewhere, but there was no woman or wife. Word was the man was a widower. Sad state, he mused. He'd be hard-pressed if ever he had to manage without his dear Caroline, after all these years together.

When was that wild buck, young Greyfriars, going to find himself a wife? Nichols wondered. He was a likely enough fellow, for all his handsome looks and fashionable ways. The man had a clever head on him, just like his father.

He frowned. Except for this one instance. For the life of him, he couldn't imagine why Lord Phillip had insisted that he invest Lady Winston's money in the Holland Drapers Company. It had been tantamount to casting the whole lot into the ocean, and wasting money went against Nichols's whole nature.

But it wasn't his job to question orders from his clients. He had served the Greyfriars since before Phillip, or even his late brother, Thomas, had been born. And he had learned that their madness most often had method, and if it did not, it was folly to contradict them. For good or ill, fortune or folly, Nichols got his commission, and more besides.

He came to the door of Lord Elyot's house and was ushered into what he knew used to be Phillip's own solar. Phillip greeted him with a distracted deference, but when the servants had left them and they sat alone at the big table, he leaned forward, his eyes shining bright and hard. "Have you accomplished all I asked?"

"I have, my lord. The account was reduced to its last five pounds this morning. The Lady Winston should hear of it within the day."

"Good. Now then, Nichols. You have served me so faithfully these last years, even when I was away. Your advice is like gold to my family, and you are held in high esteem by us all. That is why I wish to make a gift to you and your lady wife. I have it all arranged for you and she to go south to France for two months. There, by the ocean, it will be warm, and you and your good Caroline may grow young again. What say you?"

Nichols spluttered with astonishment. "It is a most gracious offer, my lord, but I don't think I could accept—"

"Come now, you wouldn't insult me, would you?"

"Heavens, no! But how can I possibly leave my business, all the accounts I carry—"

"I've seen to that. Two extra clerks are waiting even now at your offices, and your man Partridge, whom you have hand-raised from a pup to follow in your footsteps, will manage the running of affairs for you. Not a penny will be lost from your business, I guarantee it."

"But, but . . ." Nichols spread his hands. "I don't see why you should do it, but it is a wondrous gift—"

"Splendid! I'll send a messenger and two of Elyot's servants to your house to help your good wife pack your things. You leave tomorrow with the tide." Phillip rose and was escorting the banker out the door as he spoke.

Nichols tried to interject a word or two, but it was to no avail. He was dismissed with all the grace and charm of a royal visitor, ushered to a little cart at the side of the house, and with many blithe farewells and claps on the back, was sent off to his countinghouse to ready his affairs for his absence.

Phillip returned to the solar, his smile fading as quickly as the sun behind a cloud. It was done. The first stage of his plan was complete, and by tomorrow evening he would have Nichols safely out of the way, should Elizabeth try to wreak any vengeance on the poor old banker.

"So much for her money," he muttered, pacing the solar. "Now, for her position."

He went to the window and stared out at the long gray line of the river in the distance. Where was Morgana? he wondered. It was a question he asked himself a hundred times in a day and at least twice that in a night. He should feel elated, he thought, at the way his plans for Elizabeth were going, and in some part of him, he was.

But the thought that at the end of it all, when Elizabeth was broken and her trickery ended, Morgana might not be there for him to return home to, was like a constant gnawing inside him. He had men looking for her, but thus far there was no word, save that she was nowhere to be found in the north.

He hoped that was a good sign, that she had changed her mind and stayed away from Cadgwyth and the Robin's clutches. Yet his mind wouldn't be at ease until she was here, enfolded in his arms, safe and whole and warm.

"Well, Greyfriars," Elyot said, coming in from his morning's ride. "Tomorrow night will tell the tale, eh?"

Phillip gave him a thin smile. "I hope so, Peter."

"Are you all right?"

Phillip shrugged. "This is a nasty business."

Elyot's eyebrows rose. "Having a change of heart?"

"No. She murdered Jamie Winston and made me her fool and accomplice into the bargain. My name was linked to hers and to his death, and no one in my family would ever bear such a shame."

"No one?"

Phillip scowled. "You mean Thomas?"

"He died getting hot revenge on someone he thought had slighted him," Elyot said, choosing his words carefully. "Some might say that was a shame in itself."

Phillip stiffened. "Are you saying I am angered over a trifle?" His voice was dangerously calm. "Am I like my brother, Elyot?"

"No." Elyot stood his ground. "But it is revenge you're having here, and you just said that it was a nasty business."

Phillip turned away from him, his fists clenched at his sides. "You know how I felt about Thomas and the way he died."

"I do. And I know how you felt about the way he lived, as well." Elyot sat down on a bench near the window and began removing his boots. "You've always said that you'd never permit your temper to master your wits."

"And so it hasn't. I haven't chosen Thomas's way. He leaped for his blade at the slightest word. Elizabeth will not lose one drop of blood by my hand."

"Well, then, old friend, I would say be of good cheer! Your scheme will bring you the satisfaction of righting your name and end her chances of ensnaring another in her nets."

Phillip squared his shoulders. "Yes. You're right. And the sooner the better."

The party was the most glorious affair of the year so far. Many notables had returned to the city after spending the summer in their country homes, and the cries of greeting and the cheerful reunions set the air ringing with mirth. Lord and Lady Osborne had set forth the best of everything, and both circulated through the crowd, making introductions, urging all to eat and drink, and making all feel welcome and at ease.

"Lord Greyfriars! We see too little of you of late!" Lady Jeanne Osborne extended both hands to Phillip.

He bowed low and kissed both heavily beringed hands. "My deepest apologies. Various matters of business have kept me out of London until recently."

"I hear you are the darling of the court once more. The ladies must be pleased to have their favorite among them again."

"You flatter me, Lady Jeanne."

"Of course I do, dear lad! What else would you expect, when there is so much here to admire?" The older woman winked at Phillip with good-natured ribaldry and gave him a good look from the top of his dark head to the hem of his fine golden velvet surcoat.

"Lord Cecil will have me roasted for flirting with his lovely wife," Phillip said, laughing.

"Oh, well, you'd be no good to any lady then, would you?" Lady Jeanne said with a chuckle. "I'll let you go.

Off with you. But if you trifle with my daughter Melisande, sir, you will answer to me.'' She shook her finger at him good-naturedly.

Phillip moved off into the crowd. Elizabeth caught his sleeve.

"Ah," Phillip said. "There you are, pet. I wondered if I'd been abandoned."

"Never, my dearest love." Elizabeth slipped her hand possessively through his arm. "I am all yours."

Phillip smiled down at her. He wondered what was going on in her devious little brain. She had clung to him like a limpet all evening. When Lord Fray and his lady had arrived, she had hardly glanced their way. Phillip had heard whispers throughout the hall, and that was good, but if Elizabeth didn't play true to form this night, his plan would be wasted.

He knew that she had had word that her finances had slipped away like water from a leaking bucket. The word from one of her servants was that the lady had been in a rage earlier that day and had all but skinned the poor fellow who had delivered the message from Nichols's company.

If this were true, Elizabeth showed no signs of any such disruptions in her life tonight. She was as cool and poised as ever, gowned in splendor and charming to all.

She was, Phillip suspected, clinging to him out of a renewed need for security. She was desperate. If she couldn't get what she wanted from one man, she wasn't about to toss away another potential benefactor.

At last, Peter Elyot was able to spirit her away into a dance. Phillip went as quickly through the crowd as he could, greeting one and all, but making as if he were on his way to either a fire or a privy. Out in the front hall, he found a man waiting, dressed in the livery of Lord Osborne's household.

"You have it?" Phillip asked without preamble.

"I have."

"And all is arranged?"

"It is."

"Do it."

The man bowed and departed into the great hall. Phillip went round to another door and slipped inside. He took up with the first lady he met, which happened to be the young and giggling Lady Melisande, and escorted her to the tables, which groaned with the finest foods available.

He kept his eye on Elizabeth. As soon as her dance with Peter Elyot had ended, a servant of the house approached and handed her a folded note. She read it over and coolly tucked it away into her sleeve.

Phillip continued to regale the rosy-cheeked girl with silly stories as he watched Elizabeth take leave of Elyot and melt away into the crowd. Good, he thought. She was wasting no time.

He glanced across the room and gave Peter a nod over the heads of the crowd. Peter gave a small salute and went off to find another lady to partner in the next dance.

Not far from where Phillip stood with the blushing Melisande, Lord William Fray was also opening a note and reading it. With as much discretion as a stripling youth, Lord William colored up at the contents of the note, crumpled it into his fist, and made hurried excuses to his companions. He pushed his way through the throngs of merrymakers and headed for the front hall.

Phillip took a turn on the dance floor with the now-stuttering Melisande. Peter passed them at one point and muttered, "Mercy," for Phillip's ears alone.

Phillip scowled. Mercy. It was on his mind. But the wheels had already begun to turn. Let Elizabeth find mercy where she could.

In yet another corner of the hall, a third note was being delivered to Lady Fray. Her face went pale as she read it, then turned bright red. She stood on tiptoe to search the room. When she did not find whom she sought, she turned, tight-lipped, to one of her companions and the two of them marched from the room.

Phillip took leave of Lady Melisande and partnered her mother, who went teasing and scolding by turns throughout the dance. At last, he bowed and delivered the lady to her husband with many compliments, and wove his way once more to the front hall.

The commotion coming down the stairs was almost enough to rival the din in the great hall. Phillip took the steps two at a time. Following the noise to its source, he found Lady Fray in one of the bedchambers, shrieking imprecations at first her husband and then Elizabeth. Lord William was scrambling into his clothes, while Elizabeth, in the bed, was clutching the covers to her bare chest. Her eyes went wide with horror when she caught sight of Phillip in the doorway.

He turned to go. Elizabeth came flying out of the bedroom, the covers scarcely concealing her nude form. "Phillip! Please! You can't go!"

He turned to face her, his face calm. "Oh, I think I'd better. Too crowded in there for me."

She reached out for him, almost dropping the coverlet. "You don't understand! I didn't do anything! It isn't what it seems! I—"

"I know, pet."

Footsteps and calls sounded on the stairs below. Elizabeth looked at him in terror. "You have to get me out of here!" she cried, tugging at his arm. "You have to protect me. The scandal! It will be all over London. At the court. My honor!"

Phillip only stared at her. *Honor? I didn't know you knew the word*, was what he wanted to say. Instead, he only smiled and patted her hand. "You'll be fine, pet."

He gently disengaged his arm from her grasp and sauntered away, letting the crowd of curiosity-seekers stream past him. He descended the stairs at a leisurely pace and went out to find his horse.

It was almost finished, he told himself as he rode home to Elyot's house. Now, if only he could find his rose.

Chapter Seventeen

The scandal was indeed all over London by morning. Lady Fray had done what Phillip had guessed she would and let it be known that her husband had been duped and seduced by an adventuress. All fault was laid at Elizabeth's door. Later that day, when word began to break that Lady Winston had long since squandered away her inheritance from her late husband, it only added confirmation that Lord Fray had indeed been victimized most cruelly. For his part, the duke wasn't saying much of anything and he prudently stayed cloistered at home all that day.

As Phillip had also expected, messages from Elizabeth, with ever-increasing urgency, began to arrive at daybreak. He let her fret most of the day away. Then, taking his time, he rode to her house near sunset.

He was ushered into her solar, which showed fresh marks on its walls where objects had struck, and the usually impeccable Elizabeth looked red-eyed and a bit disheveled. Still, she greeted him as if he were here to pay suit to her, taking his hand and leading him to the fireside, where wine was already poured and food set out on her best dishes.

"I'm so sorry that you had to see that horrid scene last night," she purred as she served him cakes and figs. "I can't imagine what possessed Lord William to think he could seduce me in his very own brother's house." She laid a slim hand to her throat. "I was so frightened, Phillip. So . . . violated."

Phillip thought of Morgana and how she had truly been violated and how she had suffered for it. He wanted to strangle Elizabeth then and there and be done with it. But he had come this far with his plan, he might as well let it play out.

"People must be saying the most awful things about me," she went on. "Have you heard anything?"

He shrugged. "Only a little. That you had your ambitions pinned on Lord Fray for some time now, and that you had been securing information about Lady Fray's lineage so that you could prove relationship within the fourth degree."

Elizabeth gasped. "How could they know—" She caught herself. "How could they possibly know what it is like to be young and beautiful and a widow in this world? Men will ever try to take advantage of a woman alone." She beamed a smile on Phillip. "Not you, of course, my dearest Phillip."

He drank some of his wine. "There's also a rumor flying about at court that you are bankrupted."

She cast her eyes downward. "It's so . . . awful. It is as I said. They've taken advantage of me in the basest ways."

"Then you are out of money?"

She paused for an instant. "No. No, of course not." She looked at him. "How could you believe such a thing?

You and I both invested in Nichols's latest venture, am I correct? Our returns from the Holland Drapers are assured.'' She laughed. ''You saw my gown last night. It was new and trimmed with gold. If I were destitute, could I afford such a gown?''

''I don't know. Could you?''

She frowned. ''Are you saying you don't believe me?''

He leaned forward. ''Of course I do, pet. Why would you have cause to lie to me? After all, we've shared so much, haven't we?''

She looked relieved. ''Oh, we have. I knew I could count on you.''

''What is it you want?''

''Only what we've always had. Our love. Our passion for each other.'' She leaned forward so that her face was close to his, her flowery scent rising. Her voice dropped to a whisper. ''I want to please you.''

Phillip leaned in, as if to kiss her. Then he leaned back. ''What is it?''

The edge in her voice spoke of anger, as well as fear and doubt. How it must enrage her to be out of control, to have to beg, he thought.

He'd imagined that he'd be glad in this moment, pleased. Instead, he was surprised to find he was merely tired.

''That sounds wonderful, Bess.''

''Bess.'' Her smile was radiant now. ''You haven't called me that in the longest time.''

''Well, my Bess, I would love to begin our revels right here and now,'' he said, rising. ''But I promised Elyot I would dine with him this evening.''

''You . . . what?'' Her voice trailed away.

He gave a chuckle and took her hands in his. ''Don't worry. There's all the time in the world, pet.'' He kissed her hand and took up his cap.

Coral Smith Saxe

"Will you come to me tomorrow?"

He flashed her a smile. "I wouldn't doubt it."

Elizabeth paced about the solar after Phillip had left, wringing her hands and gnawing at her lips. For once, she didn't think about the cost to her looks. She had to get him back. Had to make him hers.

This humiliation and scandal with William was too much. She had to have a way to cover it up, to bury it with a coup of her own.

The best coup she could think of was to snare, once and for all, the Viscount Greyfriars. But was it her imagination, or did he seem a bit reluctant tonight?

She couldn't fathom why he wouldn't want her. He'd been pursuing her all this time.

But just in case, perhaps it was time to take out a bit of insurance.

"Hot pies! Who'll buy my nice 'ot pies!"

Morgana heard the woman's cry and gave Kestrel a glance. She hadn't eaten much that day, and the ale had gone to her head somewhat. Kestrel nodded, and Morgana opened her mouth to call the woman out from the fog-wrapped pool of lamplight by the old warehouse.

Morgana never uttered a sound. One hand seized her arm while another was clamped over her mouth. In an instant, her mouth was tied with a gag, her wrists bound, and an old, foul-smelling sack shoved over her head. She heard a thud next to her and then the sound of a body falling to the ground.

"'Oo's out there?" she heard the pie-woman call. "Anybody there?"

Then she was being pushed and prodded into a run. She tried to keep her wits about her and listen for telltale sounds of where she was and which direction she was being taken. But before long, she was yanked to a halt, spun around several times, and then shoved up into a cart of some kind.

She heard the horses start up and felt the cart lurch forward, but the ale and the spinning made her head whirl. She lost all track of where she was and where they might be taking her, whoever they were.

At last, she was hustled from the cart, hay and straw still clinging to her clothes and hair, and hurried inside some house. She heard a door open and stumbled into a cold, silent room.

She was prodded some more, until she fell forward onto some sort of a pallet. She struggled, kicking out with her feet. A sudden crack sounded, just as a fearful pain roared through her head. She slipped sideways, groaning, and heard nothing more.

She awoke to the nudge of a boot in her ribs. Someone yanked the bag off of her head and she blinked in the dim light. She was in a rough-finished room, a warehouse or storehouse of some kind, she saw.

"My God."

She whirled about to see who had spoken.

"This is what Phillip has been toying with all these weeks?"

Elizabeth looked Morgana up and down, her upper lip curled ever so slightly. Morgana met her gaze with as much calm as she could muster, tied as she was and still badly shaken by her sudden abduction. What in the name of all hell's devils did the beautiful Lady Winston want with her?

"What could he possibly see in you?" Elizabeth murmured, circling round her. "Skinny, dirty, bosomless, dark—uggh. And those dreadful clothes." She gave a delicate shudder. "And I understand that you are a criminal?"

Morgana said nothing. The woman seemed talkative enough. No doubt she would get to her purpose in having her kidnapped ere long.

It was cold and her head ached from where she had been struck. She wondered how the Kestrel was faring. She had never seen the face of her captor or captors. Was he being held somewhere hereabouts?

A sudden chill seized her. Where was Phillip? He was supposed to be with Elizabeth. That was why he'd come to London—to be with Lady Winston. If Elizabeth had Phillip, then why on earth had she, Morgana, been brought here and why was the woman going on about Phillip's interest in her? She had a sick feeling that she was once again a pawn in someone else's game.

Elizabeth tapped her cheek with one finger. "What to do with you? I don't like the idea that Phillip has another little bit on the side, no matter how trifling. I need him too much now. And I don't like that he took you to his house in Aylesbury, while I have never been so much as invited to ride past."

Jealousy? This was about jealousy? Morgana wanted to laugh. The idea that Elizabeth Winston should view her as a rival was too ridiculous. But there was something about the woman that prickled the hairs on the back of Morgana's neck. There was something out of balance in the woman's voice and eyes. She held still and listened.

"You're a dreadful little urchin, but my womanly intuition tells me that you're just what I need to help Phillip see that my interests are his." Elizabeth clapped her hands.

Morgana stared in horror as Robin swaggered into the room. She felt her stomach turn over and fought the urge to run. She wouldn't get far, and who knew what punishment Elizabeth and Robin together could concoct for her? She steeled herself, though she could feel her legs quaking.

"Well a day." Robin came to stand beside Elizabeth, his thumbs hooked into his belt. "If this ain't a merry meeting, Blackbird."

Morgana held her silence.

"Is she dumb?" Elizabeth asked.

"Naw. She's got as smart a tongue on her as any wench ever made. She's just playin' with you. Tryin' to make like she's not in it, bad."

"Oh. I see. Is what this man says true? Do you believe that you're not in grave danger here?" Elizabeth's voice was sweet and soft.

Morgana only stared at her. Elizabeth made a little moue of irritation. "She's an arrogant little bitch, whatever." She moved closer to Morgana. "Shall I give you to him?" she asked lightly. "He says you owe him."

Morgana glanced at the Robin. He was grinning like a wolf. She shook her head.

"No? Then you are not quite the little wanton, are you? You like your men taller, don't you? And a good sight more handsome. And rich. You like them very rich, don't you, little mudhen?"

Morgana eyed her warily. She was about to hear what this was all about, not that she hadn't already guessed some of it.

Elizabeth went on. "I think I shall wait before I toss you to my grubby companion. Though the pair of you are well-suited, to my eyes, I need you first." She nodded. "Yes, you will do nicely for my purposes." She gave a heavy sigh. "You see, I have had a bit of difficulty of late. My money has disappeared. And now, the man I would have married, the man who would have put me into the highest circle in the land, has cast me off and gone back to his wife and daughters. I am quite desolate." She spread her hands in a gesture of surrender. "I have only one avenue left open to me. Lord Greyfriars."

She wandered about the little room, carrying her rich wool cloak high above the dusty floor. "I have little doubt that I can win him," she went on. "But I can't take any chances. He seems to have some attachment to you, though I can't imagine why. I shall hold you back as insurance. If he is reluctant to care for me in the way he should, I may be forced to reveal that I have his little play-toy. Phillip's a bit squeamish on killing, as you may know—a failing I don't comprehend, but there you are. He won't like the idea that I may have your pretty neck wrung at any moment if he doesn't give his whole heart to me. That is, of course—" She turned to Robin with a smile. "That is, after my companion here has had his debt repaid, too."

Morgana felt anger stirring within her, mingling with her fear. The woman was a lunatic. But a most dangerous sort.

"Lord Greyfriars would not refuse you," she said at last.

"No?" Elizabeth preened. "No, I suppose not. Still, in my circumstances, I mustn't be incautious. So. You shall be my guest here for a while. Just until I become the new Lady Greyfriars."

"What of my companion?" Morgana asked.

Robin snorted. "Kestrel's dead. We dumped him in the Thames late last night. You needn't worry about him again."

"You monster," Morgana snarled. "The man had done nothing to you!"

"No, but he was trouble. And I couldn't have him comin' back, thinkin' he could take over the flock again. All that's mine now, and I keep what's mine."

Elizabeth fluttered her fingertips. "That's enough of trivialities. We must think about what I need to do next."

"You don't need me," Morgana said. She softened her voice. "There is no comparison between us. Phillip will choose you. Didn't he leave me and run to you as soon as you beckoned?"

"Yes. But I need to secure my position soon. Phillip is

most awfully honorable. If he believes that failing to marry me might put even dirt like you in danger of your life, he might be persuaded to move all the more quickly.''

Morgana felt a cold hand on her heart. She was intending to marry Phillip? A dozen different emotions welled up in her at the thought, but she fought them down. It was nothing to her, she told herself sternly. Phillip was not hers to claim, nor would he ever be. All she had to worry about now was getting out of this place, untouched by Robin's filthy hands. She thought fast.

''Ah, but will he be a loving husband to a wife he thinks dishonorable?''

''What do you mean?''

''I mean, if Phillip thinks you capable of endangering another, even if he should marry you, won't he be inclined to be more stern, even miserly, with his wife?''

Elizabeth paused to consider this. She eyed Morgana suspiciously. ''You sound as if you're concerned for my well-being. But I think you are only trying to save your skin. It's all right. So would I do, were I in your place. But it's no good, I fear. You'll stay here—untouched—see, I can be honorable—until I need you. If Phillip is pliable, I shall have no need of you and you shall go free.''

Morgana felt her heart sink. She was a prisoner of this madwoman.

''Nay,'' Robin growled. ''You said I could have my way—''

''Shut up,'' Elizabeth snapped. ''You'll do as I say or I'll hand you over to the sheriff this instant. Get out of here. I've set my own men to guard this place. You're not to come here unless I say so. Otherwise, you not only do not get the money I promised you, you don't get this girl, either. Understood?''

Robin seemed about to spring at her, but then appeared to change his mind. He nodded and swaggered out, casting dark glances at both women as he went. Morgana wondered what he knew about Elizabeth that she did not. Clearly, he knew enough to fear and obey her, and that was good enough warning for her.

"Well, now. Just be comfortable," Elizabeth said, brushing her hands off. "You shan't starve. I'll see that you get something to eat each day. Pray only that it doesn't take too long to convince my Phillip that he needs me more than life itself."

Morgana felt those words go through her like a knife. *More than life itself.* Somehow, she didn't think it was just an expression with Elizabeth.

Two burly men entered the room and sat at either door, swords and truncheons at their sides. Morgana went to the rough pallet on the floor and sat down, cursing the bonds that held her wrists.

Once again, she was in trouble and danger because of Phillip. And yet, she was also a source of trouble and danger for him. If he married Elizabeth, his life would be a hell on earth; she knew that now. Yet Phillip had always treated Elizabeth like a lover, racing to London to be at her side at a moment's notice. He's never uttered a word against her. Could he possibly be in love with this madwoman? Were her beauty and outward charm so strong that he was unaware of what she truly was? Men were blind about women, Morgana had always heard. Was that true of Phillip when it came to Lady Elizabeth Winston?

She was too tired and frightened to think anymore. She just wanted out. Out of danger. Out of trouble. Hell, out of London, if she could manage it.

Morgana scooted back and leaned against the wall. With some effort, she got her cloak pulled around her, shielding her from the chill air of the room. How long would it be before Elizabeth played out her scheme?

She looked at the two men seated silently at the doors. There was little hope of getting past both of them. She was here for the duration of Elizabeth's strange courtship.

She had best settle in and cultivate patience.

"Phillip," she whispered under her breath. "Please, please stay safe."

"Lord, Kestrel," puffed old Fletcher. "You ought to change your name to the Cat. Those nine lives're comin' in mighty handy."

"You may have something there."

Fletcher helped the man up the last of the stairs and into a room at the far end of the hall. "Here we go, just a bit more, uh, uh, ahhh, there you go."

Kestrel collapsed onto the pallet. He was shivering hard enough to make his teeth rattle, and his clothes were drenched with icy water.

His old friend the innkeeper helped him out of the wet garments and wrapped him in warm blankets. He got a fire going in the smoky little brazier in the corner and pulled it closer to Kestrel's bedside.

"Here, drink this," he said, putting a bottle to Kestrel's blue lips.

He drank, coughed and choked, then drank some more. Fletcher eyed him with concern, his lips twisted into a wry frown.

"Now will you listen to me when I tell you it's time to retire?" he demanded. "The last time, I had to hide you in a chest under the inn whilst the constables tore my place apart. This time, you turn up floatin' in the river, half-drowneded. Next time, that plaguey luck of yours could be out havin' a drink with his pals just when you need him most."

Kestrel nodded, then coughed and clutched the blankets around him. He was shaking so hard his heels were thumping on the bed. Fletcher took a brick that had been heating on the brazier, wrapped it in a rag, and tucked it under the covers at Kestrel's feet. He gave his friend some more to drink and sat with him until he was warmer, at long last.

"Blackbird," Kestrel said as he was dozing off.

"Blackbird? He's here too?"

Another weak nod. More coughing. Then, "Taken. Robin."

"Oh, that bastard. I thought we was well rid of him. You say he's taken the Blackbird? Where?"

Kestrel shook his head. "Got to find her."

"Her? Her who?"

"Find Robin. Find Blackbird." He was slipping off.

"All right, all right, don't fret yerself. I'll do what I can."

Fletcher summoned one of his kitchen boys to come and sit with Kestrel, then stumped away to get his horse and make some inquiries.

"If things don't quiet down with this bunch," he grumbled as he went, "I'm the fella that's gonna have to retire."

Phillip was growing fearful. His man had returned from the north, saying that Morgana had not been seen anywhere near there. What was more, another man had been there before him, asking the very same questions. It was not known who the man was or from whence he'd come. But one thing was clear—Morgana had not gone north as she had claimed.

"That leaves London," Phillip had muttered to himself.

He'd gone straight to the White Stag, where he knew she and the Wren had once stayed. No one there had seen or heard from the Blackbird in months, he was told. He scoured the other inns and taverns of the area, asking the same questions and getting the same negative answers. There had been no sign of her. It was as if she had vanished off the face of the earth. He did learn something at the Unicorn, when he came there at last.

"No, I ain't seen anyone like him," one of the serving maids said when he inquired. "Just like I told ol' Fletcher this mornin'."

"Old Fletcher? Of the White Stag?"

"Aye. He was in 'ere this mornin', first thing. Said he was lookin' for that Blackbird fella and one o' them others—what was it 'e called im? Starling, was it? No, I 'ave it—Robin! Lookin' for the Blackbird and the Robin, was what 'e said."

Phillip's gut tightened. Robin and Blackbird? Why the hell would Fletcher expect the two of them to be together? Was Robin back in London, too?

"You say Fletcher was in this morning. He wasn't at the White Stag when I went there three hours ago. Did he say where he was going?"

The woman shook her head. "No. Just asked to send word to 'im at the Stag if I was to see either of them." She looked Phillip up and down. "You ain't one o' them birds, are you? You don't look the type."

Phillip didn't answer. He pulled his purse from his belt and laid a healthy pile of silver in the woman's hand. "If you see them—any of them—I want you to send word to me at this place." He told her Elyot's address. "Can you remember that? Come as fast as you can and there'll be gold in it for you."

A broad smile lit the maid's face. "I will and all! You'll hear about it the moment I lay eyes upon 'em."

"Or even if you hear of their whereabouts."

"Count on me, sir."

Phillip fetched his horse and rode for the White Stag. Fletcher had to come there sooner or later. When he did, Phillip would be waiting.

His patience was repaid late that night, when Fletcher came in, dusty and weary-looking. Phillip huddled back into the corner where he was seated, his hood pulled up to shadow his face. He watched as the old man went first to see that all was well with his establishment, then turned aside and headed up the stairs.

Phillip was after him in a heartbeat, following him to the

top of the stairs and listening outside the door of the little room at the end of the hall. He heard a man's rasping cough and Fletcher speaking in gruff but comforting tones. Silently, he pressed on the door and opened it a crack.

". . . ain't no word. But he's been about, that's sure."

"Who's been about, Fletcher?" Phillip stepped into the room.

Fletcher moved fast for an old fellow. He was armed with a stout stick before Phillip could take more than a step. "You get out of here, young trouble. I recall your face and I don't want to play no games with the likes of you. Now, go on—be off with ya!"

"I'll go just as soon as you tell me why you've been looking for the Blackbird and the Robin."

"Never heard of 'em."

Phillip took a step closer. "We're not going to go through this again, are we, Fletcher? I've done you no wrong. Indeed, I may be able to help you. But I need to know why you're seeking this pair."

Fletcher glanced at the pallet. Kestrel had raised himself up on one elbow and was staring at Phillip with keen interest in his fevered eyes.

Phillip looked at the man lying before him. There was something remarkable in the man's face. It was intelligent and of an indeterminate age, but there was something else about it. A sharpness, and a cool demeanor that told him that he was utterly unafraid of Phillip, despite his disadvantaged position.

"You're Lord Greyfriars," the man said, his voice a hoarse whisper.

"And you—" Phillip's jaw dropped, then closed. "Damn me," he said softly. "You're the Kestrel."

"At your service, my lord viscount."

Fletcher was gaping at the pair of them, still brandishing his cudgel. "You mean to say you know this rascal?"

"I know of him," Kestrel said. He had a fit of coughing. Phillip came to kneel beside the pallet and help him to a sitting position. Fletcher was waiting with a cup, which Kestrel accepted with a nod of gratitude.

Phillip couldn't wait for the man to speak. "I must find Morgana—the Blackbird," he said. "It's imperative."

Kestrel lowered the cup to the floor. "Imperative?"

"Her life is in danger, I believe."

"It is indeed," Kestrel said. "Robin has her."

Phillip swore a bloody oath. "Where?"

"I don't know. They attacked us from behind, in the dark. I saw no one. But I heard the Robin speak." He gave a rueful smile. "Just before they cast me off a dock into the river."

"They took her somewhere else?"

"Aye. Fletcher's been out looking for them all day."

Phillip turned to the older man. "And?"

Fletcher shrugged. "Not much to tell. Robin was seen in Thames Street, someone said. But he weren't there when I went. And no one's seen the Blackbird."

The words fell into the silence of the tiny room. Phillip looked to Kestrel. "I've got to go look for her. Or for him. I'll send a physician."

"Why?" Kestrel asked.

Phillip gave him a tight smile. "I'm not sure. But I believe that you are dear to Morgana and that she would want me to do so."

Something like pain passed over the Kestrel's face. "You love her, then?"

"I do."

"Go find her. And the devil himself hound you through eternity if ever you harm her."

Phillip and Kestrel gazed at one another for a long moment. Then, with a curt nod, Phillip left, taking the stairs two at a time.

Fletcher looked at Kestrel with a scowl. "Now what the devil was that all about?" he demanded.

Kestrel sank back down onto the pallet. "Were you never in love, my old friend?"

"Love? Me? When would I have time for that? I been too busy runnin' this place and pullin' the likes of you out of the river and all."

"Then I fear you wouldn't understand."

Kestrel dozed off. Fletcher gave a snort as he covered him up and tucked the blankets in tightly around him. "Love! Madness is more like it, I say."

Elizabeth hummed as she dressed. Phillip would be here within the hour. Everything was in readiness. All his favorite dishes, the best wines left in her bottlery, the room lightly scented with exotic incense and beeswax candles, cushioned seats before the fire—all was perfection.

She examined herself in her hand mirror. She had bathed in milk and almond oil and had donned a gown of pale, frosted violet. Her hair she left long and shimmering down her back, adorned only with a simple circlet of silver. She had spared no pains in achieving what she knew was a most alluring presence. Phillip would be enchanted.

And if he wasn't, she told herself, she had the very thing necessary to make him yield to her plan.

There was a knock at the door. Her chambermaid ran to admit the steward. "Lord Greyfriars awaits you in the solar," he reported.

"Thank you, Edward," she sang. "Tell the viscount that I shall be with him directly."

She dismissed both servants and stood, turning this way and that before the pier glass. She gave herself a honey-sweet smile. Success was hers. She could feel it in her very bones.

Chapter Eighteen

Phillip waited in the solar, impatience gnawing at him like an animal in a trap. All he wanted was to be out of this velvet wolf's den and off looking for Morgana. He had spent almost every moment since he left the White Stag scouring London's roughest neighborhoods, asking everyone he encountered if they'd seen either the Blackbird or the Robin. It was of no avail. He knew no more now than he knew a few hours ago.

What was worse was the way his imagination chimed in to add its bit to the din of concerns ringing in his mind. No one had seen Morgana. Did that mean she was dead?

Robin had her. Visions of tortures far worse than death haunted him. The idea of the man so much as speaking to Morgana made him want to tear Robin's heart out and feed it to the dogs.

He had to find her or he would go mad.

He paced before the hearth. It was a bitter night. The cold suited his temper. He had made a decision to end things with Elizabeth once and for all. He'd done enough; she was effectively repaid for duping him into helping her murder her husband. Tonight, he would tell her that he was finished with her. It would be a relief to have this long ordeal ended. He felt he had paid a heavy price for this revenge and he wanted to rid his life of it—and her— forever.

Elizabeth glided in at last, a vision in pastel purple, like a delicate, candied violet. He was unmoved. She could be naked and lying on a bed of flowers and he couldn't have cared less. She was dead to him.

"Phillip!" she said, coming to greet him, her hands outstretched. "I'm so glad you came. I felt we parted badly the other night. I'm relieved to see that you've forgiven me for my moment of weakness with Lord William."

"You may have all the moments of weakness you like," he told her, taking her hands. "It's nothing to me."

She regarded him warily, then laughed. "You're such a silly. Come now. Sit. Let me get you some wine."

"No servants?"

She gave him a shy smile. "I wanted to serve you with my own hands, love. It means so much to me."

"Ah. Very flattering."

She poured him a drink and took one herself. She raised her cup to his in salute. "Let us drink to our future, love."

"The future." Phillip tasted the wine and then set his cup down.

"Is the wine not to your liking?" Elizabeth lifted the decanter. "I'll ring for something else. You have only to ask."

"The wine is good."

"Then what is it, my love? Why do you look at me with such big, dark eyes?"

He moved away as she approached. "I have something to tell you. I'm leaving London."

"Leaving?" The smile stayed on her face even as her voice took on a wary note.

"Yes. I'm thinking of going to Italy. Perhaps Germany, too. I shall be gone quite a long while."

"But . . . what about me? About us?"

Phillip shrugged. "I think it best we go our own ways. We both know the passion is gone between us."

Elizabeth sat down, her hands clenched in her lap. "You can't be serious." She forced a little laugh. "You're teasing me again, naughty thing."

"No. I'm quite serious. I want to get away."

"But I thought that you—that we—" She rose and came to stand before him, tears edging her eyes. "Phillip, love. I would die without you. How can you break my heart this way?"

"Sorry, love. But you're strong. You'll get over it and land on your feet. Cats like you always do."

Elizabeth's cheeks went pale. "What did you call me?"

"Come now, pet. You know what I mean. You're a survivor! You still have the remainder of James's money and his title. The silly folk at court will forget all about this little scandal in no time and you'll have your pick of tomcats to play with."

Elizabeth clenched handfuls of her gown. "But you don't understand," she said. "I don't have the money. It's lost. All of it. All my investments went bad. I—I only learned of it this morning."

"No!" Phillip feigned shock. "Well, that is a bit of mess for you, isn't it?" He reached out and patted her on the head. "But you'll be all right. You had no money when you found James, or damned little of it. You can do it again."

"I don't want to do it again."

"Well, then, you might consider convent life."

"What?" Elizabeth's soft voice became strident.

"It's where most ladies go who are in such dire straits as you. I know of several good abbeys, not far from London. You could become a wealthy abbess, with all your talents."

She drew a deep breath and advanced on him, eyes blazing. "Dire straits? Abbess? Are you insane? I'm not about to go to a living death in some nunnery!"

He shrugged. "Suit yourself. I know you'll think of something. Now—" He picked up his cap. "I have errands to attend to before morning. I bid you adieu and the best of luck, pet."

He started for the door, leaving Elizabeth open-mouthed where she stood. She found her voice as he was reaching for the latch. "I don't think you want to leave just yet."

Something sharp in her voice caused him to halt. "Oh?"

"There's something that you may wish to know."

He gestured impatiently. "Well? Spill it, woman. I know you won't rest until you have."

Elizabeth picked up a knife from the platter of fruit on the table. "I heard that you were engaged in a dalliance," she said, trying the sharp edge against her thumb. "While you were paying court to me here, you were keeping a woman at your country estate."

Phillip felt as if ice water had just fallen on him. With sudden swiftness, he knew what Elizabeth was about to say and yet he couldn't open his mouth to utter a word.

"I see you have the good sense not to try to deny it. It was shocking to me when I learned of your betrayal of my love. But not so distressing as when I learned that she was not only a little bit of a trollop but a criminal as well." She clucked her tongue. "Poor Phillip, what would your family say if they knew?"

"My family and my affairs are none of your business."

"No? Think again, love. For I know where your precious little Blackbird is at this very hour."

Phillip met her eyes, his mind whirling with images of Morgana in untold dangers. Elizabeth gave a low, murmurous laugh.

"Ah, yes. I believe I have your attention now."

"Where is she?"

"In a safe place I know of. And well guarded. Not only by my men, but by one of her thieving friends who goes by the ridiculous name of Robin, I believe?"

Phillip summoned all his will and restrained himself from lunging at her. "Take me there," he said evenly. "She's of no use to you."

"That I won't do. You'll not go near her again. Nor will I see you so much as kiss your hand to another woman."

"You're dreaming."

"Perhaps. But I think you will see things my way. Once you and I are wed."

Phillip threw back his head and laughed. "You *are* mad! Marry you? I'd rather wed your horse."

Elizabeth held the knife up before her. "You may laugh. And you may threaten. But you will marry me. And soon." She waved the knife so that it glinted in the candlelight. "If you do not, I will have your little plaything destroyed."

Phillip's hand moved to the hilt of his own knife. He'd never wished so much to use that blade as he did at this moment. Elizabeth's lovely bosom was there before him, almost bared above her low-cut gown. It would be so easy to overpower her, to—

But that would mean certain death to Morgana. He had to think, damn it! His mind raced, searching for a key, a plan, a way to get this viper in silks to free Morgana without selling his soul.

Elizabeth set the knife on the table. She came to stand before Phillip, her lovely face lifted up to his. "You see?" she asked softly. "I gave you every opportunity to do this without threats, but you forced my hand."

"Your hand has never been forced to anything," he growled.

She thought for a brief moment. "I had to take her. Not only to convince you that your life is here with me. I couldn't have her coming around you again, begging for favors, telling everyone that she was sleeping with you while I was here in London, alone and at the mercy of foul seducers and false advisors, with no idea that my love was playing me false."

Phillip shook his head in disbelief. "You actually believe yourself an innocent, don't you?"

"It doesn't matter what I think. All that matters is what you do."

Phillip knew she was right. Everything depended on what he did next. God, he had been so driven in both carrying out his plan for revenge and in searching for Morgana that he hadn't seen this coming. He was a fool, an idiot!

He moved away from Elizabeth and walked about the room slowly, pondering. She stood by the hearth, her hands folded demurely in front of her, awaiting his decision.

He was caught. He knew it and she knew it. There was no way that she was going to let Morgana escape without getting something from him, something big. And his instincts told him that if he didn't act soon, Morgana might yet be lost.

Morgana! He wanted to race out into the streets, dragging Elizabeth by that damned hair of hers, and force her to tell him where she'd taken her. But such actions would only cause a hue and cry from the neighbors and constables, and even if it didn't, Elizabeth was so utterly ruthless that she would hold out against him until it was too late for him to save Morgana. How long did he have?

As if in answer to his thoughts, Elizabeth spoke again. "I don't wish to rush you into anything so sacred as marriage, love, but if you do not make some oath to me by midnight this night, I'm afraid your little bitch will be dead. Or as good as."

Phillip thought. He had to do it. He would think of how to end the marriage as soon as he knew Morgana was safe. But he had to have some guarantee, some assurance that Elizabeth would keep her word.

A terrible thought came to him. What if she was bluffing even now? What if Morgana was already—

"Take me to her."

"Don't be ridiculous."

"Take me to her. She doesn't have to see me. If I'm assured that she is alive and well and that she has safe passage to wherever she wishes to go, I will do all that you ask. But nothing less will do."

Elizabeth pouted. "I don't like it that you're making demands. I'm supposed to be doing that." She frowned as she considered. "Oh, very well. I'll let you see the dirty little trollop. I can't imagine what you see in her, but that's of little concern to me now. When I am your wife, you won't need any other woman to keep you happy and satisfied."

Phillip shook his head at her delusions but let them slide. He put on his cap and rang the bell for the steward. "Let's be off," he said. "If this thing is to be done, let's be quick about it."

"Now, that's the Phillip I love."

Morgana had been dreaming of Phillip. It was a familiar dream, in which he was riding toward her on Saracen. She was running, laughing. He came close enough to scoop her up into his arms and together they skimmed over the ground, riding the very wind.

"Get up." She was shaken out of her pleasant respite by one of the barrel-chested guards of her cell, as she had come to call it.

"What is it?" Her words were lost in the folds of the old dirty sack as it once more came down over her face. She cursed under her breath.

"Shut up. Her ladyship don't want no talkin' 'less she says so."

She was pulled to her feet and hauled, stumbling, out to what she guessed was the middle of the room. She heard the guard step away from her and go to the door.

Someone had come in. She turned in the direction of the door, lifting her head to hear what she could beneath the heavy, rustling hood. She thought she heard two sets of footsteps on the hollow old floor, but one set could have belonged to the guard. The other steps were light, and there was the sound of smooth, full garments brushing across the floor. The scent of lilies penetrated the hood, and Morgana knew that Elizabeth Winston was once more in the room.

"Well, you are the lucky one," Elizabeth said at last. "It seems you have a benefactor. You've been ransomed."

Morgana remained silent, waiting to hear more.

"Say thank you."

"Thank you. Who—"

"Never mind who has agreed to pay your fee. Let's just say that this has worked out well for us both."

She heard footsteps leaving the room now, and the door latching. The scent of lilies remained strong. She had no time to ponder who had left the room, as Elizabeth continued.

"You will be released in a few hours' time, when all has been . . . paid, shall we say? But don't entertain any notions of having revenge or of ever contacting Phillip

Greyfriars again. You will be followed. You will leave London and you will never come here again. Nor will you go to Aylesbury and try to reach him there. Nor to Wildhurst.''

Morgana heard Elizabeth step away, then halt. ''Oh, and if you still are not convinced that I mean what I say, perhaps your friend the Robin can persuade you. That, or I turn you over to Henry himself and tell him that the outlawed daughter of Morton Langland has been troubling one of his most loyal subjects, the Viscountess of Wildhurst.'' Elizabeth giggled. ''Say, 'Yes, my lady.' ''

Morgana held her silence.

''Say yes!''

''Yes. My lady.''

''Remember it.''

The footsteps left the room and faded away outside. The guard came and removed her hood, hustled her back to her pallet. She sat, stunned, pondering Elizabeth's words. A benefactor? Did she mean Phillip? Then why hadn't she said that Phillip had agreed to marry her? And if her so-called benefactor wasn't Phillip, who could it be?

Morgana hated this game. She wanted more than ever to be free again and on her own. She was growing weary of being a pawn at every turn.

To Morgana's utter astonishment, beyond all hope, Elizabeth Winston was true to her word. Before noon the next day, she was taken, blindfolded, and transported to the Bishopsgate. She was free.

''Well? Didn't I tell you your little urchin was fine? You saw her and you heard her.''

''Just see that she stays that way. Our bargain includes keeping that vermin the Robin away until she has had plenty of time to make her escape.''

Elizabeth fluttered her hands. ''It shall be done. You

313

know, I didn't like doing this, but I was forced to take her.'' She went to Phillip and reached her arms up around his neck. "Now, let's forget all about this unpleasantness. Let's talk about our wedding. Soon we'll be as happy as we were in the old days.''

"Right. Let's be about it, then. Let's seal this bargain.'' He pulled the ruby ring off his finger. Disentangling her from his neck, he set her on her feet and took her left hand in his. With a look of dark, heated purpose, he slipped the ring on her forefinger. "Here is my token and bond. Tomorrow we'll go to the priest. We can be wed first thing in the morning.''

"Oh, Phillip, you know rubies are my favorite!'' Elizabeth held the ring up to the candlelight, admiring her long, slender hand with its new bauble. "But, Phillip, why such a hurry? The wedding of the Viscount Greyfriars and the Lady Elizabeth Winston is sure to be the event of the age! What would your family say if you were married without so much as a by-your-leave?''

"I'm sure they won't mind,'' he said dryly. "I'm going now to St. Dunstan's to engage a priest. Be ready when I return tomorrow morning.''

He felt sick as he went to the church but also relieved. He had seen for himself that Morgana was well, at least for now. He had it in his power to free her and protect her from Elizabeth's grasp. It didn't matter what the cost. He'd manage somehow. What mattered now was making sure Elizabeth let Morgana out of her web. He could protect himself. But he wouldn't let Morgana suffer one more moment for his sake.

He visited the church and rousted one of the friars from his rest. The priest had many admonitions for him about hasty marriages and passionate unions cooling soonest, but Phillip's money and persuasive words helped to soothe his qualms. He said a priest would be waiting and ready in the chapel. The wedding hour was set and a messenger dispatched to Elizabeth's house telling her the appointed time. Phillip rode home in a fog of weariness, rage, and apprehension.

The next day, Father Bernard rose from his bed before first light and knelt to begin his prayers. The single candle on the altar was the only light in his little cell of a room. He felt a rush of wind about his bare ankles, but he ignored it. The church was nothing if not drafty, especially at this time of the year. He murmured his entreaties to the Creator, asked for wisdom and blessings in performing the marriage rites that morning, and was just rising when he was greeted by the sight of a small man, all dressed in drab brown and smiling an apologetic smile.

The man said not a word, but before the friar could cry out, the fellow stuffed a rag into his mouth and tossed a sack over his head. His hands were bound, though not cruelly, and he was conducted gently backwards until he was compelled to sit on the bed. He heard the man rustling about the room. He wanted to say that he had nothing of value to steal, except perhaps his little stump of a candle, but the man had made it impossible.

He heard more soft rustlings, the thump of boots on the floor, and then a rush of wind as the door of his cell opened, then closed with a soft click.

Ah, well, he thought. Brother Leo would find him when he came to accompany him to morning prayers in the chapel.

He wriggled back on his narrow cot and was able to bring his feet up over the edge. He slid them under the blanket as best he could, and settled in for a rest.

Elizabeth had not been idle, Phillip saw when she arrived at the church the following morning. Or, at least, her servants had not been idle. She had managed to summon up a tailor in the night, it appeared, and she was gowned in the richest velvet, her cloak, hood, and gown all trimmed in ermine. She floated over the stones of the old church floor like a breath of swan's down, her expression so serene and joyfully innocent that anyone watching would have been convinced in a moment that she was nothing less than a sweet, chaste bride, going prayerfully to be wed to her true love.

Phillip's stomach roiled at the image. There was nothing left of her illusions for him. The sight of her in the pale rose gown and white cloak was the same as seeing a toad hopping toward the altar, its tongue flashing in and out with greedy abandon.

The friar, however, couldn't contain himself. "Oh, and here she is, my lord, a vision to please the eyes of the angels! A lucky man, my lord, you are this day! Come hither, daughter! Your bridegroom has been waiting here like a stallion fit to break down his paddock."

Phillip wanted to glare at the jabbering priest but forced himself to smile and hold out his hand to Elizabeth. She glided forward, took his hand, and sank to her knees in a flawless imitation of piety. Phillip followed suit and knelt beside her.

"My lord," whispered the friar. "It is, ah, meet that there should be guests at such a momentous occasion, do you not think?"

"We need no one but God to witness our loving vows," Elizabeth murmured.

"Ah, yes lady, but a mortal witness is a good thing. Should there be, God forbid it, anyone who might make a challenge to, let us say, the legitimacy of this, ah, marriage, then, if you please, it would be wise, prudent even, to have another stand here to lend his voice against any such claim as might—"

"Very well," Phillip growled. "Who shall we get?"

Elizabeth looked at him with wide eyes. "Had you or I a brother, that would be fitting."

"Peter will do. He lives not far from here. I'll fetch him."

"Oh, my lord Greyfriars, do let me aid you here. I know of one who may go as swiftly as a bird flies. Tell me where to find your friend and he will be present in the blinking of an eye, the passing of an instant, the—"

"Go." Phillip told him the address. The little friar scurried away, leaving Phillip and Elizabeth alone in the chapel. She rose and went to sit on a bench by the wall. Phillip began to pace the length of the chapel, his hands knotted behind his back, his brow dark.

The friar was back shortly, puffing and chattering about the weather and preparations for Twelfth Night and how the spiritual conditions in the city were on the most perilous decline.

"Thieves are everywhere!" he exclaimed. "And adventurers of all sorts. Bawdy women with their evil snares. It is all that we can do here to hold England for the Lord."

Phillip scarcely heard him. He wanted this to be over, now. He wanted to be sure that Elizabeth was satisfied of his intentions. Then he could be sure that Morgana was safe. But that wouldn't happen until this nattering magpie of a friar got on with the ceremony!

Peter Elyot slammed open the door to the chapel. "Greyfriars, what the devil are you doing?"

"My lord!" The priest gave him a stern look.

"I crave your pardon, father. Greyfriars, some ninny just rousted me out of bed and dragged me here saying that I'm to be a witness to your wedding. Since when are you marrying anyone?"

"He is marrying me, Lord Elyot. This morn."

Elizabeth came gliding across the floor to them. She wore her most beguiling smile. "Won't you do us the honor of celebrating the occasion with us? We have need of a friend to share our happiness and bear witness."

317

Peter shot Phillip a questioning glance. Phillip nodded. "It is even so."

Peter swept off his cap and bowed. "I am at your service, lady. Lead me to it." He looked again at Phillip, but Phillip gave him only a brief shake of the head.

The ceremony was quick, once the friar got through scuttling about, exclaiming over this and that, and arranging the wedding party just so. Each stage of the ritual added to the weight on Phillip's chest. By the time the friar had uttered the final blessing, Philip's mood was as dark as the most desperate midnight.

Morgana, he told himself again and again. This was for her.

As he stood to kiss his bride, he held Morgana's image before him, her name in his heart. It was enough to see him through.

"Now, Elyot," he said with false heartiness, "join us for the wedding feast?"

"Lead on. I am but your servant today."

Peter led Elizabeth away as Phillip turned to give the friar money for the service. The little man bobbed his head and burbled on. "Such a lovely lady! Such grace and lightness. My lord is most fortunate! Oh, and may I say that your lordship is also most generous. So kind of you to remember our humble work here at St. Dunstan's. We're all that stands, you know, between the safety of English souls and—"

"Yes, yes, I know. The evils of these modern times." Phillip turned and started away.

Something halted him and caused him to turn back. There was something about that friar . . .

The little priest had already scuttled away, vanished in the twinkling of an eye, as he himself would have put it. Phillip shrugged. The old cleric was a bit addled, that was all. He had more important matters on his mind.

* * *

"And you're sure it was he?"

Wren nodded. "No other."

Kestrel rested back against the wall. "From all I've heard, the man is not a fool. Why would he marry the Winston bitch, when he stood here and told me himself, with truth in his eyes and voice, that he loves our Morgana? And you say he loves her too, that he was with her at Cadgwyth?"

Wren nodded and tore off a hunk of bread to dip in the stew Fletcher had brought for them. He had arrived in London only three days ago, but he was already in the thick of things and happy to see his old leader and friend at last.

"She loves him," he said between bites.

"Yes. I can imagine. He is quite a man of wax."

Wren shot him a sharp glance, then went back to his victuals. "Now what?"

Kestrel wrapped his cloak more tightly about his shoulders. He was still weak and taken with fits of coughing. He shivered and cupped his hands around the bowl of hot stew.

"I want you to go to a place in Kyroun Lane," he said. "I have rooms there that I have let. Blackbird probably will come there, if she manages to get free." He paused to swallow some of the broth. "Bring her here. Robin'll be on the watch for her in both places, but you and I and our good old friend Fletcher will be able to manage him."

Wren wiped his mouth and jumped nimbly to his feet. Kestrel grinned up at him, looking more like his former self. "I'd have loved to have seen you as a priest."

Wren grinned and folded his hands prayerfully, looking to the ceiling in piety. Kestrel laughed. "God, how the Winston bitch will howl when she learns this marriage is a sham!"

"Amen."

Chapter Nineteen

Phillip paced the floor of the withdrawing room he had claimed as his own in Elizabeth's house. It had been a month since the wedding and he was about to go mad from a killing combination of boredom and rage. Had he ever imagined that life with Elizabeth might be a pleasant thing? She had little or no conversation, she was sweeter than sugar to him, acquiescing in all things as if she imagined that was how a wife should act, and she was almost solely interested in two things—sex and money. The first interest he had fulfilled with perfunctory grace, avoiding it when possible but acquiescing when he couldn't avoid her. The second he had tried to fulfill by sending for some of his coffers to be brought to London from the vaults at Cygnet House. Elizabeth had been delighted for a time, but she was already hinting that there should be more coming her way.

Worse still, she wanted to go to Wildhurst. To pay respect and get his parents' blessings, she told him. He had held her off thus far, claiming that he wanted his bride all to himself for a while. But now he knew that word was well out in London of their marriage and it would be only a matter of time before the news reached Wildhurst. His parents had to be told.

He ran his hands over his hair. He had made a deal with a devil, he knew that now. It might well cost him his soul. But one thing was certain—he now knew that Elizabeth had freed Morgana. He had exacted that promise from her and had ridden with the guard to the crumbling old storehouse where Morgana had been kept. His heart had leaped up when he saw her emerge into the light, her dark curls tousled, her clothes tattered. It had taken all his strength to stay in the shadows, unseen, as he had promised Elizabeth. They had seen Morgana safely to the outskirts of London, and then he had turned back, pondering how long it might be before he could end this farce and leave Elizabeth without fearing for Morgana's life. Or his own.

The thought shook him now. God in heaven, she'd done it before, hadn't she? Jamie Winston had met his untimely end solely because he wasn't rich enough or powerful enough for Elizabeth. Had Phillip sealed his own fate with this marriage?

He sat. He would give his life for Morgana. He knew that, to the very bottom of his soul.

Yet, he realized, he had kept alive the hope that somehow, some way, he would be rid of Elizabeth and be with Morgana again. He wanted to live, if only to see her one more time. He wanted to live in order to see that she was safe, always. He had once worried that he would not have a soul or a heart to give to Morgana when he was finished with Elizabeth. Now, he wondered if he'd even have a life to give her.

Damnation! He felt like a fly in a web, alive but immobilized. If he set Elizabeth aside, she might reach out and harm Morgana. If he stayed with her, she might indeed kill him and become again a rich and beautiful widow with her eye on an entry into the royal family. And she might not hesitate to rid the world of an inconvenient little thief who knew a bit too much about her actions.

He knew if he went out she would have him followed. He'd already tried it. He didn't even know where Morgana was. He had to get word to her, to somehow warn her to leave London. Perhaps he could send her to Judith, his sister. Whatever the case, he had to reach her.

He called for a servant and sent for Peter Elyot. When Peter arrived an hour later, Phillip greeted him with a warm handshake that laid a small, folded note into Peter's hand. They chatted in the solar, with the servants coming in and out, per Elizabeth's instructions, to insure that nothing happened in her house to which she was not privy.

Peter left, and Phillip prayed he was not followed.

"Good morrow, Master Browne!"

Morgana startled, then turned to see who had hailed her. It was Partridge, one of the clerks from the countinghouse next to the house where she and Kestrel had stayed. She was on her way past the countinghouse when Partridge called out to her.

She stopped and pulled her cloak about her, covering her ragged clothes. For weeks, she'd been hiding out in various places in the city and just outside, making sure she wasn't followed and that there was no sign of the Robin. Now, she only wanted to get into their rooms and get clean and have a rest. But the man was smiling and bearing down on her, bound to chat.

"We haven't seen you much. Nor your father. Been out of the city?"

"Aye. On family business."

"Ah. Everything well, I hope?"

"Improving." She smiled and began to move on.

"Wait, I'll accompany you to your door, lad. I've been working double since my master Nichols departed for France. Now, with our Viscount Greyfriars and his lady wife celebrating as if money could be minted just for them, well, I'm just glad to be out of the countinghouse for a breath of air."

Morgana stared at the clerk. "Viscount Greyfriars?"

"Oh, yes. The Greyfriars are our most important patrons. Lord Phillip was married only last week."

The news washed over her like a freezing fire. Phillip was married? He had married already?

"Aye, he's landed the lovely Widow Winston at last, the lucky dog."

She turned away, hiding her face. She'd never dreamed she could hurt so over something that she knew had to happen, which she had done nothing to prevent and everything to encourage. But she did. She hurt all the way down to the bone.

"Well. That is news indeed. I hope that you get a holiday, soon," she said. She turned from the man and hurried in the door of the house.

She climbed the stairs and shut herself into the empty, cold rooms. It was evident that Kestrel had not been back since the night they had gone out together for a drink and a bit of relaxation. Then it was true. Kestrel was dead. Robin had killed him. Her last friend was lost to her.

She sank onto the bed, too weary and shocked to do more than sit and stare at the wall. She ached with hurt and betrayal. She didn't know why she should be surprised when people failed her and showed their worst. She had known betrayal almost all of her life.

But Phillip's marriage seemed a worse betrayal than any of the others. For the first time in many a long year, Morgana had chosen to place her trust in someone other than herself. She had opened her heart and her arms to Phillip and had believed that he would never take advantage of that vulnerability. She had fallen in love, and this was where it had landed her.

She knew she was making no sense. She was the one who had shoved him away from her. She had been the one to run off, the one who had insisted that she would only bring shame to him and his family if they stayed together as Phillip had asked. She had let him go to Elizabeth. Hell, she'd pushed him! And Elizabeth herself had told her that marriage with Phillip was her aim. She knew that the beautiful, scheming Elizabeth would win him. Morgana was no match for her.

But how could Phillip have agreed to marry her so quickly? He had been so fervent in his loving, so urgent in his pleas that she stay with him. How could he have suddenly turned from those passionate feelings for her to passion for Elizabeth?

Her heart told her that she would never betray the deep-rooted love she had discovered for Phillip. Never. Yet was she so stupid, so naive that she had imagined that he had felt the same love for her? Why hadn't she seen that as soon as he was rid of her for good and all, when he couldn't have his little diversion, he would find a new plaything at once? And a richer, finer, more beautiful one, besides? Why was she so hurt and surprised?

Stupid! she railed. Green, foolish, stupid, and so besotted by a pair of eyes and a few kisses that she had imagined love! It was to laugh at. She was an idiot.

But she would never be so again.

She dashed the bitter, hot tears from her eyes. She might be alone, but she was not helpless. She had learned a great lesson, she told herself. There was no one she could count on in this world, save herself. From now on, she would take care of herself and let the devil take the rest.

She jumped at the sound of a light knock on the door.

324

She frowned. No one knew she was here except the gossipy clerk from next door.

Her heart pounded. Kestrel!

Or Robin?

She slid off the bed and crept to the corner. Armed with her knife in one hand and a stout stick of firewood in the other, she went to the door.

"Come," she called at last, bracing herself.

The door opened and she lunged. Her victim managed to throw his arm up in time to send her blow only glancing off his head. Still, it was enough, and Morgana stared in horror as the Wren crumpled to the floor at her feet.

"What the devil were you trying to do?" she demanded. "Scare the life out of me or merely end yours? And what's happened to your hair?"

Wren winced as she touched a cool cloth to the knot on his head. He patted the bald spot at the back of his head. "Mice. Kestrel sent me."

"Kestrel!" She looked up in excitement. "You've seen him then? He's alive? He's all right?"

Wren nodded. Morgana rocked back on her boot heels. "I'm glad of that. Robin, the bastard, told me he'd thrown Kestrel's body into the Thames." Her face darkened. "What of the Robin? Have you seen him?"

"No."

Morgana gnawed at her lip as she wrung the cloth out in the water basin. "I don't think I can go back to Kestrel," she said. "I've been thinking. I'm not going in for the old life again."

Wren patted her shoulder. "Come see Kestrel. Talk."

She looked around her. "Well, I can't stay here, that's true. I can't afford to pay for it, for one thing. And I have a feeling Robin may know about it."

"And Greyfriars?"

Fresh pain washed over her. She lowered her eyes. "That's over. He's married."

"Maybe. Maybe not."

She frowned. "What does that mean?"

"Come. See Kestrel."

Sighing, she rose to her feet and began gathering her few possessions into a rucksack. "I suppose I should go and see how he is. He wouldn't have fallen into Robin's hands if it hadn't been for me."

"Maybe. Maybe not."

"Will you stop saying that, you magpie?" She smiled at her friend. "It's good to see you."

Wren grinned and gave a salute, then winced, touching the knot on his head.

"All right, my pathetic friend. Let's go."

Wren carried Kestrel's things and Morgana carried hers as they made their way through the streets to the White Stag. Morgana kept a sharp eye out the whole way, fearful of seeing a telltale red tunic or signs of anyone regarding them too closely. She saw no one.

The reunion at the White Stag was bittersweet. All three friends were worse for the wear of the past months. Kestrel was still weak and sick, Wren was tired and thin, and Morgana's spirits had all but been extinguished. But after they had greeted one another and Morgana had tended and fussed over the Kestrel for a bit, they sat down in the dim little room and looked at one another expectantly.

"Well?" Kestrel asked. "Did you tell her?"

Wren's eyes gained some of their lost twinkle. He shook his head.

"Oh, are we back to that?" Kestrel sighed and motioned for Morgana to sit nearer. "Our friend here is pretending he can't talk. But I tell you, lass, he can chatter like a starling when given reason."

"I know." Morgana shrugged, looking at her partner with fondness. "I just assumed he was waiting until he had something worthwhile to say."

"Most perceptive." Kestrel settled in, tucking his blankets in closer about him. "Your Lord Greyfriars paid me a visit."

Morgana looked down at her hands. "He's not *my* anything. He is married to Lady Winston, the same one who had me captured and you nearly killed."

"Mm. I'd have given good odds the man wasn't such a fool." Kestrel's fingers drummed on his thigh. "He loves you, Blackbird."

Morgana shook her head. "No."

"Ah, but he told me he does, not a month ago, in this very room."

Morgana looked at him, anger kindling in her eyes. "Then he was lying. He is most skilled at that art."

"Perhaps. But he had naught to gain by telling me that."

"What's that to me? I do not love him. What's more, he's wed. And he and his lady wife can go up in smoke, for all I care."

"A fitting condition, I'd say, at least for her. I know of this woman. I knew her long before she bedded her way to the title of Lady Winston." Kestrel's lip curled. "She'd pull out her own mother's hair just to dust off her shoes."

"She's dangerous. But she has what she wants now. He has what he wants. We can go on about our business." She pulled her rucksack into her lap. "I have all the plans we made here. With Wren's help, we can be doubly secure in ridding the countinghouse of its excess gold."

Wren shook his head. Morgana raised a brow. "You don't want a part of this? There's plenty for all, isn't there, Kestrel?"

"Aye. But I don't think our friend objects to our plan or its rewards." Kestrel gave a wry smile. "I think he objects to your protests regarding the Lord Greyfriars."

"Oh, give over," she groaned. "Wren, you know I have always told Phillip that there can be nothing between us. He has finally learned the lesson, that's all."

"You care." Wren crossed his arms.

She sighed. "Well, what if I did? It's done. Now, let's plan—"

"Go see him."

"What?" She looked at Kestrel, appealing for help. "Has he lost his wits?"

"Nay. Not our Wren. But he has been brother to Tom Black a long time. He knows your heart, even if you do not." Kestrel turned to Wren. "Is this not so? And what you want is for her to go and see Greyfriars one last time, to set all matters at rest?"

Wren nodded.

"Of all the ninny-pated, lame, foolhardy twaddle! You can't mean it. I won't go."

"Then we don't steal."

"Try and stop me!" she retorted. "I know all about this job and I'll do it alone, if I must. I need this money. You know that."

"I'll raise a hue and cry."

Morgana stared at Wren, feeling herself beginning to blaze with anger. "Why are you doing this?" Her voice dropped to a pained whisper. "What can it possibly gain you to put me through such an ordeal?"

"Go to him."

She looked again to Kestrel for aid. He shrugged. "Our Wren is as stubborn as any. But I've never known him to prove faithless. Perhaps he knows more than you or I?" He looked at the wall again. "Sometimes, Blackbird, it only takes a moment to change our fates. Take a moment now."

"It's cruel." The words came out in a choked sob.

Wren's eyes were soft, but his jaw was set. "Go."

"Damn you," she said softly. "I never thought this of you."

Wren stood and took up his cap and cloak. He donned them and then motioned to her to do the same with her own things. She stood, giving one last look to see if Kestrel would come to her aid. He sat silent, still gazing at the wall.

"All right," she said, snatching up her cloak. "Let's be off and get this over with."

They didn't speak as they made their way to the Strand and Elizabeth Winston's house. Morgana could scarcely believe what she was about to do. But her curiosity was piqued, as well as her anger and fear. Why had Wren been so insistent? Why hadn't the Kestrel come to her defense in what was obviously a foolhardy demand? There was something afoot, and obeying was the only way she would learn what it was.

The house was all too familiar, though it had been months since she had been here. This was where it had all started, all this trouble, she thought.

She and Wren pulled their hoods up to cover their faces as they neared the place. Wren motioned to her to take up a place to hide while he went to scout the house and its inhabitants.

He came back a short while later, smiling and rubbing his hands together. "He's alone."

"Wonderful," she said sourly. "This is my neck you're risking."

"Off," he said, making shooing motions. "Window at the side."

She followed where he pointed and found a window left open on one side of the house, facing into the shadows of the building next door. With one last baleful glance at her partner, she boosted herself up over the ledge and into a dim little hallway.

"Solar," Wren called in softly.

She sighed and moved in the direction of the solar, which she guessed to be toward the back of the house. Cursing herself for an idiot, she stole quietly along, praying that she encountered no servants, even if Elizabeth herself was elsewhere. She didn't doubt for a moment that

Elizabeth would be as good as her word about having her killed on sight if she was seen near Phillip again.

The door to the solar was slightly ajar. She peeked in and saw Phillip sitting before the fire, twisting a cup between his palms as he slouched in a chair. Even now, the sight of him caused her heart to leap up. She had memorized every inch of him and laid it all into her soul for safekeeping. She could never deny her love for him, or her desire. Still, she resolved she would keep her distance and guard her heart from yet another bitter betrayal.

Pressing the door open silently, she entered the room. She was just closing the door behind her when Phillip suddenly straightened in his chair. She froze, her hand still on the latch.

"Blackbird?" he whispered, his eyes still trained on the fire.

She shut the door. "Aye."

He leapt up. "Angel. You shouldn't have come here."

"This I know," she drawled. "But my hand was forced."

He scowled. "Elizabeth?"

"Wren."

His eyes went wide in surprise, then his wicked, devilish grin flashed out at her, causing her heart to leap up in joyous response. She fought to maintain her anger.

"So Master Wren has returned?" Phillip came closer. "That is good news indeed. But still, angel, it's dangerous for you to be here."

"Why?" she asked, her voice hardening. "Will your wife be here soon?"

"Aye."

She studied his face. There was no apology in his eyes, but neither was there any pleasure in his answer.

"Then you're right. I should be gone."

"Wait!"

She turned back.

"You wouldn't have come here if it hadn't been important," he said, coming to stand before her. "What is it that you wish to say to me?"

She felt such a sudden overwhelming need to touch him, to reach out to him, that her head almost seemed to spin. Why did her body always seem to wander off on its own course whenever she beheld him?

"I came to . . ." She was at a loss for words. Why had she come, indeed? Wren and Kestrel had insisted that she see him, talk to him. But now that she was here, she hadn't the faintest idea what to say. At least in words. Her body was shouting messages all its own, causing her cheeks to flush and her hands to moisten, her breath to quicken, her heart to beat like a rabbit's.

"I'm glad you came, sweet," Phillip said, reaching out to touch her cheek. "I'm glad to see you're well."

She jerked backward, out of his reach. "I am well. Better than ever."

"It's good to know it. I've been worried for you."

Her lip curled. "Oh, yes, I'm sure you have. Each night when you take your beloved Elizabeth into your arms, you must worry yourself senseless."

He looked stung for an instant, then stepped back, his jaw working in anger. "Is this what you've come for? To speak of Elizabeth?"

"No! I could not care less for her. Or you! I don't know why I came. So I'll be going now. I—"

She was cut off in mid-sentence by the sound of the latch. Elizabeth stood in the doorway, her eyes wide with shock and rage.

Phillip moved to stand in front of Morgana. She felt her heart begin hammering in her chest. What had she done?

"I told you if you ever came near me or my husband again," Elizabeth said, advancing on Morgana, "that I would see you torn apart and fed to my dogs."

"I was just leaving. He's all yours." Morgana gathered her cloak around her.

"You're going nowhere," Elizabeth snapped. "You took your chances by coming here to rekindle your nasty little affair with Lord Greyfriars and now you will pay the price."

"I want nothing from him. Or from you."

"Ah, but you will get something from me, I tell you that!"

"Elizabeth," Phillip said, warning in his voice. "She's done nothing. Let her go. You have what you want. And so have I." He reached out and caught Elizabeth's hand. "We can afford to be generous, you and I."

Morgana felt sick as Phillip moved quickly to slip his arm about Elizabeth's waist. It was true, then. He had been lying. He did not care about her. He was happy with his fine lady. So be it, she thought.

"Let me go," she said. "I want only to be as far away from you both as I can get."

Phillip's eyes flashed for a second, but were quickly shuttered as he looked to Elizabeth. "She's only a poor thief, my pet. And she's stolen nothing from us."

"Nor will she. I know what she was trying to steal. It will avail you nothing, wench," Elizabeth said. "Phillip and I are married. I have the prize you sought and I do not part with my possessions, especially not to the likes of dirt such as you. Good Lord!" Her violet-blue eyes went wide. "You didn't actually imagine he was in love with you, did you?" She began to laugh, her slender shoulders shaking. "You did! Oh, it's too rich for words!"

Morgana only stared at her, contempt rising to mingle with her fear. The woman was a monster.

"It is even as she says," Phillip said. "We are married."

"This I know. And I'll leave the two of you to each other and the devil." Morgana stepped toward the door. She jumped back as it flew open before her hand touched the latch.

"Not yet." Wren popped through and whipped off his cap with a flourish. "No wedding," he announced with a grin.

"What the devil is going on here? What is this man doing in my house? Durel!" Elizabeth began to shout. "Edgar!" She turned to Phillip. "Our house is beset with thieves! Kill them!"

Phillip pulled her close to his side. "I'll not let them harm you," he said blandly. "Wren, what are you talking about?"

Elizabeth sputtered, but Wren stepped up to Phillip with a nod. "There was no wedding." He looked to Elizabeth, then back to Phillip. "No marriage."

Elizabeth cried out in derision. "Fool! Everyone in London knows there was a wedding. Ask anyone! Ask Lord Elyot. He stood as our witness."

Wren shrugged. "Aye. Witness to a sham."

Phillip's eyes narrowed. "What are you saying?"

Wren whirled about and pointed to the back of his head. His hair was neatly tonsured, leaving a nest of pale skin at the crown of his head. Like a priest's.

"No," Phillip murmured.

"Oh, and here she is, my lord," Wren piped in a querulous tone. "A vision to please the eyes of the angels. A lucky man, my lord, you are this day. Come hither, daughter! Your bridegroom has been waiting here like a stallion fit to break down his paddock."

"This is impossible!" Elizabeth gasped.

"Oh, but my lady, surely you must know that thieves are everywhere," Wren continued. "And adventurers of all sorts. Bawdy women with their evil snares." He wiggled his brows in Elizabeth's direction. "It is all that we

333

can do to hold England for the Lord.''

"What the devil—Father Bernard! Wren! It was you?"
Phillip seized the small man by the collar.

Wren raised his hands for mercy, but he was nodding.
Morgana put her fists on her hips. "Will someone tell me
what you two madmen are chattering about?"

"Oh, you will love this, Blackbird!" Phillip's eyes
were bright with mischief. "The man actually had the
cheek to impersonate a friar! Have you ever heard of such
a thing?"

Morgana gaped. "So that was what happened to your
hair! Mice, indeed!"

Elizabeth ignored them both and flew at the Wren.
"You miserable worm! You made a mockery of my wedding vows!"

Phillip held her off. "He made no more of a mockery
than you did, lady." He pushed Wren gently to one side
and faced Elizabeth. "Your marriage to James Winston
was the most vicious and callous of mockeries. And he
died paying for it."

Elizabeth went white. "You! How dare you turn self-
righteous on me! You were in on it! You were my aide
and accomplice to James's pitiable end."

"Guilty as charged." Phillip's voice had changed from
merry and mocking to stone coldness. "Unwittingly, albeit, but I did have a hand in James's death and I will
carry that stain on my soul for eternity. But blacker still
was my sin in ever falling into your web, Lady Spider."

"My web! You mewling coward! You chased me with
all the hot eagerness of a lad with his first wench. It was
you that sought me out here in London, not long after
James's death. And it was you that suggested we be married. Don't speak to me about webs, Phillip, lest you entangle yourself in one of your own making!"

She shifted moods in the blink of an eye. Morgana
watched in amazement as she went from haughty warrior
to purring kitten.

334

"Phillip," she said softly. "How can you say these cruel things to me? Have I ever given you anything but sweetness? Have I not given you hours and hours of pleasure, not just here in my bed, but in every nook and corner of this house and yours? Haven't I looked to you for advice? Haven't I given up all other suitors in favor of you?" Tears sparkled in her eyes. "How can you side with this man who played such a vile trick upon us? And in God's holy church, besides?"

She had eased up to him, floated there. Now she stood just inches from him, her tear-starred eyes searching his with wide innocence.

"In God's holy church?" Phillip echoed. "Elizabeth, if indeed you ever were born with a soul, it was lost to God in your cradle."

Elizabeth cast about for a new weapon. "So. You married me to free this—this dirty little bitch of a thief. Surely you can't love her. Look at her! She's naught but a nasty bit of a strumpet who's no doubt spread her legs for every man in that so-called flock of hers."

Phillip only gazed at her with cold loathing.

"God, you and she were in on it, weren't you?" Elizabeth snarled. "Together, you and your low-born slut! How long were you planning to keep up this charade? How long before you had me murdered in my bed so that you could rut in the dirt with this black sow?"

"Murder is *your* game," Phillip said evenly. "How like you to think that everyone else's desires are as dark and twisted as your own."

"But you had no plan to remain with me."

Phillip's lips thinned and tautened. He shrugged. "My soul be cursed for it, but I did indeed plan to stay with you. I would not break a vow made before God."

"How noble. And now that those vows have been invalidated, I suppose you plan to be rid of me as fast as you can?"

Phillip nodded. "In the twinkling of an eye. I'm sorry, Blackbird," he said, turning to Morgana. "I had meant to stay with this monster to protect you from her. But after even this long in her company, I find I have no stomach for it. I will have to protect you some other way. I can't stay with this . . . this demon in silks."

Elizabeth was vibrating with rage. "Demon, am I? And what of the child I carry? Will your son be a demon as well?"

Silence hung in the room like a winter fog. Morgana felt her heart contract with pain. A child? Phillip's child? It was hideous.

At long last, Phillip spoke. "There is no child, lady."

"There is! Even now, he grows in my belly!"

"Nay. You believe yourself clever, but I know more of women than you imagine. Women love me, remember? They tell me all their secrets. And I know two of yours, witch. The first is that you use suppositories of cotton soaked in oils and repellents to block my seed from your womb. Did you think I wouldn't notice?" He crossed his arms over his chest. "And I know full well that a woman monthly bleeds. You have only just finished your time. I have not touched you since your sudden need to sleep alone, to avoid sharing a cough, as you so weakly put it. And your maidservant has been none too careful in carrying away the soiled cloths."

Elizabeth's pale face grew redder. "You vile, mewling, white-livered vomitus of Satan!" she hissed. "You're no man! Your knowledge of women betrays your true sex! I should have known it. A man who never raises his hand in anger. A man who never makes use of a blade! You were hot for me once, but you couldn't be asked to sully your hands with a bit of blood! So I had to make all the arrangements for James's death!" She whirled on Morgana. "It is no wonder that this one goes about dressed as a man. No doubt that is how he prefers it! And does he love you like a man? Or like a weak woman?''

Morgana only stared at her. The beautiful countenance, once so perfect and smooth, had grown red and mottled. The exquisite mouth was twisted into a sneer. The lovely blue eyes were muddy with venomous hate. Suddenly, Morgana knew. Phillip had been telling the truth. He did not love Elizabeth. All those times in which she had mentioned Elizabeth's name and seen anger and pain behind Phillip's eyes—now she understood. The woman was evil. And Phillip had consented to be yoked to her for life, for Morgana's sake alone. For her. For love.

She looked at Phillip. He was looking at her, waiting for her to speak. She only bit her lip, her eyes brimming with tears at the overwhelming love she felt for him. At last, she found her voice.

''You're an idiot, Greyfriars,'' she said tenderly.

''Better an idiot than a traitor to my love,'' he said with a shrug.

''Better a living traitor than this one's next victim.''

''Better a victim than an aide in your destruction.''

''Better leave this one to the devil.''

''Amen, sweeting.''

''What babbling nonsense is this?'' Elizabeth cried. ''You sound like utter fools.''

''My lady, that's the nicest thing you've ever said to me.'' Phillip gave her a sardonic grin. Elizabeth could only splutter.

''Come, Wren. Our business here is ended.'' Morgana started for the door. Phillip turned to follow her.

''Oh, yes, run!'' Elizabeth shrieked. ''But where will you go, Phillip? Where will you go, you and two dirty thieves? I can give you all up to the sheriff—nay, to the King!—in a moment!''

Phillip shook his head. ''I no longer care, Elizabeth. A month in your house was not only long enough to sour my soul but it also allowed me to discover several other secrets of yours.''

"What secrets? If you mean Lord Fray, don't even dream of it. He loves me yet and he will hear of no evil against me.''

Phillip slung his cloak over his shoulders. "I have no need of him, though your visits to his bed while you and I were wed will not endear you to him any more than they did to me. He was one who didn't know of our nuptials, as I understand it. Or did you just lie to him about me?''

Elizabeth clenched her fists. "What, then? Are you planning to tell him? Say something, damn you!''

Phillip only guided Morgana ahead of him to the door. Wren brought up the rear, his hand rubbing slyly over his bald spot.

"I will see the lot of you in hell!" Elizabeth screamed. "Count this hour as your last! No one betrays me! No one leaves me!''

"Not alive," Phillip said softly.

He pulled the door shut just as something shattered against the wall. He urged Morgana toward the entryway. "Let's be off. She will have her revenge, somehow. We'd best make plans for your safety.''

"And what of yours?" Morgana asked as they hurried out the front door.

"I don't think she'll try to touch me just yet. My family has too much power. But she will most assuredly try to wound me by harming you. That's why you have to get out of here. Out of London. I'm sending you to Wildhurst.''

Morgana stopped dead on the street. "Wildhurst? You're mad! Your family will be shamed beyond all reckoning.''

"Let them be so. As long as they have money and influence at court, their house and horses and hounds, they'll survive anything.''

"No! I'm staying here to see that you are safe."

"I appreciate your concern, sweet. But I will be able to work more easily and with more cunning if I am not worried about you. And what I have to do cannot be accomplished with you at my side, however much I may want to bind you there."

"Then I'll go to Cygnet House."

Phillip shook his head. "That's the first place that Elizabeth will look for you. She'll never believe that I sent you to Wildhurst, for the same reasons that you do not wish to go. What's more, there are far more people at Wildhurst and far more security. I will place you in my sister's special care, and no one would dare harm a ward of Judith Redmayne, wife to Lord Gregory of Willamton, daughter of the Marquess of Wildhurst and the Viscountess of Thorne, brother to the Viscount Greyfriars."

"Titles won't turn aside a stealthy blade," Wren put in.

"True enough. You've done me more than one kindness, Wren, especially this last in bringing Morgana here to hear the truth. I will repay all, if I can, but I'm asking for yet another favor. Go with her now. You may take on whatever guise you wish so that you may have the freedom to watch over her at all times. Will you do so?"

Wren thought a moment. Then, when it seemed that he couldn't come up with a better solution, he nodded.

Phillip shook his hand. "It is well. Let's be off now, to Peter Elyot's. You leave at once."

"And what will you do?"

"I will see that Elizabeth the viper is rendered toothless for all time."

Morgana shivered at the sight of Phillip so utterly cold and bitter. This was dangerous business. She had to find a way to help him. And she couldn't do that miles away at Wildhurst.

* * *

Robin was nursing a hangover of prodigious strength when Gerald Durel found him at last. Lady Winston had paid him handsomely to stay away from the Blackbird for two months, and he had drunk at least half of his fee already. If this was to keep up, he thought, he might actually have to go to work again.

But Durel showed up just in time.

"My mistress has already found the girl," Durel told him. "She'll be in our hands before the day is out."

"Then what do you need me for?"

"My lady wishes to make a present of her to you, for all your good services to her. That is, of course, after she has served her purpose to us."

Robin licked his dry lips. "That again. Will there be anything left after that?"

Durel looked at him without amusement. "Do you want her or no?"

"Aye, I want her." He swallowed some ale, hoping to chase off the dog that was still biting him. "Oh, I want her, all right."

"Good. Then come with me now. I have horses waiting."

Chapter Twenty

There had been so little time. First, Phillip had whisked her off to Lord Elyot's house, where, at Phillip's insistence, she had changed into women's clothes for the trip to Wildhurst. They had dined with Peter Elyot, who seemed at first shocked, then relieved and amused by this recent turn of events in his friend Phillip's tempestuous life. Morgana decided she liked Elyot, who was courteous without being pompous and who clearly admired and cared for Phillip.

But there was no time to form any further assessments. Phillip bundled her up in a fur-lined cloak, added more warm clothes to Wren's wardrobe, and hustled them both out to a wagon waiting at the back of the house. He led Morgana aside and laid his hands on her shoulders.

"Sweet, it won't be long. I have to make sure that Elizabeth cannot touch either one of us. You'll be safe at Wildhurst, and my family will love you." He grinned. "You and Judith will make a pair, I trow. I wish I could be there when you meet." He gathered her quickly into his arms. "I love you, angel. I'll come to you as quickly as I can."

Morgana buried her face in his shoulder and let the sweetness of his embrace soak into her. God, she had longed for this moment for so long!

With a hard but hurried kiss, that sweetness was snatched from her again. Phillip whirled her away to Wren, who helped her up into the wagon and took the reins. Then he was slapping the horses' rumps, sending them along, carrying her away from him and to safety.

Morgana peered out a crack in the heavy canvas sides of the wagon until she could see no more of him. She sat back as they rattled through the streets of the city and began to plan.

By the time they had reached the Cripplegate, her scheme was set. She waited until they were out on the road, alone. Then, murmuring a prayer and an apology, she took the stick from beneath her skirts and neatly knocked Wren out cold. She took the reins and drew the wagon up under a tree.

"Sorry, old friend," she murmured as she trussed him up. "But you're too soft on me. I'll send Kestrel or Fletcher to you as soon as I get back to London."

She stripped off her fine woolen gown and put on some of Wren's clothes. She cut one of the horses loose from the traces and mounted up, bareback. It wasn't a long ride back to London. She'd be at the Stag long before night fell.

She urged the horse into a trot but found it hard going without a saddle. She decided to sacrifice a little time in favor of being able to walk once she reached London, and slowed the horse's pace.

The wagon was out of sight behind her when she heard hoofbeats on the road from that direction. She glanced over her shoulder and saw only a pair of travelers, trotting along and chatting to one another.

She looked ahead and saw another pair approaching. She urged herself to stay calm as she looked about for an escape.

A third pair emerged from the woods to her right, from the west. She swallowed hard. It was a trap. She kicked her horse and left the road, heading east. If she could make it to the woods, she might lose them.

They came on like the wind. There was no shouting or calling, but slowly, surely, they formed a circle about her and began to close in.

She urged her horse on, but she felt the lack of a saddle, and the horse was more worker than racer. She was soon surrounded, hemmed in, and forced to follow wherever they pressed her.

She was caught again. And there was little doubt in her mind that her luck had run out.

Morgana watched as Elizabeth paced the room. It was baffling to see someone so lovely harboring such venom inside. Even though Morgana knew that Elizabeth would end her life in a heartbeat, she still couldn't take her eyes off the woman's ethereal beauty.

"Why do you stare at me like that?" Elizabeth demanded.

Morgana shrugged, unwilling to fuel her captor's anger.

It didn't matter. Elizabeth could manufacture ammunition out of thinnest air. "Don't tell me that dressing as a boy has made you as lustful as a lad," she taunted. "Wouldn't that take Phillip aback, to know that you fancied me rather than him? Or was it that his little thief fancied him in the way of the ancient Greeks?"

Morgana remained silent.

"I suppose you think I'm mad."

No reply.

Elizabeth sneered. "Phillip does. Though I imagine with you out of the way, he might be persuaded to think again about me. Men are such weathercocks. All of them, to a man, are led by what's beneath their codpieces." She shot a sour glance at Morgana. "But, of course, you'd know all about that, wouldn't you? Living with men, sleeping in the woods with them, luring them into your snares just to rob them." She laughed. "I see I've hit upon it, haven't I?"

She came to stand before Morgana, her hands on the sides of the chair. "You see it now, don't you?" she asked, her voice soft but throbbing with excitement. "You and I are one and the same. We both want Phillip, for our own reasons. We both play tricks for our livelihood. It just happens that I play the game for far greater takings than you. But we both have used our bodies and our wits for gain. And why shouldn't we? What have *they* ever done for us?"

Morgana felt the heat in her cheeks as Elizabeth's glimmering eyes studied hers. The woman's words had hit home. She had indeed used her body as a lure on the highways. That was how she and Wren had first encountered Phillip. She did employ tricks to make her living. She played games of hide and seek, of charades. She was like Elizabeth.

The shame of it was like a hot coal in her stomach. Cedric had been right in the names he'd called her all those long nights ago. She was a whore, whether she admitted it or not.

Elizabeth peered at her; then her mouth turned down in disgust. "But you still think men are fair and just, don't you? You think that women shouldn't be allowed to look out for themselves, just as men do." She pushed away from the chair. "God, it's too rich. But you wouldn't be so forgiving if you'd had to live through what I have." She resumed her pacing.

"Men have always tried to use me for their own purposes. My own father was the first to have me. I fought him for a while and then put his dirty little needs to use to gain enough money to get out of his house for good. I was too young and stupid, though, and I ended up in a brothel soon after, working on my back for a pittance while yet another man took my earnings. I learned fast, though, believe me. I soon found a man who would take me up into society. And after him, another. And after him—my first big prize. Marriage with Lord James Winston." She laughed. "The fellow was so besotted with me I swear he thought I was a virgin on our wedding night. And don't you think I didn't take pains to make it appear so. I still carry the tiny scar on the inside of my thigh where I cut myself to make certain he saw virgin's blood on us both and on our bedsheets that night."

Morgana watched, sickened at the twisted tale that was unfolding. There were indeed strong parallels to her own fate. The advances of a father, the runaway to the streets. The bitter fear and anger at men for the crime they had committed against her. She hated it.

She wanted to run, to be anywhere but here, listening to this madwoman's ranting that could so easily be her own. But she couldn't. She had to stay and hear it out.

"Jamie was a milksop," Elizabeth said, shrugging her shoulders as if casting him off like an old cloak. "If it hadn't been for his fortune, I would have settled for marriage with another, more fiery lover, his friend Tristan Carrowe."

Morgana stiffened at the name. Tristan Carrowe had but recently wed her cousin, Ariane. Did Ariane know aught of Elizabeth's connection with her new husband?

"But Tristan was not the viscount, only the younger brother, and he led me to Jamie. Jamie, in his turn, got me presented at court, and it was there I met Phillip. No one compares to Phillip as a lover, wouldn't you agree?

Don't you wish that men could just stay in their places as bed partners and allow us women to get on with the business of running the world? Life would be so much simpler.''

Morgana hated even the faintest hint that Elizabeth and Phillip had ever been lovers. Though she knew that Phillip now despised Elizabeth, the smallest, dimmest image of the two of them embracing made her ill with jealousy and pain. She hoped that Elizabeth would move off the topic soon.

''Still, Phillip served his purpose, too. He provided me with my alibi on the night James was killed. Everyone saw us together, all of the servants bore witness that we retired to my bedchamber together and were heard to be engaged in rather enthusiastic sport. All night long.'' Elizabeth slid her a glance and gave a brief, silvery laugh. ''The word and reputation of Phillip Greyfriars is unimpeachable. He spoke right up in my defense, after James's body was found. Poor idiot. He simply was too in love to do otherwise.''

She frowned. ''I thought he and I would be married, then, since Jamie was out of the way. I would have settled for being viscountess until his father gave up the ghost. But Phillip turned squeamish when it was noised about that he and I were not only cuckolding old Jamie but that he and I might have had a hand in his death. Phillip's liver is too white, girl, remember that. He has no stomach for blood. He'll not draw a drop on your behalf or his own, you may depend upon it. Not like his brother. Now, there was a man. Pity his hand slipped that last time. Thomas would have been a worthy mate for me.''

Morgana shifted in the chair. She was growing weary of sitting and listening to Elizabeth's ranting. The bonds at her wrists were so tight they were beginning to cut off the blood to her hands. How much longer was the woman going to go on, recounting her sordid glories? If she was to die, she'd rather be done with it.

"So, that is how I came to London and set up house-keeping on my own, grieving widow as I was. It wasn't long, though, before Phillip was back from his travels, knocking at my door, begging to be my consort once again. I let him, of course, even though I had met another who outranked him in power and wealth. It wouldn't do to throw out such a rich fish as Phillip, even as I cast my nets for a bigger one. If I should fail in my mission to win Lord Fray, I would still have Phillip. And he would be the perfect cover for my affair with Lord Fray. All of London society knew that I was in love with Phillip and he with me. It was so simple."

Elizabeth picked up a vase and smashed it against the wall. "But that was ruined! Some snake-hearted, jealous person tattled on Fray and me and there we were, caught in bed together, in front of his wife, his friends, and half the royal court." She stood, shoulders shaking with the effort to master her rage. "And there I was, also, my finances in ruins. My future shattered! And Phillip insisting he wouldn't marry me to save me either from ruin or scandal."

She rounded on Morgana. "But you know all about this part, don't you? You were just the prod I needed to make Phillip see things my way. I showed such mercy and set you free, but your wretched little friend tricked us into that sham marriage. Off goes Phillip with his dirty strumpet."

There came a knock at the door. Morgana praised the heavens for the respite as Elizabeth went to answer it and confer with a servant in the hall. She looked about the room. It was an old hunting lodge, she guessed, long past its prime and falling into decay. The windows were higher than Morgana could jump, and the walls too smooth to climb. There was only one door, and Elizabeth would surely have it guarded. Still, if she could get her hands

347

free, she might have a chance to fight her way out, perhaps taking Elizabeth as a hostage.

She groaned inwardly. She was dreaming. It was as hopeless a situation as she could imagine. She would simply have to wait and see what Elizabeth had in store for her.

Speak of the devil and up she pops, she thought to herself. Elizabeth had returned.

"It shan't be long now," she said briskly. "But I wanted you to know that you may have fooled Phillip and everyone else, but not me. I know all about you, *Lady* Langland. All about you and your traitorous family."

She giggled at Morgana's proud stare. "Ah. I see you won't deny it. Do you know what else I know about you, chit? You're also Morgana Bracewell, daughter of Cedric Bracewell, a mere grocer. You stabbed the man some five years ago and fled his house, taking all the money he had in his coffers. You'd hoped you'd killed him, but it was not to be. So you've been in hiding from him ever since. There's a pretty price on your head for his attempted murder alone, not to mention what I could get from the sheriff for surrendering one of the infamous Kestrel's flock."

Morgana felt her hands growing cold and not just from the straps at her wrists. What did this monster have in mind? What else did she know about her past?

"I am prepared to be magnanimous, however. My guess is that your stepfather is as big a bastard as ever my father was and that you had good reason for stabbing him." She grinned in triumph, though Morgana had not thought that she had betrayed any emotion on her face. "It is even as I thought. You wanted to murder him, didn't you?"

Morgana pressed her lips together. She wanted to shriek at Elizabeth to get on with this, just name her scheme and be about it. Why did Elizabeth care about her so much? What use was it to prolong this chat?

"Yes, you did want to murder him. You did. As I murdered my father. How alike we are. How odd that we should have Phillip Greyfriars to bring us together. But where I succeeded and even covered my deed, you blundered and were made twice an outlaw. And that fate has followed you and brought you here to me."

Morgana gave a weary sigh. "I am here, yes. Now, perhaps you will get on with it? Or do you plan to talk me to death?"

Elizabeth's face mottled with anger. "Shut your mouth, whore!" she hissed. "I'll tell you when I'm finished! You just sit there and listen, or I'll change my plans and cut you to such an extent that Phillip will vomit just to look upon you!"

Morgana held her silence. Patience was her only ally. She had to hold on.

"That's better," Elizabeth cooed. "You're learning. As I was saying, fate has brought you to me. And I will be avenged for all the tricks you've played on me, you and your precious Phillip."

"You're insane."

"Am I?" Elizabeth considered this for a moment, then shrugged. "So many people have said that. I believe it's just jealousy. I'm beautiful, I'm smart, I'm wealthy, and soon to be even wealthier and more powerful than almost anyone in the kingdom, even the Queen." She smiled. "An old friend of yours will soon arrive. Another one of those ridiculous bird-persons. Robin, I believe you call him."

Morgana could feel the last heat draining from her body, chilling her to the heart. Robin. She should have known. She should have seen this coming.

Elizabeth looked with bright-eyed interest at her suddenly whitened face. "So. You recall him? And you recall that he has a debt he wishes to repay?"

Steady, Morgana told herself. *Hold onto your calm.* If nothing else, she would go out with some pride.

"Oh, my. Still so haughty? How can it be that one who lives in the very gutter where piss and garbage run all day can be so prideful? Well, never mind. You won't feel so mighty when your loving swain is forced to watch while you're pinned beneath the churning behind of that clod, Robin."

"What?"

"Ah, so she does speak."

Morgana struggled for breath. Phillip? Phillip here, watching as Robin exacted his revenge on her? She felt screams welling up inside her, bursting to get out. But she couldn't. She couldn't move, couldn't utter a sound.

"Oh, dear, struck dumb again. Well. No matter. You won't need to say a word."

Elizabeth turned to leave. Morgana managed to summon breath.

"Please, don't do this," she whispered. "If you've ever had any feelings for Phillip, don't make him a witness to this. I'll do all you ask. I'll leave him forever! I swear it." Morgana lowered her voice. "You're right. You and I have much in common. I don't want to die and I don't want my future lost to the wrath of either Robin or the Greyfriars family. I want to be free to gain whatever I can in this world, just as you do. Let me go and it will be as if I had died to Phillip. You can get him back! You're so lovely and desirable. And I promise before God and all that's holy that I'll never—"

"Oh, please, spare me your begging. You and I have too much in common. You are as full of desire for gain as I. That's why I can't do this any other way. You're a murderess and a liar and a whore and a thief. So am I. You can't imagine that I don't know that you'd go back on your word the instant I set you free? You've already played too many tricks on me." Elizabeth shook her head.

350

"No, there's nothing for it but to play out my scheme. It's the only way I can be sure that you're ruined forever."

"He will hate you for this."

"Mayhap. But he will learn his lesson for good and all. Same as you."

There was a knock at the door. Elizabeth called out, "Come!"

One of the men who had captured and tied Morgana stuck his head in the door. "Begging your pardon, m'lady, but Lord Greyfriars is less than a mile away."

"Is he alone?"

"As far as we can tell, yes. He's been followed all the way from London and we've seen no one else."

"Good. Go get my other guest now. See that Lord Phillip is brought here as soon as he arrives."

"As you wish, lady."

The man bowed his way out and shut the door. Elizabeth whirled around, clapping her hands. "He's almost here! Oh, this shall be a most merry meeting."

Morgana felt her heart thudding dully in her chest. There had to be a way out of this! There had to be! She couldn't stay here and face Robin, or Phillip. Elizabeth danced out of the room, leaving two guards in her place.

Morgana felt as if the walls were moving, drawing in upon her, ready to crush her where she sat. She thought about all that she'd been through since the day her father rode away to battle Henry Bolingbroke. She'd been the pawn of a king, a lust-ridden stepfather, a crazy woman, and now a violent, vicious enemy. She'd been betrayed and hurt, imprisoned and threatened, tortured and torn from all she'd ever loved. Time and again, the fates had ripped and torn at her life, taking their toll with gleeful abandon.

Morgana began to feel heat within her once again, growing in the pit of her stomach. She'd been treated as a pawn in Elizabeth's sick games. She'd been a pawn too often. A victim too many times.

It was over.

She wanted to shout it.

She was through with being a victim. Though she died for it, and like as not she would, she would die fighting with every ounce of her strength and every scrap of her wits.

She sat back in the chair, taking deep breaths, calming herself. She focused her thoughts on iron and steel, and also on the dodging, leaping swiftness of a deer in full flight. She imagined herself a falcon, soaring over her prey and taking it with viselike claws. She was a blackbird, swift, clever, a survivor.

She was ready.

And then she saw him.

Phillip was cursing himself for a fool for the thousandth time. He'd been clever enough to find where Elizabeth had gone to ground, but not clever enough to save himself from being caught by her men before he could reach her. He'd been taken on the road, bound and blindfolded and led, he assumed, into the old hunting lodge that had once belonged to James Winston.

What game was the woman up to now? Would she dare to harm the Viscount Greyfriars? Even she wouldn't be so stupid.

He hoped.

Praise God, Morgana had agreed at last to go to Wildhurst. He'd sent word to Judith that she was coming and that she was by no means to be left unattended for even a moment—both for her protection and to prevent any chance that his blackbird might once again fly away. He only hoped he'd come out of this business whole and alive and able to return to her.

"Good morrow, Phillip."

"Elizabeth." He turned in the direction of her voice. "I wish I could say well met, but you'll understand if I do not."

"No. No, I most surely understand. Just as you'll understand if I don't stay to play hostess to you. I have other matters to attend. But you make yourself comfortable, my lord. And I hope my little entertainment will be amusement enough in my absence."

Hands grabbed him from behind and pulled him into a chair. His hands were unbound, only to be tied again to each arm of the chair.

"There. I believe that will do." Elizabeth was close to him now. "Fare thee well, Phillip. Remember me always."

"I shan't forget you, pet. Every time I see a fire lit, I'll think of you, dancing barefoot on the coals."

She slapped him and then gave a throaty chuckle. "You're the one who'll be squirming over the coals, love. And much sooner than you imagine."

He heard the rustle of her skirts as she brushed past him. Heavy footsteps followed her out of the room. He was alone.

Or was he?

He thought he heard breathing. "Who's there?"

There was a scraping sound, as of a foot on the floor. But that was all.

"Come now, Elizabeth," he said. "Isn't blind man's bluff a bit childish for the likes of us?"

There was no reply.

Then the door opened behind him once more. Heavy boots clumped into the room and crossed the floor. Soft hands, hands he knew, were removing his blind.

"Enjoy, my love," Elizabeth whispered and fled the room, laughing her sweet, tinkling laugh.

"Well a day," said Robin. "If it ain't my two favorite folk, right here. The Blackbird and—" He turned and grinned at Phillip. "And the Raven."

Phillip lunged up, but the heavy chair counterbalanced him and he crashed back onto the seat.

"Morgana!" he cried out. "No!"

She had been gagged. She couldn't make a sound and the cloth was choking her besides. Her hands were bound, but not her feet.

Robin was here.

So was Phillip.

Panic and shame began to well up in her, but she fought them back. She wasn't going to abandon her plan. She was ready. She would grant no quarter.

She had managed to work one hand half out of her bonds while waiting for Robin. She was still seated in the chair, but her belt and boots had been taken from her. She knew that any chance she might have would depend on surprise, for Robin was more than her match in strength. She allowed her shoulders to sink and her head to bow low, her eyes on Robin's feet as he swaggered over to stand before her.

"Oh, this is a pretty scene. The haughty Blackbird brought low—by a lady, yet." He licked his lower lip. "Serves you right for goin' about as a boy and bein' so unnatural. If you'da been more like you shoulda been, I might've overlooked all you done against me in the band." He spread his hands. "But, then, you wouldn't have been in the flock at all if you'd been goin' about like a woman."

Morgana let out a sniffle. Robin chuckled. "That's right. Not so proud, now, are ya? Well, that's all right. You just forgot yourself for a time." He glanced around at Phillip. "And him, too. But I'm here—" He removed his belt. "I'm here to teach you all about what's what. Like what a woman's real job is."

Morgana felt her flesh crawling as Robin took off his surcoat and stood before her, his shirttails loose. He was as grimy as ever, and she could smell the stale stench of his sweat as he moved.

"Morgana."

His voice almost undid her. She wanted to scream at him to be still, to let her believe she was alone, that she could handle this. But his voice, so full of pain for her, so beckoning, cut her heart.

But there was nothing she could do. And she wasn't going to lose this moment. Robin bent to pull at the fastenings on her tunic. With all her might, she thrust upwards with her clasped hands, striking him just under the nose.

His head flew back and she leaped to her feet, swinging again. This time, she aimed for the side of his head. With a satisfying thud, her fists met his ear and he screamed in pain.

He grabbed for her in his rage and caught her to his chest, his nose bleeding profusely. This time there was no impediment to her legs. She raised her knee and slammed home with all the power of a flying brick.

Robin curled over with a gurgling cry. She danced out of his grasp, heading for Phillip.

"Behind you!" he cried.

She whirled, just in time to catch a scratch from the knife-blade that Robin had drawn. He was still clutching his privates with one hand, doubled over, but he was coming at her with the rage and power of a maddened bull. She danced out of his way again, light on her bare feet, but he was backing her, inexorably, toward the far wall, making wide, wild slashes in the air before her.

She tried to look for anything she might use as a weapon. There was nothing. She couldn't keep on backing away. She had to mount an offensive.

She dove, throwing herself at Robin's knees. The impact toppled him backward, but he kept hold of his blade. She scrambled up before he could right himself and flew to Phillip's side.

"Angel, don't—save yourself—"

"Help me," she shouted. "Grab the cord!"

Phillip needed no further instructions. He seized the loosened end of her wrist-cord and yanked so hard it nearly pulled her into his lap. Her hand was scraped raw but she was almost free.

"Bitch!" Robin roared, staggering their way. "I'll cut you to strips!"

She backed up again, still tearing at the cords. It was no use. They were too tight. She made her decision.

"Come get me," she taunted. "Come get me with your little 'soldier,' you rotted bag of horse-dung!"

He lunged. Phillip shouted in fear as Morgana raised her hands to the blade. With one slice, Robin freed his prey. Morgana danced away once more.

Phillip was tearing at his own bonds. He had to help her. She was fast and she had her hands, but she was no match for either Robin's strength or the glittering edge of his knife.

His eye fell on a bottle on the table nearby. If he could get to it . . .

Morgana was beginning to tire. She was bleeding from her arm and her hand where the knife had nicked her in cutting her cords. Her feet were sore from scraping over the rough stones of the floor. Robin, for all his bulk, was dogged and tireless. He kept up a steady assault, pressing her here and there, keeping her on the move.

If she could only get him down once more, perhaps she could get his blade. But she didn't think she could fool him again by diving at his feet. He stayed just far enough away to keep his footing, while still dodging in to menace her. She had to trip him somehow.

356

She heard thumping on the floor. She knew it must be Phillip but she couldn't spare him a glance. If only he could get free . . .

She shook off the thought. She wasn't looking for a rescue. She'd fight this fight, even to the death. The victory would be hers, whatever the outcome.

With renewed energy, she changed tactics on Robin. She lunged for him, as if she were attacking. He swung for her but stepped aside, trying to avoid another tackle. She forced him sideways, then dodged the other way, forcing him to shift his weight to chase her.

"Getting tired of this yet?"

"I'll still have enough strength to screw straight through you, bitch!"

She laughed and lunged for him again. He brought the knife up, inches from her breast, but she was too quick. She leaped to the side and Robin stumbled, falling over Phillip in his haste.

Phillip kicked out, and Robin screamed as the heavy boot smashed into his ribcage. He rolled away but Phillip caught him again, this time in the jaw. Morgana darted in, grabbed the bottle, and smashed it. She dropped the jagged bottom half in Phillip's lap and brandished the neck herself.

"All right now," she said to Robin, who was on his feet again. "Here's something more like a fight, you mewling coward."

He gave a bellow of rage and charged. She slashed out at his wrist, trying to get him to drop the knife. He twisted away just in time.

She pressed forward, taking the offensive once more. Her quick, darting thrusts caught him time and again, slashing his clothes, nicking the skin, but she could get no purchase.

He was sweating, his hair plastered to his forehead. Her lungs felt scorched by the constant motion, the lunges and

357

retreats. She didn't know how much longer she could go on, but she didn't care. She wouldn't give up. She was going to fight this to the last gasp of breath and drop of blood.

She gathered her energies and leaped past him, barely escaping the knife. Robin came about to face her just as Phillip raised his chair and swung it, with crashing power, against the back of Robin's head.

Robin staggered forward and impaled himself on Morgana's upraised bottle. He gave a gasp of horror as the sharp edges penetrated his breast to the heart. She dropped the neck of the bottle and leaped back as he crashed to the floor at her feet.

She stood, frozen, for a long moment. Then she looked at Phillip, who stood also, the chair still in his upraised hands.

She moved at last, going cautiously to feel if Robin was truly dead, as he appeared. She crossed herself and got to her feet. She raised her eyes to Phillip's.

"I love you," she whispered. And began to sob uncontrollably.

Phillip was there in an instant, holding her, kissing her, taking her into his lap on the floor. She let herself be taken up into his comfort, his love, and allowed wave upon wave of release and grief to wash over her in the safety of his arms.

She raised her head at last and wiped the tears that covered her cheeks. "Not bad chair work," she said. "For a man of silk."

He gave a short laugh. "Remind me never to trust you with a broken bottle," he said. "Not only did you finish yon dung-heap Robin, but you nearly unmanned me when you tossed that shard into my lap!"

A smile quirked at the edges of her mouth. "A sorry state for the Viscount Greyfriars."

"A sorrier one for my viscountess-to-be." He took her hand.

She looked at him and shook her head. "No. Don't start that now." She shot a glance at the Robin's still form. "It's no good here."

"You're right." He rose, taking her with him. "And there is still a viper yet to be crushed."

Morgana felt a chill race down her spine at his words. Elizabeth had outwitted them both so many times. Could she bear to let Phillip risk his life again? His soul? Elizabeth had, in her ramblings, told her all she had wondered about Phillip's past and his ties to Elizabeth. Despite his humor and his charm, he was a man with pride and a conscience. And if anyone understood the pain of being another's victim, it was she. He'd been there for her. She'd do as much for him.

She took up Robin's knife and nodded to Phillip. He pulled up one of the broken chair legs and held it at the ready as they went to the door.

They expected to find guards waiting in the hall, but the place was deserted. Morgana looked at Phillip. "I don't like this."

"I don't either. Elizabeth must know that her game went awry. She may be waiting outside for us."

"And she may be in Scotland by now."

"May you be right, love. God help the Scots."

They gained the front door of the lodge and peered out. "I don't see anyone." Morgana shrugged.

"But that doesn't mean they aren't there. Come. Let's see what the stable holds."

It held an old donkey and not much else. Phillip looked at the beast with pity. "Poor old fellow. We can't leave him out here if Elizabeth doesn't come back."

"We can't leave him if she does. I wouldn't trust her with man or beast."

"Right. Come on, Lightning. Let's be off." Phillip untied the donkey's bridle. "I don't know that he'll bear you. He's been half-starved."

"I don't need to ride. I can walk."

"Madwoman. Look at yourself."

She looked down. Her hand and arm still dripped blood. Her clothes were torn and cut in several places. She was barefoot and her feet were scraped and bruised. "Well, you're not much prettier!"

He grinned. "Never that, love. But I have more of my blood still inside my flesh and I think that should be our criteria. Don't you agree, Lightning?"

The donkey gave a wheezy sigh but stood patiently, waiting for his burden. Phillip took Morgana about the waist and lifted her up on the beast's rough back. She went without a protest, suddenly weary and sad.

She looked about the stables once more. "Phillip!"

He halted. "What?"

"Does she have Saracen?"

"She or one of her minions."

"Damn the woman! Now I know I hate her!"

Phillip stared at her sudden vehemence and then laughed long and loud.

"What's so humorous?"

"You. The woman has kidnapped you, harmed your friends, nearly has you raped and murdered, but you're not angry until she steals a horse!" He chuckled. "God save me, you're the most wonderfully cockeyed woman I've ever known."

Morgana glared at him. "Not just any horse. Saracen. He's—"

"Yes? He's what?"

"He's a friend," she muttered.

"A friend. My word. Has my rose caught my madness?" he asked the donkey. "She's begun to view animals as human beings."

360

He stole a glance her way, his smile flashing in all its wicked delight. She pressed her lips together to keep from returning it. The man was arrogant enough, she told herself, and at her expense, besides. She wasn't going to encourage him, no matter how wonderful he looked striding beside her, his dark head uncovered, his hair rippling in the breeze.

"Do you know where we are?" she asked him at last.

"Yes. We're near the Wye, not far from Clifford. Do you recall it?"

She looked puzzled for a moment. Then she gasped. "The Ruggles! No, no, Greyfriars, you're not going to get me to dance again. Nor tell fortunes. I just won't—"

"Peace, sweet. Elizabeth may have my horse, but she did not remember to take my purse." He slid a devilish glance her way. "Not an oversight you'd make, my love."

She smacked him playfully on the shoulder. "I haven't stolen anything from you in months."

"I beg to differ."

"What do you mean? I have nothing of yours!"

He kept silent but turned to look at her, a look of such intense heat and love in his eyes that she was shaken. She would have to be on her guard or her heart would be shattered forever.

He said nothing, only walked along beside the donkey until they came to a fast-running stream where they could rinse themselves off and tend to Morgana's wounds. They drank the cool water, let the donkey crop a bit of grass, then resumed their journey.

Elizabeth was seething. She had counted on that stupid Robin fellow to do the job for her, but it seemed that the little black-haired witch-girl had some magical protection about her. She might have known Phillip would have his usual luck, but she hadn't counted on the girl being so fierce a fighter.

She cantered along on Phillip's fine stallion, gaining ground toward London at good speed. It was a chilly day, with a thin, cold sun. From somewhere overhead, she heard the high, shrill cry of a hawk. Someone must be hunting on James's land, she thought. Poachers.

She tossed the thought aside. She couldn't think about that now. She was in grave trouble. Her victims would survive and tell the tale to anyone who would listen, instead of dying in a tragic lover's quarrel at an out-of-the-way hunting lodge, as she had planned. She would either have to go underground or throw herself at the mercy of some of her former friends at court. If she could just get to them before Phillip and his strumpet could get back to London, she might gain some ground. It would be a struggle, but she was used to that.

She wasn't going back to the streets, she told herself. She'd come too far, had paid too high a price to give up now. She had tasted what life could be if she just played her game aright, and it was sweeter than any honey. It was what she was made for, what was her due. She'd give it up on her deathbed, old and wealthy and powerful. And even then, she thought, she might find a way to take some of it with her.

She was thirsty. She slowed the horse and came to a stop beneath a bare oak. She climbed down and opened Phillip's saddlebags for a drink.

A powerful hand reached out and covered hers before she could reach inside. She gasped and jerked about.

"You!" she breathed.

"That's right, Bess," the man said. "It's me."

She stepped back against Saracen's broad flank. "What do you want?"

"Oh, come now. Is that any way to greet an old friend?"

362

"You're no friend. I left you long ago."

"I recall. I wasn't rich enough for you. Nor powerful enough."

He reached out and flicked one of her silken tresses. She cringed.

"What's wrong, Bess?" he murmured. "Afraid I might be here to collect a debt?"

"I owe you nothing."

"No? What about Ben Truscot? What about James Winston? Do you think they're happier in their graves than alive and free as you?"

"I didn't kill them."

"No. You merely made sure that someone else did the deed for you. I don't know who did poor Lord Jamie, but I know who did Ben Truscot, don't I, Bess?"

She tried to strike out at him. He caught her hand and pinned her, easily. "I wouldn't even dream of trying it," he said softly. "You know I'm a killer, don't you, Bess, my girl? And you know who made me so."

She sneered. "You didn't have to kill Truscot."

"No, my soul be damned for it, I didn't. But I was sick in love with you and fancied you cared for me as well. You're the finest actress ever lived, I think. I only wonder how many others have been snared by your lies."

He yanked her closer to him. "I would have done anything for you," he said, teeth clenched. "Anything to get you what you wanted. But it was never enough, was it, my lass? You're like a sucking wind that gobbles all before it and still roars on, grabbing everything in its path."

"You're mad."

"Damn me if for once you haven't said a true thing."

She tried another tack. "I'm in trouble. I have no money. No one to protect me. I'm of no use to you. Let me go, please. If once you loved me, let me go."

He gripped her tighter. "If once I loved you?" he mocked. "There's a fine sentiment. But you're right, you are in trouble. You've crossed my path again and caused me pain. I swore I wouldn't let you do it twice."

She was beginning to shake. "What do you mean?"

"You sent the Robin after me and . . . a friend of mine. Someone I care for. I ended up in the Thames, near-drowned on your orders. And my friend ended up kidnapped and tortured by you. Nearly killed." He gave her a shake. "Did you think I wouldn't demand payment?"

"Your friend?" Elizabeth began to laugh hysterically. "Good God, not that little black rat-woman! The Blackbird? You care for her?" She quivered with mirth. "This is too rich! Your little friend is a whore, sir. She's already moved on to another, richer fellow, the Viscount Greyfriars. You just can't seem to hold a woman, can you? Not even a scrawny little bitch who can pass for a boy any time of the day!"

"Shut your mouth."

"Oh, yes." She yanked herself from his grasp. "Another fool in love with that poxy thief. Well, love her if you must, you imbecile. She's probably sprawled beneath Phillip's churning arse at this very moment."

"Shut up." His voice was almost a whisper.

Elizabeth moved away from him. "No, you don't frighten me. You're an idiot! You always were! If you'd been half a man you might have had a chance to hold me. But you can't even hold onto a titless whore!" She put her foot into the stirrup, preparing to mount up. "And won't you love it when I catch her at last," she hissed. "I'll make sure that every plague-ridden sailor and scullery boy in London has his chance on top of her. Before I kill her."

His hands were on her throat. She was falling from the horse. The wind was shrieking in her ears. Shrieking until she went deaf. And blind. And dead.

Kestrel stood over her limp body, panting. He turned up his head and howled at the darkening skies.

Chapter Twenty-one

The Ruggleses greeted them with cries of joy and all but killed the fatted calf over the return of the Greys. The best entertainers, they claimed to all who were in the room, in all of England!

"Oh, but we're here this night as paying guests," Phillip said. "In payment for the kindness you showed two traveling players down on their luck."

"Looks like your luck's not much better, and all," observed Lydia Ruggles, frowning at Morgana's bare feet and poorly bandaged hands.

"Just being here has changed it for the better," Phillip said smoothly. "Now, if you will show us to a room and summon a tailor, we are prepared to put ourselves in your excellent care."

A few hours later, after all the dressing and fussing and celebrating, they were once again alone in the little room over the inn. Morgana looked at Phillip with mirth and joy. He opened his arms to her and she went to him at once.

The lumpy old bed became a heaven to Morgana. In Phillip's arms, she was soon transported to a place of such warmth and such shattering pleasure that she wondered how she managed to exist, afterward.

As they lay wrapped in each other's arms, Phillip stroked her hair and sighed. "When we get to Cygnet House," he said lazily, "I think I'll begin a mill tower. The stream could be made to run more abundantly, and drive a windmill."

Morgana was silent.

"Too mundane?"

"No. I'm sure you'll have the most elegant windmill in Christendom, as well as the most efficient."

"*I* will? Ay, me, are we back to this?"

He raised up on one elbow. "Angel, don't you know by now that I don't care about your profession, the friends you keep, or what sort of a devil your stepfather was? Nor will my family care. And if they do, the hell with them." He took her chin in his hand. "I love you, Morgana. You have said, and you have shown, that you love me. We belong together."

She gently put his hand away. "You don't know all. I am an enemy of yours."

He ran his hand over her hip. "God, that all men should know such enmity."

"Stop that!" She hid her smile. "I am an enemy of all, Phillip. I was a thief, you know that. I tried to kill my stepfather, this you also know. And now I have murdered the Robin. But what you do not know is that I am an outlaw by the very word and hand of King Henry himself." She looked hard at him. "I see I have your attention. Listen to me when I say that I am, or was, as you guessed, a lady of gentle birth."

"Even better! How can you now say my family will object?"

"Attend, Greyfriars!" she cried, pounding him lightly on the shoulder. "I am a lady, but no lady with whom anyone may associate. My father was a loyal friend to King Richard. He rode to meet him in Wales when Richard returned from Ireland—he was one of the few who didn't desert his king. He fought fiercely against Henry's forces at Flint. But they were too great to defeat, and my father, along with several others, was named a traitor and hanged on the spot. His title was given to another, his lands forfeited, and my mother and I were thrown out of our home. We were named outlaws, and no one may aid us or name us or give us protection. That is why my mother married a man who was not only far beneath her in station but in character, as well, for Cedric Bracewell was only interested in the little money my mother had in her own right and the boast that he had a noble lady for a wife."

Phillip frowned. "But this does not make you my enemy."

"Perhaps not. But neither does it make me fit company for you, let alone a wife. No one in this land would say a blessing over our union, and you would be reviled for taking an adder into the bosom of your family and society." She sat up against the wall. "I know this, Phillip. My mother, shy woman that she was, begged all our old friends in turn to help us, or at least not to shun us. Only my uncle Langland would offer succor, but he was already in Henry's disfavor and was soon killed, leaving my only cousin orphaned. As for all the rest, they could not afford the offense to Henry. Nor can you. I do not blame anyone. It just cannot be. Must not be."

Phillip slammed his fist into the pillow. "Damn it, angel! Why won't you see reason?"

She felt tears coming and looked away. "I do see it," she said softly. "And so do you."

He seized her and crushed her to him. "I will quarrel with you on this," he said darkly. "Don't mistake me."

Before she could reply, he had covered her mouth with his and any further talk was lost in the fever of their love-making.

They left two days later, after they found horses and had left Lightning as a gift to the Ruggles. Phillip didn't mention marriage again, or Cygnet House. When they passed through the Bishop's Gate, Phillip looked about them with a wary eye.

"I will take you to the White Stag," he said, "if that's where you want to go. I don't know where Elizabeth could be but I can guess her humor. I know that you don't want it, but I'm setting a man to guard you, day and night, until she is found." He held up a finger. "No arguments. Just come with me now to Elyot's house so that I can fetch a guard. Then we'll go to the Stag."

She assented and they went on to the Strand. There was much commotion when they arrived at Peter Elyot's house. "God's wounds, Greyfriars! We took you for dead!" Peter cried when he saw them.

They were ushered into the solar and servants were dispatched to see that all their needs were met at once. Peter was amazed and delighted to meet Morgana again but he had exciting news to impart.

"Your horse, Phillip," he said. "It came back riderless to Cygnet House. A messenger came here at once to inquire, but I said you had taken your Saracen on a journey north. We've had men searching for you for three days! Where the devil have you been?" He looked at Morgana. "Begging your pardon, Mistress Bracewell."

Phillip grinned. "A lovely gesture, Peter, but hardly necessary, in this case."

Morgana shot him a hot glance. He only smiled with all sweetness at her and turned back to Peter.

"Thanks for all your concern. You may call off the search now. Only tell me, has anyone come across Elizabeth in all this searching?"

Peter nodded, wide-eyed. "That's the other part I needed to tell you. She was found just this morning, not far outside the city. Dead. Strangled."

Phillip and Morgana stared at him, stunned into silence. After a long pause, Phillip spoke. "They are certain it is she?"

"Certain she is dead?" Morgana put in.

"Aye to both. Her own steward recognized the body when it was brought in, and Lord Fray besides."

"What a sorry end to his dallying," Phillip murmured.

"What a sorry end." Morgana looked to Peter. "Do they know who did this?"

"She was last seen in the company of her man, Gerald Durel, and another fellow known only as the Robin. A thief and a thoroughly low sort, as I understand it. It is all but a fact that these two were her murderers, since neither man can be found, all the lady's finances are in ruination, and she was left so brutally by the side of the road."

Phillip and Morgana looked at one another again. Something seemed to go out of Phillip's eyes, she thought. Dear God, had he still harbored feelings for Elizabeth, despite all she had done to him?

"Well, angel," Phillip said. "It looks as if a bodyguard is no longer needed. I will take you home."

They made the trip to the White Stag in silence. When they arrived, Morgana tried to hand Phillip the reins of her horse. "Keep it," he said.

He turned abruptly and rode away, soon disappearing in the crowded city streets. Morgana felt tears choking her. She put the mare in the stall behind the inn and went inside.

Fletcher and Wren were sitting in a corner, sipping warmed wine. Wren rose to greet her with a relieved grin.

"I knew you'd come."

"Of course I came. You think I'm going to just walk out on you and Kestrel? We have a job to do." She straddled a bench and poured herself wine from the jug. "Oh," she added with an apologetic smile. "Sorry I had to hit you again, old fellow."

"Kestrel's gone."

She looked up at him with a frown. "Gone? Again?"

Wren nodded. She turned to Fletcher. "What do you know of this? He was still weak. You just let him go off?"

Fletcher's long face looked even longer. "He would go, Blackbird. Wouldn't brook any denial. Said he had a debt to pay."

"A debt?" She looked to Wren again. "Who did the Kestrel owe?" Wren gave a small shake of his head. "Does that mean you don't know or won't say?" she demanded.

He looked deep into his wine cup. Then he met her eyes, his mild brown ones sad and sorrowful. "I don't know. I only know he's not coming back this time."

Morgana felt as if someone had pulled the final brick that brought the walls of her life tumbling to the ground. Phillip was gone. Kestrel was gone. Her mother was lost to her. Her life as a thief was as hollow and lonely as a cave.

She downed the last of her wine, then filled the cup again. She lifted it to the others. "To Kestrel," she said gruffly.

"Kestrel."

"Kestrel."

She drank a long gulp and then rose and went upstairs to the room she once shared with Wren. It, too, was cold and lonely. Fitting, she thought.

She pulled off her cloak, lay down on the pallet, and wrapped herself in the blankets. She lay for several long moments, shocked, hollow.

Then the tears came. And came, until she couldn't summon up another one, and she lay there, her arms wrapped about her, until sleep came and washed her out to sea.

"Greyfriars, what the devil are you up to now?"

Two long days had passed, in which she had lain in her room, grieving and trying to imagine what sort of life she now must make for herself. She had hardly cared enough to eat or drink, but she slept, taking the only respite she could from the cares she couldn't sort out and the memories she couldn't bury.

Now, here was madman Greyfriars, bursting into her room like a cheerful storm. She wanted to swing on him for intruding on her this way, bringing her fresh pain.

"Put these on." He tossed a bundle of clothes at her. "I'll wait." He sat down on the floor, his back to the wall, ready to watch with bright interest.

"I won't."

"Wren!" Phillip called.

Wren stepped in. "Put 'em on."

"No. Wren, you traitor! Will you always take another's side against me?"

He shrugged, then nodded. "Sometimes. Put 'em on."

She glared at both men. "All right. I'll put them on. But both of you—out of here! You may have me, but I'm still entitled to some privacy."

Phillip rose. "I'll turn my back."

"Like hell you will!"

"Rose, I can't trust you not to try and give me the slip. I'll make a concession to your modesty, but I won't go."

"Aiieesh! All right, you too!" she snapped at the Wren. "Round about with you!"

She climbed out of the clothes she had been wearing for the last two days and started to put on the garments that Phillip had brought her. She looked at the delicate undershift and the good brown wool gown and decided she'd better wash. She went to the water basin and began to scrub.

Phillip made impatient noises behind her. "Hush up, misery," she snapped.

At last, she was clean and dressed. "Now," she said once again. "What the devil are you up to?"

"I'm gardening." He turned to look at her, his eyes lighting like candles.

"You're wh—you're mad."

"But you knew that. Long ago."

He came and draped a fur-lined cloak over her shoulders. "Come now. We have calls to make this day."

She looked to Wren for help. He looked at the ceiling. "Greyfriars. If this is one of your tricks—"

"Tricks? Not on my soul!"

He led her outside and they mounted up together on Saracen. "I can ride, you know," Morgana said.

"I know. But humor me. If at this day's end you wish to have my ears, I will gladly give them to you for a necklace."

"Lunatic."

They didn't have far to go. He stopped before the church of St. Dunstan's and gave Morgana's arm a squeeze. "I'm sure that you recall this place?"

"Ah. You've decided to atone for your sinful life by joining the brotherhood. In truth, this time."

"Not exactly. But I have agreed to repay the friars for my impiety that night when I offered you sanctuary in this place. And Wren the same. We agreed to bring them a fresh soul to save."

He dismounted, handed the reins to the waiting groom, and lifted her down beside him. She glared at him.

"You're up to something, Greyfriars. I can see it in your eyes."

"Can you, Blackbird?"

He took her arm. She balked. "I'll not go one step until you tell me why we are here."

He slipped his arm about her waist and pulled her along with him, up the steps of the church. "I'm going to make my confession. And you, sweeting, are going to do the same."

She pulled back, aghast. "You can't mean this."

"I do."

"Does your black heart stop at nothing? It's one thing to make a mockery of the church outside its walls, but when you—"

"Mockery? Sweet Blackbird, I am in all earnest. And if my heart is indeed as black as you claim, then won't you please come in and pray for its safety? I seem to have lost it somewhere, you see, and I cannot vouchsafe its actions."

"Phillip, this is too—"

Her words were cut short by the appearance of Father Bernard at the top of the steps. He was smiling and beckoning to them. Phillip propelled Morgana up the last few steps and handed her over to the friar, who in his turn took her around the waist and led her into the church.

"Morgana, may I present the real Father Bernard?"

"I am most heartened that Lord Greyfriars has kept his promise to me," the cleric said. "It fair restores my faith in men to have this rascal here in my church to make his peace. And you wish to join with him. It is well, I say. A most judicious and merry a beginning."

"Beginning—?"

"Come this way, lady. I have agreed to hear Lord Phillip's confession. He says that I am stouter than Father Leo and will not grow faint in the long recounting. Such a rascal!"

373

Bewildered, Morgana sputtered her protests, but the cheery father wouldn't hear her words. She was led to the confessional cell and ushered inside. Father Bernard beamed in at her. "Be of good spirits, lady. Make your peace and begin afresh."

He closed the door before she could utter another word. A rustle sounded in the dim little room. "Welcome, daughter. What have you to say?"

Morgana felt the wild, sudden urge to run, run as far and as fast as she could. She could not tell all her sins. They were too black, too heinous. She had killed a man. She had stabbed another. She had stolen, lied, and more. There was no penance she could make, no absolution great enough.

"It is well, lady." The gentle voice held a slight quaver of age, but the tone was kind. "Do not fear."

A horrible thought struck her. "Greyfriars!" she hissed. "If this is another of your games, you are courting not only my anger, but the wrath of God!"

There was a chuckle from behind the screen that separated the confessor from the hearer. "I assure you, I am not he. Though it surprises me not one whit that that wild pup would dare to slip in and pretend to be a priest, wherever a young lady is concerned."

Morgana felt her cheeks flame with embarrassment. "You aren't Phillip," she said, feeling supremely foolish.

"No." There was a gusty sigh. "If I were young and a part of the world again, I might envy him. But no, I am not."

"And . . . and you're not the Wren?"

"Not I."

Morgana closed her eyes. She was standing before a real priest. Hastily, remembering her training, she went to her knees. "Father, I must beg your pardon. There's been some mistake—"

"That's quite all right, daughter. We all make mistakes. Your duty is but to confess those mistakes and make your peace with God."

"But, forgive me, Father—"

"That's right. I imagine it's been some time since your last confession. But go on. 'Forgive me, Father, for I have sinned,' " he prompted.

Morgana felt again the impulse to run. But just as quickly as it came, it vanished again. She surrendered. Phillip had bested her once again. She would simply have to make the best of it.

"Forgive me, Father, for I have sinned. It has been five years since my last confession . . ."

Some time later, Morgana emerged from the cell, drying her eyes. Father Leo came out with her, touching her elbow and saying nothing, only smiling and nodding. She went to the altar and began her penance.

She was just rising again when Phillip and Father Bernard came out of the other cell. She concealed a smile as she saw that Father Bernard's eyes were wide with wonder and his cheeks more than a little pink. She imagined that Phillip's confession would provide him with food for thought for a good long time, let alone subject for urgent prayer.

Phillip gave her a long, solemn look as he passed her on his way to the altar. He went to his knees and began to murmur his prayers.

"He, ah, he may be a bit longer," Father Bernard whispered to Morgana. "Come and sit over here. You'll be more comfortable as you wait."

He led her to a bench along the wall and gave her hand a pat as she was seated. "Much joy to you, daughter. This is the happiest of days."

He bustled away. Morgana was left staring at Phillip's bent head above the straight expanse of his shoulders. What was he up to now? For certainly she knew him well enough by now to know that his ever-flying mind had concocted some new scheme, some masterpiece of artistry and cunning that would only land her in trouble of the most serious sort.

Yet, she smiled. She felt weary after her confession, and she had shed many tears over the pain she had to relive. But she felt pleasantly empty now, as if she had been a bowl overfilled with longing and shame and anger, finding release in pouring out her story to the kind, solemn friar. And he had indeed absolved her! That was a wonder. She didn't know if she could truly accept it, but the old priest had seemed to read her thoughts. "Don't compound sin by refusing the grace of forgiveness," he had admonished her. "Your job is but to be obedient. Let the Lord take care of His mercy."

She would try. She would make her penance and she would try to accept any forgiveness that came her way. She was in need of mercy. She was in need of peace, as well as comfort, in order to face her future squarely.

She looked at Phillip, still bowed in prayer before the altar. She would be grateful to him for this. It was an act of great kindness on his part—he had wanted to ease her mind. But she couldn't stay near him and not long for him. She couldn't stay and not bring the notice of his family and the court and society to her wretched past. She had best go now, while he was busy making his own peace.

She rose and went swiftly to the door of the sanctuary. She was glad to be wearing a gown and soft slippers, for her boots would have rung out on the stone floors and given her away at once. She gained the door and slipped the latch.

"There, that's taken care of." Phillip spoke just by her ear.

She spun around. "What the dev—"

"Ah-ah. Not here." He raised his finger to her lips.

"I have to go now," she told him, pushing his hand aside.

"Yes, we do. We have yet another stop before we may go home."

He took her arm firmly and led her through the door. Morgana wanted to curse the day that she and Wren had taught Phillip how to walk like a shadow in the night. She'd have heard him coming and been able to elude him. *Not any more, damn it all.* She recalled where she was and offered a quick prayer of apology.

The groom held the horse for them at the bottom of the steps. Phillip lifted Morgana up and then mounted behind her. Tossing a coin to the lad, he started off into the streets of London.

"Haven't you made enough mischief for one day?" she asked.

"Me? No. I'll never have enough. Although I hope that today's mischief will not have to be repeated. I mean to put many things in order this day."

She groaned. "Saints preserve me, the man has a plan." She leaned back against him, savoring the comfort of his strong body next to hers—for one last time, she told herself. "So, where are you taking me now?"

"First, to Peter Elyot's house."

"Ah, yes. The house that you sold just so you could trick me into coming to Cygnet House. Did you confess that, too?"

"None of your affair. I've arranged for some food to be served while we change our clothes."

"Change? What is wrong with what I'm wearing?" She plucked at the skirt of her soft brown kirtle.

"It's lovely. But not quite correct for our next destination. Sarah will help you dress."

He'd dragged Sarah into this scheme. And what destination could require new clothes? She'd had enough of costumes and disguises to last her a lifetime. When she and Wren set up their inn, as she intended they do, she had every intention of being just who and what she was, to the end of her days.

They arrived at the fashionable home, and once again Lord Elyot greeted them at the door with great cheer. Sarah was waiting right behind him. As soon as Morgana crossed the threshold, she was whisked off to an upstairs chamber. There, lying on the bed, was an outfit of such breathtaking beauty and costly materials that Morgana could only gape. "What in the name of—"

"Lord Phillip had Lady Judith order it made for you, with his bits of instruction, of course." Sarah was unclasping Morgana's cloak as she spoke. "You'll be the loveliest, most elegant lady there this day, I'll warrant."

"Where?"

"Oh, I'm not supposed to say. Only to help you to be ready within the hour."

"But I—"

"I know, lass," Sarah clucked as she began lifting the hem of Morgana's gown. "You must be famished. Lord Phillip fair stole you from your bed this morn and you've had no chance to break your fast." She drew the garment off over Morgana's head and bustled to a table. "I've a tray waiting. Come, eat and drink, there may be a wait when you arrive."

"A wait?" Morgana allowed herself to be led to a bench. She was famished, and the arrangement of meats and cheeses and fruits made her stomach growl in eager anticipation. "Who would dare keep the Viscount Greyfriars waiting?"

"Oh, there I go again. Never you mind, lass. You're a clever one, I know, but you just remember that I've been serving Lord Phillip a good while now. I'm used to fox tricks of all sorts."

Morgana gave up and turned her attention to the meal. Sarah readied a basin of warm water, and after Morgana had eaten, she helped her bathe quickly with a fragrant, rose-scented soap.

Then, ceremoniously, the dressing began. First a dainty silk shift, then a snowy white, tight-fitting cotehardie, and last, a heavy silk surcoat of periwinkle blue, its sides open to show off the curving white waist of the cotehardie. Creamy pearls formed a thick, twining braid down the front of the surcoat and edged its angel-wing sleeves. In the lining of the sleeves and about the hem, white swans were embroidered, a design reminiscent of Phillip's own arms.

Sarah dressed Morgana's hair and laid over it a gauzy scarf of palest lavender. As the final touch, she fastened the scarf to a delicate circlet of gold, studded round about with pearls and amethysts. Morgana stood still under the older woman's ministrations, but when she was led to the pier glass, she gasped in protest.

"Oh, Sarah, no. This cannot—"

"Lord Phillip's orders," Sarah said firmly, cutting her off. "And as I said before, I know you're too fine a lady to ask a servant to disobey her master."

"But, Sarah, this is too fine! Where can I possibly go in such an outfit and not look as if I've just escaped from the royal court . . ." Her mouth suddenly formed an O. "No," she whispered. "He wouldn't." There was a sound of footsteps in the hall.

"I don't know what you're talkin' about, lady." Sarah turned her around and steered her to the door. "I only know what I'm told and I do just as I'm told."

She threw open the door and there stood Phillip and Lord Elyot, both dressed in the finest and most fashionable of garments. Phillip was laughing, but he fell silent at the sight of Morgana in the magnificent gown.

"Sweet Jesu," he murmured.

"Amen," said Peter Elyot.

Morgana could feel color rushing to her cheeks at their regard. She hid her discomfited pleasure with anger. "Tell me you're not going to try to drag me into the palace."

"I'm not going to try to drag you into the palace."

"Then where are we going?"

"To the palace."

"But you just said—"

"I said I wouldn't try to drag you. I intend that you shall walk into Henry's court just as you are, proud and lovely beyond all words."

Morgana stepped back, shaking her head. "You cannot do this. Henry hates my family. He knows I'm a thief. He will have me thrown into prison if I go before him."

Phillip stepped into the room. "I think not. He wouldn't dare imprison anyone I brought to him."

"You're a dreamer. You're so arrogant you think even the King will bow to your every whim." She backed up another step. "Besides," she said, her voice low. "Even if I'm not thrown out, how will it look for you to be seen with me? Your family are favorites of Henry's. I am his hated enemy, an outlaw and a criminal. Think of your name, Phillip, for God's sake."

"I am thinking of your sake today, little one. Let me worry about what others will say. Only come with me and see what we shall see." He stepped forward and took her hand. "We must leave now. We mustn't be late."

"No, Phillip! Please do not do this!"

Peter Elyot spoke up. "Trust him, lady. He's been hard at work to make this meeting."

Phillip pulled her to the door. "Only come. Hear what is said."

"Now I know why you dragged me to church this morning!" Morgana allowed herself to be pulled along. "You wanted me to make peace with my creator because Henry intends that I shall meet Him this bloody afternoon!"

Sarah scuttled after them, laying the soft wool, fur-trimmed cloak over Morgana's shoulders. Before she could think, they were out the door and being transported in a little cart to the palace gates.

The flurry of ceremonies all blended together as she and Phillip and Lord Elyot entered the court and were announced. They did not have to wait. As her heart and her hands grew icy with dread, Morgana was ushered before King Henry the Fourth, the man who had had her father killed and her family named as outcasts forever. The man who had taken her inheritance and left her and her mother alone and friendless in the world. She didn't know if she could ever make peace with this man, even if he were to offer it. Still, she sank into a low bow at the foot of his dais.

"I understand that you have a petition to make to me, Lord Greyfriars," the King said without preamble.

"I have, my liege."

"You may make it now."

"I would say first that your highness is well set upon the throne and justly so. Your rule in England is absolute and true. Your reign has been fair and your justice clear and tempered with mercy."

"So you say," Henry drawled.

"It is even so, my lord." Phillip went on, as Morgana listened through the whistling of fear and anger in her head. "I know that Morton Langland committed a grave error when he failed to recognize your sovereignty. He has been punished for his folly."

Henry looked to Morgana. "Do you feel your father was justly punished, lady?"

Morgana's eyes sought the King's. She saw no animosity there, only a probing seriousness. She raised her chin, about to retort, and sensed Phillip stiffening beside her. She recalled the Kestrel's words to her about taking

381

a moment to change her destiny. She needed change. She needed peace.

She lowered her head. When she spoke at last, her words were soft but clear. "My liege, it is not my place to question your judgment. All I know is that my father was punished and he is now dead."

"And for your loss, I am sorry."

She looked up at the King in surprise. He gave her a nod.

"I take no pride in the blood that was shed to gain my throne. But had I to do it over again, I would take the same course. I am the rightful King and I do what I must for England's sake." He turned to Phillip. "What else have you to say?"

"I beg for a favor, sir. I would ask that you lift the sanctions against Lady Langland and all her family. Let them return to their lands and home and resume their rightful places as good citizens and servants of their true King."

Henry frowned. "And how shall I be assured that this family will not rise up against me?"

Phillip offered a scroll of paper to the King. "In this letter, my liege, you will find my word, the word of my father, and the word of Lord Peter Elyot that we will vouchsafe your majesty's peace with the Langlands. If the Langlands attempt to resist you in any form, we shall accept your punishment with them."

Henry handed the scroll to one of his courtiers. "I see. And how shall you accomplish this?"

"My lord, by marriage with this lady, our two houses shall be joined. If she rebels against you, she rebels against me and shall pay the consequences."

Morgana looked at Phillip with mingled wonder and outrage. Marriage? Rebellion? Consequences? Who the devil did he—

"And will you, lady, agree to such terms?" Henry's look was piercing.

"I—my liege—I had no knowledge—he's never asked to marry me . . ." Morgana's voice was swallowed up in shouts of laughter. She wanted to swing on all of them.

"Lord Greyfriars, your reputation is confirmed. None so confident as you would offer up a marriage to which the bride has not yet been invited!" Henry's smile carried over to Morgana's thunderstruck face. "So, lady, what say you to this knave's proposal?"

"I—"

"She says aye!" Henry spread his hands. "What am I to do but grant this boon?"

"But, my lord, I cannot—"

"Ah. Yes, there is the matter of your recent occupations, Lady Langland." Henry's face darkened. "What have you to say on that?"

Morgana felt her hot cheeks growing chill. "I confess all, my lord. With deep contrition."

"And will you quit all such actions when you have married Lord Greyfriars?"

"I would, only—"

"Good. But you must make some restitution. In payment for all you have stolen from my lands and people, Lady Langland, I claim one-quarter of all your lands. The rest shall I return to your mother and yourself as the heirs of Morton Langland."

"My lord!" Tears started up in her eyes. The image of the King swam before her.

"Lord Greyfriars, your petition on this lady's behalf is granted. I accept your vouchsafing of her good behavior and will expect you to keep her well under your surveillance and care."

Phillip bowed. "Many thanks, gracious lord."

"Now, be gone, all of you. There's a wedding you must plan."

Two attendants were at her elbows, ready to usher her out. Morgana only just managed to remember her manners and sank into a deep curtsy. She backed away from the throne, her mind dazed from this sudden, startling course of events.

When they were outside the great hall and the doors had been shut behind them, she whirled on Phillip. "You!"

"Here it comes," Lord Elyot murmured in Phillip's ear. He beat a hasty retreat.

"Morgana, it was the only way!" Phillip held up his hands.

"You dragged me before the King at the peril of my life! You made the outrageous claim that you would marry me! You put your life, your lands, your name—" Tears now flowed down her cheeks. "You put all you had in jeopardy for me. For my family. Oh, Phillip, how can I ever thank you enough?"

He grinned. "You can't. Not in this lifetime or the next. And I intend to be right here beside you, for eternity, reminding you."

She flung her arms about his neck. "You are the plague of my heart, Greyfriars!"

"And you are the love of my life, Langland."

She looked at him with tear-starred, happy eyes. "Langland! Oh, how good it feels to be called that once more!"

Phillip gathered her closer. "Enjoy it while you may."

A few short, blissful hours later, they arrived to trumpet fanfares at Cygnet House. In true Phillip fashion, their welcome was elegant, merry, and memorable. Morgana stood stock-still in the middle of the great hall when she saw the woman standing nearest the fire, her arm around a young boy with dark curls almost the same shade as Morgana's.

She looked at Phillip, tears spilling. He nodded and ushered her forward.

"Mother?"

Katharine held out her arms. Morgana rushed to her and they stood, for uncounted minutes, in an embrace that spoke volumes and healed many wounds. At long last, Morgana pulled back, wiping her tears. "Mother. How did you—?"

"Get away from Cedric?" Katharine smiled a smile of heartbreaking sadness. "He got away from me. He is dead, my girl."

Morgana clapped her hands over her mouth. "I didn't—it wasn't—"

"No, no. He did it by his own hand. But that is not fit talk for a day like today. We'll tell each other all. But later. Right now, this fellow has something planned, I believe."

Morgana turned to Phillip with a smile. "When does he not have something planned?"

He motioned to someone, and suddenly Morgana found herself once again facing Father Bernard and Father Leo. She was pulled along with the large party of friends and family as they all trooped to the chapel. There was a smell of sweet, musky incense, and candles glowed from every corner.

Morgana hung back at the doors. "Wait!" she cried. "Phillip Greyfriars, what is the meaning of this?"

"Our wedding, sweet."

"*Your* wedding, sir. *I* have not been asked."

There was a shout of laughter, and Phillip was pushed forward to stand before her. She tried to suppress a grin as he went down on one knee.

"Morgana, you know that I have given you my whole heart. You hold all my future in your hands. I have asked your lady mother and she has given her consent. The King has given us his blessing."

385

"He's practically ordered it!" called out Peter Elyot.

Phillip ignored him. He took her hands in his. "Morgana," he said in a low voice only she could hear. "However we may have got to this place, this event, I want you to know that it is where I most want to be, where I would be, come what may. I love you, my Blackbird. I would have you for my wife even if we had to live as outlaws and outcasts for the rest of our days. Please say that you will take me for your husband."

For her answer, Morgana pulled him to his feet and kissed him. "I will," she whispered against his ear.

"What was that?" Father Leo asked loudly. "Brother Bernard, I fear me I'm getting too old for this."

"I said I will!" Morgana whirled to the brothers. "Shall we be quick about it?"

"Oh, ho, Phillip's met his match indeed!" someone called out.

In a glowing hour of candlelight, at the setting of the sun, Morgana recited her vows at Phillip's side and heard his, as well. Then, with a clash of cymbals and a beating of drums, the feasting and merrymaking began.

As the night went on, a gentle snow began to fall. Morgana slipped away to the alcove above the stairs, first to look out at the falling snow, and then to watch with fond eyes all the people she knew and loved celebrating in the hall below. Her mother and Peter Elyot were chatting, while Gareth cut capers around them both. Wren was cutting capers of his own with Sarah and with Mistress Margaret. Judith was dancing with her sons, the three of them rollicking along with joyful abandon until sober Lord Gregory could not help but join them. And Ariane had come! Ariane, her dearest friend of childhood was there, her belly swelling with her twins and her handsome husband, Lord Carrowe, proudly standing at her side. Phillip had seen to everyone and everything.

"Here you are."

"You can stop stealing up on me like that," she said with a smile. "We're no longer thieves."

He laughed and slipped his arms about her waist. He looked with her at the crowd below. "Now here's a merry sight."

"Mm. Yes." Morgana leaned back against his chest with a blissful sigh. "I didn't know I could love so many people all at once. Or that they could love me."

"I knew. I know." Phillip turned her in his arms. "I think I fell in love with you the first time you ever stole my purse."

She giggled and kissed him. "I'll not have to steal it now, will I?"

"No, love. My lot is yours."

"And mine is yours. I am an heiress again, you know."

"I do know."

She gave him a narrow look. "That isn't why you married me, is it, you rogue?"

"Better a rogue than a fool."

"Stop that, mischief!"

"At once, sweet dowry."

"Dowry! Is that all I am to you?"

He grinned. "You'll never know. If you want proof and assurance of my love, you'll have to stay at my side forever."

"I think I can manage that." She kissed him again.

"Tell me, lady wife, what would you have for a wedding present? I've seen a ring I like very much. And a horse, a fine gray. How would those suit you?"

"I've already picked out my gift."

"What do you want? Ask and I'll move oceans and mountains to get it for you."

"Your child."

He was silent for a moment, his eyes locked on hers. Then a slow, wicked smile spread across his face. "Ah! At last, something you cannot steal!"

Coral Smith Saxe

Morgana wound one arm about his neck. With the other, she laid his hand flat against the soft, new swell of her abdomen. "Don't be too sure."

She kissed him. For once, she had had the last word with Phillip Greyfriars.

Epilogue

"And so she wasn't a thief anymore?"

The old man came out of his reverie. The sun was falling below the vine-covered walls of the priory, the lad had finished digging all the holes and had planted the twenty seedlings. The evening breeze was rising, cooling the late-spring air and bearing the scent of new green growth on its breath.

"That I cannot say. Mayhap she was. Mayhap she wasn't. Such habits are sometimes hard to break. Some of us leave the world with our fingers still deep in the coin purses of others. Some of us just leave the world."

"She didn't die, did she? Oh, come now, Brother Theodore, say she didn't die after all that."

"I don't know, lad. I haven't been out from these walls in some twenty years and five. She'd be an old lady now, with grandbabes to dandle on her knee."

"But the man she married—that wasn't you. And yet you loved her."

The friar pushed himself up from the bench and stretched to loosen his tired back. He started to collect his tools, bending stiffly and straightening with a grunt. The young man moved swiftly to retrieve them all, taking them out from under the friar's nose before he was forced to stoop again.

"That's a kind lad. There's hope for you yet, pup. Mayhap you'll take my tale to heart and think twice about letting yourself in for trouble by consorting with a thief, especially a female one."

"But you did love her? And how do you know all this? You said you were in the flock. What name did they call you?"

The old man looked at the boy. His wrinkled face suddenly seemed to lose its weariness. It appeared to smooth itself and bear again the taut, blood-freshened tone of youth. The hook of his nose was more imperial than ever, more impressive. His brown eyes, usually dimmed by age, brightened and snapped. As the lad gaped, he straightened and strode away with strength and purpose, his mouth quirked into a half-smile. From somewhere high above the garden, it seemed, the whistling cry of a hawk pierced the air.

"Never," the lad murmured. "He couldn't have been . . ."

Some of us leave the world with our fingers still deep in the coin purses of others. Some of us just leave the world.

The boy looked down at his belt. His purse was gone. "No! Father!"

He raced down the path after the older man, tools rattling and banging against his sides as he ran. From out of the falling shadows, the cry of the hawk sounded clear once more.

390

Enchantment

Coral Smith Saxe

Bestselling Author Of *Silver and Sapphire*

They call her the Hag of Cold Springs Hollow, yet Bryony Talcott can't even cast a spell to curdle milk. Then she chants an incantation to bring change into her life and, to her surprise, conjures up dashing Adam Hawthorne. Beneath his cool demeanor, she senses a wellspring of passion that frightens her innocent heart even as it sets her soul afire.

Out to discredit all so-called witches, Adam is prepared to unmask the Hag as a fraud—until one peek at Bryony rising from her bath convinces him that she is not the wretched old bat he expected. Shaken by temptation, Adam struggles to resist her charms. But he is no match for Bryony or a love that can only be magic.

_51968-2 $4.99 US/$5.99 CAN

New York Times Bestselling Author
Ellen Tanner Marsh

"The Enchanted Prince, a superb novel by one of the romance genre's finest, provides a delightful twist to the *Beauty And The Beast* legend."

—*Affaire de Coeur*

As brash as he is handsome, Connor MacEowan can take any wager his friends dream up and never lose. Convinced he leads a charmed life, the bored Scottish nobleman agrees to the most outrageous gamble of all: Disguised as an unkempt pauper, he will woo and win a haughty aristocrat or lose his beloved Highlands castle.

With the face of a fairy princess, and the reputation of a spoiled brat, Gemma Baird refuses to consent to any arranged marriage. The maddening beauty will settle for nothing less than her heart's desire. But when she is forced to marry an uncouth beggar, she vows to turn the tables on her obnoxious husband`and use the power of love to make him her very own`enchanted prince.

__3794-7 $5.99 US/$6.99 CAN

ENCHANTED TIME

TIMESWEPT

Amy Elizabeth Saunders

Bestselling Author Of *Sweet Summer Storm*

With an antique store to run, Ivy Raymond has an eye for members of the opposite sex, as long as they are named Shakespeare, Rembrandt, or Louis XVI. But she is too busy to look at men from her own century. Then a kooky old lady sells her a book of spells, and before Ivy can say abracadabra, she is living in a crumbling castle with a far-from-decayed knight.

Stripped of his land, wealth, and title, Julian Ramsden is still arrogant enough to lord it over Ivy. But the saucy wench has powers over him that he cannot deny. Whether the flame-haired stranger is a thief, a spy, or a witch, Julian is ready to steal a love that is either treason or magic.

_52049-4 $5.99 US/$7.99 CAN

DON'T MISS THESE MEDIEVAL HISTORICAL ROMANCES BY LEISURE'S LEADING LADIES OF LOVE!

The Love Knot by Sue Deobold. A valiant warrior in the service of Richard II, Sir Crispin battles men to the death and never flinches. Yet he is utterly powerless to fight Catherine Clifford's hold on him. In a world filled with deception and betrayals, Crispin vows to risk all he possesses to protect the exquisite firebrand—or they will never share the sweet ecstasy that will change their lives forever.

_3745-9 $4.99 US/$5.99 CAN

For Love and Honor by Flora Speer. Falsely accused of murder, Sir Alain vows to move heaven and earth to clear his name and claim the sweet rose named Joanna. Yet before they can share a glorious summer of passion, they'll have to risk their reputations, their happiness, and their lives for love and honor.

_3816-1 $4.99 US/$5.99 CAN

Dorchester Publishing Co., Inc.
65 Commerce Road
Stamford, CT 06902

Please add $1.75 for shipping and handling for the first book and $.50 for each book thereafter. NY, NYC, PA and CT residents, please add appropriate sales tax. No cash, stamps, or C.O.D.s. All orders shipped within 6 weeks via postal service book rate. Canadian orders require $2.00 extra postage and must be paid in U.S. dollars through a U.S. banking facility.

Name _____

Address _____

City _____ State _____ Zip _____

I have enclosed $_____ in payment for the checked book(s).

Payment <u>must</u> accompany all orders.☐ Please send a free catalog.

White Heather

Helene Lehr

Bestselling Author Of *The Passionate Rebel*

She is a fiery clanswoman who can wield a sword like a man, a sharp-tongued beauty with the courage to protect her people. But when rival clan leader Thornton MacKendrick takes Diana captive, nothing can protect her from the sinful pleasure that awaits her.

Although Diana is determined to return to her beloved Highlands, her heart betrays her will, and she finds herself drawn to the rippling, tartan-clad body of her captor. But it will take more than Thorn's heated caresses to make Diana his own. Only with a love as powerful as her pride can he hope to win her trust, to conquer her heart, to make her his love's captive.

_3795-5 $4.99 US/$5.99 CAN

An Angel's Touch

Heaven's Gift

Janelle Denison

The last thing J.T. Rafferty expects when he awakes from a concussion is to find a beautiful stranger tending to his wounds. She saved his life, but the lovely Caitlan Daniels has some serious explaining to do—like how she ended up on his isolated ranch lands, miles from civilization. Despite his wariness, J.T. finds himself increasingly drawn to Caitlan, whose gentle touch promises sweet satisfaction. She is passionate and independent and utterly enchanting—but Caitlan also has a secret. And when J.T. finally discovers the shocking truth, he'll have to defy heaven and earth to keep her close to his heart.

__52059-1 $5.99 US/$7.99 CAN

Touched By Moonlight

Carole Howey

Bestselling Author Of *Sweet Chance*

Terence Gavilan can turn a sleepy little turn-of-the-century village into a booming seaside resort overnight. But the real passion of his life is searching for Emma Hunt, the mysterious and elusive creator of the tantalizing romances he admires. When he finds her, he plans to prove that real life can be so much more exciting than fiction.

To the proper folk of Braedon's Beach, Philipa Braedon is the prim daughter of their community's founding father. Yet secretly, she enjoys swimming naked in the ocean and writing steamy novels. Philipa has no intention of revealing her double life to anyone, especially not to a man as arrogant and overbearing as Terence Gavilan. But she doesn't count on being touched by moonlight and ending up happier than any of her heroines.

_3824-2 $5.50 US/$7.50 CAN